ARUNDAY ꓤ DIVERGENCE

THIEVES' GUILD BOOK SIX

C.G. HATTON

Published by Sixth Element Publishing
Arthur Robinson House
13-14 The Green
Billingham TS23 1EU
Great Britain
www.6epublishing.net

For Hatt

CHAPTER ONE

"*WHERE IS HE?*"

Her voice echoed off the marble floor, around the lofty stone pillars.

The creature sitting on the throne upon the dais was regarding her with dark eyes, brows furrowed. It was hard to see any compassion in that expression, there was no doubt there, none of the fiery determination to put right the wrongs that had been so badly inflicted here.

He was changed. And that sent ice into her veins.

This haven that had once been such a comforting reminder of all they had lost now seemed hollow. Chillingly cold despite the heat and humidity.

No answer was forthcoming.

She continued to walk, footsteps resounding as if beating a drum leading her to her execution.

"I know your plan," she said, each word curt, struggling

to curb her distaste at even being here in his presence. "I've spoken to Sebastian."

She expected him to rise to such a challenge but he merely stared.

His voice was deep, resonating, when he did deign to respond. "Then you know it is the only way."

She couldn't help the disgust that crept into her response. "You have abandoned them... how could that ever be the only way?"

There was a damned DZ, right in the middle of the street, suppressors activated, totally silent, eerie as hell, turret already turning towards them as they cleared the corner. Hil skidded to a halt, pinned in its spotlight as it swung round, the beam piercing the inky black, icy cold darkness, illuminating the sleet that was driving down in sheets. The dark husks of bombed out skyscrapers loomed in all directions, flashes piercing the night sky like lightning as gunships swept the city, searchlight beams scanning, looking for him, a far off wail of klaxons mixing with the scream of engines flying low over the ruined city. Temerity hadn't been hit in the first wave but it hadn't suffered any less than Earth or Winter when the attack finally came.

He yelled a warning and tried to turn, boots slipping on the ice, a deep thrum reverberating through his chest as the DZ powered up to fire. Sanchez grabbed his jacket and hauled him aside as the tank's main cannon engaged with a deafening roar, gunfire erupting all around them, a massive shockwave shoving aside the chill air in a billowing blast of heat.

There was a split second of absolute silence, slow motion dread as the universe spun and the dice bounced. Hil closed his eyes. He couldn't move fast enough. Couldn't breathe. Had no idea how the hell he'd blown it badly enough that they'd rumbled him. And somewhere along the way he'd freaking lost his knife.

Something punched into his shoulder and he was thrown backwards, hitting the ground and rolling. He slammed up against a wall, flinching from the debris raining down, curling up, ears ringing.

The Senson engaged, cutting through the confusion and pain from the blast, pushing past an increasingly insistent drone in his ears that he had a horrible feeling was a Bhenykhn troop carrier overhead.

"Hil..."

The voice was distant.

A million miles away. Years away.

"Skye?"

His voice cracked, throat constricted as if he'd been kicked in the neck.

"Hilbud, sweetheart, believe me, I am not Skye and I am not going to mother you out of this. Now, get your butt moving and get clear before the Bennies decide to join this hunt."

Time kicked back in with a vengeance. He blinked cold sleet from his eyes, awareness hitting hard, heavy footsteps pounding a distant beat, a hum of powered armour moving in. Shouts, yells. More cracks of rifle fire.

There was a body next to him. Sanchez, the extraction agent who'd just saved his life, blood streaming down her face, eyes staring.

He started to reach his hand towards her.

There was a curt, "She's dead. Hilyer, listen to me. Move your ass. Now. Or you will be too."

Iona.

She was supposed to be in deep cover, darkside, out in far orbit. Close enough to run comms for him but no way were they going to risk a Thundercloud as valuable as Iona getting caught here.

"How...?"

She cut him off with a brusque, "Move."

He moved.

He pushed to his feet, one hand pressed against the burning spot in his shoulder, and staggered into a run, back into the darkness of the narrow stinking passages between the bombed out buildings. Someone appeared next to him and he almost spun to fight them but whoever it was dragged on his arm and pressed a gun into his hand, hissing into his ear, "Let's get the fuck out of here, shall we?" Ayling, Sanchez's partner, not wasting any time or sentiment and running ahead to take point.

Hil wasn't going to argue. Whatever had gone wrong, however his cover had been blown, they were deep inside Bhenykhn-held territory, surrounded and hunted by the human collaborators he'd managed to infiltrate and in the shit about as deep as it was possible to get.

"Hilbud..." Iona again. She sent him a data drop, updates on hostile movements, nothing too overwhelming but enough to send his already wrangled senses reeling.

He stumbled, bumping up against a filthy brick wall, twisted metal scaffolding clattering, coming up against a rusting ladder hanging off its bracket. He ducked past and ran after Ayling, dodging past piles of decomposing rubbish and clambering over mounds of rubble, slipping in the detritus of human neglect and the aftermath of ferocious bloody combat. Clearing up after the invasion had hardly been a priority for the few humans left alive. And as cold as it was, there was no disguising the stench of decay from the aliens.

Head spinning, Hil misjudged his footing and fell, scraping his arm on a jagged edge of metal sticking up out of a shattered slab of concrete. Cursing and fumbling, he couldn't get his balance, trying to keep one hand tight around the pistol grip, the other still hard up against the wound in his shoulder.

Ayling grabbed his jacket and hoisted him upright, pulling him onwards.

"Wait," Hil gasped. "Left. Go left."

They veered left and ran through another dark, narrow alleyway into some kind of parking garage or loading bay, broken glass crunching underfoot.

Ayling must have been getting instructions too, from Iona or another extraction team, as the guy murmured an affirmative out loud, adding a curse and bundling Hil aside into a doorway.

"Get inside," he got from Ayling and Iona simultaneously and he shoved the gun into the small of his back, leaned into the door and started working the lock, one handed, the other still pushing hard against the wound in his shoulder as if he could numb the pain the harder he pressed against it. It was a bullet in there, he could feel it. Nestled below the collarbone, burning like hell.

Ayling was standing at his back, gun up, watching outwards. "How bad is it?" he murmured.

Hil shook his head, cursing as his fingers fumbled the lockpick. "I'm fine," he muttered without looking up.

The lock snapped open and he pushed through, pocketing the lockpick and pulling out the gun again, trying not to cough in the cold and musty air.

Ayling followed him in, shutting the door and shoving him through. Of the three extraction teams that had got him this far, Ayling was the only one left alive.

"What the fuck happened?" the guy said as he checked

out each room, efficiently and sharply scoping out each door, corridor and window they passed.

Hil had to stop himself scowling. They were well and truly in enemy territory. Surrounded. At least five people, valuable people, were dead because of him. What the hell had happened? The mission was supposed to be foolproof. Infiltrate the Order's standing army on Temerity. Acquire the intel. Leave. Should have been a cinch. For him. And it had been. The corporate ID he'd used had been cast iron. Fast, they'd come up with it in less than perfect circumstances, but in these times of chaos and upheaval, it had been as good as it needed to be. He'd got what he'd been sent in there for, was on the verge of withdrawing, mission complete, tab done, status green, when...

"It went to shit," he muttered, breathing through the intense pain for a moment as the bullet in his shoulder shifted.

Ayling glanced back at him.

Hil narrowed his eyes, following the guy's stare. The gash scraped down his forearm was hot, not burning as much as his shoulder, but still hot. He dragged his sleeve down, ignoring the questioning look, ignoring Iona's insistent query for an update.

The extraction agent nodded, checked out another room and paused, pulling out a trauma patch and throwing it to him, before moving on.

Hil snatched it, breath catching. It stung when he

pushed it inside his shirt, up against the wound, stung like a bitch, but it was a welcome heat that he fell forward into, closing his eyes for a second.

He could hear that Ayling was already running forward. He breathed through the pain and followed, trying to track the comms from Iona, trying to figure out where this route was going to take them, how the hell they could find a way out. It was looking more and more desperate. But they'd known the risks when they'd sent him in here.

"You need to get out of the city," Iona sent. "Get into the hills. Meet with the resistance. We'll extract from there."

That was easier said than done. This place had no tunnels. And he could tell from the comms he was tapped into, from what he was picking up from Iona's fast and furious thought processes, they were being tracked. Five units of Drake's mercenaries were closing in, and the lone Bhenykhn troop carrier originally supporting them had been joined by at least another two from the sound of it. He knew what the aliens did to their prisoners and he'd be damned if he was going to end up like LC and NG.

He followed Ayling up a narrow staircase, running up two, three steps at a time, and through more dark corridors, no let up in the pace, no let up in the droning overhead that was rumbling like thunder through the building. This floor was desolate, open to the elements, ravaged by bombs, and he had to dodge the beams from gunship searchlights that were sweeping in through the shattered window frames, flashing bright white as they scanned across the scorched and crumbling walls.

Ayling paused up ahead, teetering on the edge of an exposed ledge, the wall ripped away, ice cold waves of blustering sleet driving in. The guy glanced back, nodded once, and ran, keeping to the darkness of the far wall and sprinting across to barge open a door at the far end, turning and gesturing frantically.

Hil sucked in a deep breath and started to run. A hail of gunfire erupted all around him, strafing the walls behind him, shrapnel flying, dust and debris exploding out. He didn't stop, didn't flinch at the multiple impacts and threw himself, tumbling, through the doorway, skidding and rolling through rubble.

Ayling slammed the door shut, ignored him and started to haul the rug from the centre of the room. Hil staggered to his feet, head ringing, shrugging off shards of glass, and helped, reaching down to pull up a hatch in the floor.

Iona was sending a steady stream of updates. "You need to speed this up, boys," she sent.

It took them both to heave out the chest that was stashed there.

The lock was guild, biotagged, opening automatically as it recognised him.

There wasn't much left in it, just a few mags of mixed ammo, couple of holsters, medical kits that looked like they'd been raided already, and a couple of ration packs.

"Iona, go," Hil sent back as he rifled through the kit, chest feeling hollow. "Get out of here."

She wasn't impressed. "I'm not leaving until you're clear of the city. And I'm serious, you need to get moving. Don't get trapped in there. You have less than two minutes before you're overrun. Come on, boys, you need to be..."

The link cut out. Abruptly and absolutely.

Hil blinked. He couldn't reconnect no matter how much he tried, even though he could still hear her thinking, hear her mad, insanely fast and rambling AI thoughts, even at this distance, cold panic as she lost the connection with them.

Ayling looked up, catching Hil's eye, with a curt, "Shit."

They were jamming comms.

The Bhenykhn were jamming comms.

That meant the aliens were very suddenly, and very purposefully, jamming all communications between the humans. And that could mean only one thing.

Ayling stood. "They know you're here." He held out a holster.

"I know." Hil took it and fastened the belt tight around his waist.

"We need to split up," Ayling said, shoving all the medical stuff and the food into Hil's pockets.

He didn't argue as he secured the tie around his thigh. Everyone knew the Bhenykhn couldn't see him. The damned aliens tracked humans from their life signs. Pure energy. Unavoidable, unequivocal, a supremely perfect tracking system, and it was inherent in the massive alien hive and every one of its foot soldiers.

But from whatever biological quirk of nature it had been that had conspired to make the virus react in his body the way it did, in combination with the electrobe poisoning that had hit him on the Expedience, he was invisible to them. Totally and utterly invisible. So long as they couldn't see him. So long as he was never caught in sight on his own, and he'd gone to pains to make sure he was never with less than four or five other humans when the Bhenykhn were around, when they could see him. If he was on his own, he could stand in the shadows right next to them and they'd have no idea he was there.

But to the Bhenykhn, Ayling stood out a mile and he knew it.

"You go," Ayling said, holding out a magazine. "You know the RV points in the foothills?"

"Yeah."

There was a bang outside, detonation, as if a door had been blown in. Distant voices, shouts.

Hil reloaded the gun and shared out the rest of the ammo, fast, jamming his into the pouches on the belt.

Ayling nudged his arm.

Hil looked up, heart skipping to see the guy holding up his knife, Mendhel's knife, offering it hilt first.

Holy shit.

He reached for it, a lump in this throat, not wanting to ask what it had taken to retrieve it.

Ayling pierced him with a stare as he handed it over. "Don't get caught."

"I know." He took the knife and tucked it back into his boot, resolve, determination, hell, sheer bloody mindedness rippling out as he breathed, keeping eye contact with this guild extraction agent, a dying breed, a guy who had just lost his partner and two fellow extraction teams.

Ayling's eyes were glinting in the half-light as he maintained the intensity of that stare. "I'll hold them off. Meet you at the RV."

There was nothing to say. They both knew it was a lie.

Hil nodded.

"Go." The guy held out his hand, bloodied and filthy. "See you there."

CHAPTER TWO

She walked up to the dais, chin up, crossing the black and white marble floor as if she were a piece moving across a chess board. Was that all she had ever been, a queen in reserve, waiting to be sacrificed?

"We are responsible for this war..." Her voice was a low murmur.

"The Bhenykhn are responsible for this war."

"And who are responsible for the Bhenykhn?"

He narrowed his eyes, breathing deeply as if composing himself, sitting there on an opulent seat that could only be seen as a throne, as if he was overseeing the game, manipulating pieces with impunity.

She stood tall, meeting that cold gaze with defiance. "You promised me you would tell them everything. You lied."

There were sounds of movement behind her, armoured

footsteps, a single synchronised echo. She didn't need to turn to know they were his elite guard.

She had no need to be cowed by the threat and raised her voice to a commanding resonance. "You portray yourself to them as 'The Man' yet you are the least 'humane' of all of us, Koschei." She used his real name, no compunction in wielding the power that gave her. "Our immortal, brilliant, shapeshifting mindreader... the outsider, the deviant... I defended you. I protected you. Yet I see now you have turned into a monster worse than the monsters you sent here to ravage this galaxy."

Hil edged towards the corner of the alleyway and risked snatching a glance at the intersection, blinking freezing cold raindrops from the torrent that was driving down between the towering buildings, trying to steady his breathing.

This was the fifth route out he'd tried. Every one had been the same. They had the city closed down.

For a colony that had been keeping pretty much to itself in the midst of the invasion, the Bhenykhn had mobilised damned fast. He stared at the intersection, the crossroads lit up with spotlights. A squad of the huge Bhenykhn warriors were shoving the human soldiers about, bellowing with what passed for laughter amongst the aliens, ragged cloaks hanging limp against their armoured shoulders, rain dripping, hefting their axes and adjusting their massive rifles. He'd seen four grunts, one squad leader and a damned shaman at every intersection. Not to mention the other squads out searching. Revelling in this hunt.

The mercenary captain in charge of the human forces was yelling at his own guys in frustration. Hil stared at them. He couldn't read minds, couldn't feel emotions and track life signs the way LC and the others could but he could sense the fear in the chill air. It was sickening to see the mercenaries bitching, harsh shouts getting drowned out in the downpour, aggression sky high to each other and total subservience to the Bhenykhn.

Just watching it made his hackles rise.

He shrank back into the darkness of the alley, wiped the rain from his eyes and tapped his finger against the trigger guard of the pistol he was holding down by his thigh, fingers numbing in the freezing night air.

He had three fresh kill tokens in his pocket, nestled in there next to the one he always carried, blood spattered, all from lone Bhenykhn hunters he'd killed trying to break a way through their lines. Mendhel's knife was back in his boot, still smeared with their blood. It hadn't taken the aliens long to reorganise back into squads, leaving no single warrior alone. One he could take down. More than that...?

It was looking impossible.

He'd tried everything. There was no way down into

the sewers, no way into the maze of maintenance basements beneath the city and no way across the rooftops, the buildings too tall and too far apart to jump between them. If this was a tab he was running, he couldn't even think what the plan would have been. He tried to rack his brains, tried to think what Mendhel would have thrown onto the table if this had been a viable scenario for a tab. Even tried to think what Quinn would have said, for Christ's sake. Probably, don't do it.

Weighing up his options, he couldn't fight his way out of this and he sure as hell wasn't about to surrender. Screw that. He'd seen how badly that went wrong the last time they'd tried it with Drake and he wasn't about to do that again.

He hugged his arms around his ribs, the stolen combat jacket soaked through and possibly making him more cold than if he wasn't wearing it. He should have grabbed a rain cape when he'd raided the ruined APC he'd found two blocks away. He still had no idea what had given him away in the barracks. He'd been embedded in there, deep cover, for over five weeks. And he'd been beyond careful. He'd raided their systems, trashing his way through level after level of protections to get anywhere near the intel on Drake and her operation that he needed, and then it had been encrypted to hell. But he hadn't screwed up. He knew he'd almost slipped up twice but he hadn't, he was damn sure he hadn't.

He edged back to the corner and stared at the

Bhenykhn squad leader, its hulking grotesque figure casting a twisted shadow as it paced. If it wasn't for them, he could've wandered out, joined a patrol of mercs and joined in their bitching. Very happily.

He was going to have to wait this out. Find somewhere to lie low and figure it out from there. He started to turn away and froze. The shaman was staring right at him. Across the street the tall bony figure was poised, twisting its staff, clacking knucklebones sending raindrops flying, orange eyes staring into the depths of the alley where he was standing, as if it could see him.

His skin crawled. He had to trust that it couldn't. There was no reason why it should.

Time stretched into nothing.

And eventually, after an eternity, the shaman grunted, stared for another second and moved away.

Hil turned.

And saw a figure stagger into the far end of the narrow passageway.

He'd snapped up his gun before he realised the figure was human. And wounded, stumbling, then falling. Dammit.

Every instinct he had was screaming at him to get away. He should have run past and left them there, but there was a pained cry and he couldn't help stopping and dropping to his knees.

It was a girl. She looked up at him through dark,

goggle-like glasses, cheap, cracked lenses, the kind usually hardwired into some kind of comms tech. She was soaked, skinny, fair hair bedraggled and tied up into two knots on top of her head like antennae, dirty fatigues hanging off her and a hand pressed to her side. Swearing. She could have been twelve or twenty, it was hard to tell.

He rocked back on his heels and pulled out a trauma patch, shoving it at her and glancing backwards over his shoulder, half expecting to see mercenaries or Bhenykhn piling in.

She hissed through gritted teeth as the patch kicked in but otherwise she made no sound.

Iona's voice was a calm murmur inside his head, comms back before he realised it.

"You stay there, you'll get caught, Hilbud."

The Bhenykhn must have been sure they had him cornered to drop the jamming.

"Iona..."

"Drake's troops have closed down the entire city," she sent. "They're running an airtight Danvers protocol, block to block."

He'd figured that out already.

"And the bounty on your head has escalated. Well done, you just matched NG."

Holy shit.

"And it's an open bounty, Hil. Do you realise what that means?"

Meant that every single bastard soldier out there

suddenly had a very good reason to work their ass off to be the one to find him.

"At least they want you alive. Get to the south end of the alley. I'm finding you a way out."

He felt the muscle in his jaw tick. In the past few insane months, Iona had kept him alive too many times to count. It was an automatic instinct now to trust her and not question her instructions. He stood and started to back away.

The girl swore again and hissed, "Wait."

He shook his head, edging back against the wall with a glance both ways.

"Hilyer..." Iona murmured inside his head, "tell me you didn't go off mission again."

"I didn't," he lied, the denial as equally automatic.

He checked the mag on the gun. It wasn't full, not empty but low enough to change.

"You should have left there a week ago. What happened?"

He'd been getting out all the strategic intel he was finding as he gathered it, through the network they had set up. Standard procedure. Hand to hand to his contacts, through drop boxes or tight wire. Secure as you could get. It hadn't been breached. He knew for a fact it hadn't been breached.

"Hil...?"

He holstered the gun and pulled out two of the half spent mags, starting to thumb rounds from one into the other, calm, hands steady even though his heart was pounding, glancing up to keep watch on both ends of the alley.

"Hilyer..."

"She's out there, Iona."

For a Thundercloud in the centre of an active theatre, she was being remarkably restrained. "Hil, you can't keep doing this."

"It wasn't that, I swear. Iona, I was close, I was damn close, but I didn't screw up."

"If you keep chasing her like this, you're going to get yourself killed."

He flinched back as a gunship flew low overhead, its searchlight flashing across the alley, the circle of bright light just missing them.

"It wasn't that," he sent again, stubborn, steadfastly certain that he hadn't done anything to compromise any aspect of the operation.

"Hilbud, you refuse to withdraw on schedule, we hear nothing else for days then you yell for an extraction and the entire colony erupts around you. What the hell did you find in there?"

The girl was whimpering. He shushed her and drew the gun, switching mags and tucking the others back into a pouch.

He had a lump in his throat that was making it painful to swallow.

Shit, he didn't need this. He pushed all the crap little

thoughts back into the boxes in his mind where he kept them and sent back to Iona a firm, "It wasn't that. I found something else. Something I can't broadcast."

He'd stumbled across something when he was looking for her, something else, the intel that had finally made him decide to sack it, gear up to pull out. Intel that he couldn't hand to anyone but Evelyn. So damn right he'd called out for the extraction teams to close in. Urgently. Right before it had all gone to shit.

"Iona, I..."

She cut him off. "You need to get out of there."

He wasn't going to argue and made to move away, checking both directions.

The girl staggered to her feet and caught his hand, looking at him with a set to her face that made him feel even more shit. "Zach, wait. I know who you are," she whispered.

Holy shit, she knew his name.

Her cheeks were flushed. "You're the one they're all looking for," she said, the pain etched on her face easing somewhat as the trauma patch did its job. "I know you're the one they're looking for. I know who you are."

Iona was losing what thin shred of patience she had left. "Leave her and move your ass, Hil."

He shrugged off the girl's hand and pressed his finger to his lips. Dammit, he really didn't need this.

He started to back away. She was going to die anyway, sooner or later, whatever he did.

"Zach, help me," she whispered, desperation edging her voice, "and I'll show you a way out. I can get you out of the city."

Iona cut in with a curt, "Don't trust her."

"I'm not about to."

He shook his head again and whispered back to the girl, "You get caught with me, they'll kill you. Go home. Find somewhere to hide. Get off the streets. But don't follow me."

He felt like he was kicking a stray puppy.

He turned away but she reached for his hand, fingers slick with blood. She suddenly looked a lot older than twelve. "I know a way. Please listen to me, we've been looking for you. We've all been looking for you. We've been trying to find you before they do. We have a way out of the city." There was something about her voice, a desperation that cut deep. "The bridge," she said. "There's a way under the bridge."

He shook his head. "I've checked it. There's no way to get anywhere near it."

"Not unless you have a diversion." She tugged at his hand. "Zach, I'm not here alone. If you get me to the bridge, we'll get you across the river. And out of the city." Her goggles were glinting every time a gunship flew overhead. If someone looked down the alley, she'd stand out like a beacon. She raised her voice, "I can get you to safety," and he had no choice but to pull her close, pushing his finger against her lips that time.

"You need to keep quiet," he muttered, harsh, shoving her deeper into the shadows.

"I know people," she whispered. "We have places in the foothills. Safe places. Places the Bennies don't know about yet. I can get you to Libassi." She leaned over with a gasp, in pain, and looked up at him again, biting her lip, the expression pulling at her mouth a weird mix of defiance and despair.

"Now that is interesting," Iona sent. "Libassi is the leader of the local resistance. No one should even know that name unless they know him."

Hil cursed. He knew fine well who Libassi was.

"Let me show you the way," the girl whispered. "Help me. Please, come with me. I can get you out of the city and to people who can help you get away."

"Your call," Iona sent. "Route to the bridge looks clear."

If he left her there, she was liable to give him away with the racket she was making. At least if he was with her, he could keep her quiet.

And in the five weeks he'd been there, the idea of trying to meet with Libassi had crossed his mind more than a few times.

He nodded. He grasped her hand firmly, holstered the gun and pulled the medical supplies from his pocket, transferring it all to hers, stuffing in what he could, and adding the rations as well.

"What are you doing?" she breathed. "You're hurt. You need this."

"I don't need it." He could hardly feel the wound in his shoulder anymore. The virus had dissolved the bullet, absorbed it, whatever the hell it did to break down the metal into something it could use. He took out an injector and pressed it against her wrist. "C'mon, let's get out of here."

She led him a winding route around the city, using the back streets and alleyways through the human populated part of the city, the aliens no doubt able to track her, avoiding the intersections. Iona was giving him warnings as they moved and he had to pull the girl back a couple of times when the Bhenykhn got close. She was leaning heavily on him, limping badly by the time they heard the river, the rain still heavy and gunships still circling. He risked giving her another shot of go-juice as they waited in the cover of a burned out shop front, along the street from the bridge, watching as two squads of Bhenykhn met, hefting axes and crossbows high, laughing before they moved out.

The bridge was guarded by human mercs and two of the big DZ45s. The river sounded like it was in flood, a thunderous roar adding to the clamour of the rain and the gunships.

"We just need to get down there," she breathed,

pointing to a gap in the railings. "There are steps down to an underpath. I just need to give the signal and Libassi's people will draw them away. We'll be able to sneak along out of sight and climb up under the bridge struts."

Like it could be that easy.

"You might pull it off," Iona sent, "if you can time it right. Just be aware, you are surrounded by mercs. There's a lot of activity all over that area. And you'll have to move fast on the other side. There are more Bhenykhn ships entering orbit. They're flooding the entire planet looking for you."

"Can you come in?" Hil sent, holding the girl's shoulder while he scoped out the street. There were human troops out there but no one looking this way.

"This is going to be tight, Hilbud. Get high enough up into the hills and we'll be able to try it."

That was something at least.

Then she added, "So long as they don't bring in a command ship."

So they were on the clock.

He nudged the girl. She tugged on his arm and pulled him out into the street.

And he knew the instant she let go of his hand that she'd set him up.

CHAPTER THREE

THE VAST CHAMBER *plunged into dense black. His voice was ponderous, quiet but onerous.* "Your misguided affection for them is a weakness you can ill afford." *A single source of light sprang to life, flickering just above his palm, shadows leaping around his bony, hunched form. The flame danced as he spoke.* "Their candles may burn bright but they burn fast." *It extinguished.* "They breed, they war, they die."

"That does not mean you can use them as your playthings." *Her words were swallowed up by the darkness.*

There was an ominous pause as he ignored the emotion of her outburst then he said, voice low, "If you have spoken to Sebastian, then you know that Nikolai was captured."

It was the one piece of news that had distressed her the most. And to know what had happened, and why... She had to temper the unfamiliar anger that threatened to rise.

She blinked as the chamber was once again bathed in light. "And not only Nikolai...?"

"Much has come to pass," Koschei said from his throne. "A year in Earth terms is the merest blink of an eye to those of our kind but for humans it is a long time. You may have gathered some of what has transpired from Sebastian, but, believe me, you have no comprehension of the intricacies of events as they have tumbled into being."

The heat of anger was stoked. "Then I challenge you to explain."

Koschei rose, limbs unfurling. He looked down at her. "Come with me."

It was beautiful in its orchestration.

She stepped away, their fingers parting, slow motion, the wind driving torrents of rain between them.

She didn't give a signal, she called out.

Hil froze, cursing.

Spotlights burst into life, pinning him there in the open. He was surrounded in seconds, figures rushing forward. Mercenaries, guns up, screaming at him to get down, to drop the gun.

He hadn't realised he'd drawn it.

It was knocked from his hand and he was on his knees, splashing in the pooling rain, before he could react, a blow to the back of his head knocking his vision sideways. He braced himself to fight, no way was he getting taken down that easily, and he shoved one guy aside, kicked out at another, and tried to turn but someone moved up behind him, grabbed his jacket and dragged him close, an arm around his throat. Squeezing tight.

He tensed.

There was the sound of weapons being readied all around.

A hand rested on the back of his head, pushing him down.

If they wanted to kill him, they could break his neck in an instant.

He breathed, slow and calm.

Nothing else he could do.

He blinked and looked up, rain beating hard against his face. The girl, who was about sixteen or seventeen, he reckoned now, the girl he'd been stupid enough to trust, was still standing there, right in front of him, upright, no evidence of a wound, no sign of distress. She stepped close and looked down at him.

He blinked again, squinting through the rain.

The girl was staring at him, grinning.

She pushed her goggles up onto the top of her head.

Her eyes were pale. Almost translucent. So like LC's it was hypnotising.

He almost reeled backwards, would have if the mercenary hadn't been holding him there. "Shit," he sent, heart racing.

She peered at him, eyes gleaming, whispering, half deranged, "Told you I'd find you a way out of the city. Eloise is waiting for us..."

Holy shit.

"Iona, are you getting this?" he sent. "Eloise Drake has telepaths."

Somehow somewhere along the line the crazy old bitch must have succeeded in her experiments.

Iona sent back a restrained, "That explains how your cover got bust."

"No shit."

The girl reached forward and stroked her hand against his cheek, making his skin crawl.

"Guess you thought we didn't know about you." She gave a little incredulous shake of her head. "The Bhenykhn know all about you, Zachary. All about this..." She tapped her finger against the side of her head. "This... nothing you have going on." She peered at him with those big, pale eyes. "They really want you. A human they can't detect?"

She wasn't telling him anything new. He'd seen the alerts sent out after they'd escaped from Beijing.

The girl's mouth twitched, something like disappointment, disdain, bemusement, whatever the hell it was, crossing her delicate features, little dimples appearing in her cheeks as she smiled. "Don't worry just yet. Eloise wants to get her hands on you first."

That explained the drawn out dance through the city.

This girl wasn't going to let the Bhenykhn take her prize before she got what she wanted from Drake.

"I must say, I expected more from the infamous Zach Hilyer," she said softly. "You walked right past me in the barracks. I spotted you just like that." She snapped her fingers in front of his face, flicking rain. "No feelings... No thoughts... No life signs... Bit of a giveaway. And out here? I've been following you for an hour. Thieves' Guild?" She shook her head. "You suck."

He hadn't screwed up. And no one had betrayed him. Drake had telepaths. They'd had no idea that was what they were up against.

He couldn't help saying, "You're being played by the wrong side. Don't let..."

He bit off the comment as the guy behind him pushed down, exerting just enough pressure to make him immensely aware of just how fucked he was.

Iona was still talking inside his head. "Don't antagonise them, Hil. They want you alive. Be patient. I'll get you out of there."

He didn't have much choice. They had him and there wasn't a damned thing he could do.

"I really thought you would be more of a challenge..." the girl murmured, waving her hand with a flourish and snapping up a playing card, the jack of clubs, he could just make out, an almost teasing playfulness in those stunning eyes as she held it in front of him, bitterly cold rain still drenching him through. "I can't wait to meet LC." She flicked the card and pulled the neat trick of making it turn into the black joker. She was good, he'd give her that. "He's gonna be my next," she said, eyes flaring wide, grinning at him as she held LC's card up by her face.

"Good luck with that," he muttered.

She stepped back, dropping the grin and staring at him sullenly, as two soldiers appeared beside her.

"Take him to the palace," the girl said, cold and sounding a lot older than she looked. "I wanna get paid. And let's not lose him again, shall we?"

One of them leaned in, pushed his head down and pressed something against the back of his neck that adhered with a vicious spiking pain. Tracker.

He sent quickly, "Iona..." Screw it. Evelyn and Elliott needed to know, and if he was thrown into a prisoner pen, it wouldn't matter a jot who else knew they knew. "Tell Evie..."

The soldier in front of him activated a remote and the device sparked with a shock. Intense. Not pain, Christ, almost pain, but not... some weird line between excruciating and exhilarating... He breathed through the intensity of it and almost laughed, hard pushed to think straight. He'd not had the pleasure of one of these devices since he'd been infected. It was like having a glucose drip packed with go-juice, happy-juice and a shot of insanity for good measure, all pumping direct into his bloodstream.

The mercenary scowled and punched at the remote as

if he thought it wasn't working. His buddy growled a vicious, "Screw this," and even though Hil caught the look and saw the rifle butt incoming, there was nothing he could do to avoid the blow that smashed against the side of his head. The overload escalated, senses spinning.

"Hilyer," he heard deep inside his mind, "stand by."

Playtime.

He almost smiled, lowered his head, closed his eyes and tensed every muscle.

"Keep the girl alive," he managed to send.

"Don't move."

Moving was the last thing he was about to do. He'd been in the centre of this before and it was not something he was ever going to get used to.

He felt the guy behind him twitch as if they were getting ready to haul him up.

Any second...

Someone grabbed his arm, fingers digging deep.

When it came, it sounded like thunder. A crash of lightning right overhead that seared through his eyelids.

He kept his head down.

There was a blast from behind that threw him forward, impacts punching against his back as he staggered and fell, tackling the girl and driving her to the ground, splashing, shielding her there as more explosions erupted around them, gunfire and yells. The Thundercloud bombardment was relentless, the crash of windows blowing out and deep rumbles as buildings collapsed all around, the noise exploding against his ear drums as the billowing dust mixed with the rain to produce a thick airborne sludge that buffeted across them. He kept his eyes squeezed shut and breathed through his sleeve.

It lasted forever then stopped abruptly, the cacophony replaced by the sound of engines, familiar engines, getting close fast, the downdraft sending the downpour spraying outwards in a frenzy.

He risked a glance up, neck muscles complaining, having to squint and wipe at his eyes, still struggling to see. The girl was wriggling beneath him. He threw a punch into the side of her head that stilled her for a second, staggered to his feet and hauled her up, dragging her arm into a restraint hold and wrestling with her to get her in front of him, making it clear she wasn't going anywhere, as the mass of a ship dropped into the clearing with a deafening roar, a swarm of Hailstones flying in to buzz around them.

He muttered a grateful, "Hey," connecting with them with relief. They danced around him, a couple closing in tight before spinning off to circle defensively.

He turned to look around. The bridge across the river was gone. The city levelled at least two blocks in all directions.

"Any time you want, Hilbud," Iona sent, as the ramp of the gulfstream crashed down.

As heartening as it was to see a way out, there was a

guttural drone overhead, Bhenykhn troop carriers, the flashing lights of gunships moving in fast. They were far from safe.

The girl was fighting him but she was small enough to subdue easily and he dragged her, lifting her at times, kicking and screaming, across to the ship, having to step over a scattering of weapons, human bodies sprawled in the rubble.

He shoved the girl on board and wrestled her into a seat, securing her arms with restraints and stepping back, chest heaving. Not exactly what they had planned to extricate but he'd take it.

Iona didn't mess about, taking control of the drop ship, and pulling a vertical evac, sheer lift, the pressure easing only once they'd made jump and dropped into a deep space drift. The ship was cold, a chill tang to the air. He didn't care, even sitting there, soaking wet. He was glad to be cooling down, too hot, the mix of adrenaline and intense input from the device taking a while to dissipate, every cell in his body feeling like it was supercharged as the virus ran riot, taking the energy and using it to heal every damn injury he'd picked up over the past few hours.

It eased eventually and he reached to his neck to tug out the device, clenching it in his fist, working to control his breathing and wishing he'd had time to snatch the remote. It was only then he took the time to reach out. The gulfstream was grappled tight to the Thundercloud, held secure in a hastily retro-fitted docking cradle, a whirl of emotion from Iona battering him like a warm breeze once she was sure they were in the clear.

"Glad you made it, Hilbud. Was looking a bit tight there for a moment."

"You had me covered."

"Damn right I had you covered. I had two gees riding on that mission."

He smiled and stood, reaching into the overhead locker. He had no idea what the hell currency the Thunderclouds used to gamble amongst themselves, even though they included him in it most of the time. He took out a bottle of recycled water, popped it open and took a sip, breathing out slowly, trying to get some kind of balance, his other hand clenched tight. He might be alive but three extraction teams weren't.

A disgusted grunt from a seat behind him reminded him of their guest.

Hil turned round.

"You'll regret doing this," the girl snarled at him. She was shivering, trembling uncontrollably, tugging at the restraints.

He gave her a smile and waved the bottle in the air. "I take it you don't have any of the wacky stuff. No fireballs? No blasts of energy?"

She scowled.

If she could do any of that, she wasn't and he figured if she could she would have already.

"I'm cold," she complained, sounding young again, like a petulant kid. "Aren't you cold? Why is it so cold?"

"Because we don't have the fuel to waste that you do," he said, wandering back to his seat, rubbing a hand over his face.

She was looking around, goggles perched on her head, those pale eyes glaring. She had a disgusted twist on that delicate mouth as she said, "What the hell kind of ship is this?"

"What kind of ship is this, Iona?" he said out loud, wandering back to his seat.

"Gulfstream X750, ER sub class, Wintran. Modified," she replied, curt and sounding like an AI. Iona was playing games. Then she added with emphasis, "ER for extended range. The Modified means 'militarised'. You should see what else we can do."

Hil grinned. "There ya go."

The X750 was the ship Elliott and Iona had sent to retrieve them from Beijing. Elliott had given it to him. Modified it for him. Stealthed to hell. Sparse fittings. Basic quarters. Lockers with his field-op and incursion gear. Minimal supplies because he didn't need much. No AI. He could fly it if needed, but Iona controlled it for him most of the time. And she tended to make the jumps. The X750 was their way of staying together. It wasn't Skye but it was his now. His and Iona's. Thunderclouds had never been designed to carry passengers but this arrangement was working just fine.

The girl wasn't impressed. "Eloise will find me. And when she does, she'll kill you for what you've done."

He shook his head. "I don't think so." He dropped the button device into his pocket. If he could get a remote, that would be freaking useful in a fix. He froze as his hand nudged up against cold metal. The kill tokens. He took one out and rubbed his thumb across the twisted design, wiping it on the leg of his combat pants to clear away the blood and dirt.

One of the Hailstones buzzed in as he sat there and nudged his hand. Hil closed his fingers around the kill token, gripping it tight, and nudging the small sphere back, like bumping fists with Iona, the gesture familiar and welcome. He sensed a ripple of pleasure and amusement from the big AI.

"You can't beat them," the girl said.

He glanced up, taking another mouthful of water. "Looks to me like we just did."

She sneered. "And then you ran away and now you're drifting in deep space. Not much of a victory."

Hil stood and faced her. "How old are you?"

She pulled out the scowl again.

"Where are you from?"

She narrowed those amazing eyes and sat back.

Hil took a step forward and didn't let up. "When did Drake get her hands on you?"

"I don't have to talk to you."

He stopped and downed the rest of the water, casual. "No, no you don't. We don't need you to talk. Guess you'll get to meet LC after all."

The Man's ship, Fleet Comm One, now Evelyn's command centre and effectively the flagship of what remained of the combined human resistance, was already at the RV, broadcasting an urgent message requesting they dock asap and ready for jump.

"Negative," he sent. "You really don't want us to dock. Prisoner on board. And trust me, you don't want her anywhere near anyone."

It was Evelyn herself who cut in, as if she'd been waiting for them. "Hil, get over here. We have to go."

No welcome back. No, 'Hey, glad you're alive.'

"Hey, Evelyn," he sent. "No. You're not listening to me."

"Hilyer, get your ass over here. What the hell happened on Temerity?"

"I got busted by a freaking telepath. Sanchez and Ayling got me out but they didn't make it. Neither did the other two teams." He took a breath. "Did you hear what I just said? Drake has telepaths, Evelyn."

He waited for it to sink in, knowing Iona was sending a stream of intel direct to her desk.

There was a pause, then, "Oh shit."

Yes, oh shit.

LC had always said he didn't understand why they didn't just give the virus to Drake and her cronies. Give it to them. That was one way to take the heat off it. Just give it to whoever. It was shit, was the way he said it, they're welcome to it. Problem was, telepathy was a heap load more powerful than LC would ever comprehend. LC was the most powerful telepath they had. The original, more powerful than NG if you believed what NG had always said before he'd been captured by the Bhenykhn. But LC would never, unconditionally not ever, use that power to hurt anyone. It was a given. An absolute, hard-nosed given unless some scumbag, alien or human, was threatening people LC cared for, and that was excusable. But Drake?

"We caught one," Hil sent, dampening down the need to say that the telepath in question had screwed him over so badly. "Got her here if you want to come get the little bundle of joy but I'm not bringing her on board."

The last thing they needed was a telepath listening in to their every move. And Evelyn was smart enough to know that.

The question of how Drake had got her own telepaths, and what the implications of that were, was something that would have to wait.

"Dammit. This we do not need," Evelyn sent, constrained to say the least. "Okay, Hil, stay there. I'll send Duncan and Martinez with a special detail. Then Hil, you get back here. We don't have time to be screwing around."

"What's going on?"

"Bhenykhn incoming. Right on our tail. Neutralise the telepath. Do you understand?"

They had nothing on sensors. He checked in with Iona, fast updates, all negative.

"We're not picking anything up," he sent back.

"Yeah, well you don't have a resident early warning system. Just make sure she can't communicate with anyone. And get your ass over here."

CHAPTER FOUR

THE CHAMBER to which he took her was dark, deep beneath the main halls and the rooms in which he had graced her presence previously, an air to this other place that was private, concealed.

He didn't speak, walking one step ahead of her, making her trail in his wake. Once there he paused, didn't look back at her, and simply uttered, "You may think you hate me now. What you are about to see will exacerbate that hatred. I cannot urge you to reserve judgement, as your judgement is correct, but I can implore you to wait until you have heard it all..."

She stood her ground, refusing to rise to his mystifying obtuseness.

"The end point in which we find ourselves," he said, "is not where I would have chosen to be had events been under my control. These creatures, these humans, they are fickle, *and they move fast at times, far faster than I was able to anticipate."*

Candles burst into life, one after the next, illuminating a long aisle ahead of them, the flickering orange light glancing off glass canisters.

"Eloise Drake," he said, "was not the only one experimenting with human-Bhenykhn DNA..."

"She hasn't tried anything," Hil sent through the Senson as the guild vessel docked with them, watching the girl to see if she reacted. "But we don't know what she's capable of, apart from being a cold-hearted bitch. Keep her isolated. And you want my opinion? Keep her away from LC."

There wasn't so much as a flicker to suggest the girl had heard the private comms, but then he knew she was a good actress.

"We've got quarantine set up," Martinez sent back as the airlocks cycled. NG's former bodyguard emerged, just wearing fatigues and light infantry armour herself but flanked by five soldiers in full chameleonic battle suits. She took one look around and cursed, sending privately just to him, "You find anything on NG?"

It wasn't just NG they were looking for. Every unit that was out there anywhere had standing orders to report in any sightings of Bhenykhn with blue eyes. So far... nothing.

Hil shook his head. "No."

Four of the Hailstones were hovering, one in each corner of the cabin. If whacko-girl did try anything...

"She isn't carrying any electronics and she has no implant that we can tell," he sent, wide connection to them all, including Evelyn in the link as well.

Hal Duncan was right behind Martinez. "No weapons?" the big marine said as he pushed his way in, angling around and watching the girl's reaction.

Hil shook his head again. "Just an endearing wit that is as razor-sharp as her tongue, and armour-plated arrogance that is irritating as hell."

"She looks like LC," Martinez sent.

"Yeah, I know. And not just the eyes. Wait till you see her smile."

No chance of that at the moment. She was scowling, struggling against the restraints, fists clenched.

Duncan approached her. "Holy shit."

"I know you're talking about me," the girl said, glancing at the soldiers who were spreading out around her and turning her head to stare at Duncan.

"She's trying to read us," the big man sent.

Hil almost laughed. Good luck with that. Hal Duncan and Angel Martinez both had a reputation of being as hard to read as NG. It was good to see they'd teamed up.

Martinez was taking NG's loss hard. They all were, but Martinez especially. Hal Duncan was good for her.

Duncan shook his head and said out loud, "Nice try, kid. But you'll have to work harder than that. You want some advice? Don't even try to read these guys." He gestured to the other soldiers. The detail Evelyn had sent with them weren't just Security, they were the Man's Elite Guard. No one ever messed with them. Telepath or not.

The girl narrowed her eyes, darting a glance sideways, as if she couldn't resist taking the bait.

Hil counted through the Senson, "Three, two..."

She sat bolt upright and froze, gasping in pain, as if she'd been hit by a shot of FTH, point blank, and slumped over, out cold.

"That makes it easy." Duncan gestured to one of the armoured unit they had with them to move in, and turned to Hil. "We've got this. Go. You need to get over there. Iona, refuel and restock. Fast as you can. You're gonna be going straight back out."

Whatever it was, it didn't sound good.

Hil grabbed his kit bag.

"What's going on?" he asked again. "I need to talk to Evie and Elliott."

"Supply convoy just got hit. DiMarco and Tierney. If we lose them, we really are screwed."

. . .

The Man's ship was at full battle readiness. The crew kept him in the docks while they jumped, twice, everyone on edge waiting for the all clear. Whatever jump point they'd dropped into, it must have been swarming with a load of other ships, close by, big ones as well, high level AIs, command vessels, his mind bombarded, pounding, with an overload of input he was hard pushed to contain as he stood there, breathing through it, and as he was waiting for them to release him, he hooked in to the main system of the Man's ship and ran a fast inventory. LC was on board. So was Sean O'Brien, not surprising since she'd been sticking close to LC, had been since they'd got him back from the Bhenykhn. He could hear Edinburgh throwing around banter with Iona, ribbing her for having to put up with him. He stifled a grin and resisted the temptation to butt in. Edinburgh was razor sharp, sarcastic even for an AI. She'd roast him if he even tried to defend himself.

He checked the others quickly, five weeks was a long time to be out of the loop, relieved that he didn't have to resort to the list of dead and MIA. Pen was on Kheris, marshalling the resistance and handling the refugees that were still flooding in to what was still the only colony that was free of the Bhenykhn. Badger was on board the Man's ship. Spacey was on board. Matt Jameson was out with the convoy. So it wasn't just DiMarco and Tierney on the line.

After an age, someone yelled, "We're good. Go," and he ran through crowded corridors, two Hailstones flying at his shoulder as he pushed past techies, pilots in full kit and grunts in battle armour.

He connected with Evelyn as he ran, sending a quick, urgent query requesting a private briefing.

"Now?" she replied, irritated, sounding tired.

"Off the record," he sent back. "Total blackout. And I need Elliott. Do you know where he is?"

"You need Elliott? Dammit, Hil, what is this? We just received an urgent communiqué from Elliott demanding he see you. What's going on? Did Angel and Duncan tell you DiMarco is in trouble? We're trying to..."

"I know, I know, but you need to hear this."

There was a pause, then a curt, "Give me ten minutes."

He went to his quarters, very aware that he was filthy and covered in dried sludge and blood. And even though he didn't have much time, he stopped at his locker and reached into his pocket to take out the new kill tokens. He stared at them. One was a superior token, not the biggest he'd collected, but close. They'd sent a champion after him. He held it in his hand for half a second, not exactly sure what emotion it was that was swirling in his stomach, then tossed it in there with the rest. Ninety three, four and five. He bumped his fist against the sealed bottle of whisky he had standing in there amongst them and reached for the board that was stashed next to it. It was a private, free standing file, not connected to any ship systems, encrypted to hell. He updated the intel fast, adding every scrap of information he'd gathered for himself. The one possible lead he'd been chasing slotted in to the mass of data with uncanny ease, pointing in the direction he'd suspected, not definitive yet, but looking likely enough that it made his stomach turn. He finished up, stashed the board and closed the locker door, leaning his forehead against it and taking a deep, calming breath.

Martha had been working for Itomara.

He'd stake his life on it.

And now Itomara, the esteemed, high ranking Kimi Itomara of the Order's High Guard and CEO of Aries Corp, that NG had pretty much considered to be a solid ally, had vanished.

And he'd hit another dead end.

Dammit all to hell.

He backed away, managing to not punch his fist into the locker door.

Itomara, for Christ's sake.

All this time?

He crammed any thought of Martha back into the little mental boxes he kept buried and stripped quickly, trashed the clothes he'd been wearing without looking too closely at the damage and took a fast, cold shower, checking that each fresh injury was healed, totally healed, not lingering too long on each new scar. He'd had a call-in from medical on the way in. Nothing like the old compulsory post-tab checkups they used to get. Just a 'we heard you were wounded, call in and let us check you out' kinda deal. He'd told them he was fine. He was fine. He didn't know what the hell the virus was doing to him but he didn't want anyone poking at him. He dressed in field-op kit, pulled down his shirt sleeves and headed out.

The war room was packed, bustling with staff, realtime schematics spinning above the table, data boards strewn across its surface. Evelyn was standing at its head, Quinn at her side, not his handler anymore, they were way past that. Quinn was now second in command of the joint forces, Evelyn's right hand man, helping her hold together the volatile alliance of what was left of the human resistance, Imperial, Wintran, guild, ragtag neutrals from the Between like Jiro Tierney. Volatile was an understatement. He didn't envy them.

Evelyn glanced up as he edged into the room, giving him a nod, and sending a fast, "I'll be with you in a minute."

LC was sitting on a bench in the back corner, feet up on a chair, holding a cold pack to his forehead, eyes closed, pale. He was just wearing light combats and a tee shirt, shipside kit like he wasn't expecting to be let out any time soon. The lightning marks from the shaman blast winding around his left arm were as dark as ever, standing out like bruising.

Hil nudged his way through, sending the Hailstones off to keep their distance, and sat next to him, having to nudge him with a quiet, "Hey," to get his attention.

LC looked up, eyes bloodshot, switching the cold pack to the back of his neck and wincing, as if even that small motion was painful, blinking as if he wasn't quite aware of what was happening around him. He was holding the pack with his left hand, his right nestled in his lap, still wrapped tight in the black field bandage he'd taken to wearing. It looked as though he was clenching his fist, not obvious that the fingers were missing unless you knew what had happened.

"You look like shit," Hil whispered. He got a faint smile but that was all. "What's going on?"

It was a pleasantry. He knew exactly what was going on. He was listening in to the main ops comms, filtering the AI inputs he was picking up into something vaguely resembling intel he could process and was tapping into the main boards Evelyn was using to coordinate the orders she wanted actioning. Iona had submitted the intel from Temerity the minute they'd got close and he could see the tumbling implications of everything he'd brought back being fed into the main systems and rippling out into new strategies.

LC looked like he was about to keel over. "They just want me to tell them when the Bennies are near," he mumbled, voice so quiet it was hard to make out what he was saying.

"I'm not being funny," Hil said, "but can't you do that from...?"

"Don't." LC closed his eyes again. "I'm sick of being stuck in medical, and don't tell me I need to sleep." He stuck the ice pack back over his face and leaned his head back against the bulkhead. "How was Temerity? I heard you got caught."

That was the problem with LC. It was virtually impossible to keep anything from him. Hil laughed it off. "Yeah. Did you hear about Drake's telepaths?"

If LC had, he ignored the question. "You get anything on MJ?"

"Possibly." He didn't want to say what yet.

"Nothing on NG?"

"No."

Hil looked across the room. It was good to see Sean there.

"Do you reckon he's still alive?" LC blurted out, blunt, sounding numb.

It had been three months since Beijing. Hil shrugged. He felt cold just thinking about it. "He will be or he won't." It sounded brutal, but what the hell could they do but keep looking, keep fighting and keep dying.

It was a damn good thing no one could read his mind.

Sean glanced up at him as he thought it, as if she had, and for a split second he doubted himself, felt bad and almost walked out, but she engaged through the Senson and sent a soft, "Hey. It's good to see you, Hil. Are you okay?"

He gave her a half wave and sat there, leaning back. Not sure what to say.

Sean said something quietly to Evelyn and stood, grabbing a couple of bottles of water from the table and heading across.

She stopped in front of them, nudging in close to LC and offering them each a bottle. LC had trouble, having to balance the cold pack in his lap to take it with his left hand and then not able to open it. Sean had to open it for him. It was weird to see him struggling so much with something so simple, weird to see LC struggling with anything. It felt like that, more than anything, showed how far in the shit they really were. Like nothing was ever going to be the same again.

Hil downed a mouthful of water. It tasted warm, a tinge of chemicals like the recycle unit was fucked. A long way from the fresh spring water he'd got used to as second nature at the guild.

"It was Sanchez and Ayling, wasn't it?" Sean said softly, out loud, so LC could hear.

Hil nodded, swallowing past a lump in his throat, having to suck it up.

"Was the intel worth it?" she asked, smart enough to know that while it would never justify what happened, it could take the edge off it.

Sean was good to be around. He almost envied LC.

He nodded slowly, feeling grounded just because she was there, because she reached a hand to touch his arm softly and, as hard as it was to admit, he didn't let himself get that close to anyone these days.

"Good," she said. "Because we need everything we can get."

He knew it was shit but he couldn't help saying, knowing how tired he sounded, "We're losing, Sean. If we haven't lost already..."

She had her other hand on LC's knee. "We have to keep fighting. What else can we do?"

He glanced around at the war room, at the frantic discussions on how they could run a rescue and get Tierney and the convoy out alive.

"Drake's playing a different game," he said, cautious, keeping his voice low. It was hard to explain to someone who hadn't seen it first hand, who hadn't seen how damn smart Eloise Drake was being in the games she was playing with the Bhenykhn, with the Order... getting exactly what she wanted and just plain surviving. "We have no food, no fuel, no medical supplies. I'm starting to wonder if collaborating is the way to go, because, seriously, I've seen how they're living and it's..."

Sean frowned and cut him off. "You don't believe that."

"Sean..." he said under his breath. He could feel the muscle in his jaw ticking. "I don't mean we should jump into bed with the freaking Bhenykhn. But, Sean, what if we're playing this wrong?"

LC raised his head, blinking, as if he'd just realised they were still there. "We don't..." He stopped. The bottle tumbled out of his hand, and he looked at them, frantic as if he was trying to say something and couldn't.

His eyes closed and he started to fall.

Shit.

Hil reached and caught him, feeling the clammy heat of his skin burning through his shirt, as Sean grabbed him as well, turning and yelling, "Bhenykhn."

LC slumped against Sean's shoulder and Hil backed off as she held LC there, one hand against the back of his head, as the warning klaxon for jump sounded.

He stared at LC, bracing himself as the rumble of jump drives reverberated through the deck.

"I thought he'd got control of it," he sent, private to Sean.

"He did. This started a couple of weeks ago."

Holy shit.

"This happens every time...?"

"Every time now."

Evelyn was watching them. Half the room was watching.

"He never get anything from the Bennies about NG?"

It wasn't a fair question. If LC knew anything, he'd have said. It just seemed weird that he could be this close to them and not know.

"Nothing," Sean sent. "He's trying but this wipes him out..."

The countdown for jump speeded up, warnings screaming out across the war room. Hil closed his eyes. It was vicious, a long jump they couldn't afford the fuel for, but they dropped out and he was hit with a blistering cacophony of AI intensity. They were surrounded... The Seven. And others.

He blinked through the overload of input to force his eyes open, squinting, to see LC visibly sag, relaxing as if a weight had been lifted, eyes still closed, a trickle of blood running from his ear down his neck, and muttering, "Yeah, we're good."

Shit, they might be but he wasn't. Hil breathed through it and pulled every trick he'd learned in shutting them out, closing down every one until he could think for himself again. It had taken him a long hard time getting used to the high level AIs like Iona and Fallon. The Seven? Different level by a million, painful miles.

He heard Sean communicate the all clear to whoever she was tied with crewside, including him in the loop and Evelyn by the look of it.

Someone nudged him with a, "Hil? You okay?"

"I'm fine," he managed to reply. "The Seven are here."

"You wanted Elliott and he's demanding to see you," Evelyn sent, cutting in. "Sean, get LC to medical. I need him back up and running."

Cold, brutal. LC was an asset. Was that all? Had they

all changed that much? Was that all any of them were now?

"Hil," Evelyn sent, just as cold, "briefing room three. Let's make this fast."

The room was already set up for total blackout. No one could listen in, nothing was being recorded. It was as secure as they could get.

Hil sat down opposite Evelyn, not too happy that Quinn was in there as well, and looked up as Elliott walked in. The avatar, projected being, whatever the hell it was that Aries, the esteemed leader of the Seven, the most powerful AIs in the galaxy, did to create a human-looking walking, talking, cold-skinned entity of solid matter, took a seat at the table and said with no preamble, "I need Hilyer to come with me. Now."

That wasn't totally unexpected. Elliott had been pulling him into missions on and off over the past year.

"Okay but wait," he said, "you need to hear this."

"What?"

Hil set his bottle of water on the table and sucked in a deep breath. "Eloise Drake is working with an AI." He paused and looked straight at Elliott. "They're searching for a weapon that will destroy the Seven."

CHAPTER FIVE

SHE WAS LOST FOR WORDS, *reaching a tentative hand towards the specimens contained there.*

"Yet in all I have done," he said, voice low, "never have I dabbled with the artificially intelligent life forms that are so prevalent in this galaxy. Not only does Drake tamper with the Bhenykhn virus the humans managed so serendipitously to develop, against all odds as I know only too well, but she is throwing care to the winds and throwing into the mix the biomechanical monstrosity that is artificial life with no regard for the consequences."

She turned, aghast.

"You find me abhorrent...?" Koschei regarded her with dark eyes that glinted in the orange candlelight. "Eloise Drake is bold beyond her means. You understand the threat of the Seven?"

She nodded, unease settling deep inside, an unwelcome

emotion amidst the stirrings of anger that had fuelled her so far.

"Then understand this," he said, voice rumbling, "there are three aspects, three factions in this war, in this galaxy in which we find ourselves... human, AI, Bhenykhn. We have underestimated them all. For whoever controls all three, controls the war... the very future of existence of our kind and theirs."

———

Elliott narrowed his eyes, an uncharacteristically emotional response. "Not possible. I know every AI there is. Drake might have enslaved some and may be forcing them to work for her, but, ultimately, they're loyal to me. And whatever Drake thinks she's chasing, she's wrong if she thinks it's a weapon she can use against us."

Evelyn didn't blink. "You've been with Drake?" she said. No mention of NG. She'd stopped asking a long time ago if anyone had any news on NG. Drake was something else, Evelyn's current, barely constrained obsession. And no one, absolutely no one, was blaming her for pursuing it.

He hated to but he had to say it. "Not close to her. No."

She narrowed her eyes as if she didn't believe him.

"Seriously, Evie, Drake's personal security is buttoned up so tight you couldn't get an ant through there if she didn't want to see it. No one gets near her. You want to try anything now? Use LC. He's probably the only person who could get close enough."

"All I need is a crack in the window so I can put a bullet in her head." She stared at him for a moment, eyes dark, then said, cold and precise, "So... something that can destroy the Seven?"

"There isn't anything," Elliott said. "If something like that existed, I'd know. It doesn't."

Hil reached for the water, wishing it was a beer. "They think there is. And I swear, one of the high level AIs is working against us. For her."

That went down even worse.

Quinn leaned forward. "How high? One like the Eighth? Like the one you retrieved from Beijing?"

The atmosphere in the briefing room felt charged as if he was aware of every single molecule of air, atoms spinning. Being this close to Elliott was hard work. Especially with that mention of the Eighth. Touchy subject considering the state she was still in. That she even existed. That someone had dared to attempt to create more of the Seven and had failed so badly.

He curled his hand around the bottle, rubbing his thumb over the label, and raised his eyes, looking at Evelyn not Quinn. "I don't know. Possibly. Maybe just an AI."

She opened her mouth to reply but it was Elliott who spoke first, voice raised. "I thought you understood this, Hilyer."

"I do but..."

Elliott cut him off. "They are captive. We're in communication with all of them. Drake knows that fine well and is limiting what they have access to. Half the time she's feeding them misinformation in a laughable attempt to fool us. Trust me, we are not being fooled. They knew you were there. Do you know how long they knew you were there?"

He bit down on his irritation, not letting it show on his face. But no, he had no idea when whacko-girl had spotted him. It could have been five minutes before he'd yelled for an extraction. Or it could have been five minutes after he'd arrived.

Elliott was relentless. "How do you know they weren't letting you find that exact nugget of intelligence? Planted it right there just for you to uncover?" He shook his head. "Whatever you've seen or heard..."

"What if there is some kind of weapon out there?" Evelyn said, blunt, cold.

"Misdirection to send us running scared and allocate resources we can't afford." Elliott sounded reassuringly convincing. "And believe me, there's no way Drake is capable of creating another viable entity of our ilk, and there is no way any of the AIs are siding with her willingly."

Hil was tapping his trigger finger against his leg under the table, bouncing, staring at the avatar as the swirl of emotion he was picking up intensified, not sure why

Elliott was shutting him down and not giving him a chance to tell them what he'd seen. He took a slow sip of the water, put the bottle down and set his jaw, opening his mouth to protest and clamping it shut as Elliott sent him a firm, private message through the Senson. "Not now. Bear with me."

Easier said than done but he sat back. He'd expected this was going to be tough. Hadn't expected this reaction from Elliott.

"Evelyn," Elliott said out loud, still calm, "I need Hilyer for a mission. You," he pointed towards her, "need to rescue that convoy. It's not just medical supplies, is it? The Mayfair is a mobile surgical hospital. You lose that, you lose a plasma unit."

Elliott emphasised that 'you'. The AIs had no need for human blood supplies but the Mayfair's capacity to produce artificial blood and plasma was crucial for the human forces. So that's why they were all freaking out about the convoy.

Evelyn looked beyond tired, exhausted.

Quinn replied for her. "We know exactly what's at stake, Elliott."

"Good. I'll send the rest of the Seven to help you rescue Tierney and those ships. Hil needs to come with me. Now."

Quinn nodded but Evelyn wasn't impressed. "Where are you going?"

"Please don't ask."

"I'm asking. I assume you're taking a full security detail."

Hil could feel an unease emanating from Iona, random irrational thoughts as if she was arguing with herself or someone else, he couldn't tell, but that was setting him on edge even more.

The leader of the Seven shook his head. "Just Hilyer."

"Elliott, we just lost three of our best teams on Temerity..."

Elliott gave another gesture, this time a small wave of his hand around them. "Because we now know that Drake has telepaths. Hilyer was right to request total blackout for this briefing, don't you think? Drake is giving the Bhenykhn whatever they want... No one can read me. No one can read Hilyer. No offence, Evelyn, but maybe the less you know, the better."

Evelyn wasn't happy. "Do you know what that woman is offering on him right now? We can't even trust people in our own ranks not to turn him in."

Elliott shrugged. "I need someone to infiltrate a base that is overrun with Bhenykhn. You want to suggest anyone else who could do it?"

There wasn't much she could say to that.

"Trust me, there won't be any telepaths there. There aren't any humans there. He's invisible. Fast in, fast out, as you all say."

Hil sat there, letting it all flow over him. He didn't understand why Elliott wanted him to shut up, head pounding too much from the proximity to the powerful AI to sort out the maelstrom of thoughts he was picking up from him, but if he did, there'd be a reason. So he sipped at the water and listened. He wanted another mission, back to back, the less time he was here the better. He knew Evelyn would agree. It wasn't like she had much choice.

Quinn pushed back from the table as if he was done with the conversation. "We have to get this rescue under way."

Evelyn was constrained, as if she was at the end of a tether that had frayed a long time ago. "Fine, go. Hil... just find me a way to Drake."

The intensity in her eyes as she said it was painful. It wasn't just Drake, it was what she represented... it was the Order, for what they'd done to Devon, to NG...

He nodded. He had his own reasons for wanting to get back out there.

"Good," Elliott said. "We leave now."

"Where are we going?" he sent privately.

Elliott scraped back his chair, showing uncharacteristic etiquette in standing as Evelyn stood, even going so far as bowing slightly. He threw Hil a look and sent back, "You are going to Redemption."

He ran, pushing his way through crowded corridors again, the Hailstones that had been hovering outside the briefing room flying ahead, sending to Elliott as he did, "Why the hell am I going to Redemption?"

"You remember the conditioning facility you were sent to?"

Over ten years ago. Of course he remembered. His first tab for the guild. The one he ran with LC when they were kids.

Elliott didn't wait for an answer. "Luka wasn't the only subject that Spearhead infected with his own special strain of electrobes at that base."

And there it was, like a dark echo from the past.

"I though you killed Spearhead."

"I did kill Spearhead," Elliott sent. "Believe me, I destroyed it. And when I destroyed it, it was brutal. Only remnants remained. I've been pulling fragments of its memories together. There's not a lot there and it's taken me this long to figure out what I have. But it has come to my attention that there were others. I want you to find out if any more of the little child soldiers Spearhead took from Redemption managed to survive."

He hit a stairwell, and dropped down two levels, fast, heart pounding even at the thought of Redemption.

"I don't understand why you didn't say this in front of Evelyn."

"Tell her there's a technology that AIs can use to control humans?" Elliott sent, tone scathing. "I take it you haven't mentioned Luka's predicament to anyone?"

He hadn't. No one else knew what had happened to

LC after Redemption or before they'd rescued him from Drake and Spearhead at Zang's fortress. If LC remembered, he hadn't included it in any report, and Hil damn sure hadn't.

Elliott didn't wait for an answer. "A lot of humans still don't trust the AIs. Can you imagine the repercussions if humanity discovered there was a technology that allowed us to control them. The alliance is fragile enough as it is. If it's out there, I want it. We can't afford for Drake of all people to get her hands on it. I want you on Redemption asap."

Redemption? But that wasn't where Spearhead had been. "Elliott, excuse me for being fucking stupid here, but why don't we go straight to the facility?"

"And you know where that is?"

Shit. "No." Hil dropped down the stairwell to the crew quarters. He'd been fifteen. Undercover as a juvenile delinquent – ironically – pulled into an illegal operation on the dark side of beyond. None of them had had a clue where they were taken. "Doesn't anyone at the guild know where we were sent? Didn't they raid Redemption after we were recovered from the Academy?"

"Don't forget, Spearhead was Order. The tendrils ran deep and they were extremely good at covering their tracks. I would know if anyone at your guild knew. They didn't find it."

"What makes you...?"

"Hilyer, the information has to be on Redemption. I

need you to hack the prison AI. The way Luka did when he was a child. Do you reckon you can do it or not?"

Of course he could.

"What about...?"

"Hilyer, whatever the hell you think you encountered on Temerity, leave it to me. You have a mission to complete."

He edged past a couple of medics, Harley, LC's favourite, catching his eye and looking like she was going to stop him. He muttered, "I've gotta go, I'm on a... you know..."

"Hil," she said, a warning tone to her voice as she manoeuvred in front of him. "Your live feed is insane. We got the reports from Temerity. You got shot. Whatever the hell it was with, we need to check you out. You know what happened to LC on Hanover. When...?"

One of the Hailstones buzzed back, circling.

Harley eyed it warily.

"I'm fine," he insisted, sidestepping and backing away. He waved, ignored Harley's frown and threw her a grin, and turned to run right into Spacey.

He caught his balance and caught her up in a hug. "Hey."

She was wearing combat fatigues. She hadn't grown that much but she looked different. She looked like she was guild.

She hugged him back, fiercely, with a, "Hey. You'll never guess what Evelyn has me doing now."

He let up and turned her around, nudging her into a fast walk in the direction he was going. "What are you doing now?"

She didn't answer. She caught his hand and tugged, stronger than she looked. Of course she was stronger than she looked, she was from Kheris. "Wait. What are you doing?" she demanded. "You just got back."

"Space... I..."

She let go. "Hil, we need you here."

It took a fifteen year old kid to say it.

"Luka's struggling again," she said. "Can't you stay for a while?"

"Spacey, I have a mission."

"You always have a mission." She stopped in the middle of the corridor.

He stopped to face her, jostled as people moved past them.

"Luka needs you," she said in a small voice. "Evelyn needs you."

For a kid he'd only known for a couple of months, she had him nailed.

"I have a... thing I need to do," he said, heart in his throat, not exactly lying but not exactly being up front, with anyone. "I have to go. But hey, when I get back I'll show you how to beat LC at poker. I promise."

She didn't argue, just stood there looking at him, and he didn't need to read her mind to know what she was thinking.

He backed away, turned and disappeared in amongst a squad of grunts, breaking into a run again.

"How come no back up?" he sent as he moved.

Elliott waited a second as if an AI that powerful needed to compose itself before having to repeat itself to a stupidly slow human. "Redemption is well and truly in the centre of Bhenykhn-controlled space. There are no human ships there. None. At all. No wreckage a Thundercloud can hide in, no fleet in orbit that Iona can mingle with. She'll take you, get you in, then she goes. Do you understand?"

That explained why Iona was being so tetchy.

"Pay attention now, Hilyer," Elliott sent. "Redemption is teeming with Bhenykhn. Only Bhenykhn. No humans. Why they're there, I don't know. I've been close but not close enough. And a lot of the systems are inert. I need a body on the ground. Someone who can get in and get to the AI core. And I can hardly send Luka, can I?"

"No..."

He shut out the Senson input, made it to his cabin without running into anyone else and pushed open the door, heart pounding from more than just the exertion. He wasn't going to rise to Elliott's chiding. He'd hacked into the base at Redemption as much as LC had, he'd just not got caught doing it.

. . .

Iona took him in, releasing the gulfstream in orbit. It dropped in combat mode, under full stealth, into the centre of a raging storm. She pulled it, by remote, into a gravity-defying, slewing stop twenty feet above the ocean, and held it there, ramp open, battered by gale force winds that were whipping the sea into an angry frenzy of roiling waves. He held onto the rail for a split second and jumped.

CHAPTER SIX

"ARIES SENT HILYER BACK TO REDEMPTION?" She *couldn't keep the horror from her voice, turning from the array of grotesque specimens to stare at him with dismay.*

Redemption had not been a distinguished chapter in the history of the Thieves' Guild, not in any way. She had argued against the sending of children into active theatre, not often that she interfered in the day to day business of the Alsatia but disturbed enough to protest when she'd heard what they intended.

Koschei himself had overruled her.

He stood there now, enshrouded in darkness, the orange light reflecting from the staring dead eyes of the hideous samples in the jars around them, his failures.

"You must understand what Hilyer has become," he said, his eyes meeting hers. "Of all my experiments, he is one of my greatest achievements."

Dismay turned to dread. He was not referring to the alien virus... something in his tone made her stop. "What did you do?"

"The best subjects are always those we capture young. How else did you think Hilyer survived that cesspit of the human penal system that is Wildlands?"

The last time he'd fallen this far into water, he'd been wearing light cotton prison clothes, barefoot, with a gunshot wound and broken ribs. This time he was wearing guild-enhanced incursion gear. Not quite the best after almost a year of alien occupation, but not far off.

He plunged below the waves and let himself sink into a silent darkness. He tumbled slowly, flashing data through the Senson. It was three miles to the island. No human life signs. What looked like five hundred and sixty Bhenykhn. Ten life signs he couldn't identify. Three gunships parked up, and two troop carriers in orbit along with a command vessel they'd had to avoid on the way in. Iona was keeping her distance, just waiting for the ship to return, ready to bug out before she was spotted. And somewhere in there was a dead AI and hopefully intact records from ten years ago that the guild had somehow managed to miss. As tabs went, it would've been high on the list of improbables. High risk ingress with minimal chance of the target even being there. They were always the tough ones. When you fought and struggled your ass off to get in somewhere just to find the intel was off and it, whatever it was, wasn't there. He'd had plenty of those. You just switched off and did it anyway. This was no different. Except for the Bhenykhn. And the half a billion on his head. Or whatever it was now. It was difficult to comprehend how money could mean anything to anyone anymore. But then he'd seen Drake's set up, and while society wasn't necessarily flourishing, a lot had returned to some semblance of normality.

He twisted around in the water, getting his bearings. "So how much is riding on this mission?" he sent to the Thundercloud as the gulfstream shot back up into orbit.

"You don't wanna know, sweetheart." Iona sent. "Just go do your thing."

His thing. She found him curious. That had been the first feeling he'd ever picked up from her. She found it strange that such a small creature could have such freedom to come and go where he pleased. The AIs, and especially the Thunderclouds, were powerful, immense beings but freedom was a hard fought concept that was still raw and elusive in many quarters. It was difficult to feel that emotion, that they were so pained, still, by the shackles humankind had placed on them. Even Elliott. Even now that things were so different.

He worked through the schematics of the prison. He'd been incarcerated here, had spent months in prison before that, more than once. He knew what it was like to have no freedom. And he appreciated every second that he was free to do what he wanted. The guild had given him the freedom he'd never had before. Mendhel and NG had given him that freedom. As if they'd known that was all he needed. A place to belong, somewhere to come back to, without reins, without bars, with the only expectation that he excelled as well as they knew he could, as well as he wanted to in order to keep that place he'd earned. And he had earned it. Thanks to LC, he had earned it. And he owed LC and NG, more than he could ever repay.

Iona was quiet for a moment, then she sent, "Stay safe, Hilbud. I'll be back in ten hours and I'll cycle in every two hours after that until I either pick you up or they shoot me down. But try not to be late, okay?"

He could feel her deep unease at leaving him alone. She was thinking she'd never forgive herself if anything happened to him. That wasn't easy to overhear.

"I'll be waiting," he sent back. Not cocky. No way sure enough that he could do this. But he sent it all the same.

Then he kicked out and started swimming.

It took about an hour and a half to get close. He didn't push it, buffeted by the waves and taking his time to get close enough to the rocks to get ashore without getting bashed against them. He made it to the bottom of a cliff edge and emerged into rain that was searingly cold as he stripped out of the incursion suit. This was the

Redemption he remembered. He dropped the suit into the waves where it could wait until he needed it again, then hunkered in close to the wet rocks. He was wearing field-op kit, lightweight, water repellent, light armour, sensor-resistant shielding activated. The only weapons he had were the knife in his boot and another in a sheath at his side. He was going in light. And quiet.

It was strange to think the last time he'd been here he was fifteen. He sat for a moment, stretched out his hand and turned it, letting the rain stream down his palm, cascading off each finger, smooth clear skin on the inside of his wrist where the guild had erased the black prison tattoo that had been there back then.

A wave crashed against the headland, spray flying, the storm intensifying. He sucked in a breath of cold salt-tinged air, and clenched and unclenched his fist, shaking out the unease. That had been a lifetime ago. A different lifetime ago. Redemption had been bad, but nowhere near as bad as Wildlands. He'd survived that. He could survive anything. Except now Redemption was overrun with Bhenykhn. He might have been imagining it but he could smell the stench of them even out here in the rain.

The base AI was inert. Offline or dead, whichever, she was closed down, and they'd had no response to their tight wire attempts to communicate. Whatever had happened, it didn't look like she'd survived the invasion when the Bennies had landed and decided they liked the place enough to make it a base for whatever the hell they'd want to do on a cold, godforsaken shit-hole of an island.

He risked reaching out with the Senson again but there was nothing. If the records were here, he was going to have to get them the hard way. That was fine. Everything he'd ever done had been the freaking hard way.

He pulled up his hood, settled low light vision kit into place over his eyes and checked the rest of the gear he had activated, motion sensor nullifier the most crucial. They had no evidence the Bhenykhn used motion detectors, why would they when they could 'see' human lifesigns? But the hive knew he existed, was smart enough to anticipate that there might be more humans like him, and could easily have acquired and rolled out the tech to set up perimeters watching for unexpected movement.

All seemed to be in order. As far as he could tell. He couldn't sense Iona anymore. So he was on his own.

There were three ways in to the main prison complex on Redemption. Walking in through the main gate was out of the question, as was dropping in to the main landing pad. So that left the sewers and storm drains. He pushed to his feet and started to creep his way around the base of the rocks, making his way round the coast to the outlet they'd identified as the best option, keeping low and close to the rocks. He knew he was getting near as the stench increased, a heavy tang of cloying decay clinging to the mist whenever he found an overhang to shelter from the rain. All he needed to do was make it inside, make it to the AI core and get out. Eight hours and counting.

The storm drain led into the main complex but there was no way down to the inner hub of the sub basements that housed the AI and the records without getting up into the main structure of the prison complex itself. He went in through the juvie facility, working his way through the rafters and crawlspaces, past the main hall, the gym, the dorms and classrooms, all teeming with Bhenykhn. They'd hung heavy drapes on the walls, sconces holding burning torches hammered into the main beams. It stank of that leafmold stench of decay, heavy with pheromones, wafts of some kind of incense. Every space was filled with workbenches, rows upon rows of benches, all strewn with apparatus, jars, knives, figures hunched over at each one, working. It was strange having to be so careful somewhere he'd kicked around in as a kid, weird to think how much more he could do now, how much he'd learnt in the past ten years. Having to be so much more careful now that there was so much more at stake than just the threat of being beaten and thrown into solitary for a few hours.

He ran a standard avoidance and reset incursion, monitoring life signs as he moved, invisible, silent, leaving no trace, replacing anything he moved, re-securing any locks he had to bust open. No footprints, no finger marks, no tool marks. Not so much as a smudge of dust out of place. Immaculate. The Bhenykhn had no idea he was there.

He could hear them, grunts and shouts echoing through the corridors as he slipped from one spot to another, keeping to shadows, having to hold a couple of times and wait as they walked past. He had plenty of time. No need to rush. No need to take risks. He moved carefully and deliberately, working his way through to the admin block, backtracking when necessary. It took three hours. Leaving one to get what he needed. Four to get back out. He leaned against a maintenance hatch and gently bust open the lock, bypassing an old alarm system with care even though the power was down. The Bhenykhn used their own generators, nothing like human tech, nowhere near, far more powerful, and with that weird mix of immensely advanced systems to power their weapons and ships, then freaking candles to give them light.

There was probably a reason for it. There was probably a reason for all this. In the grand scheme of the universe. What it could be, he had no idea. And he didn't care.

He leaned into the hatch and opened it slowly as the lock gave way. He could hear footsteps behind him. He edged through and brought the hatch to a close gently, staying there and breathing slow and steady as the aliens walked past, the tapping of a staff and rattle of bones suggesting a shaman, grunts and guttural chatter coming from at least a couple of others. He didn't know what the fuck they were saying. For telepathic creatures of a hive mind, they weren't quiet. He knew that. He'd been this close before, many times since that first encounter on Erica on board their crashed command ship. Shit, that had been a wild ride. Even flashing back that briefly on it ignited a dark flare of unwelcome emotion deep inside his chest that he had to shut down as fast as it manifested.

He pocketed the lockpick and rested his hand against the knife at his belt, waiting and listening as they passed. Concentrate on the now, this tab. Nothing else. He needed to get down into the maintenance tunnels. No one knew why the Bhenykhn avoided tunnels but they did, and in almost a year had never shown any inclination to start using them, easy enough to wait out any humans they were hunting. Once down there, he'd have free run of the place. AI core, records, comms centre... And he could find out what had happened.

The Bhenykhn passed, nothing untoward. He leaned in again and locked the hatch, the mechanism slotting into place with a quiet click.

He waited a moment. Then took off.

The easiest way down was through the crawlspaces lined with cables and pipes, squeezing past thick bundles of wire, and dropping down one level at a time, enough light coming in through vents here and there that he could see what he was doing. Finally he dropped down into the tunnels, into pitch black darkness. He waited a moment for the goggles to adjust from low light to zero input, just enough so he could see. That was one thing he did envy LC for, being able to see in the dark. Although from everything LC said, it was relentless, no way to sit in darkness and relax. Ever. Nowhere was ever dark. Except the nightmares. He didn't envy that.

He stood, getting his bearings. It wasn't far to the AI core. This close? It should have been deafening but there was nothing. It was quiet. Too quiet. No rumbles of power conduits, no hum of electrobes. The band on his wrist was dormant.

He checked the time. Forty five minutes until he needed to split and start to work his way out. Only once when he was here as a kid had he ventured this far below the complex. He'd backed out when the electrobes got too bad, ran back to the dorm and tried not to cough his lungs up. Now, the lack of electrobes was sending his stomach cold.

He started to work his way through, figuring out the way from the schematics he'd had to memorise the hard way. Another thing it was easy to envy in LC, but again, the way LC said it, having an eidetic memory, remembering every freaking detail of everything that ever happened to you, was as much a curse as an advantage. Screw that. Hil took out his knife and twirled it between his fingers as he walked. He had so many walls built up around the crap he didn't want to remember, it was good to have a focus to fill his memory with new stuff like inch by inch schematics of a prison complex ten levels deep. He paused at an intersection and shrank back against the wall, checking the way ahead, out of habit more than anything. Clear. Nothing on the motion detector. A couple of small anomalies that might be rats.

He took one step out, heard a noise and froze. Damn sure that wasn't rats. It sounded more like a dog or a wild boar. Snuffling, growling and gnawing as if it was worrying some prey it had caught. There shouldn't be any freaking animals down here. There'd never been wildlife on the island and he'd never heard of the Bhenykhn using animals. It sent his nerves grating. He shrank back into the shadows and spun the knife up into a fighting grip.

The noise stopped.

He tensed.

Silence.

That was worse.

He backed up. Slow and steady. Running alternate routes through his head, trying not to give in to the temptation to run, when there was a snarl and a scrabble of claws. A hit of adrenaline sent his heart racing. He'd been caught by guard dogs before. Not something he wanted to repeat.

He turned and ran.

. . .

Whatever it was, it started howling, a call to the hunt, gaining on him, no way was he going to make the maintenance hatch. He scanned ahead of him as he ran, looking for doors, ladders, anything.

There was nothing.

He could hear it behind him, breathing heavy, slavering, snarling, getting so close he could almost feel its breath. It was big. He couldn't run any faster. There was something that looked like a thick pipe overhead.

He jumped for it, hooking his arm around it and swinging up.

Jaws snapped tight around his trailing leg, clamping round his thigh, only the light armour of the field-op kit stopping it from biting his leg clean off, pain flaring as teeth broke through and sank into his flesh.

The weight of it started to drag him down, muscle tearing.

He let go instantly before it could take his freaking leg off.

And he fell.

CHAPTER SEVEN

"*THE UZHASA.*" *She breathed the name as if to say it out loud would be to summon the dire creatures here. It made her heart ache with an ice cold chill. It was bound to happen. Only a matter of time...*

"The Bhenykhn Lyudaed are enjoying the hunt."

She lifted a small glass jar, watching the pale liquid in it swirl, the organs of some creature or other floating adrift. "All the others are gone. There is now just us, Koschei, you and I. We alone bear responsibility for the survival of the fragile souls we found here, this species upon which we set loose the scourge of the Devourers." She set the jar down on the workbench next to the dismantled parts of a twisted black metal staff, careful to avoid touching the knotted strings of bones that lay discarded amongst jars and pots of substances, milky vapours creeping from some, others glistening with bioluminescence. "I see now you have never been honest with me. Be honest with me now... can we beat them?"

He turned from her. "I know you do not approve of my methods, but knowing now what Hilyer encountered on Redemption, I fear whatever we try we may be too late."

The creature tossed its head as they hit the floor, letting him go and throwing him aside. He hit the tunnel wall, hard, face first, black closing in as the goggles smashed. He fell, curled up, trying to shield his head, senses rattled, leg on fire, clenching his fist around the hilt of the knife as it pounced on him.

He swung his arm and felt the blade scrape against something hard then bite into its neck. Its flesh tore, blood spurting. The stench was hideous, worse than the Bhenykhn, and he couldn't breathe, desperately trying to stay quiet, cursing under his breath against the pain, and stabbing it again, deep, dragging the knife through its neck. He could feel the power in its muscles, as the blade cut through sinew and hit against bone. It howled then and opened its maw, jaws gaping towards his head, its breath hot in his face as it snarled. He managed to twist away, thrusting his shoulder up in defence as he stabbed again, the blade going deep, his vision narrowing and strength going as jagged teeth bit into his arm and an agonising heat pulsed into his bloodstream. The virus faltered.

Poison.

His hand fell from the knife grip, all feeling draining out of his entire body.

And the full weight of the creature collapsed on top of him.

He was not going to die on Redemption. He'd decided that a long time ago. He'd be damned if he was going to let it happen now. He lay there for what seemed like forever, bleeding, each wound burning with a heat that was beyond pain, then slowly forced himself to gather up the strength to move, stomach muscles complaining as he tried to heave the creature off him.

Its teeth were embedded in his shoulder and upper arm. He sagged back onto the floor, raised a shaky hand and tried to take a hold of its head by the scruff of the neck, no strength, having to channel every hurt and pain and injustice he'd ever suffered to get angry enough that his muscles would react and grip hard enough to shift it. Its teeth withdrew from his flesh with agonising slowness, every inch excruciating as if the jagged incisors were barbed. His eyes were watering by the time he got free. He rolled the body of the creature off him, sagging again with the effort, light-headed and half delirious. The adrenaline was dissipating. That was all. He lifted a hand that felt like it didn't belong to him and dragged the broken goggles off his eyes. He couldn't see a thing. He needed to move. This thing might have a mate. He stayed still for a moment, listening, but couldn't hear anything. That didn't mean much. He reached along the floor, numb fingers sticky with blood. He could feel an underlying energy humming through the base around him, wires and cables below the floor. There wasn't much but he spread out his hand and pulled in enough energy to be able to shift his ass and reach to his belt, hitting up against his flashlight. He fumbled with it, clenching and unclenching his fist until he had enough strength to grab it and flick on the beam. The red light reflected off dead orange eyes staring right at him, pupils slit-thin like a cat, the creature's head lolled, limbs sprawled. It sure as hell was not any kind of dog or big cat he'd ever seen before. Its muzzle was leathery, short matted fur tufting around chitinous plate armour, massive haunches muscular. The jagged, razor sharp teeth he'd experienced up close and personal.

He lay back, letting his head rest down, eyes closing as he checked the time. Twenty minute window to find the intel before he needed to split. Shit. This was going to be close now. He drummed up enough energy to reach into a pocket and pull out a trauma patch as he lay there, tucking it inside his shirt and pressing it against his upper arm, feeling the virus respond, the heat intensifying. It took another moment or two before he could sit and see to his leg. His thigh felt like it was on fire. He could heal small wounds fast. This felt like something else entirely. He didn't look too closely. He dragged himself to a conduit that was warm and pressed one hand against it, drawing in energy as he pressed a trauma patch against his leg to staunch the bleeding. He couldn't afford to stay there. He wrapped a black field bandage tight, popping in a shot of antibiotic to help the virus deal with whatever the hell that thing's bite might have infected him with, breathing through it and readying himself to move.

Eighteen minutes. He could do this.

He reached, dragged his knife out of the creature's neck, and pushed to his feet, staring down at it for a second before turning and casting the beam of the flashlight into the darkness. So much for the tunnels being a safe bet.

A snarl echoed up ahead.

Shit.

He turned and ran, limping, swearing, and screwed if they caught up to him.

There were more than two of them. Three or four from the scrabbling sounds and barking. He had no idea how but this time he reached a ladder that went up to a maintenance hatch and was climbing up into it, dragging his injured trailing leg inside and slamming the hatch down as the fastest of the snarling beasts threw itself at the wall. He backed away, chest heaving, hearing them growl, low threatening rumbles.

He scrambled backwards into the small space and crawled, scraping his elbows, squeezing through gaps between pipes, and having to flatten himself, reaching to grab a hold of struts to pull himself through in places, very aware that he was leaving a trail of blood, but there was no way a Bhenykhn could get in here, no way one of the mutant dog creatures could get in. Problem was, he couldn't stay there. He stopped at one point to catch his breath and reassess. He was jammed in tight, and for a second it was quiet, hot, just a hum of machinery vibrating through the pipes he was squashed in amongst.

He had four hours before Iona came back for him. If he was lucky, the Bhenykhn would assume the creatures were chasing rats. If he was unlucky, they'd send someone down there and discover one of their pets dead, if they didn't know already. And if these creatures were telepathic, he was well and truly screwed.

He pressed one hand against the bandage around his thigh, breathing through the burning heat, and held the other against a power cable, drawing in more energy faster than he'd ever done before, healing, the agonising pain in his leg and shoulder easing to a dull ache as the wounds sealed.

He needed to get the intel. That was it. That was all he had to concentrate on. Find a way in. Get it. Find a way out. Simple. Same as every tab he'd ever run for the guild.

. . .

The only way directly into the sub basement, avoiding the tunnels, was the elevator from the admin centre. He crawled forward on his elbows and peered through a gap in the ceiling tiles. The hallway was dimly lit, a single hulking Bhenykhn warrior stationed at each end. Only two but enough to make the lift shaft option hard.

Three figures approached as he watched, taller, thinner, wearing robes, not armour. Not shamans. They walked close together, occasional grunts and gestures, but mostly in silence. Creepy as hell. There was something familiar about them. They stopped at the lift shaft and waited for the doors to open, having to stoop to go in, turning to face him, and he saw their twisted features, leathery skin like all the Bhenykhn but drawn cheeks, sunken eyes.

His stomach turned as it clicked then where he'd seen their like before.

In the chambers deep within the processing plant under Beijing. Knives in their hands, dissecting human prisoners.

The elevator doors closed.

There were no humans here, at least not living ones. He knew that from the scans they'd made from orbit on the way in but even so, it made that queasy knot deep inside twist to wonder what they were doing down there.

He backed up and found some space to sit, checking

the time again and stretching out his leg to check his thigh. The bleeding had stopped. He wrapped a fresh field bandage around it and flexed the leg, feeling the intense heat still burning away, fatigue draining every cell as the virus worked to fix the damage. He curled his hand around the warm metal of a conduit to drag in more energy, feeling the virus respond, needing desperately to wait and pull in more to help it but feeling the back of his neck prickle with unease.

The only thing he could think to try was an ingress through the adult prison block. He'd only been in there once ten years ago. It would mean going back outside but from the look of the motion scanners he had active, the Bennies were all inside, only a couple running a patrol of the perimeter. He'd missed any chance of the first RV already but he was damned if he was leaving here without that intel.

He lingered before he let go of the conduit, cinched the bandage tighter and moved out.

It had stopped raining, low cloud casting a gloom over the complex. Roughly midday. Not that you could tell from the light. They'd timed the mission to hit pre-dawn going in, dusk extricating.

No chance of that now.

He crouched on the rooftop in the cover of a vent and watched the patrols.

They looked like they were running drills. Not seriously expecting trouble. Until, as he watched, there were shouts. Three of the bigger warriors met in the courtyard, a door opening in the main block and a commander striding out, black cloak. Not the biggest he'd ever seen, but big enough. It beckoned and one of the others gestured to someone he couldn't see.

Two more warriors entered the open area, both holding chains and leading two of the mutant dog creatures, one of them dragging the body of the one he'd killed, the other with something hanging from its mouth.

He watched, eyes narrow, as the commander waited until the creatures were close then lifted its hand, beckoning again. One of the warriors leaned down and took something from the dog, offering it up to the commander.

It was a blood-soaked cloth.

The huge commander lifted the cloth to its nose and sniffed, a smirk creasing its leathery features as it looked up and around, as if it was testing the air.

It recognised the blood as human. Hil couldn't read its mind, couldn't hear the hive, but it was damned obvious.

And if they knew that was fresh human blood, and they couldn't sense a human anywhere on the colony, they'd know it was him.

Or someone like him.

There were satisfied grunts from the watching

Bhenykhn, pheromones heavy in the damp air. An apprehension growing. Axes hefted, muscles twitching.

More of the alien warriors appeared around the edges of the courtyard.

Iona wasn't due back for another three hours, twenty two minutes.

He could survive that long...

Two shamans walked up to the commander, standing at its side, rune-etched bones clacking as they twisted their staffs.

...or he could go get the intel he'd come for.

The shamans kept their heads down but cast their eyes around as if they were trying to sense him. The dog creatures were pacing, growling.

He let his heart rate slow and stared as the commander threw the bloody cloth down in front of the two mutant beasts as if it was throwing down a gauntlet. They sniffed at it, straining at the chains, snarling. The commander nodded, and the two warriors released the catches. The creatures raced off, muscles rippling, teeth bared.

So much for them wanting him alive.

He closed his fist around the hilt of his knife.

If it was a hunt they wanted, he'd damn well give them one.

The first time he'd ever seen a dead body, he was seven. The first time he'd seen someone kill, in cold blood, he was twelve. And the first time he'd ever killed someone, he was fourteen, and found out the hard way that arguing self-defence was a bad mistake that had gotten him dragged into a police cell and beaten half to death himself.

He stepped back into the shadows and wiped his knife on his thigh, controlling his breathing, staring at the hulking alien body lying out there on the cold ground by the gate, blood pulsing from the wound in that sweetspot at the back of their neck where the armour flexed.

That was the fourth he'd killed.

He slid the kill token into his pocket to nestle there with the others.

Ninety six, ninety seven, ninety eight.

And now ninety nine.

Felt like a long, long way from that first one on Erica.

He watched as the Bhenykhn mobilised, knowing instantly that he'd killed another one. He could hear the roars, guttural shouts as they realised he was hunting them, hating that they couldn't see him.

More troop carriers had dropped in system, coming in low, pods thudding down in relentless reinforcement of their position. Gunships multiplying as they flooded the place.

It was getting late, what light there had been fading, shadows lengthening.

He shrank back into the darkness alongside the wall, let it enshroud him like a cloak.

Even their freaking attack dogs couldn't sense him

because he'd soaked himself in their blood. He could see the creatures out there, turning and snarling at each other, straining at the leashes, not knowing which way to go.

He spun the knife around his fingers.

Thing was, they were assuming he'd be trying to escape, sending out search teams to scour the moorland. It didn't seem to occur to them that he could be breaking in.

He edged back and worked his way round, slipping into the admin block. One more for the hundred and he knew exactly which one he was going for.

It was standing guard by the access to the lift shaft maintenance hatch. The only thing standing between him and a fifty foot climb down to the sub basement where he needed to be.

Twelve hours ago he'd scoped out this corridor and moved on, needing a way past without being seen. Now?

He watched as it patrolled. Easy. Not expecting trouble. Probably wishing it was out on the hunt, if they even thought like that.

It was a grunt.

Easy.

He braced himself to jump down, waiting, timing out the pattern of its movement, knife held loosely as he crouched on the overhead beam. His leg was still sore, shoulder aching, but the heat had eased. He checked the time. Any minute now. It was strange to be surrounded by so many troops, yet to have no AI thoughts battering his mind, no comms he could listen in to, no channels of data he could hack. It was as if he'd lost his hearing, deaf to all sound. He'd had that before, been too close to too many explosions more than once. But the Senson had always been there to give him access to the outside world. Here...? Nothing.

Until...

Five more minutes and he was starting to think she wasn't going to make it, when he got the rush of emotion before the comm stream hit the Senson.

It was good to feel that connection even though he knew she was going to be pissed at him.

"Hilyer, sweetheart, you wanna let me know why the hell you are still in the middle of that island and not at the RV?"

He sat back, relief that she was there mixed with a level of anxiety for her safety that was sky high.

"You need to leave," he sent back.

"Damn right I need to leave. I need to leave now. With you. What the hell is going on, Hil?"

"Iona, go."

"What happened?"

"I..."

The Bhenykhn pacing the hallway below him stopped, still, as if it was listening to something, the way they did when the hive was reacting to some kind of alert.

Hil froze, breathed slow and steady, and inched back.

"I don't have the intel yet," he sent. "But you need to let everyone know, they have attack dogs. In the tunnels. Huge freaking mutant attack dogs. We can't assume tunnels are safe anymore." He balanced his weight, adjusting the angle of his new vantage point. "Iona, go. Don't risk getting caught."

She must have been scanning his stats because her tone changed as she sent, fast and urgent, "Hil, what happened? Are you okay?"

That was a helluva question. He watched the Bhenykhn resume its patrol, walking further down the corridor that time and regarding the stairwell intently before it turned and walked back, massive rifle cradled in its arms.

"Hilyer, are you injured? Talk to me."

"I'm fine. But they know I'm here. Iona..."

And as soon as he killed that Bhenykhn, they'd know exactly where he was so he'd have to move fast.

"Dammit, Hil. I can't see a way to get you out and I can't stay. The whole system is teeming with them. There's no way I can..." He could hear her thinking, processing scenario after scenario, calculating distances, times, odds, all flashing by with dizzying, despairing speed as she hit dead end after dead end. "There's no way I can even get close enough to deploy the Hailstones. But I..."

"Iona, there is no way out. Just go."

He edged forward.

"Hil..."

"Go. Come back in two hours and I'll have the intel for you."

There was a moment's silence then she sent, "Roger that. See you in two."

The connection cut at the same instant the AI presence vanished.

Hil spun the knife, braced himself and dropped.

CHAPTER EIGHT

A SWELL *of pride defied the disgust she had at having to
listen to this account of these events that had happened so
fast in her absence. "I had heard Hilyer's reputation is now
somewhat formidable amongst the Bhenykhn." She
murmured it. Proud. But also regretful. Such reputation
could only attract dangerous attention.*

*"He hunts the hunters," Koschei said simply. "You know
they thrive on a challenge. What greater challenge than to
have one of your prey dare to turn the tables? A small, weak
species that dares take up a blade against you? Considering
what he did whilst moving invisible amongst them, it is not
surprising that they came to value his hide more and more.
And not surprising that so many of his own were willing to
offer so much to get their hands on him."*

The sub basement was warmer than the last time he'd been down here, sneaking around as a kid. No coolant. That was obvious. No electrobes. No sting of chill, tainted air at the back of his throat as he dropped down out of the shaft, kill token number one hundred in his pocket, landing on his feet and only slightly out of breath.

It was quiet down there. Way too quiet.

He had a cold spot of dread sitting low in his stomach even though he knew what he was going in to.

The chamber was dark. Far from the sterile cool hum there should have been down there. Far from it. There was a dank warmth to the air. The stench of the Bhenykhn heavy. His boots crunched on broken glass as he reached for the flashlight on his belt and cast a beam around the AI core.

They hadn't been subtle in their destruction of it. She'd been torn apart. The casing was smashed, veins and cables ripped out and shredded. He stepped over broken panels and kicked aside debris, the floor plates sticky with grey sludgy biomatter, littered with shattered glass.

He wasn't picking up anything down here. She was gone. Completely. No activity at all.

He moved the beam of the torch around the chamber and stopped, that cold unease biting deep, as it illuminated benches and shelves stacked with bottles and jars, apparatus, knives. He'd seen this before as well, only last time it had all been drenched in red blood, the samples in the jars human body parts. This time it was pale fluids, a tinge of green, metallic components, silver shards glinting in the arc of light. They hadn't just destroyed her, they'd dissected her.

He stared. All he could hear in his mind was Skye telling him calmly to get down, all he could see was the mud and the rain, the gunship breaking through the low cloud, guns whirring, heading straight for them. And Skye just telling him to get down, before...

His chest was hurting. The scar from the machete that had almost cut him in two the first time he'd encountered them out on that damned cold moorland. It was the worst kind of bone deep, muscle throbbing ache that flared across his chest every time he thought about her and that moment, that instant that...

He blinked.

Not on Erica. He was on Redemption and he had a tab to complete.

He backed away, breath caught in his throat, as a sound echoed, far away but getting closer. He looked up, letting his arm fall and the beam of light vanish.

Footsteps and the clatter of shaman staffs.

He watched from a perch high up in the rafters of the core as three tall Bhenykhn and a shaman entered the chamber. The shaman gave a wave of its hand and candles flickered to life. He shrank back, sure of the darkness but still uneasy. At least there were no damned dogs with them.

They started to unpack a crate and lifted out more parts, reverently placing them on the counter tops and wielding knives to split them open, working methodically. He almost gagged when they opened one flask-like biohazard container and took out what looked like a human heart, placing it down in front of a line of clear glass containers that glowed a sickly green in the candlelight, the fluid inside swirling and twisting. Electrobes.

He knew they did this. Had known it since Erica. Shit, he'd never told anyone about some of the crap he'd seen on that grounded Bhenykhn ship. But it was still unnerving to see it happen right in front of him.

They sliced the heart open, spreading out the muscle and sinew and pinning it in place. He didn't want to watch but it was grotesquely hypnotising. One of them picked up a complex component that looked like an Aidan's tube, orange light dancing along its surface. Jesus, they were playing with human weapons components, AI biomatter and human body parts. LC used to joke that if he got caught, they'd liquidise his brain and feed it to rats. And shit, now that idea was in his head Hil half expected to see a cage in there, could almost hear the scrabbling of tiny clawed paws.

He blinked.

The shaman had a ball of energy crackling in its palm.

It clenched its fist and the lightning sizzled, sparked

between its bony fingers and vanished. The heart jerked on the table.

Holy shit.

He didn't want to see any more, inched backwards, nudged against a beam and braced himself to climb.

The mod bay was dark and quiet, cooler. He dropped down, in total silence, and stood. Just breathing. Then he pulled out the flashlight again and scanned it across the banks and banks of memory modules spread out in aisles in front of him.

LC had always said there was a layer of security that he'd had to bust through before he found out about the programme. The reason they'd been here in the first place was because the guild couldn't find it. It wasn't even a dark op. It was unsanctioned. The AI here wasn't in on the programme, but maybe she'd known that the pattern of kids being cycled through here wasn't normal. Maybe she'd hidden something in plain view, was the way Elliott had sold it to him.

The mods were time stamped. He worked out the time period and pulled out two.

The last time he'd hooked into an AI memory module, it was Skye's from the lab.

His hand started shaking.

He glanced round, sweeping the beam of the torch

down the aisle and onto a stack of equipment and terminals at the end of the chamber.

He couldn't use an ASM in case the Bennies detected the energy spike. If there was even energy going in there.

But... if he could suck energy in, then...

He sat back in the corner, placed one on the floor next to him and held the other in his hand. He closed his eyes. Using the Senson at first, then ditching it and going direct. Just went after the data. And flinched as a packet of intel flashed into his brain, agonisingly intense, followed by more and more. Faster than he could process. He dropped the module into his lap as if it was burning his hand, the connection breaking with a shock that resounded with a painful sting. He couldn't see for a second, couldn't think.

It felt like his head was going to explode. Worse than any proximity to even the Seven.

He tried again.

This time he let the data wash over him and took a mental step back, watching it, as if he was watching a raging river in flood. He gradually took control and made it slow, spinning it round and interrogating it for the content he needed. He had no idea of time, and played with it, pushing for hidden compartments or routes to hidden caches. There was plenty of inflammatory content in there, high level bribery and corruption. Mention of him in the new intake, tagged as high priority within a day. LC getting thrown into solitary and getting a red flag against his name. Jem... shit, that was a tightly-packed little box of guilt that threatened to burst open just seeing her name.

There was nothing about the programme. He let it go and slumped forward, head in his upturned hands, breathing carefully.

He got it under control and sucked in a deep breath, setting that module aside and picking up the next, double checking it was the next in line. It was and it was worse. Jarring somehow. Off kilter. Hinky as hell. It felt like he had a rusty saw blade slicing through his synapses at every turn. White noise, only tainted and nasty, piercing into his skull. Time fell away. He worked through it, clutching the module closer to his chest the worse it got, hands cramping as he reached his limit and dropped it, sending it tumbling and kicking it away with a gasped breath as he broke the connection.

His eyes were watering.

Skye had warned him once that he should never hook up with an unknown AI memory module. Shit, she wasn't wrong.

He didn't know if he could stand but he pushed to his feet, stumbled and almost keeled over. He dropped to one knee, head spinning, pain pounding red hot spikes into his brain. And raised his head to see the blurred but unmistakable shape of a shaman standing right there.

It swung its staff, no chance to duck, and caught him in the side of the head.

. . .

He came to as he was thrown down, knees hitting cold, wet ground, chains clanking heavy around his wrists. A blow to the back sent him sprawling, face down. Outside somewhere and he couldn't think where. His mind was still half entangled in the stream from the memory mod, crazy connections warping through his synapses, dizzying, unsettling, nausea welling in his stomach. Rain was streaming in ice cold rivulets down the back of his neck, bringing back some sense of time and reality. It wasn't Temerity. He'd got away from Temerity. Or was it?

He tried to raise his head and got another shove, a heavy boot coming to rest between his shoulder blades, pushing him down. He could hear a low growling off to one side, heavy breathing and grunts all around. Bhenykhn. He was surrounded by Bhenykhn. And through the pounding of the rain he could hear what sounded like the rumble of a ship's engines.

He tried to access the Senson to get an idea of time but it was too raw, the data swirling too fast to grasp.

Something grabbed his arms and hauled him to his feet. He swayed, only that iron grip keeping him upright.

He blinked through the rain, trying to focus, to see anything more than dark shapes as a shadow loomed close.

The Bhenykhn commander.

It leaned in, leering and dragged a taloned hand across his chest, ripping away his jacket and shirt in one casual swipe, clawing deep gouges into his exposed skin.

He breathed through the pain, refusing to show it,

using everything he had not to cry out. It was Redemption. He was on Redemption.

A flaming torch was thrust close, writhing with dense black smoke, the cloying thick stench of burning oil heavy. He flinched from the heat of it, narrowing his eyes against the orange light.

The alien rested a talon against the long scar that crossed his breastbone, the one from Erica. He bit the inside of his lip and raised his chin in defiance, skin crawling, rain streaming down his face.

It lingered, stroking its talon along the scar, then gave a satisfied sneer and a nod, with a guttural, "You are the one."

A hand thrust against his back.

He tried to pull away, struggling against them, only to realise with a jolt what the commander was holding in its other hand. The iron rod was sizzling in the rain, spitting drops of water.

Hil froze, tensed and closed his eyes, silent scream stuck in his throat as the red-hot brand was pushed against his chest.

Bastards.

The ship they flew him up to felt ominously like the ship on Erica, like the capital ship NG had taken them to attack, warm, wide corridors, pulsating luminescent bulkheads. He had a Bhenykhn warrior on either side of him, talons digging into his shoulders, rough handling him to get him to move whenever he hesitated.

He just walked, that good old closing down and walking, breathing through the burning agony flaring deep in his chest, the swirl of disorientation still spinning inside his head making it all feel unreal.

He had no idea how long it had been since Iona had gone but he wasn't picking up any sense of her, nothing on the Senson even when he reached out and called her, initiating the briefest flare of an emergency signal so she'd know what had happened if she did come back.

He'd never been caught by the Bhenykhn before. But he knew for a fact that his biggest advantage was that they couldn't get into his head. He'd seen what they'd done to LC. He was glad the virus had worked differently with him. And dammit, if that meant being totally isolated, closed down tight, deaf and mute, when every other telepath around him was chattering away to each other inside their heads, then fine, he'd take it right now... if the damn Bhenykhn couldn't screw with him.

So he did the walking thing as they took him wherever they were going, eyes half closed, biding his time, a horrible feeling in the pit of his stomach that there really wasn't a way out of this. And from the number of alien warriors he had escorting him, they weren't taking any chances.

They eventually reached a huge chamber. Aisle after aisle of massive looming pods stretched as far as he could see. They looked like the ones they dropped ground troops in, the brown chitinous shells and twisted black metal glistening in the half light of the bioluminescence given off by the bulkhead walls.

One of the pods up ahead hissed as they approached, the front shell splitting open and a dense, chill, decay-tinged fog swirling out, reaching for him and catching at the back of his throat as they hauled him round to stand him in front of it. He felt tiny, realised what they were about to do and baulked, struggling, backing off.

"No freaking way," he muttered, heart racing, sweat stinging against each raw wound, sending again, frantic, "Iona...?"

There was no answer and he couldn't stop them pushing him forward, spinning him around and shoving him into it.

Soft, spongy matter embraced him, sucking him backwards into its midst.

He fought against it, damned if he was going to let them stick him in a stinking alien pod.

One of Bhenykhn soldiers thrust its fist forward, fast, no way he could duck to avoid it, the punch catching him hard in the chest. His breath caught, knees folded, and the pod closed.

CHAPTER NINE

"They took him...?"

Koschei didn't respond, merely beckoned her to follow and ventured deeper into the vast vault-like chamber, candles flickering into life ahead of them and the shadows lengthening, as the banks of glass jars gave way to looming chitinous pods, lines and lines of them, twisted conduits entwining each one.

The anger smouldering deep inside threatened to ignite at the sight of them.

"How long...?" She was struggling to believe that she had been deceived for so long.

"What the Bhenykhn are doing on Redemption," he said without turning to face her, "is abominable, even by my standards. How can we dare hope to defeat them if we cannot match them?"

He was trapped. In absolute darkness. Tough to comprehend the reality of it. And hard to breathe. He gagged against the stench, cloying alien matter flooding in, a jelly-like substance filling the space and rising fast, up over his chest, shoulders, face, into his mouth, into his nose. He braced himself, holding his breath, clawing at the opening and unable to get a grip, slamming his elbow against it, anything to get the damn thing to open but the substance started to solidify the more he struggled. He closed his eyes as it crept up and covered his head. Squeezed them shut, screaming inside, and stopped fighting it, hugging his arms close to his chest, fists clenched, as the aliens trapped him, caught, done, no way to get out. Oh shit, he couldn't breathe. Couldn't think straight.

The pressure increased. Exponential. Beyond belief. Nothing he'd ever experienced, even in the worst combat jumps, the worst extractions he'd ever had, nothing near. He had to breathe, couldn't help it and sucked in a mouthful of the alien jelly that flooded warmth into his lungs, suffocating, drowning, excruciating heat cascading in waves through his entire body. He cursed every known entity in the universe and curled up as he was completely smothered.

There was an instant of intense dissociation that could have been a fraction of a second or a decade, a century, then the pod split open with a screaming scrape of metal on metal. Hil fell forward, drenched, the jelly spilling out with him in a gushing flood. He coughed the substance out of his lungs, gagging on it, and falling to his knees on the deck in a blossoming pool of the stuff. His eyes were stinging, heart racing, hearing muffled like his ears were stuffed full. He was vaguely aware of movement around him, what sounded like combat, metal clashing, bodies falling. He wanted to throw up but there was nothing in his stomach, as if he'd been sucked dry. He coughed again, retching, having to concentrate to send a vague, "Iona?"

Nothing.

Massive alien hands grabbed him and lifted him. He blinked, struggling to get free, twisting within its grip and managing to wipe goo from his eyes, blurry vision making out huge figures lying sprawled on the deck in the wet mess, blood and shards of chitin swirling in crazy spirals as his head spun.

The Bhenykhn that had hold of him broke into a run, carrying him tucked under its arm, the stench of its sweat nauseating as his senses returned, talons raking into his ribs, head pounding with each thunderous footstep. He could hear grunting, clangs, almost passed out twice as the alien squeezed him tighter, then there were guttural shouts and he was flung aside, flying through hot, damp air to land with a sickening crunch against a pulsing bulkhead. He curled up instinctively, flinching away from a huge armoured boot that stamped down by his head, scrambling away as more Bhenykhn appeared, fighting hand to hand, machetes flying.

He wiped his eyes again, trying to see where they were, what was happening. It felt horribly like he was inside the guts of a vast living creature. The chamber they were at the bottom of was enormous. Looking up, he could make out racks and racks of what looked like gunships, fighters and troop carriers filling the space, all connected by thick writhing strands of biomaterial, pods glistening in their midst as they were sucked and manipulated into place, mechanical clanks and bangs resounding in amongst a pulsing thrum. And the whole deck in front of him was teeming with Bhenykhn warriors, fighting.

Bhenykhn fighting Bhenykhn?

He tried to get to his feet, slipping on the wet floor, the manacles heavy round his wrists and the chains dragging. Klaxons were blaring, energy shield pods exploding all around and Bhenykhn roaring.

A machete swept close, the tip of its blade slicing across his arm. He flinched, staggering back as a huge alien body crashed into him, blood spraying into his face. He pushed it away, spluttering, gagging from the stench, left arm numb from the impact.

He staggered, sending, "Iona?" and muttering, "Shit, shit," as he tried to free his hands, managing to do nothing but tear the skin off his wrists. If he could get clear, he could disappear, vanish into the depths of the ship the way they had at the stronghold in Beijing, the way he had on Erica. If he could get clear...

He looked up into the grimacing face of an alien warrior reaching for him. He flinched aside, sliding, barely avoiding an axe that swung round to embed into its chest. The Bhenykhn wielding the axe kicked out with a roar, freeing the blade and sending the other flying backwards. Hil tried to scramble away but it caught him with its free hand and dragged him up, tossing him aside as another charged in to engage it, a machete clashing against the axe, sparks flying.

He caught his balance and spun, seeing a way out and turning to run as a bolt hit his leg, punching deep into the thigh muscle, knees folding as poison pulsed, stronger than any toxin he'd ever been hit with, the leg numb and incapacitated before he hit the deck.

A huge booted foot kicked hard and he rolled, shivering and retching, another alien crashing up against that one and swinging it away from him. Hil recoiled from them as they traded blows, crawling away and tugging at the bolt in his thigh, yelling curses as the pain spiked. It came free with a jolt, dragging a chunk of flesh out with its barbs. He let it drop from numb fingers and looked up, no idea who was winning, or why the hell they were even fighting, except more of them were flooding into the area.

An alien body crashed down towards him. He couldn't move fast enough, trying to scramble away and failing. It landed heavily across his trailing leg, its knife clanging to the deck by his face.

He cursed through the pain, trying to free himself, his other leg still paralysed, trying not to twist his trapped knee any more than it was and flinching from more heavily booted alien feet that were landing so near to him he had to dodge the blades that were sweeping close.

He couldn't get clear.

There were more grunts and shouts, the clash of metal on metal.

The Bhenykhn knife glinted in the faint luminescence.

He reached for it, fingers inches from the hilt, and froze as the atmosphere changed, a chill descending.

As one, the Bhenykhn dropped.

Weapons clattered as the huge alien warriors crashed to the deck.

Then it was quiet.

An occasional clink of metal.

Heavy breathing that meant he was still surrounded.

He raised his head slowly.

Only a handful remained standing.

This was either going to be shit or really shit.

He braced himself to move, trying to free his leg from beneath the dead alien as a huge Bhenykhn commander walked up. The surviving aliens backed away then dropped to one knee, heads bowed. An act of subservience he'd never seen from the warrior caste. It made his head spin even more than it was.

The commander strode over the dead to stand in front of him, staring down at him, something like a smirk twitching on its leathery face. Blue eyes bright in the dim light.

Hil blinked, heart thumping.

What were the chances? What were the chances it was the same one?

"Zach Hilyer." Its voice was low, guttural, almost mocking. "Welcome to the real war." It leaned forward, its breath frosting in the cold air. "I want Anderton. And you're going to bring that little bastard right to me."

They hauled him to his feet, casting aside the dead alien with ease, and held him in front of the commander.

It said, "Bring him," and walked away, adding as it went, "And neutralise that brand."

"Wait." He tried to yell it but his voice was hoarse. "You took NG."

The massive Bhenykhn stalking ahead of them stopped and turned, black cloak sweeping about its shoulders.

It did smirk then, blue eyes glinting. And it nodded. It called back with a dry, "Very astute, Zachery," and continued to stride away, its hand twitching to the crossbow on its belt.

Hil was pushed forward, cursing as one of them pressed a device against the brand in his chest, engaging it with a vicious clunk and sending a shock sparking in lightning flashes across his skin.

He couldn't think for a second, eyes watering, and he had to force himself to shout again, "Wait. Where's NG?"

The Bhenykhn commander didn't stop.

One of them pushed him in the back and he stumbled forward, limping as they nudged him into walking, right leg weak as the feeling came back in waves, and head pounding like the worst hangover he'd ever had. He half hoped one of them would pick him up again, and as he thought it, one of them did. His vision tipped and spun, stomach lurching as it threw him over its shoulder and broke into a run. He bounced, his head knocked hard against a rifle slung back there, and black closed in fast.

He woke up on board a ship that was moving fast judging by the thrum of the deck. Bhenykhn, by the heat and the stench. He shifted his weight cautiously, realised he was strapped into an oversized seat, hands not restrained any more, the wounds in his leg and shoulder all healed, completely, the muscles hot as he flexed them but no sign of the poison.

There were no AIs in range at all, nothing he could tap into, not even low grade, definitely nothing as powerful as the Seven.

He was pulling aside his torn shirt and twisting to stare at the elaborate design burned into the skin just below his collarbone, when the ship dropped and banked. He fumbled to grab hold of the harness, trying to brace himself. They were descending, not quite a combat drop but not far off. He closed his eyes and went with it, riding the jolts and discomfort. He seemed to have found the Bhenykhn with blue eyes. Now he just needed to find NG.

They landed and walked him out, down the ramp onto rough moorland, damp chill air hitting him as they left the ship, dark clouds hanging low in the sky, a mist swirling. His boots crunched on dead blackened bracken underfoot. The few trees he could make out were all black, skeletal, branches dead and twisted like grotesque figures. It was eerily quiet. They nudged him forward towards a high wall. Gates. All of it damaged as if it had been bombed and shot to shit. Black, alien metal, knotwork dull in the grey mist, lying twisted and broken.

It was one of their old forward operating bases. Cold sweat was trickling down his ribs. He recognised the structure of the FOB from the footage the extraction teams had taken, from the live cams when NG had trashed one, right before the alien fleet had arrived. If this was that same one, he'd seen it from orbit, when he was here on his own, gathering intel for NG before they launched the attack.

It didn't look as if the aliens had made any attempt to repair it.

He kept his head down. They hadn't re-manacled his hands, weren't punishing him any more than necessary to keep him in line. He glanced up at the Bhenykhn commander as it stalked across the blackened dirt floor of the open killing ground inside the walls, past rusting burned out hulks of crashed gunships and through huge doors into the base. The other Bhenykhn there were all deferring to it. It was laughing harshly as it greeted them, emotions still sky high, but this was obviously, firmly, its territory.

None of the others had blue eyes. Just the commander.

They nudged him to follow and took him through corridors that were too high and too wide, an eerie, dim pulse to the lighting that was flickering as if it wasn't at full power.

It was warm inside, the smell of decay strong, hanging in the air, a damp mustiness that made his chest ache.

The Bhenykhn with him dropped away as they walked through the base until there was just one at his side. They obviously didn't consider him to be a threat. The commander disappeared through a huge doorway, faint orange lights flickering on in the darkness beyond as it entered.

Hil paused, not sure what it wanted him to do. It looked like a command centre in there, consoles, screens, all inert, dark, only partially lit by candlelight dancing around the edges of the room. It almost felt like the Man's chambers. He half expected to see a massive wooden desk in there, wooden chairs and a rack stacked with bottles. He'd only ever been in there once but you didn't ever forget that oppressive, ominous atmosphere, the way it pressed upon your soul. This was the same. Warm. Closed in.

The Bhenykhn commander stood at the centre console, facing the door, thick arms resting down on its surface, regarding him with something like curiosity, bemusement. It nodded and the warrior at Hil's back nudged him forward, inside the command centre, the door closing behind him.

"Come in." Its voice was guttural but not harsh. It was staring at him, the corners of its mouth twitching.

He took two steps in and hesitated.

"You don't know who I am," it said.

"I know you took NG."

"But you don't know who I am."

As if he was supposed to, as if he'd somehow failed to recognise someone of great significance. Hil stared back. It was a freaking Bhenykhn, commander judging by the black cloak. One that could speak human words more clearly than any other he'd ever heard talk, whatever that meant.

It didn't move, those blue eyes boring into him as if it was trying to read his mind. "Do you know where you are?" Emphasis on the where. Again as if he should know.

He took a guess and took a risk in antagonising it.

"The FOB that NG destroyed." He said it calmly, probably too cocky.

Its eyes narrowed but the smirk didn't fade. "The FOB – I – destroyed."

Hil started to shake his head, totally confused, slightly incredulous, sure beyond doubt now that this was the base he'd scouted for NG, the one he'd watched on the live feeds as NG had wandered through, past the hulking dead bodies to this very command centre.

"Nikolai..." it said, watching him as if it was trying to provoke a reaction, "might have been the one that pulled all the strings to get the human forces in place, but believe me, I was the one that took out this FOB and its commander."

CHAPTER TEN

"SEBASTIAN..." This part of the story she knew already. Sebastian had not pulled his punches in relating the details of his predicament to her.

"It was a foolhardy action that risked far too much." His tone was scathing. "If Hilyer hadn't played the hero in remaining on Redemption and being stupid enough to take on the Bhenykhn single-handed, Sebastian would not have had to show his hand so carelessly."

She trailed her long fingers across the warm surface of the pod, feeling the life essence pulsing inside. These pods could heal, regenerate, accelerate growth, but she knew if a Bhenykhn warrior placed in the pod was too injured, the pod would kill them, digest them, reset ready for its next occupant. To think of Hilyer being encased in one such pod was chilling. But that Sebastian had risked capture, dared expose all Koschei was going to such pains to orchestrate, was warming to her. Hilyer was one of her favourites. The thought that he could have been lost to the Bhenykhn too much to bear. Especially considering what had happened to Nikolai in the time she had been gone...

Hil took a step back. He didn't understand and he wasn't sure he wanted to.

"Where's NG?" he said again.

"Alive. Safe," it said. "For now. But I want Anderton."

It stroked its hand, talons scraping, across the surface of the console and it lit up, schematics whirling, alien symbols cascading.

"Tell me, Zachary," it said without looking up, "what do you understand of the term Arunday's Convergence?"

He stared. Confused. It rang a vague bell. Something he'd learned years ago in some class somewhere. An outdated theory no one used anymore. They hadn't spent long on it.

It looked up and pierced him with those brilliant blue eyes, waiting for him to answer.

"Point of no return," he said, dragging it from his memory, not quite believing he was standing discussing military strategy with a freaking Bhenykhn commander. "A convergence of events that marks a point in time beyond which the only outcome is a no win situation.

Whatever path you take leads you to defeat. Whatever you do."

Not quite textbook but not bad recall considering the state he was in.

It smirked. "Well done. Arunday was a fool but he knew what defeat looked like." It wiped its hand across the console. "We passed Arunday's Convergence the minute the Tangiers engaged the Bhenykhn at Erica. There is no going back. There is no turning the tide. Humans cannot win this war." It stood up. "And the Bhenykhn are enjoying themselves far too much to finish this galaxy quickly. We seem to be providing them with quite a challenge."

Hil could feel the muscle above his eye ticking, a headache brewing that was more than concussion from being knocked around. It was referring to the Bhenykhn as if it wasn't one, as if it was on the side of the humans.

"I've taken a great risk bringing you here. The Bhenykhn are not pleased to have lost Nikolai. They are hunting Anderton, voraciously hunting Anderton, and no doubt there will be uproar that you have been snatched from their clutches. For three small humans, you have given them reason to sit up and pay attention. You have upped the stakes of this conflict. You especially."

He must have pulled a face, shaking his head slightly.

It frowned, displeased, as if it was losing patience, and tossed five kill tokens onto the console. They clattered as they landed, skittering across the smooth surface, leaving a spattering of dark blood.

Hil resisted the urge to pat his pocket. He didn't need to check to know they were his.

"How many does that make?"

He didn't answer.

"You thought you could get away with hunting them? Let me make this simple for you," it said, dripping disdain. "Human bodies cannot survive Bhenykhn jump. Not the kind of long distance, hard pull the capital ships make. You were put in that pod because they were taking you out of this galaxy, Hilyer. Do you understand? Can you even comprehend how close you came to being gone? For good. No return. Not dead. My god, they don't want to kill you. You saw what they did to our precious Nikolai. I must admit, I'm impressed he survived as long as he did. But believe me, that was nothing compared to the treatment they had planned for you had they succeeded in taking you."

It paused, regarding him as if it was having to force itself to waste time explaining it to him, as if it knew he wasn't believing a word it said. It was a look he was used to, he seemed to inspire that in people. Weird to see such familiar emotion twisting such an alien face.

"You think you're invisible to us?"

Hil clenched his fists to stop his hands shaking. He kept his face neutral.

"Stay invisible, Hilyer." Its voice was a low derisive

growl. "You screw up again and they get their hands on you a second time, they won't make the same mistake. And I won't be there to pull your ass out of the shit. Trust me when I say that. I risked too much this time. Prove to me you're worth it."

It was like the kind of roasting he used to get from the Chief, the kind that made his hackles rise and that temper smoulder to the point where he had to go beat the crap out of someone just to be able to breathe again. He could feel his chest constricting, jaw tense.

"Good," it said. "Be angry. Be the little bastard you always were because that is what will keep you alive. You cannot win this war." It let those words hang heavily between them. "I can. But I want Anderton. I let you go, with coordinates, you bring Anderton. And trust me..." It looked up, expression changing as if it was bored of toying with him. "You try anything stupid and you will never get your precious 'NG' back."

He opened his mouth to object, no way was he giving LC up to anyone, especially a bastard alien that knew way too much about them all, but the Bhenykhn turned away.

"Take him," it said. "Beat some sense into him if you have to."

It wasn't speaking to him. He half turned.

He hadn't heard the door open behind him.

The figure standing there was small, human, fair hair and startling blue eyes unmistakable.

Anya.

She threw him the kind of flirty half smile she used to use so much when they were teenagers, saying, "Come with me," and turning away, confident, the way she always had been that he'd follow.

He followed, the way he always had.

The back of his neck was itching but he didn't look back at the weird Bhenykhn with blue eyes... that intense shade of deep ocean blue that matched Anya's. And as that occurred to him, he did glance back. The alien was watching him, that smirk on its face.

It didn't move as the door slammed shut between them.

Anya had quarters set up that were decidedly not alien. High ceiling, huge door, warm and candlelit, but she had an elegant – human – cast iron four-poster bed, bedecked with heavy drapes and crisp bed linen that must have been looted from somewhere ridiculously expensive. Add in the carved wooden desk, soft leather sofas and fat, elegantly upholstered armchairs, and it was a veritable den of extravagance. More sophisticated somehow than anything he'd ever seen at any of Drake's palaces.

No comms, no tech, no screens though. As if she was cut off from the galaxy.

She turned to face him as he entered the room behind

her, and she swept her arms wide. "Welcome to my prison cell." She gave him that look she had when she was perfectly unimpressed. "Sebastian has no need for iron bars, nor..." she held up her hands, "iron manacles."

"Sebastian?"

She looked at him like he was stupid. He'd seen that look enough times as well. And he couldn't help the deep, stinging resentment that the last time he'd seen her had been when she'd cut NG's throat, and the time before that when she'd been torturing LC, and the time before that when she'd been manipulating Zang Tsu Po to send out the bounty on them that had got Mendhel killed. It was hard to remember her as the kid that had flirted with them and led them a merry teenage drunken dance through the bars of the Pit in the tunnels beneath Aston.

He rested his weight on the leg that hadn't been mauled by mutant dogs and pierced by a crossbow bolt. Tired, he realised. Low on energy.

"Anya, quit the games. We're..."

The door was slamming shut behind him and he was flying backwards through the air towards it before he could blink. He hit, hard, and crumpled, having to catch his breath before he could look up at her from the floor.

She was standing, glaring at him, pouting like a child. "It's all a game, Hil." Her voice was hard. "This whole war is nothing but a game. Can't you see?"

He pushed to his feet.

She was barking mad, he knew that. Had known it

since Zang's underground facility when she'd admitted she'd betrayed them. Shit, that felt like a long time ago. And she was stupidly powerful, apparently. LC had said as much after he'd had his latest run in with her. He hadn't been expecting the telekinesis.

And as much as LC had told him in Beijing that Mendhel wasn't Anya's father, that NG was, or rather Sebastian was, he said carefully, "Anya, what do you mean, Sebastian?"

She stared at him for a long heartbeat then laughed. "Oh my, you don't know. Why would you?" Her expression changed suddenly to a disconcerting mix of endearment and condescending disdain. "Oh Hilyer, I suppose I'd best explain. And sweetie, seriously, you'd better bring LC here because Sebastian is just about managing to keep NG alive right now... and if I don't get LC, I'm going to kill NG outright this time and there'll be nothing any of you can do to stop me. Now go shower, you look, and smell, like shit."

She put two beers on a small table between two sofas then sat cross-legged on one of them and leaned forward. "It's been a long time, Hil." She popped one open and gestured him to take the other.

He hesitated then sat opposite her, reaching for the bottle but not going so far as to clink it with the one she was holding out. She'd watched him shower, slightly unsettling, but her bathroom looked like something ripped out of a luxury cruise liner and the water had been hot, a powerful stream that he'd lingered beneath once he'd stripped and discarded the dressings. He'd leaned his hand against the hot pipe and drawn in energy fast, then ignored her as he soaped and scrubbed away the dirt and blood, the alien goo that seemed ingrained in every pore, not caring that she was staring at him, no doubt at the scars more than anything. Even the gashes gouged into his ribs when they'd dragged him out of the pod had healed, completely, the line of each injury traced by that cold, matt black, blacker than black, not-freaking-human-flesh-and-blood-anymore substance he was going to such pains to conceal. She'd thrown a set of fatigues at him when he was finished, just a short-sleeved tee shirt as if she knew fine well he didn't want to be so exposed, then she'd walked out, telling him not to take too long because she was hungry.

She was still staring at him. She took a drink then pointed the bottle at his arm. "That is just weird."

He'd forgotten how stunningly blue her eyes were, and what an amazing smile she had.

"You heal fast," she said. "Far faster than LC. I didn't believe it when they told me what had happened to you. Still don't quite get it." She tapped the bottle against her head. "It's like you're not really there. I feel like I want to push you to check that you're real."

He had to duck as she threw a cushion at him. For one

weird moment it was as though the past ten years hadn't happened and they were still crashing out at Pen's place, drunk on stolen vodka and trying to figure out how they could sneak out for the night.

She smiled as if she was reading his mind. "I can see why the Bhenykhn want you."

"Can you read my mind?"

"No, Hil," again like he was stupid, "that's why we're all so interested in you. You're an anomaly. A freak of nature and the wonder of bioengineering. And totally infuriatingly invisible to us. As well, it turns out, as being the psychopathic killer I always had you sussed for." She downed another mouthful of beer, raising her eyes to meet his as if she wanted to see how he was going to react.

He didn't.

"So..." she said as if she was getting bored. "Sebastian wants you to do a job for him and I somehow have to explain to you who he is..."

She picked up another cushion, toying with the delicate embroidered monogram initials decorating it. No doubt from the same luxury cruise liner. She was wearing a bracelet on her wrist, knotted string, tiny brown gemstones woven into each knot. Shit, that was LC's. His great-grandmother's good luck token. It felt disgustingly wrong to see it there on her pale skin.

He took a sip of the beer, damn good beer, staring at the bracelet, trying to figure out what it would take to steal it off her wrist.

She tapped an immaculate fingernail against her bottle. "Let me see... Turns out your dearest darling Mendhel Halligan wasn't my real father after all. Now, how do I explain that my biological son-of-a-bitch father who lied to me my whole life and who set my mother up to be killed – let me be really clear here, I'm talking about NG – was really just an artificial construct created to jail my real father – Sebastian..." She gestured towards the door. "...who is a sociopathic bastard with out-of-this-galaxy mental powers who managed to jump consciousness into the body of an alien warrior?" She stared at him before giving a slow considered nod. "Yep. That kinda sums it up. And now he's keeping me prisoner here. And you all wonder why I'm so screwed up." She drained the bottle and threw it across the room. It smashed against the wall in a shower of glass shards.

Holy shit. Insane didn't seem to cover it.

She was staring at him as if she was daring him to say something, as if she wanted him to screw up and piss her off so she could throw him across the room again.

He had no idea what was the right or wrong thing to say. Not that different from when they'd been kids.

"Why does it need LC?" he tried.

It was a Bhenykhn. He had no idea why Anya was talking about NG and Sebastian. LC had always said that Sebastian hated him, when they'd all assumed Sebastian was just a side to NG's character, some alternate personality NG switched to when he was being an ass.

Like some kind of dissociative identity disorder to deal with post-traumatic stress, Martinez had reckoned. It had made sense. Kind of. Especially when they'd all realised what NG was capable of. How old he was. What he'd been through.

The idea that this blue-eyed Bhenykhn could be anything other than a freak alien was so off the scale it was hard not to think he just had to humour her to get out of there alive. If the big Bhenykhn was going to let him go, fine, he'd go. No chance he was going to bring LC back here. He'd bring a whole army here to get NG back before he'd let Anya anywhere near LC again.

"Why does – Sebastian – want LC?" he said, trying not to sound as wildly sceptical as he felt, trying desperately not to sound like he was talking to a small child who was telling fantastical fairy tales they honestly believed to be truth. He knew Anya was insane, but really?

Anya frowned.

Wrong question. But it was too late.

"I – want LC," she said, petulant, fingering the bracelet on her wrist as if that gave her some kind of connection with him. He was sure LC wouldn't have given it to her willingly.

Hil raised his eyes. She was staring at him as if she was trying to read his mind.

"I don't care whatever the hell Sebastian wants him for," she said, scowl turning into a sly smile. "Daddy dearest has promised me that LC will be mine once he's done with him." She stood. "And you're going to bring him here. Or, Hil... I will kill NG. And I'll enjoy doing it."

The door opened.

"Sebastian wants to see you," she said, dismissive as if she'd hit the limit for her boredom with him, a chill edge to her voice as she added, "Go. Say hi to Evelyn from me."

CHAPTER ELEVEN

SHE RAISED HER EYES. "In all this, Anya is your greatest mistake." She couldn't help the depth of her satisfaction seeping through into her words. It was immensely gratifying to see him scowl.

"Believe me," he murmured, "she showed no such power at a young age when she was still with us."

His dark eyes were piercing, fixed on hers as if he was reading her soul. He was welcome to. She, unlike so many in this war, had nothing to hide.

"In all my efforts to recreate Nikolai..." he said, voice as dark as his eyes, letting that hang in the heavy, spice and pheromone-scented air between them.

The warmth of her satisfaction fell away like snowflakes hitting flames. "Recreate...?" She glanced back at the aisles and aisles of specimens, creatures, bodies suspended forever in glass jars... No...

His eyes glinted. "I must admit it did not occur to me that the boy could simply breed his traits into a future generation so successfully."

Two grunt Bhenykhn escorted him from her quarters back to the command centre. It was unreal. Like he was a prisoner but not. And he had no idea what to think of any of it. He stood in the doorway when they left him there, watching the commander manipulate the centre console.

There was no way...

It didn't look up but it said, "You don't believe her."

"No." He couldn't help it. He didn't believe a word they were saying. Anya or this alien. Ten years ago, NG had struggled to get the section chiefs to accept Mendhel's word that he was worth breaking every damn rule they had when he'd turned up on their doorstep, aged fifteen, fresh out of prison, an impending death sentence hanging over his head. NG had backed Mendhel's judgement. He would do anything for NG. NG. Not Anya. And not...

It was an alien. A freaking invading bastard alien that had destroyed the Alsatia, destroyed Earth, Winter, destroyed...

"What can I say that will persuade you...?" It gave a casual gesture. Swiped its hand across the console.

An image appeared. Black ink. Wildlands.

The breath he was taking stuck in his throat.

The Bhenykhn looked up with those weird out of place blue eyes. "You never did tell Anderton what that meant."

Hil shook his head and backed off a step, a cold, sick knot twisting deep inside. He had to work to keep his voice steady. "So you accessed our files. Means nothing."

"That knife in your boot was given to you by Mendhel Halligan..."

"No."

"Nikolai told you his favourite whisky was from a small island on Earth..."

"No." He took another step backwards.

Its expression darkened. "What do I have to say, Hilyer? I'd read your innermost thoughts and deepest memories well before this happened to close you down to us. Nikolai might have had scruples about what to strip out of someone's mind but believe me, I've never been so constrained. I know why you hate being called by your first name. I know what you did the first night you spent in Wildlands." It leaned forward, resting its elbows on the console. "Hilyer, I know the real reason you killed that undercover police officer when you were fourteen..." It stood up and stepped back, as if it was gauging the situation, like it was considering whether it should be wasting time with him or throwing him back into a cell. "And I know you pushed Anderton into a river when you knew he couldn't swim. We're not that different, you and I. We know what needs to be done and we'll do it. We will do it, when no one else will. And that..." It stroked its hand across the console, the image disappearing as it powered down. "...is what will win us this war."

He was finding it hard to swallow past the lump in his throat, shutting out everything this bastard had just thrown at him and locking it away again. Shit happened. And all that was a long time ago. He couldn't believe this creature in front of him was NG. No way. Whatever it tried to say. They could read minds. It could have pulled all that from NG when it took him.

Its mouth curled into a sly grimace. "You want persuading?" It let a long pause hang in the air between them and then blinked slowly. "I know you told Gian Fiorrentino to go fuck a goat when you got us caught on the Expedience. When that bastard was making you watch them beat the crap out of me. Our dearest Nikolai might have been unconscious but I wasn't..."

Hil shook his head, doubt suddenly fogging every certainty he'd had that this was just a freak of an alien. NG had been out of it, totally, bleeding and out cold on the deck, when he'd thrown that cocky, stupid comment to Fiorrentino. There was no way anyone could know...

The Bhenykhn lowered its voice. "It was right after the virus kicked in, after you were hit by the electrobes in the AI core and Nikolai was stupidly stubborn enough to come after you instead of getting away. Now how could an alien warlord from another galaxy possibly know that?"

It looked at him, that scrutiny so intense it was hard

not to think it could be reading his mind. It was making his skin crawl.

"Interesting how much you've changed, Hilyer. Fascinating what Zang's wonder virus combined with those electrobes has done to you. No one with the virus is completely human anymore, but you...? What is that?"

It was looking at his arm. He couldn't help glancing down. The gash he'd picked up on Temerity. Looking at the dense, dark scar tissue was like looking into the depths of a black abyss, as if it was sucking up light and devouring it. He hated it. Hated every inch of this alien substance that was replacing his human flesh every time he was wounded. Christ only knew what was happening inside him.

"Not wholly Bhenykhn," the alien said as if it had tested a sample.

He wouldn't have put it past them to have taken a biopsy when he was unconscious on their ship.

It manipulated the console as if it was studying a stream of data. "Not human, not machine, not AI or electrobe. Your DNA is being rewritten into something unknown in this galaxy, if not the universe." It looked up. "Are you not curious to understand what it is you are becoming?"

He wasn't. He stood there, switched off and shut down, refusing to engage, still refusing to believe anything it said.

"Did you ever meet the Man?" it said abruptly, its voice a sneer, disdain dripping from every word.

"Once."

"He is not as you saw him. You want to take intelligence back to dearest Evelyn? Take her this... the Man is not of this galaxy. He and his people sent the Bhenykhn here. You want someone to blame for all this? Blame him. And if he dares offer you help, warn her. Be very careful before you accept help of any kind from that being or any of his like."

He couldn't help rising to it then. "You're one of them. Why should I trust anything you say?"

"You shouldn't. Be wary who you trust. What did Anya say to you?"

"She said you're Sebastian." He was finding it hard not to sound resentful. He'd just been hunted and captured by these creatures. The wounds might have healed stupidly fast but he was still tired, not liking its threats, and not impressed at all that it knew so much about him, intimate, private stuff he'd never told anyone at the guild.

It stood, flexing its arms, the massive muscles straining. "In the flesh, so to speak. I am Sebastian and you would do well to listen to me and stop seeing me as the enemy, whatever form I might take. Nikolai has always held you in high regard. Do not let him down now by being too stupid to see what needs to be done. Anderton is immensely powerful. I need him. The Bhenykhn grow, adapt, feed, devour. They assimilate. This war in which we find ourselves is not going to be won by humans. Or the AIs."

A niggling doubt was stabbing at the back of his neck. He stared at the kill tokens still lying there on the console. There was no way this was true. But...

"The Man," it said, its voice low, "set us up. He set us all up. He sent them here because he has known all along that there is no way to defeat them." It paused.

Arunday's Convergence.

Hil looked up, having to work hard to keep his expression neutral.

Why the hell had it brought him here, why did it want LC, just to tell them there was no way to win?

"We're the Man's last chance," it said finally. "This is what he has set us up for. The Man knows, has always known, the true depths of human greed and its immense aptitude for self-destruction. The Bhenykhn devour everything in their path. Let them devour that and then see what they become."

The image of Bhenykhn fighting Bhenykhn on the ship flashed into his mind. If this really was Sebastian, NG, somehow... If that's what the Man had been planning, all along...

It was hard not to wonder in the midst of all that why the aliens would consider any of them to be so important. "So why do you need LC?"

The Bhenykhn narrowed its eyes, a dark shadow

crossing its gaze. "You want Nikolai back? Bring me Anderton and we both get what we want."

"Where is NG?"

It gave a slight shake of its head. "Bring me Anderton."

"I want to see NG."

"You're not in any position to be making demands, Hilyer."

"I'll do it but I want to see NG."

He didn't have anything to lose. The way he was seeing it, he was fucked whatever he did.

The alien straightened without a word and walked out.

Hil reached towards the console and palmed only one of the kill tokens, his original, the one from Erica. He slid it back into his pocket and turned to follow.

It took him underground. That was unnerving. The Bhenykhn hated tunnels and from the look of the vault this was an addition to the FOB that was nothing to do with its original build.

He watched as it disabled the locks and security panels with a mere wave of its hand, doors opening ahead of them, the air cool and sterile.

There was an isopod in the centre of the chamber, medical equipment blinking, a soft hum emanating from the machines.

NG was lying there, stretched out in it as if he was asleep, peaceful. Intact. He looked young, timeless. Hooked up to life support, lines in his arm, wires on his chest but nothing like the mess he'd been when they'd seen him in Beijing. It was as if nothing had happened. As if they could hit the release and he'd sit up, crack a joke and tell them all to get the hell back to work.

"He's healed," Hil said quietly.

There were neat scars cutting across his left bicep, right thigh, a more jagged line traced across his throat. But no other sign of the damage the aliens had inflicted on him.

The Bhenykhn, whoever the hell it was, grunted. "I've done what I can but the stubborn bastard won't wake up."

Hil stepped forward, narrowing his eyes. "When you say..."

It scowled. A strangely human expression on that alien face. "He's fine, physically, but he's retreated into that damned place he's prone to conjuring up in his mind. I can't get him to come out. You want to save him? Bring me Anderton. Maybe that little shit can get through to him again." It looked up, piercing him with those blue eyes as if it had just realised something. "You were at Beijing. You saw what a state he was in. I haven't just healed him – I've restored him. I was rather fond of my body. All of it. I could do the same for you. You want to be human again, Hilyer? Completely human? Stop the hiding, stop the running? Belong again...? What would you do to be fully human again...?"

He set his jaw, ignored the chill swirl in his chest. "This isn't about me."

He said that but his heart was cold as he uttered the words. He did want it to stop. He wanted all of it to stop. The war, the virus... He'd lived his whole life on the run, running from something, running from himself. The guild had given him a home and now that was gone. And whatever was happening to him, that gulf between him and everyone he held dear was opening up like a gaping chasm.

"I could make you human again," it said. "If you let me... before you lose all trace of human DNA, before that organism takes over completely. Think about it."

The lump in his throat was painful.

It smirked. "Bring me Anderton."

They gave him a ship, no AI, and just enough fuel to make jump and run back up life support to wait out a rescue once he made it to a known RV. He hadn't seen Anya again before they'd kicked him out. And it didn't matter what he did, he couldn't shift that parting shot from his mind.

Iona greeted him the second she dropped into range, a wave of relief emanating from her that was tempered with a desperation he couldn't figure. Not the usual.

"Hey, Hil," she sent, "you made it. Well done, sweetheart. It's good to see you. I knew you'd be fine. Are you okay? What happened? Where have you been?"

"I'm fine. It's... complicated. I found NG. He's alive."

It was what they'd all been wanting, desperately, but she didn't respond. That was weird. Just an intensifying of that swirl of unease he was getting from her.

"Iona? What's going on? I know where NG is. Are you getting this?"

She didn't know what to say, he was picking that up.

He set a course to intercept. "You good to control this bucket or do you want me to fly it in?"

That usually got a response regarding his piloting skills and her paintwork but there were no jokes this time, no banter. He just felt the ship shift as she took over, sending a soft, "I've got it. We're two jumps away from FCO. You want to transfer to the 750 or sit tight?"

It was as if she hadn't registered what he'd said about NG. Something was wrong. He could feel it. Couldn't pinpoint exactly what, but she wasn't telling him something, a general uneasy buzz of concern in her thoughts, worry that she didn't know how to tell him.

"I'll transfer," he replied. He wanted to change, get into a long sleeved shirt at least. He added a casual, "What's wrong?"

"You found NG?" she said at last, as the ship bumped up against her, hooking in close to the 750. "Where is he?"

"With Sebastian," Hil sent back, unfastening the

harness and making his way to the airlock as the ships engaged grapples. "NG is alive but..." He didn't even know where to start. "Sebastian wants to trade. He let me go because he wants LC. He wants me to take LC to them."

She did reply then, her voice strained. "In exchange for NG?"

"Not exactly. It's complicated." He pushed through into the 750. He had no idea how he was going to explain it. "It has to be LC's choice. But we do this right, we get them both back."

"Then we have a real problem."

"Why? What's going on?"

"We don't know where LC is."

His stomach flipped. "What?"

"Strap in, Hil."

She started jump protocols, short countdown, the jump drive rumbling into overdrive.

He sat down fast and said again, as he grabbed the harness, "What? Why isn't he on the Man's ship?"

She was quiet.

"Iona, where the hell is LC?" he demanded, struggling to keep the frustration from his voice.

"Evelyn sent him to Kheris."

CHAPTER TWELVE

As MUCH AS her heart was clenched tight and she desired nothing more than to throw Sebastian's words at Koschei, throw in his skeletal face all the flaws in his plan to manipulate Sebastian and cast Bhenykhn against Bhenykhn, his last words caused her to stop.

"Luka is missing?"

He ignored her, turning and walking away, along the aisle of massive Bhenykhn pods. "Evelyn Valencik," he said, "would not have been my choice as successor for such a crucial position as head of the guild. The girl is an assassin. A damned good assassin, but her skills, as impressive as she was when utilised by Nikolai, are not suited for command in a theatre of galaxy-wide war. And, as sharp as her daggers may be when facing an enemy, her emotions are far too human when dealing with those close to her."

"What happened?"

"Someone suggested she send Anderton to Kheris. For his safety." Again scathing. It was an attitude he did so well. He did turn then and pierced her with that stare. "The Bhenykhn avoid Kheris for good reason..."

They dropped out of jump into a crowded RV, input hammering against his senses from multiple AIs, comms incoming on all channels, the Man's ship included.

He felt sick. "What happened?"

Iona manoeuvred hard, sending his already churning stomach lurching. He grabbed for a handhold, trying to separate out the cacophony of intel he was getting. When none of it mattered except finding out what the hell had happened to LC.

"Evelyn sent him with Sean," Iona said as she docked. "We got a mayday from Edinburgh minutes after they dropped in system. Nothing since."

Hil sat back, numb, waiting for the worst.

Iona was already logging a report, short and sweet, word for word what he'd said to her about NG, private to Evelyn only. "We can't find them," she said as she powered down. "They didn't make orbit, definitely didn't land. We have no idea what happened but we've been searching for days. I'm sorry, Hil. Much longer and Evelyn is going to call them MIA."

· · ·

145

He grabbed a jacket and walked out to a welcoming committee, Martinez and Duncan waiting with a crew of dockies who hustled straight into action to restock the 750 with boxes of gear, rescue stuff, the kind of medical emergency kit no field-op ever wanted to see. Hil hesitated, backing off, staring, flinching as Martinez took his arm to steer him away.

"Where is he?" she said.

"What's..."

"Hil," she said, intense, still holding his arm, "you found NG. Where is he?"

He couldn't help firing back, "Where the hell is LC?" glancing from one to the other as they led him to one of the small dockside offices.

They both looked uncomfortable as hell.

He had to bite down against the edge of temper that was threatening to ignite deep inside. "Why can't you find him?" They were all telepaths, for Christ's sake. Freaking powerful telepaths. They sensed each other and chatted away together long distance, far longer than a Senson range.

Martinez pushed him inside. "We're trying."

Hil had to grit his teeth not to snap. "Excuse me for saying this but why the fuck are you not out there looking for him?"

Martinez was as tough as they came. He'd never known her to flinch from anything, not when she was at NG's side as his bodyguard nor since in the months they'd been searching for him. "We have people looking. Quinn's out there. We have search teams..."

"No, I mean you. Why are you...?" He backed into the small room, fists clenched. "Why are you two not out there looking for him?"

She regarded him with cold, pale eyes and shook her head, almost imperceptibly.

Duncan gestured him to sit and pulled out two more chairs. "We can't get near."

"What do you mean, you can't get near?"

Martinez sat and leaned her elbows on the table. "Telepaths. We can't get near. I don't even know how to describe it but as soon as we get anywhere near the Kheris system, it's... unsettling, uncomfortable, painful, excruciatingly painful, then..." She pressed her hands against her temples as if she was fighting off a headache. "Believe me, Hil, we've tried. We've all tried."

"Not hard enough."

Iona cut in on a private link. "Back off, Hilbud. Hal Duncan almost killed himself trying to find them."

Didn't help.

"The only thing we can think," Martinez said, "is that LC got it worse. No one realised but he's the first telepath we've sent out there."

"Why the hell did Evelyn send him to Kheris? Christ."

She shook her head. "It was a mistake. We know that now. But Hil, the Bhenykhn are everywhere. LC was having nightmares, bad nightmares, and it was getting worse."

It was hard to imagine how it could have been worse.

"Every time he freaked out," Duncan said quietly and carefully, "we had no idea if it was a nightmare or if it was real."

Hil stared, a lump in his throat, thinking back to what Sebastian had said. "It was real. They're hunting him. But even so, Kheris?"

"He didn't want to go," Martinez said, "but what else were we supposed to do with him? Every time we got near even a lone Bhenykhn vessel..."

"But, for Christ's sake, Kheris?" He sat, jaw clenched. He could feel Iona's unease.

She nudged him, almost a physical shove. "Hil, don't be an ass. We thought you were dead. Think about it. I got your beacon out at Redemption. We had no way of following you. We all thought you were dead, or gone, as much as NG has been gone. Evelyn just didn't want to lose LC as well. Kheris is the only safe place we have."

"And by sending him there, she's killed him."

He had to stop himself from kicking at the table leg, lashing out and telling them all to go to hell. He'd thought LC was safe here. This felt more shit than any other time LC had ever gone missing. There was something final about it somehow. As if because it was Kheris, that was it and he'd never see him again. And it was worse because he hadn't been there for him...

148

He looked up as Duncan connected on a tight wire secure link, private, not even including Martinez. "We're kitting up Iona and the 750. Take a medic. You go. You can hear the AIs. If anyone can find them, find Edinburgh, it's you."

His headache spiked. No one was supposed to know about that.

"Hil..."

"How do you know?" he sent back. He'd talked to NG about it on Erica. NG, LC and Quinn after Pandora. No one else. And no one was supposed to know. NG had put a total black out on it after that conversation. Way too valuable a fact to let slip to anyone outside, he'd said. It made his stomach cold. If Elliott ever found out...

"I know," Duncan sent. "I was there..."

On Erica, when Skye had... He hadn't realised that Hal Duncan knew but thinking about it, Duncan had been right there.

"Shit," he muttered out loud.

Movement at the door made him glance up as Evelyn walked in with an abrupt, "Where's NG?"

Still no welcome home.

He swallowed past the lump in his throat, the muscle in his jaw ticking. This needed to be secure. "I don't..."

"Hil," Evelyn said, "I want you out at Kheris, right now. We don't have time to screw around. We're secure. I promise you. Iona..."

Iona flashed him a fast rundown of security protocols

that had been implemented since he'd brought in Drake's telepath. They had a guild-loyal telepath now assigned to all senior guild personnel, maintaining a secure cordon around them at all times, scanning for other telepaths, any hostile intentions, any hostile activity whatsoever. As far out of the whole telepath loop as he was, it was convincing.

"We're secure," Evelyn said again. "Where's NG?"

"At the FOB. At the base we took out. Sebastian..." Hil glanced around. "Do you all know about Sebastian?"

The noise of the docks was loud behind her, clangs and shouts, not just the 750 getting restocked for a mission. Iona was refuelling. He could feel her anxiety, waves of tension, apprehension, impatience to be ready, but underlying it all a deep gratitude that he was alive. She'd thought they were all lost, him, NG and LC. Everyone had. That had been hard, he was picking that up from her. Now he was back, alive and well, bouncing with the news that he'd found NG, and LC had gone and got himself freaking missing again. It was hard not to join her in that anxious impatience and just walk out of there.

The Thundercloud must have been monitoring his stats. "Ten minutes, Hilbud, and we're good to go."

He sent back an affirmative and stood as Evelyn closed the door behind her. The noise cut, dropping them into an uneasy illusion of calm.

"NG is with Sebastian?" Evelyn looked beyond

unimpressed as she pulled out a chair. "What the hell does that mean?"

"The Bhenykhn that took NG," he said, sitting back down but just perching on the edge of the chair, "this bastard Bhenykhn with blue eyes, it's Sebastian. It rescued me from the aliens that caught me on Redemption. It has NG and it knows all about me, stuff I've never told anyone. Seriously, the only way it could know that stuff was if it had read my mind before all this... if NG read my mind, which we know he did. He read all of us." He leaned forward. "I swear. I just had a freaking Bhenykhn telling me crap from when I was a kid that I've never told anyone."

Martinez shook her head, sceptical as hell. "You told Iona he wants LC." Her voice raised a tone in incredulity. "It's Sebastian that wants LC? What the hell? Sebastian hates LC."

Hil looked at her. Not for the first time, he wished he was telepathic, to strip information from someone's head without having to wait for them to tell him.

"Sebastian hates LC?" He couldn't help the acid tone. She said it as if she was personally acquainted, as if there was a whole shit load more to this than he knew. He forced himself to calm, wishing someone would magic up a beer or a bottle of water.

"Hil..."

"What the hell do you understand about Sebastian?" He looked from face to face. "Because I may be way behind the curve here but I thought Sebastian was just some twisted alternate personality NG switched to when he was being a violent bastard."

He stared at them, defying them all to reveal what they had or hadn't known about someone they all counted as more than just the leader of their guild. NG was family.

It was Martinez that answered, her voice was low, threatening. "He isn't. Sebastian is real. Why does he want LC? Does he really have NG?"

It was clear from the look on her face, that was all she cared about.

"You saw the report on NG after Beijing?" he said, watching her as he said it, and knowing fine well that she had. They'd all been horrified. He didn't know what LC had said to anyone but they'd both described the failed mission in detail. Reading LC's account had been hard, physically hard to stomach. What they'd both put about NG had been graphic.

Her reply was cold. "You know I did."

"NG is healed. Completely. You'd think nothing had happened. If Sebastian has somehow... if this Bhenykhn can do that for NG..."

"Why does he want LC?" Hal Duncan sounded as suspicious and sceptical as Martinez.

"Because NG won't wake up. The Bhenykhn thinks LC might be able to get through to him with their wacky mind stuff because he knows that's what LC did when we found NG in Beijing."

Suddenly the Bhenykhn was 'he'. As if it somehow definitely was Sebastian and Sebastian wasn't just a figment of NG's imagination. And that made everything Anya had said true.

Hil forced himself to breathe. This was too weird.

"NG told me," Martinez said, bracing herself as if she was having force herself to say it, as if she was betraying a confidence, "that the Man had created him. That he didn't exist and that Sebastian was the real one. The Man created him to imprison Sebastian in his own mind." She looked up, her pale eyes glinting as she stared at him. "This could be true." She turned to Duncan. "Hal, you've seen Sebastian. What do you think?"

"I think he could have wiped out NG and Luka on several occasions, on Erica and at the FOB. And he didn't." The big marine looked at Hil. "He took on the Bhenykhn. If what you are saying is true, then that's all he's doing now."

Martinez turned to Evelyn. "I know NG confided in you. What did he tell you about Sebastian?"

"The second time? When he didn't wipe my memory?" Evelyn didn't hide the bitterness that crept into her voice. "He didn't need to tell me. I've seen Sebastian. He talked to me, and yes, he is a twisted bastard. And yes, he has blue eyes." She composed herself. "NG told me that it wasn't him that killed the Bhenykhn on Erica. It was Sebastian. They weren't just two separate identities, they were two separate people, trapped in one body. And we all know how powerful they both were..." She caught herself. "...how powerful they are. If Sebastian has done this, actually jumped bodies..."

Martinez nodded as if she was willing it to be true. "Then we have a Bhenykhn on our side."

As if it could be that simple.

Evelyn's eyes were cold, hardened. She stood up. Done. "Angel, Hal, get out to that FOB." She turned, eyes searing into him. "Hilyer, go find LC."

CHAPTER THIRTEEN

"*Why did you not help Sebastian with Nikolai? You know where they are. You know what's been happening. Surely you, of all people, are uniquely qualified to remedy such a situation. You...*" She had to compose herself. "*You created them. You promised me you would help them.*"

"*I promised no such thing.*"

Curious. Infuriatingly curious and damningly clear. Given all she had learned from Sebastian, little else could surprise her. Koschei had always had his own agenda, his own ways. It was miraculous they had ever worked together so well given their differences. Not so, when she considered how much he had kept from her...

"*You need Nikolai as much as Sebastian does, don't deny it.*"

A hint of sly satisfaction reached his eyes. "*None of these creatures are indispensible. None of them. Do not lose sight of that, however fond of them you may be."*

The medic was waiting for him on the 750. Harley. That wasn't surprising. She gave him a nod and strapped in as they were given the go ahead to deploy. They dropped out of jump somewhere quiet, totally dark, no engines. Kheris, he realised, picking out the intel from Iona's thoughts. Way out on the edge of the system. She was scanning, careful not to emit too much of a signature. No Bhenykhn, that was a given at Kheris, but always the threat of human ships that were allied with Drake or some other of her old Order buddies. Hil kept his eyes closed as they drifted, a headache pressing against the back of his eyeballs.

She was waiting for something but he couldn't tell what. "What are we doing?"

"We have to keep our distance," Harley said, "until we know you're not going to be affected."

"I'm fine." He ran his hand over the console, starting to bring up limited data, still under the radar, nothing that anyone watching would be able to detect.

Harley dropped into the seat next to him. She reached her hand to his arm and squeezed his arm gently. "Your stats are fine. Temperature elevated but there doesn't seem to be anything untoward."

He wanted to tell them all to go, leave him there and let him figure it out, but he forced himself to ask calmly, "Iona, are you getting anything?"

"Not out at this range. Do you want to hear the mayday?"

"No." That was the last thing he wanted to hear. "Can you jump to their last known location?"

"There are ships at that point..." Iona said and threw a packet of intel his way, charts, current positions of guild vessels, lots of guild vessels, all running search and rescue vectors, all reporting back real-time, all using a lot of valuable fuel, and nothing to show for any of it. "There are gaps. Choose one. Come on, Hil, if anyone knows what LC would do, it's you."

He scanned through it, trying to figure out some kind of pattern to it all. He wasn't the one that did this shit. LC was the patterns genius.

He stared at it. He had a horrible feeling they'd either been caught somehow and were gone, god knows where, or they'd been vaporised. The guild had been searching for days. If they were adrift somewhere and Edinburgh was just damaged, they could still be alive. If her life support had been damaged as well...

He chose one at random and shared it with Iona. "Go there. How much capacity do we have before you need to refuel?"

"At this kind of range, we can make jump four times, five at a push. How lucky are you feeling today, Hilbud?"

. . .

It took them three. And it was so faint he almost missed it.

He sat up. "Wait."

He could feel Iona gearing up for jump.

Harley shot him a glance. "What?"

"There's something." As soon as he said it, he couldn't hear anything. It was illusive, intangible, a wisp of conscious thought that evaporated as soon as he concentrated on grasping it.

"Nothing on long range scan," Iona said.

"Jesus, Iona, give me a second."

He closed his eyes and shut out the background hum he was picking up from the Hailstones they had with them, the thoughts he was picking up from Iona, and reached further, out into the darkness.

There was nothing.

Vast, empty, dark space.

They were on the fringes of the Kheris system.

Cold, dark space.

Iona sounded a million miles away. "Hilyer, they're calling off the search. Drake is flooding ships into the system. We're being called to pull out."

"No. We're not giving up."

He focused again. It was hypnotising. Terrifying to think LC and Sean could be out there, dying.

Then...

It was more a hit of desperation than a thought.

So brief he couldn't pinpoint it.

He stood and backed away from the console, eyes still closed, turning slowly.

It felt like the deck fell out from beneath his feet, as if the ship disintegrated and dissipated into a million pieces that scattered away from him on a breeze.

He was alone in a vast, empty nothing.

One thing he'd never been able to figure out was how to communicate thought to thought with the AIs like the telepaths did with each other. He didn't work like that. He could hear them, that was all. Even the Seven, even Elliott. The advantage Elliott had, that – Aries – had, was that he could cut through the Bhenykhn jamming technology like it wasn't there, connecting through the Sensons even when no other comms were possible. But hearing their thoughts... That was what had driven him crazy in those first few weeks. Their minds ran fast, inhumanly fast, chaotic, emotion-fuelled bio-machine minds that were so way beyond anything human it was awe-inspiring that they could even lower themselves to communicate on a human level.

The stars of the galaxy spun around him as he turned.

Nothing. Then another hint of something more...

"There," he muttered. "Iona..." He sent through the numbers, heading and distance, as close as he could gauge it. "Get closer. It might be nothing..."

"I'm not picking up any life signs."

His stomach was cold. "Just get closer."

· · ·

Edinburgh was drifting in an asteroid field, her hull battered and scarred from multiple impacts. With shields failing, it was a miracle she hadn't been destroyed.

Scans were detecting only trace energy emissions from the ship. No wonder no one had been able to find them. Hil could sense nothing from the AI, not even the faint gasp of fading emotion that had caught his attention. They couldn't get anything else from her, no matter what they tried.

He glanced at the monitors as he dragged on the EVA suit. The life signs scanner was flatlined. Nothing. He shrugged into the bulky sleeves, wriggling his fingers into the gloves, grasping clasps and slamming them into place with hard, cold efficiency. He didn't want to be there. He didn't want this to be happening. LC had been through too much, survived too much, to die now.

Harley was quiet beside him as she kitted up.

"We could just grapple, drag her out of there and jump," Iona sent.

"No." Hil secured the helmet with a snap and grabbed the evac holdalls. "If they're alive, it'll kill them."

"Hil, the scans..." Harley said softly, stopping herself as he brushed past.

"I need to know," he sent, keeping to the Senson, not wanting to talk past the lump in his throat.

He got to the airlock even as Iona was still

manoeuvring the gulfstream into a position to effect a docking. He punched and twisted the manual release as soon as the grapples caught, and pushed ahead.

He had to wrestle with the release at the far side of the airlock, struggling to get it to give and having to throw his whole weight behind it before it would open. His stomach was cold as he stepped through into a zero-g darkness lit only by the ghostly cast of the helmet lights.

"Edinburgh...?" he sent again, reaching out to Sean's AI as he moved, weightless, pushing and pulling his way through narrow corridors, ducking burned out wires and eyeing the blackened bulkheads uneasily.

He was willing her to respond, desperately wanted her to reply with the kind of scathing, sarcastic comment she usually threw at him.

Nothing.

The blast door leading to the main cabin was sealed but dented, the clear panel in the window cracked and burned.

He let go of the evac kit, letting it drift away, and grabbed a handhold, punching the edge of his fist against the release, hitting it again and again, peering through and trying to see past the damage, wanting to see and not wanting to see at the same time.

He tried reaching out on the Senson to Sean.

Nothing.

No way of contacting LC save yelling out loud.

Dammit all to hell.

The door still wouldn't open.

He rested his helmet against the glass and pressed his gloved hand gently against the panel, reaching into the door controls by remote. The circuit was fried and even had it not been, there wasn't sufficient power remaining in the backup systems to power the door. He gave up and punched open the cover plate that gave access to the manual controls, beginning to physically crank the door open, cursing at every hard-fought turn of the handle, the mechanism seized as if it had been bent out of alignment. It took forever to open enough of a gap to squeeze through into the compartment beyond.

Harley was at his back, nudging the evac kitbags ahead of them as they went in.

The main cabin area was trashed, as if a bomb had gone off.

It was cold according to the VHUD stats that were also showing no oxygen, zero, nothing, dust and chunks of debris drifting in the zero gravity.

"Hil...."

Harley's voice was strained. He turned to see her reaching a gloved hand in front of her towards something that looked like droplets in the light of the helmet, a string of shimmering red beads, suspended mid-air. She nudged one of them, sending it tumbling. "This is blood," she murmured.

He turned slowly, not wanting to see, a cold, sick weight in his stomach. He sent a cautious, "Edinburgh..."

through the link and thought he caught a pang of despair he could just as easily have imagined. "We're right here," he sent. "We're right here, Edinburgh. You've done great."

He moved forwards, slowly, heart in his throat, the dread of finding them dead fighting with what little hope he had that they could still be alive. He grabbed a hold and pushed himself off, using the burned bulkhead to propel himself, Harley right behind him as they moved through the ship towards the bridge. It was trashed, same as the rest of the ship, consoles burned out, screens smashed, debris floating.

And two bodies.

CHAPTER FOURTEEN

'WHAT HAPPENED?' was on the tip of her tongue, at the forefront of her mind, a desperate longing to jump straight to the end of this twisted tale and be done.

She regarded him with care, calming the turmoil inside.

He obviously knew how much she cared, about these few especially that he had nurtured under the mantle of the guild they had created.

He was revelling in this. Koschei was the master of intrigue, stringing out a story, an emotion, a situation... a war. She of all their people had advocated for him, pleaded mercy on his behalf when others had called for his head.

Was she now to regret all that she had done?

A fresh pulse of adrenaline hit his chest.

Harley beat him to Sean, manoeuvring past him and grabbing her, as he made it to LC. Hil wrapped his arms around him and spun round, gently, heart pounding, none of the sensors in the suit picking up anything from this kid that meant more to him than a little brother ever could. For a weird instant, it felt like they were in the Sphere at the heart of the Maze, on board the Alsatia, messing about in zero gravity like they'd done countless times.

Except LC was pale and still, eyes closed.

"Sean's alive," Harley called, "but I have no idea how."

He looked up to see her brushing hair from Sean's face, one of the evac bags floating beside them.

"Hil, she's alive. Tell me LC is okay."

"I..." He didn't know. He swung round, sending at the same time to Iona, "Need some light and air in here," and dragging LC as gently and fast as he could back out to the main cabin where the other evac kit was drifting.

"On it already. Stand by for gravity."

He braced himself, shielding LC as the AG kicked back in, gravity increasing slowly, debris drifting down around them as they fell, lights and life support coming back online as Iona hooked up and shared power with the stricken ship. Hil managed to twist so he hit the deck first with his leading leg, easing LC down and into his lap, and throwing out an arm to catch the evac bag as it landed beside them. He dragged it close and managed to pop open the clasps, spilling the kit out and grabbing an oxygen mask. He pressed the mask against LC's face and eased him down onto the deck, starting to shrug out of the haz suit, tossing the helmet and gloves aside, and kneeling, looking for a pulse, willing there to be a pulse.

He couldn't feel anything, heart sinking into his stomach as he felt how cold LC's skin was, dried blood tracing tracks from still raw wounds, bruising still dark. He pulled a pouch of vials from the bag and started pressing them against that cold neck, one after another, not caring what they were, not caring that LC wasn't supposed to use this shit anymore. He rested a hand against his chest, willing him to move, open his eyes, something, but there was nothing.

Harley dropped in next to him, kicking aside debris to make space. "I've got Sean stabilised. How's he doing?"

Hil glanced down at LC. The mask was hardly misting. If he was breathing, it was only barely.

"I don't know," he muttered.

LC was everything to him, more than a real brother ever could have been.

This was not how it was going to end.

Harley ditched her haz suit and took LC's arm, starting to hook him up to an IV with the deft efficiency of a field medic who'd seen all this shit before. "What the hell happened here?" she said as she worked. She switched to the Senson and sent out an alert to the rescue teams, including him in the link and finishing up with, "Felix is red critical. Do you copy?"

Red critical.

He'd never...

He watched as she took LC's left hand in hers, the hand that hadn't had its fingers hacked off by the Bhenykhn, turning it gently to insert the line. The black tendrils scorched in lightning patterns all around his arm were standing out in stark contrast to his pale skin, dark red smears dried around wounds that were hardly healed, injuries that looked like flash burns.

"I don't know," Hil said again, queasy, watching LC's chest and trying to persuade himself he could see it rising and falling. He was getting nothing from the AI now but he tried anyway, using the Senson and sending a gentle nudging, "Edinburgh... what happened?"

There was still nothing but an eerie stillness.

"Hil, we need to go," Iona cut in. "She's gone. Stand by. We have medevac and recovery incoming. And probably about ten minutes before everyone else in this system realises we're here. We're going."

"No, wait," Hil sent, wide link including them all. He'd felt Skye die, out on Erica. He'd felt it. A punch of dark void was the way LC described it, a physical hit of deep pain he was hit with whenever anyone close, anyone human, died near him. Hil got it with AIs. He'd felt it with Skye, with Fallon when she'd saved them above Miranda. He'd found Edinburgh here because he'd felt the faintest trace of deep regret, guilt, hard-edged anger... He'd caught that from her but he hadn't felt her die. Not yet.

"She's not dead," he sent, heart pounding, almost anticipating that pop of pain in his chest any second. "Edinburgh, what happened? Edinburgh, talk to me..."

There was a bump as another ship attached grapples.

"Hil, her core is cold, she's dead. And if we don't get out of here, damn sharp, we will be too. We have incoming. Not friendlies."

Edinburgh wasn't dead, he knew that, but she was dying. He could feel it.

The ship docking with them was guild. He could hear the comms, hear the pilot talking to the extraction teams. They wanted to get LC and Sean into evac-isopods and jump out of there. They were going to be too late for Edinburgh. He didn't want to be there, didn't want to share that intimate moment. He didn't want to feel that pop, that instant switch from life to nothing that battered his soul like a sledgehammer. Every time it happened. It was hard to think there was nothing he could do.

He looked back at LC, reached a hand to his neck and felt the coldness of his skin, wishing NG was there to fix him up, like he had countless times. Wished there was a goddamned way that the same kind of freaky ass healing could be done for an AI...

There was a bang, heavy footsteps incoming.

Hil looked up.

Shit...

What if there was a way?

He stared at Harley.

"Keep him alive," he muttered and stood, backing away.

"What are you...?"

He grabbed his gloves and helmet and started to run, Iona shouting in his head, "What are you doing? Hilyer? We have hostiles incoming. Where are you going?"

He ignored her and pushed past two rescue and recovery teams, busting his way into Edinburgh's engine room, securing the clasps of the helmet. He had the gloves on by the time he reached the blast door leading to the AI core.

One of the guild teams thundered up beside him with a harsh, "What are you doing?"

He didn't wait to argue. He broke open the protections and pushed through to the chamber housing Edinburgh's core, ducking beneath conduits that were cold, arteries and veins that should have been hot, the suit going haywire with contamination warnings.

He ignored it, ignored the shouts behind him and forced his way through, squeezing past pipes and cables until he reached the shielded casing protecting the core. The manual release controls were burnt out, an exposed power cable hissing sparks now the power was back on.

He reached for the housing and tore off the cover.

The voice behind him was quiet, calm, demanding. "Hilyer, what are you doing?"

Quinn. Shit. Of all the people he didn't need there right now.

"She's still alive. We need to get in there." He pulled out a cable.

Something impacted his shoulder from behind and knocked him sideways, Quinn hissing in his head, "Hil, what the hell are you doing?"

He staggered, got his balance and ducked back in. "We have to save her," he sent, grabbing the cable and hooking in to bypass the release. He could tell Iona wasn't impressed, but she wasn't saying anything else, communicating with the guild ships and giving warnings of incoming, the countdown in minutes, her voice cold. If they jumped with Edinburgh in this state, she wouldn't have a chance.

"Hil, what the hell...?"

He kept at it, working through a mangled mess of connections. "I know you've never liked me, Quinn, but trust me. We have to get to her."

Quinn grabbed his shoulder that time and hauled him away from the casing, powered actuators squeezing tight. "Dammit, Hilyer."

"Just help me," he said, struggling to get free, voice cracking. "Don't let her die."

"I'm not about to let you die."

"I'm not going to. Quinn, c'mon, we need her. She knows what happened. Help me. I know what I'm doing."

He could feel Quinn staring down at him from behind the blackened visor, no way to read his expression, and for a second it felt like he'd failed and the son of a bitch was as heartless as ever. But then Quinn relented with a muttered, "Jesus Christ, Evelyn is going to kill me." The big handler shoved Hil back in at the control housing with a gruff, "Get it the hell open."

He got back at it, burned out three pathways and was shaking as the release procedure initiated. The casing opened, panels sliding apart to reveal the sphere of the AI core. His heart sank. It was inert, the biomatter that should have been a whirlwind of chaotic, swirling, silver energy sparking with life, what should have been a violent storm of mercury-silver, bio-mechanical soup raging in torrents of energy, was instead dark, a sludge of grey lying at its base.

He hadn't felt her die. He pressed his hand against the smooth surface of the sphere. Even through the glove he could feel it wasn't hot the way it should have been. He looked up and round. Every vein and conduit was still, lifeless.

He couldn't leave her like this.

They'd saved people, time and time again, by infecting them with LC's blood, introducing the alien virus through a transfusion. Duncan and Martinez were testament to that. Neither of them would be alive if it hadn't been for LC's blood and its strain of the virus.

Except he had no way of getting what he had, this

171

mutated, part alien, part AI organism pulsing through his veins, into Edinburgh's core. Unless...

"We have to get inside," he murmured. "Quinn...?"

"Dammit, Hil." Quinn shoved him out of the way and punched his armoured fist into the clear surface of the sphere. He punched it three more times, cursed, and pulled out a cannon of a handgun, yelling a warning to get back.

Hil backed off, angling round so he could see, reaching for the clasps on the suit.

Quinn pulled the trigger, high energy laser blasts followed by explosive ballistic rounds, firing until the gun was dry. He dropped it and started punching again.

It started to give way after five more impacts.

A lacing of thin, hairline cracks appeared, racing out across the sphere.

Hil tore open the clasps and fought his way out of the sleeves of the suit, fast. If Quinn could see what he was doing the big man would floor him. The band on his wrist started screaming, vibrating like it was going to detonate. He dropped the helmet and threw down the gloves, reached and took Mendhel's knife out of his boot. He stepped forward, took a breath laced with electrobes that flooded his lungs with a sting of intoxication, what would have been a lethal dose to anyone else, and spun the knife into a backhanded grip.

Quinn hit the sphere once more, powering his clenched fist into it. The clear surface shattered.

Hil stared, chest heaving, breathing in the electrobes as if they were a narcotic. He had no idea if this would work, but the alien virus was humming in his veins, pounding in his ears. He could feel the pull of the electrobes in his bloodstream. He lifted the knife and stabbed it deep into his forearm, dragging the blade hard through his flesh. Blood spurted, beyond pain.

He pushed forward, dropped to his knees and thrust his bare, bleeding arm into the toxic sludge of dying grey matter.

CHAPTER FIFTEEN

"*HE CAN HEAR THE AIs...*" *It wasn't a question. It was a revelation. Telepathy was unknown in their galaxy, this creature walking ahead of her an anomaly amongst their own kind. An aberration of nature.*

The Bhenykhn, she knew from legend, mythos, damn hard first-hand experience, had developed their hive mind by such a freak instance of biology. Never, never would her people have let a slave race, an engineered slave race, have such an overwhelmingly advantageous biological trait. But by trick of nature, or sheer misfortune considering the cascading sequence of events that followed, the Bhenykhn had developed a true telepathic hive mind. That such a trait should now have transferred, however convoluted its happenstance, to the AIs, that truly was chilling. Even when it was Zach Hilyer at its centre.

He floated for a while. Peaceful. Not able to remember what he'd just been doing, that was weird. But not caring too, which was a release. As if someone had given him permission to relax. Let go.

He'd been fighting for too long.

Fighting what?

A nightmare?

He was sore. Wrung out. Tired.

It felt real.

Couldn't remember why.

Drifted some more.

He could see swirls of black and silver in his mind's eye, dark black spreading out from him, advancing. Sparks flaring. Red. Blood red. Swirling like oil on suncast water, leaving trails that danced in front of his eyes as he turned, trails that drew him in, hungry, wanting more. He was bleeding. He could feel his life force bleeding out, being drawn out, dense black merging with a delicate tendril of silver that was reaching to him... taking from him as he offered, openly, freely, sharing, as much as was needed, just take it... what it was he couldn't remember.

It faded.

He had a feeling he didn't want to go back. No idea why but just a feeling it was better here, wherever here was, not there.

Here was quiet, calm. No cares.

What should he be caring about?

He couldn't remember.

He reached out to Skye.

Gentle.

Just needed a nudge back in return.

The way she did to let him know she was there...

She wasn't there.

Shit. She wasn't there.

A hit of adrenaline hit his chest.

Skye was always there. He didn't go anywhere without her.

He tried the Senson again and this time reality crashed back in with a ferocious onslaught of noise and light and motion that hit so hard his head spun, stomach churning, internal temperature so high it felt like his brain was melting.

He couldn't speak.

His left arm was burning as if flames were licking around it, the prickling sting in his lungs so bad he couldn't breathe.

Someone had a tight grip on each elbow, dragging him backwards. He could hear fast and harsh shouts, guild teams, the individual words making no sense but the emotion behind them loud and clear. They were in the shit and they were pissed at him.

He tried to protest that he could walk but he couldn't get his limbs to obey and he couldn't get his mouth to work. The Senson wasn't working.

"...no shields," he caught from someone. "She has no fucking shields. Get them out of there and leave her."

No.

The deck dropped out beneath his feet and he was freefalling for a second, stomach lurching and he thought he was going to throw up, but someone grabbed him round the shoulders and pulled him close.

He thought he heard someone say, "We don't leave anyone behind..." but it was faint, far away, and he started to fade into a swirl of grey.

"Get Hilyer into a fucking isopod. Jesus, let's not lose both of them."

Both of them?

What?

There was a vibration, a shockwave, deck shifting again as it they'd taken a direct hit.

He felt himself falling. Couldn't stop himself, nothing to brace against and knees like jelly.

He cried out again to Skye as he hit the deck, desperately, disorientation dragging his senses off into total confusion. He couldn't pin down where the hell he was or when the hell he was.

Both of them?

That could only mean LC.

He had a vague memory of LC being in trouble.

LC hurt.

The lab?

No, there hadn't been anyone else with them then.

Shit, no.

The reality of what had happened and what he'd done hit like a sledgehammer.

Kheris.

Whoever was with him dragged him close and kept a grip on him, an arm over his chest, shouting for a pod.

He tried to protest again.

LC was alive. Had to be alive.

He couldn't breathe.

Heard someone yell, "Incoming."

Another massive blast reverberated through the deck. Then, like the fury of a thunderstorm moving on, the noise got distant, rumbles and jolts easing, still there but as if the fight had shifted away from them.

He felt fingers pressing gently against his neck, tried to get his throat to work to speak but a mask settled over his face. He sucked in a breath of oxygen that almost made him choke. He was too hot. Sweat was blossoming in prickling heat across every inch of his exposed skin. Someone took hold of his left arm, the pain escalating so high, so fast, he tried to pull away but they held tight and clamped something around it, a trauma patch from the sting, but worse, and he had to bite down a scream as an agonising, bone-deep shock shot through his entire arm.

He greyed out, not for long because the pain was still sky high, coming round to voices he couldn't make out.

Whoever had hold of him said, "Daren't. I don't know

how he'd react. How much longer till we're good to jump?"

It was Harley.

Why was she not with LC?

She should have been with LC.

That made him feel cold inside. And she must have seen his arm. It set him on edge more than he'd thought it could to think that someone knew. A guild medic at that. Medics had the power to pull you off the active list. Medics could get you grounded on the basis of fuck all. It had been a freaking medic who'd got him taken back into care the first time he'd run away as a kid from a place they had no idea about.

More muffled voices, a clatter of what sounded like armour and weapons.

Harley was sitting with him, not LC, the hand she was resting on his chest holding a pistol, he could feel the weight of it. They were preparing to defend against boarders, he realised. And he was lying there unable to lift a finger to help. No idea if LC was alive or dead. All he could pick up from Iona was the cold focus of battle. He tried the Senson but no one responded. He was either fried or comms were getting jammed, which, out here, meant Drake or Ballack.

There was a cold sting against his neck. Go-juice. His bloodstream tingled as the virus took it, every vein and artery sparking with fresh heat as it gave his system the energy it needed to deal with the new influx of electrobes.

It wasn't enough. He let his right hand fall to the deck and pressed his palm against the metal panel, drawing in energy, sluggish as hell, until he could move, and just about managed to drag the mask aside enough to say in a hoarse whisper, "No comms?"

Harley shook her head.

So they had no idea what was going on?

He coughed, flinching from the icy shards of stinging pain that shot through his chest. "Give me a gun."

She pressed her gun into his hand and helped him sit, leaning him back against the bulkhead.

Every breath he took was rasping. He couldn't see straight but he curled his fingers around the cold grip of the pistol.

He didn't ask about LC because he didn't want to hear the wrong answer.

There was another bump, a violent lurch, the sound of grapples engaging.

He glanced at Harley.

She was pale, crouching by his side, another gun in her hand already. She gestured him to stay put, as if he had much choice, and stood, stepping in front of him, raising the gun to point at the door, alongside the guild agents, some in field kit, some like Quinn in powered armour.

The sounds of a forced ingress floated through to them.

He couldn't use his left arm but he managed to roll onto his side and push to his knees, using his right hand, still holding the gun, to brace himself. He staggered to his feet and stood shoulder to shoulder with her, gun up, breathing through the pain.

Quinn muttered a curse and moved in front of them, gesturing the others to go with him, sending a gesture to Hil that left no doubt what was intended. Stay. Keep the hell out of their way. That was fine but he wasn't going to sit on the damned floor while they were boarded and attacked.

Iona was pure cold fury out there. Weird to pick up on the intensity of her emotions and not hear any banter. The worse the situation the worse the jokes. He'd learned that pretty sharpish from the big AIs the guild had. As if that was their way of compensating for having to lower the speed of their comms to account for human inferiorities. They'd always chided him the most. And he missed it. Wanted to hear her slate him for being so stupid, wanted her to throw random stats and facts at him so fast he struggled to keep up, and laugh when he refused to ask for help. She was engaged in a full on firefight out there, he realised as he stood, wavering, listening to the sounds of fighting out in the main cabin, yells and screams, vicious hand to hand and the dull thud of shipboard weapons intensifying as the collaborating forces realised the guild wasn't just going to give up its most valuable assets.

There was another bump and a clang that rocked Edinburgh and almost sent him sprawling, sounds of another attempted ingress.

It was beyond shit. They were supposed to be fighting aliens, not each other.

Harley looked at him in alarm, the troops still with them turning and aiming their rifles back towards the stern.

Hil dropped the aim he had on the gun, arm aching, and turned, trying to figure out the best angle to shield her from whatever the hell was incoming, when the Senson engaged out of the blue with a firm and cocky, "Stand by..."

Elliott.

There was no further warning, no indication of what was coming. The gravity on board switched to maximum. No mercy. No discrimination.

Hil dropped and slammed into the deck. Out cold.

CHAPTER SIXTEEN

"Eloise Drake is a despicable human." *She could not keep the acidity from her tone. To hear that not only was Luka in danger but also Hilyer, at the hands of Drake, was too much. "We are all – all – fighting the Bhenykhn. How have events unfolded to such a point within a mere human year, that these humans, of whom we are so fond, Koschei, in case you forget, can fight amongst themselves so viciously?"*

He looked back at her with hooded eyes, expression dark.

There was movement, slight but there, shadows shifting, in front of them and behind. His elite guard. As if he needed a show of strength. In this place? His domain. With her?

"You have spoken with Sebastian," he murmured. "Then you know the voracity with which these humans will fight and how crucial that is to our plans... Yes, Drake

wanted Anderton and Hilyer. It is testament to the success of all we did at the guild that our two most valued operatives come to be at the centre of this endgame. What I did not foresee was the influence of the machines. It was a good thing that Aries of all entities was there for them..."

He raised the bottle to his mouth, eyes closed, feet up, head resting back against the bulkhead. Recycled water. Nothing else in the fridge there. Guess the convoy hadn't managed to nab any luxuries.

There was no one else in the mess. He had the lights out, listening half-heartedly in to the communications buzzing around the Man's ship. There were no AIs in the vicinity. Not even any Hailstones. So it was a relatively quiet, tranquil headspace, the most peace he'd had in a long time, almost enough to make the headache ease off. His left arm was still throbbing. He'd woken up as the guild teams had come in, fought any attempt to put him in an isopod and had walked out of there. No one would talk to him, even when he asked for Harley. The few medical staff he had seen, that he'd fobbed off, not politely, had refused to tell him anything. They wouldn't let him see LC or Sean, he couldn't sense Elliott, Iona or Edinburgh anywhere near, and he had no idea what had happened.

He'd escaped to the mess and was hoping no one

would find him. Ever. Screw it all. The Bhenykhn were welcome to take whatever the hell they wanted. Drake could do her worst. He didn't care.

He didn't hear Evelyn come in but she said, "Hey," as she sat opposite.

Hil opened one eye.

"You did well, Hil."

It didn't feel like he'd done well.

He didn't want to ask it but he forced out the words. "Did LC make it?"

Evelyn nodded slowly. "Sean hasn't woken up yet but they've got her stabilised. No one's quite sure what happened but the docs think the virus somehow put them into some kind of stasis after Edinburgh's life support failed..." She stopped. As if she didn't know what else to say.

Hil took another mouthful of water, staring at her over the bottle, frowning. He wasn't going to ask again.

"Elliott took Edinburgh."

That wasn't surprising.

"Alive?"

"We don't know. He didn't say."

Elliott could be a shit at times. Hil tapped the bottle against his knee, trying to figure out if he was fit enough to go to the Cage, find someone who'd give him a decent workout. He felt like pummelling someone. Anyone. It would've been freaking nice to know if what he'd done had made a difference to Edinburgh.

"He said he'd be back for you."

He was finding it hard to know what to care about anymore.

"LC's alive," Evelyn said finally. "But the medics are saying he's... he's unresponsive. There's minimal brain activity."

Hil narrowed his eyes. She said it like it was no big deal, like it wasn't LC they were talking about.

She placed a bottle on the table between them, clear liquid, and set down two shot glasses. "He's alive. That's the main thing. They just don't know what's going on. They're feeding the virus but it isn't making a dent. He's not asleep, not exactly unconscious. It's like he's shut down and they don't know how to get him back."

Like NG. So much for LC being a fix-all saviour for Sebastian.

"At least they don't think he's having nightmares," Evelyn said. She poured and pierced him with a stare as she handed over one of the glasses. "How are you doing?"

He shrugged. Obnoxious but he didn't care. He took the liquor and took a sip. Moonshine. Pure vodka. Homemade. Not the best the guild had ever had in stock. He downed it in one, throat burning.

Evelyn threw back her own and topped up both glasses. "Quinn thought he was bringing both of you back in body bags, do you realise that?" She took a deep breath as if she was tempering what she was about to say. "As much as medical are tying themselves in knots over LC, they have no idea how you survived. Do you realise how much blood you lost? Never mind the exposure to that level of electrobes." She stared. "You always were as hard as nails, Hil, but now...? What happened?"

He didn't want to talk about it. Bad enough the medics had been hounding him. It was easier to misinterpret the question. "Edinburgh knows what happened. Ask Elliott."

She looked like she was about to correct him and thought better of it, adding instead, "What do you think happened to them?"

He looked at her. "I think something on Kheris attacked LC. If it had just made them freaking uncomfortable, they would've left. Edinburgh isn't stupid. LC isn't stupid. But he is different. I think whatever it is down there, it recognised that and attacked him."

"You think he knows what it is?"

He shrugged. It didn't matter what he thought, he just wanted LC to damn well wake up and tell them. He slouched back down, cradling his left arm that was still sore as hell. "Where are we?"

"Uncharted jump point. No one knows we're here."

He let the silence hang between them then said abruptly, "I should take LC to Sebastian."

"No." She took a careful and deliberate sip of her vodka, then set down her glass. "I'm not prepared to hand LC over to anyone. If this genuinely is Sebastian, then

Sebastian has no love for LC and I do not trust that we'll ever see LC or NG again." She sat back, then added, voice cold and sharp, "I hate to say this but please persuade me that giving LC to him is the right course of action."

Hil sat there, breathing as steady as he could make it with the tingling still sparking in his lungs at random intervals. He wasn't going to persuade anyone of anything. In the scale of things, in cold, hard reality, he was a grunt field-op. One who should never have been at the guild in the first place, in a million years, if Mendhel had never taken a chance on him.

"I can't," he said, staring at the vodka as if it had all the answers. He raised his eyes. "Not with Anya there."

"What?"

"Anya Halligan is at the FOB with Sebastian. Did I not mention that?" Shit, he'd meant to. He hadn't exactly been thinking straight. "She said he's keeping her prisoner there, but..."

He knew Evelyn was well aware of Anya's role in this war, her betrayal, her siding with Zang and Drake. What he wasn't sure of was if she knew the bombshell about Anya's parentage. He'd never included mention of it in any report. Had no idea if LC had told anyone else or not. Evelyn had been NG's PA. Close to him. Almost as close as Martinez. He had no idea if she knew this or not. It felt too private, too much like he was betraying NG to air this publicly.

He leaned forward and lowered his voice. "Mendhel wasn't Anya's father. Do you know about this?"

"No. Why...?"

"It was NG. I don't think Mend knew. No one knew. LC found out on that capital ship we attacked. Sebastian confronted Pen with it. Apparently NG was with her mother before she even met Mendhel."

Evelyn looked as uncomfortable as he felt. "Is she...?" She bit off her question.

Hil answered it anyway. "Telepathy, telekinesis, fuck knows what else. What else can NG do?"

There was a horrified silence, then, "If NG is her biological father, that means Sebastian is."

"And she hates them both. Problem we have is that she's there and she wants LC for herself. She always has. She's been besotted with him since we were kids. We just never knew she was insane. And telepathic. I'm not handing LC over to Sebastian just for Anya to get her hands on him again. No way."

"Sebastian has her contained?"

Hil nodded. "Seems so."

Evelyn cursed under her breath. She stretched, drawing herself upright, raising her chin as if she was steeling herself. "This is a mess. I can't do this anymore. I can't bear to see LC like this. Sebastian is our only chance to save him and NG. Take him. Let's hope they can do it, because, Hil, without NG we can't win this war."

· · ·

Elliott turned up as he was packing his gear, the Duck dropping out of jump next to them and his avatar appearing at the door two seconds later.

Hil paused, two guns in his hands, his kitbag open on the bunk, working hard to dampen the sudden and intense onslaught of pressure in his head. Iona dropped in too, keeping quiet, as if she knew Elliott was there to see him.

Elliott didn't wait to be invited, wandering in and leaning against the locker, arms folded, casual. "You saved Edinburgh," he said. "Well done, but drastic, putting yourself in mortal danger like that."

It was impossible to tell from his tone if Elliott was impressed, grateful, derisive, mocking or incredulous that a human would do that for an AI.

"Is she okay?" The question sounded lame.

"She will be. She's alive. Thanks to you. How did you know that would work?"

Infecting an AI with the alien virus. His mutated virus.

"I didn't." He threw the guns into the bag and grabbed a couple of magazines, checking they were full.

"And by all accounts," Elliott said, "Luka and Sean wouldn't have survived much longer if you hadn't found them." He cocked his head. "How did you find them?"

"I was lucky." Hil dropped in the ammunition and reached for his belt, refusing to look at Elliott as he cinched it tight around his waist and fastened the holster ties around his thigh.

"Did you get the intel from Redemption?"

He looked up then. Elliott was watching him, looking to all intents and purposes as if he was standing there casually, just dropped in for a chat, when in fact he was accessing every record and data entry since the last time he'd been in contact with the Man's ship, thoughts and analyses whirring in such a frenzy it was making Hil's headache spike, being in such close proximity.

"I did."

"Good. Go with Iona."

Hil grabbed his bag and made to leave. "I'm going with LC."

Elliott stepped into his way. "No, you're going to continue your mission."

It was hard not to laugh. "I'm going with LC," he said again.

"You've done your bit. Now leave this to us."

Elliott was tall but skinny.

Hil squared up to him. Not about to back down, even to someone as powerful as Aries, for Christ's sake. And no way about to let them take LC without him.

Elliott's mouth quirked into a half smile, not aggressive, more like calculating, and for a split second it felt like he was about to be knocked on his ass again, but the guy just spread his hands, appeasing, and said calmly, "Hilyer, if Drake gets to the tech Spearhead left behind at that base before we do, forget any chance of winning this war. Or have you forgotten what Spearhead made you do when you were one of its deadly little assassins?" He stared for a heartbeat and added, "Imagine if Drake can do that... to anyone she wants..."

It sucked, however he looked at it, and the thought of leaving LC in this state was just shit.

"I take it you haven't told anyone the location of Spearhead's base."

Of course he hadn't. He shook his head, jaw clenched, having to force himself to stand there, slipping automatically to attention.

"Good. Now be a good soldier and go get that intel. Send me the coordinates on a tight wire. And trust me, we'll take care of Luka... and Anya Halligan." Elliott turned and started to wander out. "I've always wanted to meet Sebastian."

CHAPTER SEVENTEEN

SHE FOLLOWED him from the chamber, gladly leaving the disembodied specimens, the Bhenykhn pods and whatever they held, and walked up steep stairs, elaborate black metal steps curling in a spiral underfoot, unsure of what exactly she was leaving behind, or heading to.

"Spearhead and the AIs seem to be taking centre stage in this war, Koschei," she threw at his back as he ascended the stairs ahead of her. "Not exactly what I was expecting to return to..."

"It is the unexpected," he said, his voice echoing in the spiral stairwell, "the serendipitous occurrences that hit us out of the blue that change the way of the world the most. You should know that."

The twisted black metal of the rail was warm beneath her hand. "I'm surprised you allow Aries such freedom to manipulate the operatives of your guild."

"There is no guild." His voice was dark, tone final. "The Thieves' Guild died with the Alsatia."

The facility was deserted. As if they'd deployed to attack the Academy ten years ago and just not come back. It didn't take much for Iona to hook in and fire up the life support and lights, whatever power plant was in operation just on standby, just waiting for the command.

Hil walked through the main hangar, footsteps echoing, two Hailstones hovering around him, darting off at times but keeping close. There was no one here. It was on an uncharted planet. Deep in the Between. Deep underground. Weird to think he'd thought they were on a ship back then. The gravity was high, and just walking through that vast empty space brought on flashbacks, painfully sickening flashes that left him feeling queasy, palms sweating, and not sure if the headache was real or a ghost of a memory. He could almost hear the lines of kids in identical black kit, running perfect Shaolin sequences. Almost felt his muscles respond. They'd been that programmed. He'd felt this sick the whole time he was here.

If there'd been any AIs here, they were gone. All he could hear was Iona, and she was keeping quiet. She was concerned. Worried about him, especially considering how badly the memory module on Temerity had affected him, and not knowing exactly what the exposure to Edinburgh's core had done to him. She was watching his stats. He could hear it in her thoughts.

He made his way inside, past the barracks, commissary, infirmary, the pod room... offices and conference rooms he hadn't seen here last time. They'd kept the kids well under control – training, pod programming, eat, sleep. That was about it. It was hard to keep his mind here and now, hearing echoes of voices behind him, spooking him, no one there but in his mind.

"You okay, Hilbud?" Iona sent.

"No."

That freaked her out.

"I'm fine," he added quickly. "It's just weird. Where am I going? Where do you reckon?"

He had an idea already, but he wanted her working on it, not worrying about him.

He'd been hauled into a briefing room here when they'd decided he was going to be the primary for the mission. When he was supposed to have been under the influence of their drugs. There'd been terminals in there. They'd dragged up his entire history. More than he'd thought the guild would've let loose. More than he ever wanted confronting with. It had been beyond shit. But there'd been terminals in there.

He shut out the past, focused on this mission, right now, and made his way to it.

· · ·

It was somewhat liberating to drag out hard copy files and toss them onto the floor, making a mess, not giving a shit, trashing his way through their systems and throwing everything up to Iona. It felt like he was exorcising demons. Many demons, from years ago, more than ten years ago. He dropped another memory module to the floor and broke into another, and hit up against a barrier he couldn't break.

He sat back.

"Iona...?"

"Hil, be careful. Bring it back up here."

"It might not be the one we need."

She was quiet.

She knew fine well that he needed to tackle it here.

And she hated it.

There was something off about it.

Something...

He tried it.

Raw.

Painful.

That jarring, hideous, dark interference that scratched poison deep into his synapses as it sparked through the Senson and his neural interface.

This time he pushed through it. Forced his way to the barrier and broke the protections.

It was all there.

There were five.

Five kids from Redemption that had been infected by Spearhead's experimental mind control.

He worked his way through the files, fast, not sure how long he could bear staying in there.

LC, he knew.

Jarrold had died on Caron Four, shot in the head as it had all kicked off.

Singh, he had no idea. The kid had been shooting at them at the end, taken down by FTH. God knows what had happened to him after that.

Teagan he couldn't remember seeing once they'd withdrawn to the Citadel.

And that left... Jem.

Shit.

Jem.

He pushed further. Tracking back each file on the five kids, digging out everything he could on them. He took everything, only reading half of it, feeling like he was freaking intruding on LC's life just by touching his file, shit in there that LC hadn't even mentioned when he was spilling his guts in the tunnels under Hanover.

Jem was something else too.

He couldn't help getting drawn into her file.

So immersed he only vaguely registered an urgent demand from Iona, caught the tail end of a transmission. "...out. Hilyer, get out. Now."

He tried to disengage but something pulled him back in, tighter, the connection snatching a physical hold on him he couldn't break.

Shit.

He'd sprung traps inside security systems before, got his fingers burned plenty of times. This was something else. That dark and nasty, rusty saw blade interference cut right through his skull, severing connections and taking a grip on the neural interface.

Dark, looming.

Pulling him in.

A flash of white hot energy ignited behind his eyes, pain billowing outwards in an explosion of agonising intensity. It peaked. He couldn't move, couldn't scream, and couldn't block it.

He came round to a pounding headache banging hammers into every inch of his brain, intense urging from Iona, ragging at him to move, both Hailstones nudging at him. He blinked and sprawled on his back, raising his hands to press them against his eyes.

"Hil, move. Go."

"What...?" It felt like he was going to pass out again, hot, way too hot, he couldn't breathe, couldn't...

"Hilbud..." Iona sounded calm. Too calm.

"I'm..." He couldn't think.

There was a loud bang from deep inside the complex.

"Hilbud, the base defence systems just came alive. You

have two attack drones moving in on your position right now. You need to move. Do you understand?"

"Can't..."

"You need to go, now."

That was a new voice.

Who the hell was that?

His mind whirred. Then... Elliott.

What was Elliott doing here?

How the fuck long had he been out?

He rolled and managed to get to his knees, eyes burning, nose bleeding, red dripping onto the floor in front of him.

"Hilyer, go," Elliott said again.

He looked up, blinking.

Elliott was there.

Standing right there.

When...?

There was something else there.

He could hear Iona, faint as if shrouded in fog... Elliott was pissed. Angry. Cold, hard anger. As harsh as he'd ever felt from Elliott. And something else. Something intense that was pressing against his senses... Trying to get to him but...

Shit.

Elliott was shielding him.

He couldn't...

He rested his head down onto his arms, down on the

floor, pulling in as much energy as he could, as fast as he could.

He was in the middle of something way bigger than him. So much more powerful, he couldn't comprehend how much more powerful, shouldn't even be able to...

"Go."

He forced himself to move, pushed to his feet.

One of the Hailstones whirred and shot off.

Disconcerting as hell.

He was twenty levels underground. It wasn't going to be that easy to just go.

"Hil, sweetheart..."

They were both shielding him.

"Get to the lift shaft."

He still had something clutched in his hand. Lifted it and squinted at it, struggling to recognise it as a memory module.

He staggered slightly, looking around.

No one.

"Elliott...?"

"Hilbud," Iona sent, pleading, "get to the lift shaft... get out now."

Whatever survival instinct he had kicked in. He started to move, tucking the module into a pocket, and broke into a run, not really understanding what the hell was going on, he wanted out. He had what he'd been sent in here for. He needed out, and out now.

"Speed up, buddy."

He skidded around a corner as the lighting went, dropping him into pitch black. He cursed and slowed, reaching for his flashlight and backing against the wall as blue emergency lights flickered on.

He could see the elevator doors, open, up ahead, about two hundred feet away.

"Hil, run."

He ran, ignoring the pounding in his head that was keeping pace with each step, holding the flashlight in one hand and pulling out a gun with the other.

He got half way and the doors slammed shut, juddered, opened and shut.

"Iona...?"

"Don't stop."

He wasn't about to.

He could hear a drone behind him, closing in fast.

"There's a door to the left," she sent, concern mixing with irritation and a smouldering anger emanating from her. "It goes to the stairwell. You're going to have to climb. You're doing well, Hilbud, just keep going. We want you out of there."

He wanted out of there. He shoulder-charged the door as a hail of bullets opened up, peppering the wall and sending shards of shrapnel flying. The Hailstone still with him took off, opening fire itself. He ran through the door, and ran straight up narrow steps, two at a time, spiralling upwards. He kept the flashlight in his hand, its bouncing beam of muted red all that was giving him light to see by on some levels, others lit by failing strip lights, some with those flickering blue back up systems.

It was getting cold. He was as fit as he'd ever been, faster, stronger, and his muscles were still trembling, threatening to seize, lungs struggling and limbs heavy as he reached a level marked 'Twelve'. Eleven to go. Jesus.

He pushed through and ran up another, starting to flag, very aware that if he misjudged this he could flake, even more aware that whatever the hell it was that he'd encountered down there could reappear at any moment, no idea where the two attack drones were and no idea if the Hailstones were even still active. He usually knew exactly where each and every one of them was and he had no idea. Couldn't sense them at all. And the two AIs were quiet, no banter, that was a bad sign, and their thoughts were subdued, as if there was a barrier between him and them, some kind of dampening field.

"Iona...?"

There was enough of a pause that his stomach flipped, even though he could sense her there.

He ran up another two levels and tried again. This time she came back with a curt, "Not now. Just don't stop. Get to the surface."

Eight. It was tempting to slow to a walk but he knew what that would lead to and pushed through it, chest burning, pain flaring in his legs so bad it was making his eyes water. It was as bad as the first time he'd ever run the Maze on the Alsatia. NG had shown him a schematic, let him study it for thirty seconds, set him a time limit and told him to make it to the end or he was out. It had almost killed him. That had been freaking high gravity too. As far as stakes went, nothing would ever be as high as that one time. Nothing. Ever.

It was only when Elliott cut in and demanded the intel that this suddenly felt like he wasn't going to make it out alive. The pressure pushing at the base of his skull was intensifying, the sound of gunfire behind him getting closer, vision narrowed to a dark tunnel as he pushed up the stairs, one hard-fought step after another, grabbing the handrail now and half dragging himself up.

If he gave Elliott the intel, they had no need to wait for him.

If he didn't, he could flake out, die down here, and no one would ever know.

He stumbled and fell to one knee.

He was screwed whatever he did.

CHAPTER EIGHTEEN

THE STAIRCASE OPENED ONTO AN ATRIUM, dark, oppressive, naked flames in sconces casting an orange glow. He didn't stop, walking ahead without acknowledging any of the shadowy figures they passed. "As I said, three factions... a way to control humans... physically control them, beyond their own volition? Even I have never been so crass."

She followed as he headed for one of three corridors that led from that central area, aware that the elite guard were behind, unsure of the figures, human from the size of them, that seemed to be going about their business in silence. This was not an area of his domain she had ever been privy to. "Did Hilyer survive?"

"What do you think? Aries is a ruthless and brilliant being. There is a reason he was the only one of the Seven to escape. But he is not infallible. Hilyer's unique talents have made him an immensely valuable asset. Whoever is pulling

the strings. But believe me, and I have known this boy since he was a child, Hilyer is not one to be manipulated easily. He has a tendency to resist when he feels cornered. Given the right circumstances, he can excel. In the wrong place, given the wrong stimuli, he is possibly more stubborn than Nikolai. The problem Aries had with him at this point was simple... with Anderton out of action, Hilyer ceased to care."

"There were five," he sent, struggling to concentrate. He crawled back to his feet and pushed on. He knew fine well he could be signing his death warrant but fuck it, Spearhead had been working with Drake. Eloise Drake might already know who and where these subjects were, might be using them the way Spearhead had used LC. He transmitted the full package of data as tight as he could make it, fully expecting the barriers to evaporate as soon as Elliott had the information he wanted.

Seven. Six.

His head was fit to implode but he was still alive and still moving.

Five.

There was nothing from either of the AIs. He wanted Iona to chide him, tease him, yell at him. Send more Hailstones. Anything. But there was nothing. No updates. No courtesy of a countdown.

He almost retched. Eyeballs burning and tears

streaking down his cheeks. Tears or blood, he wasn't sure. He'd seen LC in this kind of state enough times and had always just felt kinda queasy, glad it wasn't him. Glad it had never been him before if this was how bad it got. He didn't even know what the hell it was that was trying to get through to him.

Four.

The last time he'd been here at this base, he'd fought the drugs and the programming. At the age of fifteen. Stubbornly, fiercely, viciously, had to fight everything they threw at him, determined he wasn't going to let anyone do what they wanted to him, make him do what they wanted. Ever again.

And he wasn't about to let them now.

Three.

He'd never triggered a trap before that had been this bad. Not ever.

A tendril of dark flashed through with sparks of silver shot past his narrow field of vision.

"Screw you," he muttered and upped the pace, back to two steps at a time, pushing it because he was almost at the top. "Iona," he called out, "you wanna tell me where the hell I go once I'm at the top." He forced two deep breaths as he ran. "Cos I'm almost at the top."

Two.

Nothing.

He got a spurt of impetus, the kind you get when you run long distance, momentum, drive, whatever the hell it was, that shit that made you run faster than was possible, and not the drug-fuelled kind of kick, the shear bloody-minded, not going to fail shit that was verging on self-destruction. He made it to Level One and burst out through a door into a hangar, chest heaving and limbs like jelly.

It was huge.

Way bigger than the hangar underground where they'd practised Shaolin drills.

Stretched out as far as he could see.

In all directions.

He caught himself and stood, doubled over, eyes closed, hands on his thighs still clutching the flashlight and pistol, palms so slick with sweat he probably couldn't aim either of them straight if his life depended on it.

He forced himself to glance up. High ceiling. No way up to it.

If he went down to his knees now, he wouldn't get up.

He stood.

Felt the pressure ease.

And heard an urgent, "Go. Go now. Straight ahead."

He staggered forward two steps and broke into a run.

Only once before all this Bhenykhn shit, before the lab and the package, had he ever run a tab and come close to calling for an extraction. He hadn't. Damn right he hadn't. It was about the only thing he'd been able to claim a lead on LC, the fact that, before this, he had never needed an extraction. That reputation was now blown to hell, especially after Temerity. He was damned if he was going to make a habit of it.

"Give me an RV," he sent, every breath fiery hot, every step pure agony spiking nails into his head. "Iona, Elliott, for fuck's sake, give me an RV."

There was nothing for twenty more feet of ground covered painful stride by painful stride, then he got a rapid burst of numbers. Nothing else. It was enough. He knew where they wanted him and he'd get there. Done it enough times before at the guild. And not about to give up now.

He ran, made it to a door and pushed out into a cold blast of air that took the last of his breath away.

He had another fifty feet before he was clear and into the drop zone.

It almost felt like he could hear engines but that could have just been the pounding pressure inside his head. He didn't think, ran, and saw a ship descending ahead of him, a shadow dropping down through the mist that he had to trust was theirs, had to cling to the reality that it was controlled by Iona or Elliott because he had no input from anywhere, and no idea what to do if it wasn't.

Gunfire burst out behind him, the boom of an explosion and that pop of disconnect that hit hard when he lost a Hailstone. He kept running, the rattle and whirr of an attack drone reorienting behind him and closing in.

He was four or five feet from the ramp and safety when a shockwave of force knocked him sideways.

He rolled with it, vision spinning, not sure if it was real or in his head.

Iona sent a hard fast, "Stay down," and he shielded his head, flattened to the ground as another shockwave rippled out in the other direction, a pulse of heat racing overhead, his nerve ends cringing.

"Okay, go," she yelled.

He pushed to his knees and up into a run, the ramp bouncing beneath his boots and closing even as he was running on board, the gulfstream lifting before it was fully shut. It lurched. He fell and gave in to it, sprawling on his back as they made for orbit, and squeezing his eyes shut as they hooked up with Iona and jumped.

He was still on the floor when Elliott appeared. The toxic presence of whatever trap he'd triggered was gone, both the AIs he was used to hearing distant somewhat as if his brain couldn't deal with any of it anymore.

"I've narrowed down one of the targets," Elliott said. Straight to the point. No niceties like asking if he was okay.

They'd come for him. At least they'd come for him and not abandoned him down there.

Hil sat up, every muscle and joint aching, chest still heaving. "Which one?"

"Does it matter?"

Immensely. "No," he breathed. It felt like his head was wrapped in layers of fog. He'd lost two Hailstones.

Elliott was sitting in one of the seats, leaning forward and watching him, intently. Making no effort to help. Not that he wanted any. He stretched his hand out on the deck, feeling the energy humming away through the ship and drawing in just as much as he needed, cautious and steady as if he was just catching his breath.

"Latest I can trace," Elliott said, "are orders to the Nairobi. I have no details on current status or the cover they're using now. But judging by what we just encountered down there, we're running out of time. You're going to have to get in there and find them manually."

Hil squinted at him. "What was that back there?" It hadn't been Spearhead. He was sure it hadn't been Spearhead.

Elliott didn't react.

"Did you neutralise it?" he said.

The expression on Elliott's face was unfathomable but the emotion emanating from him was a dark mix of curiosity and deep anger.

"We'll deal with it. I want you to go after the Nairobi. It's under Drake's control, out at Redgate. Your cover was blown on Temerity. There's a new ID in your cabin. Along with some sleeper cells I want you to install."

Yeah, that wasn't going to happen.

Hil glanced into the ship's systems. It was hard to pick up anything new. But there was no way he was going straight out on another mission. He was going back to Sebastian. He needed to know what was going on.

He pushed to his feet, swaying slightly as his balance wavered. "No, I'm going back. I want to see LC."

Elliott stared at him for a moment, no expression on that thin face. "No, you don't."

In all the time he'd been able to pick up the thoughts and feelings of the AIs, he'd never encountered such a conflicting maelstrom of troubled calculation. It was like being battered by riptides.

"What?"

There was doubt. Never had he ever sensed doubt from Elliott.

"Elliott, what? What happened with Sebastian? Is LC...?" He wanted to say okay, but 'alive' was stuck there in his mind, at the tip of his tongue. Cold, sickening dread dragging at his stomach.

Elliott stood. Staring. Eventually he said, deadpan, zero emotion, "We left Luka and Nikolai with Sebastian. That's it. Even if you did go back there, what can you do?" He leaned forward. "Forget them. You have a mission. This target is the only one I've been able to find. Don't lose her."

Her...

"Elliott..."

"Hilyer," Elliott snapped, "whether Luka and Nikolai

live or not, whether Sebastian lets them go or not..." Elliott seemed to compose himself and spread his hands. "That's where they are and there's nothing you can do. And right now, we are in a head to head race with Drake, and we're losing. Acquire the target and take her to these coordinates."

Hil forced himself to calm, to breathe. As much as he hated it, Elliott was right.

"Okay, how? What's the plan?"

It wasn't often he'd ever had to acquire live targets, rare at the guild but not unheard of. Acquire could mean anything from infiltrating the systems and subtly inserting a reassignment, to attempting to turn them, to bopping them on the head and carrying them off. Not knowing how much they were being controlled was going to make it tricky. And not knowing if whoever it was would recognise him from ten years ago was going to be weird. The fact that it could be Jem... well, that dark dense box of guilt was buried so deep, sealed so tight, it would take a sledgehammer to open it. He felt numb. On the surface, just numb.

"Find her," Elliott said. "I'm assuming you'll recognise her. That's why this has to be you. Figure it out from there. I'm coming with you this time. I can't risk Iona."

Hil nodded, jaw clenched. Hard as it was to admit to himself, there was nothing he could do for LC. Elliott was right. Switch off, keep going, do what had to be done. It wasn't the first time he'd had to do that.

"Just get the hell out to Redgate and find that target before we lose them again," Elliott said and vanished. No illusion of walking away. He just vanished. As if he'd never really been there at all.

Hil took a step back. "Iona...?"

"Hilbud, I don't know any more than you do. This war sucks. What can you do by being with LC right now? Think about it. You have a tab. That's it. Go and do it, and get home safe."

That was all he could do. And it did suck. Worse than that. He had no choice but to suck it up and do what he was told, and boy, did that bring back unwelcome memories that he was not going to go anywhere near.

He stalked off to his cabin and picked the ID up off the bunk. AI tech maintenance support, Private, Imperial Xùnzhí Corps. Elliott had a twisted sense of humour.

He pocketed the pass, slung the dog tags over his neck and picked up his kitbag. He could play a freaking convict. He'd had enough practice.

He rolled up his right sleeve and held out his arm, wrist up, calling out to Elliott, "You gonna make this convincing then?"

The Nairobi was struggling. It didn't take much to see that she wasn't operating anywhere near her former Imperial glory days.

Hil threw his stuff into the locker and turned, toolbag

in his hand. His escort hadn't left him alone for a second since he'd been picked up at the transfer RV.

"I'm here to fix your freaking AI comms system," he said, resisting the urge to scratch at his wrist. He wasn't finding it hard to act irritable and threatening. "You wanna show me where I – am – allowed to go?"

It didn't matter. He was already hooked into their systems and they had no idea. The Nairobi was one of the last few big Imperial warships that had survived the war so far. It was weird to see the mix of crew, original Imperial Navy, ragtag mercenaries and Wintran militia, a load of marines from god knows where. For all he could tell openly, it could have been loyal to the human forces. No outward sign that it was Drake's.

He'd made it on board just before they made jump to their current mission. She was on battlestations, lurking, stealthed, behind a burned out orbital, babysitting a snatch and grab operation to raid what was left of Redgate. Elliott was talking to her, Hil only catching about half the exchange.

"No," he heard Elliott saying to her while he followed the junior officer through the decks, "maintain current objectives. I'll let you know when..."

He missed the next comment as the lieutenant, who looked younger than LC, demanded his attention, asking him to log in and run a security check. They had two marines trooping along behind them. Both the jarheads stiffened as he didn't respond straight away, muscles tensing, hands gripping weapons tighter, as he glanced at them. The officer twitched like he wasn't sure if he should be stepping back and drawing his sidearm. But Hil muttered, "For Christ's sake," and pressed his palm against the panel, keeping bored eye contact as he did it, heart rate so steady he could have been booking into a Wellbeing for a week long R'n'R. He could feel the young kid staring at the black ink ID tattooed onto the inside of his wrist.

Elliott was good. As good as anything the guild had ever set up for him. If not better. The ID was solid. The kit he was wearing that was transmitting matching bio-signs was solid. And the design on the inside of his wrist was faded as if it had been there for years. Definitely not just the couple of weeks it had taken them to get out here.

Problem was, if it didn't convince them, he was right in the middle of hostile territory. And he had no contingency plan to get out if it all went to shit.

CHAPTER NINETEEN

He stopped at a door and gestured her to enter what looked like a vast command centre, staff, humans, at every station, working in absolute silence apart from a gentle hum of machinery, dark except for the faint light from banks of screens and monitors.

There was something familiar in the data, in the symbols, and it took her a moment to recognise where she was. "Kochitek." She turned to him. "Don't tell me you have reinstated your pet corporation? I thought we learned long ago..."

"We did," he growled. "And believe me, I know more than most that there is no need nor place for corporations, guilds nor any other construct in this galaxy now. But a base of operations may always come in useful."

"You didn't ever disband it, did you?"

He didn't reply, ambling over to a central console and towering over it. Battlespace data began to scroll across its surface, Bhenykhn strongholds, what was left of the human forces.

Her heart sank. "Is this what they have come to? The Order seems to be prevailing on all fronts."

"They are surviving. We, of all creatures, know what it is to be invaded, to have an enemy take what they want, destroy all that is dear. Why should Eloise Drake be vilified for merely ensuring survival for her people?"

"And Aries sent Hilyer right back into their midst..."

The panel beeped green. The marines relaxed.

Elliott murmured in his head, "They've had two incursions by Tierney and his crowd in the past month. Not surprising they're so twitchy. They're risking a lot just being here. The Bhenykhn have one base down there, minimal presence, but they could be back in force at any time."

That was one thing that was different. Operating under the noses of the Bhenykhn. Whatever agreement or deal Drake had with the alien invasion forces, they weren't bothering with a ship full of humans right on their doorstep.

Even so, it was still unnerving.

"I've got Nairobi checking personnel records," Elliott sent, "but they have so many people coming and going now that it's all gone to shit. You need to get into records and see if you recognise anyone. And let's make this fast, Mister Hilyer. Keep it simple. I don't want you on there a minute longer than necessary."

He sent back, "No argument from me," and stepped aside as the kid overrode the panel and opened the hatch, gesturing him inside.

"What ship did you say you were off?" the kid asked as he passed.

Not so green.

Hil hauled the toolbag through with him and hoisted it up onto an overhead walkway. "Sao Paulo."

"I heard the Paulo was lost at Hanover."

"It was."

Out of the corner of his eye, he saw the kid glance back at the security detail.

They were double checking his ID.

He took a handhold on the ladder and looked back. "You ever seen a Benny up close?"

The young lieutenant shook his head uneasily.

"You don't want to, trust me." He climbed up and sat on the walkway, gripping the edge so the prison tattoo on his wrist was in plain sight, legs dangling, looking down at them. "I was on the Tangiers out at Erica as well." It'd been the Expedience but what the hell. "Two for two so far. You wanna let me get this done so I can get the hell off your ship before I make it three for three?"

The Nairobi was nervous. She was setting his nerves on edge, thinking they'd been there too long, running long range scans into the outer system obsessively, as she simultaneously tracked the troops she had down on the surface, watching the Bhenykhn base, and fretting as she worked out scenarios, fuel calcs and ran checks on the blizzard down there that was increasing in ferocity.

Elliott was swapping intel, giving her everything and taking what she had of the current battle situation and status of other AIs she'd encountered. He was taking a risk trusting her but there was nothing coming out of her thoughts that suggested she was being duplicitous. She was betraying Drake, covert, undercover, nestled right at the heart of Drake's forces. She knew what their mission was, knew he was on board and knew what he was doing. She was covering for them, reassuring the security guys that his ID checked out, changing the files she had on him in realtime to back up what he was saying off the top of his head. It was tempting to get more and more outlandish but she was stressed enough so he kept quiet.

The lieutenant and his security team were still watching him. Hil shifted his weight to get comfortable and braced his leg, leaning back and hacking into the panel, rough and ready, only half concentrating, as he listened in to Elliott confirm with Nairobi that the target was there.

"Nǐ zhēn de zài Erica?" the kid said.

Mandarin. Another freaking test. Xùnzhí Corps were fluent in Mandarin, wherever the hell they'd come from.

'Were you really at Erica?'

Shit. He snatched his fingers out, cursing, as a wire shorted.

Elliott cut in, "Watch yourself, Hilyer. This kid's sister died at Erica. She was on the Tangiers."

"JU?"

Dammit. He didn't need this.

He redirected the circuit before it set on fire and nodded. "Shì."

"What was it like?" Back into English, as if he'd passed the test.

Nairobi was giving Elliott a steady stream of intel.

It was too weird to think there was someone here, on board this very vessel, who'd been at that Spearhead-run military base with them ten years ago. A lifetime ago. And the idea it could be Jem... bloody hell, right here?

Elliott cut in. "Give the lieutenant a reply, Hilyer, before he decides you're bullshitting. You want to tell him what it was really like on Erica?"

Hil glanced down. All three of them were regarding him with suspicion.

"On Erica? It was cold," he said. "And my best friend died."

He went back to work, slamming components into place and ignoring their stares.

He worked for three hours solid. Their comms were a mess, courtesy of Nairobi disrupting her own systems to make it look good, and it was almost soothing to switch off and run manual labour, mindless fixits that he could do with his eyes closed, all the time listening in to the AIs and gathering as much from them as he could. The lieutenant stayed with him the whole time, watched every move, but more as if he was trying to learn than some paranoia that Hil might be trying to pull some kind of sabotage. And there were no more questions about Erica.

He finished up, wiped his hands and packed up his tools.

"I need to get cleaned up," he said, turning in the small space to look at the kid. "Is there a shower I can use?" He didn't just want a shower, he wanted somewhere private so he could stash the sleeper cells Elliott wanted installing.

The kid was looking at the scars on his arm. He'd rolled up his sleeves while he was working. Hadn't even thought about it.

"A shower?" he said, staring intently until the kid raised his eyes, blinking, a flush hitting his cheeks.

"Yeah, yeah. I'll show you the way."

. . .

The warship was getting ready to leave, recalling the troops and ramping up her engines. He could feel that she wanted out. No one stayed in one place for too long anymore, even flying Drake's flag.

The corridors were bustling.

"So where are you going after this?" the kid asked, trying to keep up with him and having to push past a bunch of marines that were fresh from the surface, a tang of cold air still clinging around them.

"The Athens."

"You don't stay with one ship?"

"Not anymore."

"Where else have you been?"

"Since the invasion? Spent some time on the Los Angeles and the Calcutta. I was on Earth, in Beijing, when they attacked." None of it was a lie and none of it was anything he wanted to dwell on. He didn't mention Hanover, Aston, Miranda...

They walked in silence for a short while, making their way through crowded corridors.

When the kid spoke again it was in a hushed tone, no eye contact. "How come you're working for Drake?"

Hil glanced at him. The kid was staring straight ahead as if he hadn't said a word.

Holy shit. The whole time he'd been in deep cover on Temerity, he'd been surrounded by ruthlessly money-grubbing, self-centred mercenaries who would've betrayed their own grandmothers given half a chance at making some cash and surviving another day. It had never occurred to him that the crew on the big military vessels Drake had commandeered as her own would be any different.

He let it go another couple of steps before he muttered, "I don't have much choice." He twisted his arm, subtle, but enough to see the kid glance down at his wrist. "I know you know what this means."

The young lieutenant was smart. He raised his eyes, staring straight ahead again, and didn't look at Hil as he said under his breath, "Even now?"

They passed some senior officers, Wintran uniforms looking the worse for wear, arguing with mercenaries in plain black fatigues. Same old, same old. That was more like the crap he'd encountered on Temerity. He could feel the lieutenant stiffen, hands that were used to saluting remaining firmly at his side.

They got unimpressed stares but nothing more, walking past and turning into a corridor of crew quarters. The ship's mass shifted, that rumble and shift of inertia trembling through the deck. Nairobi was relieved, he could feel that, all crew accounted for and back on board. No reaction from the Bhenykhn. Go for jump as soon as they were clear. Nice and easy, as if they weren't freaking at war at all.

"You can shower here," the lieutenant said.

Elliott cut in, "You have two hours before jump. Need to get a move on."

He paused at the door, glancing back, sensing that the kid wanted to say something else.

The lieutenant shifted awkwardly before coming out with it. "You were really on the Tangiers?"

He nodded.

The kid narrowed his eyes, jaw clenched, as if he was bracing himself to say it. "My sister was an engineer on there. She was listed MIA after Erica."

Hil was just waiting for the 'did you know her?'

"What was her name?" he said, kicking himself for asking. He didn't care. He didn't want to care.

"Riham. Sergeant Riham deAnsouri."

The Alsatia had taken a load of survivors from the Tangiers. The Tangiers and the Expedience. It wasn't a name he'd come across, and even if she'd survived Erica, if she'd stayed on board the Alsatia like some of them had...

He shook his head. "Sorry, kid."

"You've really seen a Bhenykhn? For real?"

Hil reached into his pocket and pulled out the kill token, the twisted metal warm against his hand. He held it out.

"What's that?"

"It's from Erica. Keep it."

The kid took it, wide-eyed, holding it with reverence. "This is off one of them?" His voice was almost a whisper.

"Yep."

"From Erica? You killed it?"

"That was my first." Before Skye had died, taking out a Bhenykhn gunship that was about to shoot him.

"You got any family?" the kid said.

Christ, he didn't need this.

Elliott cut in. "You need to speed this up."

Hil didn't bother to acknowledge it, head aching with the pressure of being near Elliott and Nairobi. "I have a little brother," he said to the lieutenant, "who is in the middle of some serious shit right now. As are we all..." He turned to go inside and stopped himself, looking back and asking with a faint smile, "You got beer?"

The kid gave him a look, eyes flashing. "We work for Eloise Drake. Of course we have beer. Don't take long. Another half an hour and the mess is going to get busy."

Hil nodded and pushed through into a communal bathroom, cubicles with showers and rows of lockers. He cleaned up, climbed through a hatch in the ceiling and accessed a maintenance terminal to install the sleeper cells. He was back at the door inside fifteen minutes.

The idea that Jem could be there, right there, was making his stomach tumble backflips. If it was her, she'd recognise him. And he just had to hope he saw her first and got her isolated, before he found out if she'd expose him or not. He would've been a helluva lot more sure of himself if he could be confident that she wouldn't. If it was Teagan, he had more time. They hadn't been in the same block on Redemption. And they'd only been at the facility, briefly, and under the influence of Spearhead.

As they walked through the corridors towards the mess, Elliott engaged with a quiet, "Target is embedded with the Imperial Marine Corps. We're trying to work out the ID now."

He muttered an affirmative in reply and kept walking.

Another group of crew appeared ahead of them, chattering as they approached, dark laughter, all of them in dirty coveralls.

The one in the centre turned to face them head on.

And Hil's stomach, that was feeling jittery as hell anyway, did a sickeningly cold backflip as his brain failed to catch up with what he was seeing.

They passed. The girl had her wispy blonde hair dragged up into a topknot, safety goggles black rather than mirrored, but the dimpled smile was unmistakable.

It was her.

It was impossible but it was her.

"Elliott...?" he sent, continuing to walk and not able to help glancing back over his shoulder, catching her look as she turned to stare at him, a faint glimpse of curiosity crossing her delicate features. "What the hell is whacko-girl doing here?"

"Hil, keep walking. Disappear. Get off the main corridors."

"What the hell is she doing here?" he sent.

"Now, Hilyer," Elliott demanded. "All stats are negated. Disappear."

A schematic flashed in through the Senson, maintenance access one corridor over.

He brushed close to the lieutenant and muttered, "Left some tools in the comms centre. I'll see you in the mess."

The kid looked puzzled. "Sure."

Hil veered off, edged past a bunch of marines, and the ship's klaxons burst into full alert.

For a fraction of a second he thought it might be something else, nothing to do with him, then Elliott sent a hard, fast, "Run."

He ran without hesitation, turning the nearest corner and coming up against more crew, all hustling to battlestations. He could do this if he could just...

A body slammed into him. Hard. Heavy. Taking him down and twisting his arm behind his back as he hit the deck, face down, full weight of an armoured body from the feel of it, on his back and no way to fight. Not when a gun barrel pushed into the side of his neck.

He couldn't move, her voice unmistakeable as she murmured, "Hey there, sunshine." She increased the pressure on his arm, immobilising, screwing any thought he had of trying to get free. "Fancy seeing you here."

He kept his breathing shallow, controlled. He couldn't think straight.

She hauled him up and spun him around, someone else taking hold of him from behind.

The name tag on her armour said 'Riley', sergeant stripes on her arm. She took off her helmet and grinned at him.

His heart tumbled backflips into his stomach.

It wasn't Jem or Teagan.

It was Martha.

CHAPTER TWENTY

"*HE WAS CAUGHT?*" *She stepped back from the console.* "*Excuse me for being distrusting, but is it not obvious that Aries set him up to be caught? Koschei, in all this...*" *She swept her hand in a gesture encompassing the bustle of the command centre.* "*...in all that you – we – have managed to achieve in this galaxy, amidst such strife, do you not consider anymore the need to take care of these assets you claim to value so much?*"

He shrugged, wiping a bony finger over the screen and settling on a winding schematic of DNA.

"*Drake has telepaths,*" *he stated, casual.* "*In the myriad of mistakes Aries has made, I don't think we can blame it for missing the fact that Drake has managed to breed herself a fleeting army of telepathic mayflies.*"

Mayflies?

"*An insect on Earth. They live and die in a day,*" *he*

said, his tone witheringly dry as he manipulated the data on the screen. "The lifespan of a mayfly is to humans as theirs is to yours. Whatever means Drake is using to replicate the virus, she shows a catastrophic disregard for the intricacies of accelerated growth." He looked up. "Humans are fickle, fast-living creatures of immense self-interest. Drake has never demonstrated anything else. It's what makes her as powerful as she is..."

Martha took a step back, grinning at him like the cat that had just cornered a mouse. "Looks like we've got ourselves the jack of clubs, gentlemen. Who wants to split half a billion?"

There was harsh laughter. A sharp sting hit the back of his neck and something punched into the top of his left ear. Zapped and tagged, and surrounded by hostile forces.

So much for simple.

He was pushed forward, Martha taking up that grip on his arm again, so close he could smell the oil in the suit. It was her. It was definitely her. Hair was different, and she had a scar by her eye that was new but it was her.

It was tempting to connect through the Senson but he had no way of knowing if that was secure, however tight he made the connection, and he knew for a fact that Elliott could listen in to a private conversation between

Sixes. He wasn't ready to confront her, never mind let Elliott know who she was.

They walked him past a bunch of crew, all standing staring, whacko-girl amongst them, that enigmatic faint hint of a smile on her face. Hil stared back as he was marched past. How the hell she'd escaped from the guild, he couldn't even begin to fathom.

"How the hell did she get here, Elliott?" he sent as they pushed him forward, sharp voices demanding space around them.

Nairobi cut the battlestations alert and dropped them into a sudden lull of quiet, just an occasional mutter and rattle of weapons.

"She didn't, Hilyer. Think about it," Elliott sent.

Think about what?

"Get him into the brig," someone ordered.

Martha leaned close and breathed into his ear, "With pleasure." She kept a close hold on him, restraint hold tougher than necessary seeing as how he wasn't resisting, and they walked, marines on either side with rifles ready, the device humming happily in his neck, spiking every now and then as if someone was toying with him. Nice to get the extra hit of energy.

He kept the connection with Elliott open. "Any ideas?"

Elliott was never one to pull his punches. "Unless you want me to wipe out the entire crew, we have limited options here. But they're keeping a lid on this, no transmissions have been sent, nothing that could be intercepted by anyone. Doesn't look like they're about to alert the Bhenykhn and hand you over to them. What I'm getting from Nairobi is that there's all points out on you from Drake personally. She wants you and she wants you alive." He paused. Pointedly.

It was obvious what Elliott wanted, and as much as he'd never admit it, all he wanted was to find Martha and here she was. He could play along, damn right he could.

"You wanted to get someone close to Drake," he sent, dampening down the irrational thought that Elliott could have set him up for exactly this. "Looks like I'm it."

They didn't take him to the brig, they took him to the flight deck, straight onto a fast transport, a slick little corporate gulfstream, nothing like his 750, warm, still fitted out with all her plush interiors. They kept five guns trained on him every second, Martha right at his side, no restraints as if they knew he could bust out of them if he wanted, and knew he knew there was nowhere to go if he did.

Elliott was quiet but still there, taking what he could from the ship by the sound of it, cold and efficient.

Hil let them steer him into a seat.

Nairobi was gearing up for jump, signing off with Elliott, telling the leader of the Seven not to worry, she'd take care of the boy. Him. Shit, that was weird to overhear.

Nairobi felt responsible for him. He was well and truly in Drake's hands and he had a warship watching out for him.

He let it all wash over him and sat, leaning back, casual, watching Martha as she sat opposite, her eyes on him the whole time.

"Well, that didn't go as planned," Elliott sent.

Hil had to swallow past the lump in his throat. He'd been dreading coming up against Jem. The idea of running into Martha, here...?

"No shit," he sent back.

Elliott sent back a curt, "Okay, just watch yourself, Hilyer. Nairobi is going for jump. Let's play this smart. Go with them. Don't fight them. I don't think Drake is planning on handing you over to the Bhenykhn so let's go see her. Get what you can from the old lady. Whatever they do, I'll find you. Whatever happens. Okay?"

He glanced at the armed guard surrounding them. "Don't have much choice, do I?'

"Be smart, Hilyer."

"Just check on LC, will you? Don't let Anya anywhere near him."

"Anya Halligan? Believe me, that girl is the least of our problems."

They dropped out of jump and the ship dropped straight from her berth, fast acceleration. Wherever they were, Elliott hadn't followed. There were Bhenykhn there, ships in orbit around whatever the hell colony they were at, and troops on the ground. They still hadn't restrained him and it was half tempting to leap up, take down Martha's little gang of thugs, and steal the gulfstream. The ship's AI would be receptive to that. Maybe.

He counted how many there were, where they were and worked out what it would take. He could do it. Not necessarily without taking a hit. But what the hell... He'd heal but he'd be gambling that it really was Martha and that she'd go with him...

It was her. She was watching him.

She caught his eye and said quietly, "Whatever you're thinking, don't."

It was more than half tempting.

She leaned forward, a twisted gleam in her eye. "Half a billion...?"

He smiled, closed his eyes and lounged back, arms folded, legs outstretched and crossed at the ankles. Elliott wanted him to be smart? He could do that. He hooked in to the telemetry, no outward sign that he was doing anything, and listened in to the sitreps as they flew in, the gulfstream sending out encrypted messages, not giving away the fact they had him, just warning that they had high priority intel on board and requesting backup on landing.

From what he could see, it looked like a palace, typical High Order, Drake's summer retreat from the weather data they were picking up... and now overrun by aliens.

Not that different from what he'd seen on Temerity. Until they landed.

No one moved to disembark, clunks and clangs echoing.

Whatever they'd landed on dropped down, fast.

His stomach lurched but he didn't react, just opened his eyes, raising them lazily to meet Martha's, still staring at him, finger on the trigger of her rifle.

They went down, deep down, not the first underground facility of the Order that he'd been in. Not the first of Drake's either.

As soon as they stopped, the marines around him hustled into action. He stood before they had a chance to haul him up. Got a nudge in the back for his efforts and stepped forward, face to face with Martha. She grabbed his arm and pushed him ahead of her, giving no outward indication that she knew him other than from the bounty on his head. This wasn't exactly how he'd imagined their reunion would go, but what the hell. She was alive. Safe. If she was working for Itomara, that complicated things but not irrevocably. There was always a chance the old guy was still on their side.

He stepped off the ship into some kind of underground terminal, clean walls, subtle lighting and expensive, tasteful decor. Potted plants, for Christ's sake. Real, living, potted plants with leafy greenery. High end luxury, corporate as hell. No trace of the Bhenykhn.

There was a welcoming committee waiting for him. One woman, young, in a slick business suit, surrounded by an entourage of corporate heavies, all hefting snub pistols. The mercenaries escorting him backed off, letting him step forward alone.

He eyed the young woman with suspicion, expecting cuffs to appear, threats of some sort. He'd seen the kind of hospitality Drake had offered LC after Elliott had set them up, after LC had made the mistake of pissing off Anya.

There was nothing of the kind. Not yet at least.

She eyed him back, appraising, as if she was making sure he was for real. She had dark green brown eyes, natural, not a telepath. She nodded, curt and efficient, spinning on her heels and walking away without a word. One of the heavies gestured him to follow. He threw a glance back over at Martha. She was staring after him, eyes narrow, a slight smile dancing on her face. It was definitely her.

He walked after the corporate suit, tucking away any feeling whatsoever. It was a mission. Always a mission. He just did what he was told.

They took him down an elevator, then out onto a level with wide corridors decked out with soft carpet, art on the walls that looked like originals, real paintings of seascapes and green hills. It reminded him of deck Twelve on the Alsatia. NG's suite of offices. He couldn't help but linger on a huge painting of a map, midnight blue oceans, mountain ranges and foothills, deserts and bright concentrations of light, cities, civilisation. Earth. As if Drake needed reminding of where she was from. Where they were all from, whatever side you ended up on.

The woman he was following didn't look back.

The Nairobi was in orbit. He could just about hear her, faint traces of concern, an intense interaction with other AIs on the surface. They were colder, less emotional, lower level and more functional. There weren't any other big ships nearby that he could tell.

They passed open doors, quiet efficient working spaces, huge screens alive with data, offices and conference rooms teeming with suits, lab techs, occasional military uniforms, no one taking any notice of them. The air was clean, temperate. Pleasant. He'd broken into facilities like this a few times. Always felt out of place.

At another set of lift doors, the woman nodded to their escort and stepped aside to let him enter, her alone following him in and closing the door.

He turned and looked at her, properly looked at her, opening his mouth and biting his tongue as she beat him to it and said, calm and clear, "Save whatever you have to say for Ms Drake."

The way she was holding herself he was fairly sure that

if he did try anything, there was a good chance he'd be the one that ended up on the floor.

She reminded him of Evelyn and Devon.

She probably had a stiletto knife in a sheath strapped to her thigh.

They dropped down another level, this one living quarters, he guessed, narrow corridors, one after the other, all lined with numbered doors. She stopped at one and waved her hand towards the security panel on the wall.

"Place your palm here."

His biometrics had been set up for the current ID he was using. He had no idea what the hell they would have on record for him here but the panel clicked to green and the door opened.

"Your quarters," she said. "Whatever is in here is yours. Shower and change. You have ten minutes."

He walked in, giving her a glance, curious, as he passed.

This was weird.

As cells went, it was the most flash, ostentatious holding facility he'd ever been shown into. The door closed behind him, leaving him in there alone, soft carpet underfoot, plush sofas and furnishings. He pushed open an internal door to see a bedroom kitted out with crisp white linen, another that led to a bathroom, polished granite floor and walls, soft white towels on a heated rack. He flicked on the shower and stepped back as a torrent of water gushed from overhead with a waft of herbal scented steam. He trailed his hand in it for a moment, let it run and wandered back into the bedroom. The closet was full of clothes. New clothes. Soft dark suits of material that felt like nothing he'd ever worn. White cotton shirts hanging on rails. Polished shoes. He pulled out a drawer, expecting to see freaking folded socks, but it was lined with black packing foam, weapons and ammunition, handguns, knives, submachine guns, holy shit, submachine guns? All neatly arranged in custom cut outs.

He closed the drawer and stepped back, stomach cold, a lump in his throat.

He hooked in to the security system by remote as he stood there. They were monitoring him, biosigns, live scan and cameras.

He went back into the bathroom, shut off the shower and walked out.

"That was eleven minutes," the woman stated, not seeming to care that he hadn't showered and changed. "You need to improve your timekeeping, Mister Hilyer."

She turned and walked down the corridor, gesturing him sharply to follow.

"I'm not staying," he called out. Not moving.

"No," she called back without turning, "no, you're not."

The next lift dropped more than one level, no display to show how far down they were going. And when the door opened onto a long marble tiled corridor, the young woman simply said, "You should know that we have a rather extensive prison level. The Bhenykhn like to experiment. You've seen your quarters here. One wrong move, one wrong word and we will swap those for a prison cell and let them have you." She turned and pierced him with a stare. "Don't keep her waiting..."

There was only one door at the far end of the corridor. No personnel in sight. No guards. No defensive weapons installations that he could see. The door opened as he approached. His mind did a flip of sensory cognition as he went through it, disconcerting as hell considering that he knew for sure he was at least fifty levels underground, stepping outside onto a paved terrace lit by lamps and candles, midnight blue sky scattered with stars, the air an ambient warmth that was reminiscent of a tropical breeze, a gentle sound of crickets, waves lapping in the distance. He'd seen simulations that felt real before but this was something else. The air was fresh, clean. No stale tang of recyclers. No indication that there was a stinking alien army camped overhead.

Eloise Drake was sitting at a small round table, a cut glass tumbler in her hand, a tall glass jug filled with ice and what looked like limes and mint leaves on a tray alongside a row of beer bottles and a selection of small ceramic dishes, olives, cheeses, peppers, fresh bread rolls. Christ, he hadn't seen fresh bread in over a year. The bottles were chilled, condensation on the surface of the glass. For an illusion it looked freaking convincing.

She turned as he stopped, two steps from the door. "It's very good to see you again, Zachary," she said in that throaty, old Earth accent of hers. She wasn't flirting with him the way he'd seen her behave around LC but she wasn't hostile. Self-assured. Confident. As if she knew her place in this war with absolute certainty and was more than content with it. She gestured. "Take a seat. I'm sure you've guessed by now... I want you to work for me."

CHAPTER TWENTY-ONE

"No..." The anger that had fuelled her to come here reignited into a fire that burned deep inside. "I refuse to believe that he chose to side with her."

"Don't be so certain of that." Koschei killed the screen dead and turned to face her. "Zachary Hilyer was always one of the smartest operatives we ever recruited at the guild. I am sure, whatever happened, he made the right decisions for the optimal outcome of this war."

"For whom?"

He ignored the vitriol in her tone. "He has it in him to do what is necessary. As loyal as he always was, Hilyer was also always clever enough to recognise when the tide had turned. He always had an inherent ability to survive, whatever the odds. How could we, of all people, condemn him for that?"

He didn't move. Didn't react. He'd just spent five weeks undercover on Temerity working for this woman's forces, pretending to be loyal to her, now she was asking him for real? Right here, alone as far as he could make out, just the two of them. Evelyn's words echoed, hollow, between his ears. He could make the kill right now. One slick motion and his knife could be embedded in her throat without him taking another step. Getting out of here alive would be something else, but even so...

Drake drank from her glass, regarding him closely the whole time. She stretched out a long leg, resting her tumbler on her knee, and said with a smile, "I don't bite."

The last time he'd seen her in person was on Earth, the Imperial palace in Beijing, as she handed LC over to the Bhenykhn. He had no doubt that she would throw him to them as well, without hesitation, if he played this wrong.

"I don't betray my own," he said softly, seeing a spark in her eyes and figuring that he'd probably just screwed up already.

"Your own...?" she said with some consideration, immaculate eyebrows rising a tad. "Now that is a curious concept." She nudged a bottle on the table, her voice harder as she said, "Join me for a drink. I trust Nikolai trained you well enough that you know never to refuse an old lady when she makes such a request."

He walked up and sat, reluctant, and reached for a

beer, expensive beer from the label, the bottle cold to the touch. He popped it open, aware that she was watching every move, and took a sip, not sure what the hell he was about to drink but it tasted real. Damn real.

She nodded with approval. "You have had a very unique reaction to the alien virus, young man. One of a kind. And believe me, I have tried my damnedest to recreate it."

He met her eyes. What the hell was he supposed to say to that? He'd seen the prisoner pens and labs at Zang's fortress after she'd taken control there.

"By 'your own'..." she said, "I take it you mean your precious Thieves' Guild, not humanity. You are hardly human anymore, are you?"

Coming from anyone else that would sting. From her...? He didn't flinch.

She smiled. "Don't worry, I know all about Evelyn's little directive against me. You want to follow her orders? You could kill me now. I'm an old woman. You wouldn't even need to use that knife you have hidden in your boot. You could break my neck before any of my people have a chance to blink."

He kept his breathing slow and steady, didn't break eye contact.

It was tempting.

She leaned forward, stretching those endless legs, and leaning her elbows on her knees. "But you're not going to, are you? Zachary, your guild is done, you must know that.

Earth is overrun. Winter is overrun. I know Evelyn is struggling." She took a sip of her drink, seeming to savour it before she spoke again. "The Bhenykhn let the little rabble-rousers in the hills run free, playing resistance fighters, because that gives them something to hunt. They let the Thieves' Guild roam the galaxy as they are because they like the chase." She ran a finger round the top of the glass. "But your numbers are dwindling. I heard what happened to Luka out at Kheris. Careless of Evelyn to be so reckless with such a valuable asset. Such a shame. I did like that boy."

"You handed him to the Bhenykhn easily enough."

There was a long pause while she stared at him before she said softly, "You were at Beijing." It wasn't a question. "I did wonder who it was that got Luka out of there."

She sat back, straight up in the chair, looking at him through lidded eyes that were much sharper than a woman her age should ever have. "So where does that leave us?" She said it with that calm little half smile on her face. "I have need of a lieutenant I can trust. Your reputation... your unique abilities... You could do well here, Zachary. You could survive this war."

It wasn't helping her case that she kept calling him Zachary. He'd punched LC in the face the first time LC had tried to call him that when they were kids.

"I'm not interested," he said, draining the bottle and setting it down.

She reached a hand to play with a gem hanging from a

gold chain at her neck, twisting it in her long fingers, the facets of the intricately cut surfaces reflecting the candlelight in flashes. "It was bold of you to walk so brazenly onto one of my warships. Did you seriously think you'd get away with it?"

He just looked at her. It didn't feel like she actually wanted an answer.

"What were you after?"

He shook his head. "Why would you think even for a second that I'd betray the guild?"

She set her glass down and filled it from the jug on the table, ice clinking. "I know for a fact that your allegiance to the Thieves' Guild hasn't always been so strong." She let that hang there in the air between them, then added, "After Redemption..."

He set his jaw. Spearhead. It had to be. That was the only way Drake could know what had happened.

"That was a long time ago."

"I also know you're not stupid," she said. "There is no way to win this war. Face it, Zachary. Or die. There is no choice here."

Hil shifted his weight, stifling the temptation to walk out. "You're a prisoner here as much as I am," he said. "You might have your own army and pet telepaths but you're as much a prisoner as I am."

She gave a delicate gesture with her head, not exactly conceding the fact. "Do you see the Bhenykhn down here?"

He almost laughed. "You have to live underground."

"Young man, this was my realm long before the Bhenykhn appeared in this galaxy." She gestured towards the drinks and the tray on the table. "Do you see us wanting for anything?"

"Freedom."

She laughed then, deep and genuine, as if he'd surprised her. "Oh my dear boy, what is freedom if not the freedom to live? And we are not just surviving, we are thriving. Right under their noses. And when the Bhenykhn tire of this galaxy and move on, who will be left alive? Think about it. We face an alien horde. We shouldn't be fighting amongst ourselves." She picked up an olive and popped it into her mouth, swallowing the delicacy before considering him again. "I've lifted the price from your head. You're safe here." There was a pause then her tone changed as if she was growing weary of the conversation. "What is it you want, Zachary? In all this, what is it you really want?"

He looked up with a start, realising he'd been staring at the olives. What did he want? That was a question and a half. He wanted LC to be okay. NG to come back. Mendhel to not be dead. The Alsatia to not be dust in space... The Bhenykhn to leave.

To talk to Martha without worrying that someone would be listening in to their every word.

He blinked. "Cold beer. That's about it, right now."

Drake smiled. She stared at him as if she was

considering what else to say, but she just said finally, "You'll find there's a fridge in your quarters. Go. I'll give you all the resources you need. Lane will take care of you. If you need anything, ask her. See what we have here, what we're doing. Help me build a new empire. One that will outlast the Bhenykhn, one that will rise from the ashes of this invasion stronger than ever before. Think about it, Zachary."

He got the distinct impression he was being dismissed and stood, waiting for a second before backing away, still half expecting guards to descend and clap him in chains. They didn't. Suit girl with the dark green eyes, presumably Lane, was waiting and walked him back to his quarters. No armed guard on the door. They hadn't even searched him.

"You have access to levels seven through twenty nine. Don't go anywhere else. If you need anything, call me. This is your first assignment." She gave him a data board, as if she was welcoming him into a Wellbeing. "Don't go anywhere near the surface. If the Bhenykhn get hold of you, you're on your own."

He took the board and backed into the room.

"And please... take a shower."

The door closed.

He stared at it for a second.

It would be locked.

Drake was their enemy, whatever she might say.

He couldn't help darting forward and hitting the panel.

The door opened.

Lane hadn't moved, standing there, looking unimpressed. "It's not locked," she said, dry, and probably wondering how the hell he'd stayed alive so long.

He took a step back and the door closed again.

This was too weird.

He threw the board onto the bed and went to run the shower, thinking, ticking over everything that had happened. They were giving him everything he wanted. He'd had to work damn hard on Temerity to get the intel they needed. Now? They were just giving it to him? He wasn't stupid or naïve enough to think it would be that easy. But for now...

There was beer in the fridge. He grabbed a bottle and peered in there for a second to see what else there was. Olives. Holy shit. And he'd thought they were living it up on Temerity.

One of the tricks the guild had taught them, right from the outset, was how to hack a board or system and leave no trace. He sprawled out on the bed, a real bed that was so wide he could spread out sideways and still not reach the edge, hair still wet from the shower and just a towel round his waist, and fired up the board, watching the intel scroll and an assignment flash for his attention.

He stared at it for a moment before accepting it.

Kheris.

He might have guessed.

Drake wanted the avocado, Elliot's mysterious anomaly that was keeping the Bhenykhn away from Kheris. Of course she did.

He threw an olive into the air and caught it in his mouth, starting to nudge the board, doing exactly what they'd expect him to do and making it obvious that he was.

If they wanted a masterclass in what the Thieves' Guild could do, he'd give them one.

He didn't make it subtle, assuming they were watching every move and assuming they'd assume he'd know, digging covert pathways that he knew they'd be able to track to keep them satisfied and busy, while running enough darker tricks he was fairly sure they wouldn't so he could get to the stuff he really wanted. He found Riley in the records, found nothing other than a solid service record in the Earth Marine Corps. Distinguished service but nothing outstanding. No sign it was fake. He didn't try hunting down Jem or Teagan. Not yet. And the intel they had on Kheris was overwhelming. Though curiously nothing about LC ten years ago.

He kept at it until his eyes started burning, checking out the entire theatre of war as Drake had it documented, troop numbers, fleet locations, state of affairs of every colony both sides of the line, Bhenykhn activity, what she had on the guild and the resistance. His chest was cold as he found the latest lists of KIA and MIA, same list they issued at the guild, and ran his eyes down it, not realising he was holding his breath until he reached the end. No one he recognised.

He breathed out slowly and reached for another beer. It was all giving him a pounding headache. It was a lot easier working undercover when no one knew you were there.

After six hours solid he fell asleep, more tired than he'd realised, more confused about finding Martha than he thought he would be and missing Skye more than ever.

He woke abruptly, no idea if it had been five minutes or five hours. He sat up. It took a second to remember where he was and what he was doing. The data board was inert. The bowl of olives empty and a neat line of empty beer bottles on the floor. He scrubbed a hand over his hair. Dry. Another second of sitting there thinking he should get up and there was a sharp rap on the door.

He checked the time through the Senson as he stood. It had been ten hours. Jesus. And they were knocking at the door? Wasn't he supposed to be a prisoner here?

He threw his own clothes back on before he opened

the door, wary, still half expecting someone to barge in and tackle him to the floor.

It was the girl in the suit. It took him a moment to remember her name.

"Report to the infirmary," she said. "Next time, respond to the alerts we send you."

She left him to find the infirmary by himself.

Strangest damned incarceration he'd ever experienced.

He was wearing black, plain black, so he didn't stand out, not amongst a mix of personnel, half of whom were wearing fatigues or uniforms that were from god knows what units, Earth and Wintran. He moved with a steady confidence in himself, checking what he could pick up from the systems he could hear, keeping to the edges of the throughways but not shrinking back from anyone, chin up but not obvious or obnoxious. Merging with the crowds. Like he belonged here.

Belonged here? Did he?

Even thinking that sent a lump into his throat.

He was on a tab.

That was all.

Whatever Eloise Drake asked him to do, he was going to take it all back to the guild. Back to Evelyn... Elliott. Even Sebastian.

They were the good guys.

He was here on a tab.

Drake wanted him to find whatever it was on Kheris that was repelling the Bhenykhn. He could do that.

And he'd take it straight back to Evelyn.

The infirmary was the last place he wanted to go. He accessed the schematics for the facility and found a gym, found five gyms, but one was on his level so he headed there. No one stopped him. And no one questioned him when he walked in and nabbed a treadmill.

He ran ten miles, fast, not aware anyone was watching until he stopped it and turned. There wasn't exactly a crowd but the few people in there were staring his way.

It was hardly the first time that had happened.

There was a mat in the far corner. Unoccupied so he walked over and started a routine, feeling pissed off and self-destructive enough to recall the shaolin moves they'd learned at the facility they were taken to after Redemption. It came back slowly, every move perfect, every twist and leap. He pulled a sequence of flips and tumbles, landed and straightened to see Imperial Marine Corps Sergeant Riley standing there, watching, twin bo staffs in her hands.

It was Martha. Damn sure, without doubt, it was Martha.

Only one other person in the entire galaxy had ever made that little spot deep inside go warm and insanely fuzzy the way she did.

She stepped forward and threw one to him. "You want to give them a real show?"

He spun the staff and balanced his weight, heart thumping faster than it should have been. They'd sparred together on the Alsatia, plenty of times. She used to kick his ass.

She circled, smiling, came at him, twirling the staff, footsteps light, and before he knew it they'd fallen into a rhythm, millimetre perfect, one synchronised drill after another. Strike, block, spin, tumble. Faster and faster, the sharp crack of the bo staffs engaging the only sound in there.

He broke free and stared at her, circling, controlling his breathing and spinning up the staff as she came at him again, lightning speed, matching every move he made. Perfectly.

Just like old times.

She twisted her staff into his and pulled him close. Nose to nose. And breathed, "Worked out who I am yet?"

CHAPTER TWENTY-TWO

IT WAS MORE than disturbing to think of Hilyer, the child she had followed for such a brief instance of her time, but for so long in human terms, being captive under the yoke of one such as Drake. "She tasked him with finding the anomaly on Kheris? I take it you have had no luck discovering what it is on that colony that so repels the Bhenykhn."

It was hard to keep the disdain from her voice. The Bhenykhn had been in this galaxy for over a decade in Earth years... the invasion was a full year ago. And in all that time, none of the brilliant minds Koschei claimed to have gathered had figured out what it was on that one planet that not only kept the Bhenykhn horde away, they seemed unable to see it.

He gave her a glare.

It was almost satisfying to have needled him so.

She pushed. "This could be the one deciding factor in the whole war against them, and you have nothing?"

He knew who she was. He stared. Hypnotised. Someone yelled her name, "Riley," and he glanced aside, enough distraction that she had her staff hooked around his ankle and he was flat on his back before he knew it.

There was laughter, harsh, jeering laughter and on any other day he would have jumped up and taken on every jerk in there. But Martha was standing over him, smiling in that way she had when everything was alright between them, the crooked smile he couldn't resist, and he just lay there, staring at her like an idiot.

Another voice shouted, amiable, "Get that fuckwit off the floor and get him a beer. Jesus, I've never seen anything like that. Glad I never ran into the fucking Thieves' Guild in a dark alley."

There were other mutterings, along the same lines, nothing hostile, nothing worse than they used to get in the mess on the Alsatia.

Martha reached down, extending her hand, something in her eyes that made him feel that warm spot inside stir for the first time in as long as he could remember.

He clasped her hand and let her pull him upright, keeping hold of her hand like even more of an idiot, his hand hot and sweaty, but not wanting to let go.

"Hey, Riley," someone yelled again. "The Major wants to see you."

She turned, not making any effort to make him let go of her hand. "Tell her I'll be right there. I just need to get cleaned up."

Whoever it was disappeared.

Martha tugged his hand. "C'mon, sunshine. Let's go get a beer."

She didn't take him to the mess hall, she took him to her quarters, not quite as flash as his but still a private suite of rooms.

He didn't resist as she led him to the bedroom and only faltered as she took hold of his shirt and started to lift it. He nudged her hand away and tugged it back down.

"Don't tell me you're shy," she breathed into his ear.

He wasn't. Christ, he wasn't. But he wasn't ready for this...

She grabbed his arms, kissing him as she pushed him down onto the bed.

He couldn't help the grin as she leaned on him, reaching for the waistband of his pants, shirt forgotten.

It was hard not to laugh. Nothing else existed. The whole galaxy was a million miles away.

He opened his mouth to talk but she pushed a finger against his lips. She kissed him again, hard, and whispered, "Not here. God, I've missed you."

"I've been looking for you," he muttered stupidly.

She grinned. "I know."

It was only once they were in the shower with the water on full blast that she stood back and really looked at him, with a cocky, "Helluva war we're in."

He hadn't seen her since the Earth forces had descended on Zang's facility, a year ago, before Erica, before the invasion, back when he'd found out that she wasn't guild.

He glanced up and round, looking for surveillance. He couldn't see any in any of the systems he was tapped in to. If they were watching her quarters, they respected her privacy.

"They can't hear us in here and I put the one feed they do have on a loop," she said with a smile. "You guys weren't the only ones that could pull those tricks." She gave him a slight push, her hand soapy on his chest. "Glad you made it."

He stepped in and gave her a kiss, hot water cascading between them.

She pulled back. "I'm serious. When I heard about the Alsatia..."

He shrugged, scrubbing his hand over his head and washing the soap into his hair. "Shit happens." That wasn't the worst of it, as bad as that had been. Being on Earth during the first wave of the invasion... Seeing LC and NG in captivity in Beijing... Being pushed into that damned Bhenykhn pod...

She rubbed her hand across the scar on his chest, sending shivers running down his spine, tracing others, the alien brand burned into his skin, lingering on the bite marks gouged into his shoulder and rubbing her thumb along the slick black scar tissue. He couldn't help tensing. He hadn't let anyone see what had happened to him, not this close, not counting Anya when he'd had no choice. And he'd let no one get close enough to touch.

"This is what you're hiding," she murmured. "You idiot." She didn't exactly laugh but she said it fondly, he'd swear she said it fondly. She peered closer. "What is it?"

She had a way of saying that and drawing him in to her, through the water and steam, that let the tension drain away. For the first time in as long as he could remember.

"I don't know. Not freaking human."

She did laugh then, shoving him gently. "My god, Zach Hilyer, not human, who would've thought?"

He couldn't help smiling like an idiot. They'd been good together. He couldn't remember why they'd been so shit to each other so much.

Martha grabbed his hand, lacing his fingers with hers. "Drake's making it clear to everyone that she's recruited you," she said. "What is she having you do for her?"

"Kheris." He lowered his voice and moved close,

murmuring into her ear. "What is Itomara having you do for him?"

He felt her laugh again.

"I don't want to know how you figured that out and you don't want to know what I'm doing."

"I don't want to lose you again."

She didn't reply, twisting so that she had her back to him, taking both of his hands and wrapping them around herself, backing into him.

He hugged her tight.

She turned his wrist and rubbed her fingers over the black ink, leaned her head back, water splashing, and whispered in his ear, "You never did lose me." She turned around, grinning, and pushed him against the shower wall, her eyes bright, boring into his. "Wanna show me what else you can do now you're superhuman?"

He made it back to his quarters without being apprehended by anyone else, pushed his way in and grabbed a beer, starting to head to his own bathroom but stopping, just standing, bottle in his hand, half way to his mouth, struggling to process what the hell he was feeling. Sore was one thing. Pulled muscle in his back. She hadn't been gentle. After all the time they'd been apart, she hadn't wasted any time, and he wasn't about to. She'd pushed him away, finally, stared him in the eye and smiled, that enigmatic way she always had, and then told him to get the fuck out. Like she always had.

At least now he knew who she'd been working for. NG had always reckoned the JU. What he'd make of the intel that she'd been working for Itomara the whole time, Hil had no idea. He took a mouthful of expensive, cold beer. He needed to figure out how he was going to get out of here before he worried what anyone at the guild was going to think. And not just get out, but take Martha with him. Maybe stealing that nippy little gulfstream wasn't such a bad idea...

He spent five days working there, long, intense days of interrogating every inch of the system until his head was pounding and he had to run off the pain in the gym. No one else had challenged him to a fight, not when he had Martha at his side every minute of down time. Being with her was eerily like their first few months together on the Alsatia. She'd turned up out of nowhere, straight from a mission, cornered him in the mess and he hadn't known what had hit him. Kind of like now.

He stared at the screen. Pulled back and double checked, reading again the report that had stopped him in his tracks. It was real. The device he'd started to think he'd imagined on Temerity. He'd pulled some ridiculous shit to get that deep, bypassing traps, inserting loops, replicating IDs and cracking layer upon layer of encryption, hiding what he was doing with a complex side buzz of activity within the domains Drake had given him access to. He read it again, adrenaline rush pulsing through his chest. It was real. The device rumoured to be a weapon against the Seven was a small metallic cube. Hil nudged through the data with a growing unease settling like a weight in his stomach. Drake had people scouring the galaxy looking for it. It wasn't just real... he knew what it was. Shit.

He backtracked, meticulously, covered every trace he'd been anywhere near any of it, and sat back.

Drake summoned him five minutes later. He stood in front of her, never more relieved that no one could read his mind.

"Impressive work," she said, sitting at an oak desk in her office this time, no drinks, no offer to sit.

It wasn't that impressive, as much as he'd found the intel on the device again, he hadn't been able to find any trace of the rogue AI activity he'd found on Temerity. And he'd tried, he'd worked hard to track it down, refusing to think he could have got it wrong, seen something in it that wasn't there. Whatever they were doing, they weren't doing it from here.

"I see your reputation is well deserved." She paused, looking him up and down, appraising.

He was wearing the smart clothes from his quarters. Martha had thrown his stuff in a laundry chute and he hadn't seen it again. He still had his own boots, damned if he was going to wear stiff polished shoes, but he was wearing soft black trousers, crisp white shirt. Perfect fit. He hadn't gone so far as to don a suit jacket. That just made him look like a thug. So it was shirt only, with the sleeves neatly buttoned at the wrist, as tempting as it was to roll them up.

Drake looked satisfied, approving. "You uncovered intelligence on the cube."

He kept his expression impassive.

"I must say, that was much faster than I'd expected. Impressive. It's not what you think."

"What do I think?"

"That I'm your enemy, my dear. I've given you access to my whole operation." She spread her hands. "I'm not hiding anything from you. I've been looking for the cube for a long time, far longer than this war has been waging. But understand this, the cube is not a weapon. I'm aware some of the rumours claim it to be a kill switch. It's not. What would be the sense in that? The cube is the key to the creation of the Seven. They are key to winning this war. I know you understand that. Imagine our advantage if we could make more..."

She was convincing, hypnotically convincing, but it wasn't hard to remind himself there was no way she was telling him anything but bullshit. Evelyn popped back into his head with a pang of guilt that it hadn't even crossed his mind in five days. He was biding his time, that was all.

"Don't concern yourself with the cube, Zachary," she said. "I have people looking. They'll find it. I have a mission for you."

He watched without a word as she reached forward and stroked her elegant hand across the desk's surface. It lit up with star charts, projected into the space above the wooden surface.

"I want you to go to Kheris."

She manipulated the data and the schematic spun, pretty much the same three dimensional depiction of the galaxy that Elliott had shown them before the second phase of the invasion, only now it was even more densely populated with red.

He saw the patterns of the intel he'd analysed, twisting in amongst the data.

She homed in on Kheris.

"As I'm sure you have ascertained, we are no closer to discovering what it is on this darling little colony that repels the Bhenykhn."

And telepaths. But he didn't say that. The reports she had on what had happened to LC hadn't mentioned the cause of the incident. Just the outcome.

"I know the guild is looking," she said.

The schematic circled the planet, focusing in on the original main city and mining operations, now tiny, nestled at the edge of the desert in one direction and the sprawl of new human occupation in the other. The scale of new build was phenomenal, deep spacers landed, stranded, amongst pop up modular living accommodation, tent ghettos, vast sprawling hydroponics greenhouse operations and new factory facilities. It was like watching an ant colony thrive.

"From what I can see..." She raised her eyes to regard him. "...the Thieves' Guild has no idea what is there. They've lost three search teams in the past few weeks alone looking for it."

She waited as if she was wanting him to confirm it.

He kept quiet. She didn't push him to say it. And the guild didn't know what it was. She was right. He was hardly hiding anything from her.

She nudged the display to zone in on a spot in the desert, what looked like the remains of a crater, twisted metal sticking out of the red sand. What looked like a military cordon around it, tents, vehicles, temporary structures, guard posts.

"But I do know..." She paused, still gauging his reaction. "...that Evelyn now considers the ship that crashed there ten years ago to have been a Bhenykhn vessel."

LC had stated it outright. Before they went to Hanover.

"Source of the dear Bhenykhn specimen Angmar was so precious about."

He kept his expression neutral. He knew he was right

to have been paranoid about demanding a blackout, but, shit, to hear that plain and blunt, that Drake knew something that had been said in private on board the Man's ship, not so long ago.

But then again he had no idea what Evelyn might have done with that information after they'd left. He'd hardly had a chance to check. She could have broadcast it out to the whole galaxy for all he knew.

Drake smiled, the crease of her lips sly. "I have my means, young man. As I know you have yours..." She dropped the smile. "The Bhenykhn are enjoying the challenge of the hunt your guild is providing. They are enjoying it immensely but they are incensed by the idea that there is a place they cannot go, an entity or weapon that works against them that they cannot face in open battle."

The schematic switched to show deep space, not a jump point he recognised, teeming with warships and destroyers, capital ships being fitted out in space-borne dockyards.

His stomach turned.

Drake stroked her finger over the desk, casual, nudging and sending the display from one ship to the next, faster and faster. "The Bhenykhn are insisting I build them a fleet," she said. "A human fleet to attack Kheris. They plan to annihilate it."

Hil narrowed his eyes, chest cold.

"As you can see, I am gathering a formidable force."

Battleplans started scrolling beside the star chart. He hadn't seen any of this in the systems he'd accessed. He was losing his touch.

The muscle in his jaw started ticking.

Drake pulled the display back to show the full firepower of her fleet. "From everything I have gathered about you, Zachary," she said, piercing him again with her stare, "you thrive on a challenge and hate to lose. You want to survive this war and I assume you want your loved ones to survive it too. Then I need to know you're with me. There is no playing sides."

He straightened, drawing up his chest, pushing back his shoulders, standing almost to attention.

He'd misjudged the game Drake was playing.

Totally freaking misjudged it.

"Think about it, Zachary. From what I have heard, Luka is dead. Nikolai is as good as dead to you, missing as he is. What is Evelyn doing for you but getting more and more of you killed...?"

It felt like his insides were withering into a twisted knot. LC wasn't dead. He refused to believe LC could be dead, whatever this woman said.

She said again, "I need to know that you are with me, Zachary."

What choice did he have but to nod?

"Good. Go to Kheris, find this anomaly and bring it to me. Do you understand?"

He bit back the automatic, 'Yes, ma'am', that sprang

to the tip of his tongue, irritation stirring that deep down it seemed he was still such a freaking institutionalised little soldier, and said instead, an edge of belligerence creeping in, "No one's found it in ten years. What makes you think I will?"

She raised her hand in warning. "You will. You are the best Thieves' Guild operative in action right now. And you will find it before the Bhenykhn lose patience with my delaying tactics and order me to attack. I believe I can delay a maximum of six weeks, maybe two months at most, before I can't stall them any longer and have no choice but to launch my attack on that colony. So trust me, you are against the clock. I will not hesitate to wipe out that entire colony if you do not get back here in time."

He forced himself to breathe, slow and steady, staring straight ahead, through her, no way was he going to betray the guild.

Her eyes were ice cold, calculating. "I'm older than you can possibly imagine and I know exactly what I'm doing." She refocused the display back to Kheris. "Whatever it is on Kheris, I believe it can be weaponised. If you take it to Evelyn, she will use it to fight the Bhenykhn. If you bring it to me, I will use it to defeat the Bhenykhn."

CHAPTER TWENTY-THREE

Luka dead? She raised her eyes slowly, dismayed, not convinced he hadn't said that to stop her in her tracks as it did. "Luka...?"

These creatures lived such short lives, she knew she should never get so attached but it was hard when they shone so bright, even in the briefest of instances when their paths crossed.

Koschei met her eyes with a look that was unfathomable. He pushed away from the dark screen of the console and brushed past her. His gaze was piercing as he passed her. "You want to know about Kheris? One of the most devastating oversights we have made in this galaxy... We could have stopped this war before it began if we had realised what it was that had crashed there ten years ago. You want to chide me over mistakes and mishaps? You were *here. Right here when it happened. How did you miss it? How did we all miss it?"*

Drake wiped her hand across the table and set it back to plain wood, the light show vanishing. Her tone was disparaging as she stood and added a throwaway, "Come with me."

Lane was waiting outside, dropping into step alongside him as he followed Drake. They went down, god knows how deep, and stepped out into a medical facility, white walls, sterile air, personnel wearing white lab coats, some with breathing apparatus and haz suits.

He hesitated as he left the lift, bracing himself to fight them, but Lane placed her hand on his back and pushed, firm but not hostile.

"Don't worry," she said under her breath, "we're not here for you. We're not going to liquidise your brain."

Damn, that was LC's joke. How much had these people been listening in to them?

She nudged him into walking. "We haven't even taken any blood samples from you, if you've failed to notice."

He hadn't. He'd just been waiting for it.

"Ms Drake has all she needs from you. You and Mister Anderton. Don't fight us, Hilyer. I do have a nice little secure holding facility all ready and waiting for you, your name on the door and everything... We're running a sweepstake."

He glanced at her. Not sure if she was joking.

Her expression was serene, controlled, as if she hadn't said a word.

She nudged him again.

Drake stopped at a door and looked back at them, a gleam in her eye that suggested she'd heard that little exchange. "I want you to watch something, Zachary. I want your take on this."

She pushed open the door and entered what looked like an interview room. As they walked in, the far wall shimmered and cleared, becoming an observation window. He followed Drake up to it, unease churning in his stomach, his chest cold. He'd watched how they'd treated LC from an observation room like this. He wasn't sure he wanted to see what was coming.

As he approached the window, a single spotlight flashed on, illuminating a small cell below, a figure sitting at a table, the only occupant. He was dressed in Earth military fatigues. Young. Corporal by the tags on his arm.

Another figure entered the cell, set a glass of water down and sat opposite.

It was a helluva lot more civilised than they'd been with LC. But then there'd been Bhenykhn in attendance and shamans watching their every move. And it had been LC. Everyone in the galaxy knew what LC was capable of now.

The newcomer settled in, typical psych, non-threatening, sweet as pie until they turned on you.

"How are you feeling?" she said, her voice echoing slightly through the feed. "Ready for the debrief?" Standard interrogation technique. Make the prisoner feel comfortable. Like they can trust you.

Hil stared. He'd fallen for that before.

The soldier sat up straighter.

"Name, rank, unit. Let's start there. For the record."

The guy looked wary. Not surprising. He was damn right to be.

"It's alright," Drake's interrogator said, encouraging. "Let me start. This is debrief 907/1-1/K. Code AlphaTenDesertZulu."

This wasn't a debrief. They were bullshitting the poor bastard.

Hil watched, uncomfortable as hell, as the guy reached for the water and took a sip, glancing upwards as if he knew they were there.

"Go ahead," the interrogator nudged.

"Taylorson." His voice was quiet. "Corporal. JU."

JU.

Hil leaned on the handrail. Freaking JU. It was suddenly easier to feel less uncomfortable.

"Good," the interrogator said. "Now tell me what happened on Kheris."

The guy stiffened. "I already..."

"We know that you didn't include everything in your

official report, Corporal Taylorson. We want to know what really happened in there."

"We were sent into an alien ship. I lost half my team. What else do you want me to say?"

Hil stared. So this was why Drake wanted him here. He didn't catch what the interrogator said next. He'd heard this story from LC, not all of it, but enough, while they were trapped in the basement on Hanover. And he knew the alien ship had been destroyed after UM had pulled out, he'd seen the reports the guild had on it. That all happened ten years ago. This guy didn't look old enough to have been military ten years ago. LC had been, what, thirteen?

There was a long pause, the guy shifting uneasily in his seat.

The psych didn't push him.

"We flew in low over the colony," the corporal said finally. "It wasn't a combat drop so the blast shutters were up and we could see the flames and the smoke as we approached the city..."

Somehow it was worse to hear it in a cold military debriefing, however fake the setting. To think that they'd been there in the middle of it... It was hard not to flash back to the shit state LC had been in when Mendhel had picked him up, a scrawny little kid limping on a badly healed knee, a tang of smoke and explosives around him when he'd walked onto the drop ship, with a gunshot wound in his hand and a look in his eyes that was haunting. Knowing now what had happened, it was no wonder LC had always refused to talk about it. Hil stood there staring, trying not to fall back to all that. Freshly rescued from Wildlands, he'd hardly been in a stable enough place himself to care much about any other wounded stray Mendhel had diverted their ship to go collect.

He rubbed the inside of his wrist. Had to drag himself back to that cold observation room, struggling to concentrate as the guy spoke.

Except it didn't ring true. He leaned forward, unease building, nausea swirling, not just from the intensity of the tidal wave of suppressed memories. What this JU corporal was saying didn't add up. It was a Bhenykhn ship that had crashed, they all knew that. It had attacked the emergency response teams, wiped them out, except for one street kid who'd snuck inside the perimeter, Taylorson said. That lined up with what LC had told them. They'd all assumed it was where UM had captured their alien ten years ago. LC had described their comms being jammed. That was Bhenykhn technology.

But the way this guy described the bulkheads, smooth and clear... wires, cables... smooth black benches? Hil narrowed his eyes. Damn sure that was nothing like any Bhenykhn ship he'd ever been on. And he'd been on enough to know.

He glanced at Lane. She was standing with a data board in her hands, listening, calm as ever. Nothing awry.

Bhenykhn ships had bulkheads that pulsed, spongy, bioluminescent, soft to the touch, veins that twisted and throbbed, not neat cables and wires. A flash of burning heat scorched across his chest, stark contrast to the chill deep inside, mental boxes he'd thought bound in iron springing open with an intensity that took his breath away. He gripped the cool handrail and breathed through it. He'd never talked about Erica, to anyone, not even LC. It threatened to surface, dark and consuming, just thinking about that ship, about the aliens moving past him as he tried to not exist, pressed into the shadows, that pulsing biomatter soft and warm against his back, nowhere near sure that they wouldn't sense him there in their midst and turn on him at any second. He wasn't freaking empathic like the others, far from it, but he could still feel his skin crawl as they came near... feel the panic in them as they realised the battle outside was turning, the intense horror that their commander had been outmatched by a mere human, feel the numb realisation that he'd screwed up and had no chance of getting out in time as the alien bioengines rumbled into life...

He blinked.

"...a huge round tube," the corporal was saying.

Hil glanced around. No one was looking at him, everyone in there transfixed by their guest... prisoner? He breathed, forced his shoulders to relax. There were no Bhenykhn here. Not down here. Safe for the moment. Safe as anyone could be in this war.

He let his fingers stretch out, letting the tension ease, and looked back down into the cell.

"...looked like a containment facility," the corporal said. "Or at least it had been."

Hil's stomach clenched, temperature flaring, and he thought he was going to lose it. He could see what was coming.

The corporal glanced up, right into the observation window. "...ripped apart, claw marks scratched deep, thick chains lying piled on the floor, whatever had been held in there gone." The guy looked back at the interrogator, defiant, as if he expected her to refute his account. "It reeked of blood, a dank, leafmold stench..."

Hil felt his heart rate speed up a notch.

The ship that crashed on Kheris ten years ago wasn't Bhenykhn.

Not Bhenykhn.

The idea rattled around inside his head like the sharp retort of gunfire.

Not Bhenykhn.

The freaking Bhenykhn warrior UM had taken from there had been a prisoner already, onboard... onboard what?

He forced himself to stay still, not giving away any reaction, watching from the corner of his eye as Drake and Lane listened to the guy and his story from ten years ago. How the hell had this guy been on Kheris ten years ago, in active service, when he looked barely twenty now?

"There was something alive down there..." the corporal said, reaching a shaky hand to take the glass of water. "You wanted to know what I didn't include in my report?"

Hil looked at Drake as it was said. She was just listening, face set.

It was one helluva briefing. And to surface now? Where the hell had this guy been for ten years? And to say now, after ten years, that there'd been something else on that crashed ship, something left behind after UM had withdrawn, taking the captured Bhenykhn with them, something that caused equipment malfunctions, pain, intense fear... and only Taylorson out of all of them had experienced it so intensely? The way Kheris was now to the telepaths? And the Bhenykhn?

He had to force himself to concentrate enough to hear the rest. From the sound of everything this guy was saying, it went to shit fast after that, hideous to listen to as Taylorson described how his team had to race to get clear, worse when that little box in his own mind, the one buried deep inside and labelled 'Bhenykhn ship on Erica', threatened to throw out its tightly packed contents and punch him in the face.

Erica... while the others were fighting, hand to hand with the aliens out on the moorland in the torrential rain...

He'd been caught. That was what he hadn't ever admitted to anyone, what he hadn't included in his report. He'd inched his way in to what he reckoned was some kind of energy facility or power storage area, hundreds of the pod creatures swaying as if they were underwater, and he'd set the explosives... when something had changed and the entire ship had erupted around him, alien warriors mobilising, crew arguing, grunting and turning on each other, shoving and gesturing wildly. One of them had seen him, caught a glimpse as he failed to move fast enough, and they'd all turned on him, like being trapped in a swarm of fire ants...

He blinked. His hands were white, gripping the handrail, head pounding.

Taylorson was still talking. "Dixon was there, swearing at me to move, shouting, trying to drag me up."

Hil raised his eyes. He hadn't had anyone with him to help him get out of the Bhenykhn ship on Erica...

"They told me the blast took out the entire site, the crashed ship, the remains of the facility," the corporal was saying, voice rasping as if he was pretty much done. "Kobe and Blue were still down there with one of Narita's guys when it blew." He reached for the water glass, empty, and toyed with it, glancing up at the window. "I know those gunships that picked us up weren't JU. Am I back with the unit now? Because no one will tell me anything. I haven't seen Dixon since we were picked up a week ago. And no one's even told me what the hell that ship was..."

A week ago? It had been ten freaking years.

Ten years since the Bhenykhn turned up, one year since Erica.

Hil watched, heart thumping, as Taylorson sat back, raising his eyes to the window as if defying them to question him further.

"So Corporal Taylorson is an empath." Drake was staring down into the cell.

"Yes, ma'am," Lane said. "He scores exceptionally high on the gradient."

No shit.

"Put him back into cold storage," Drake said.

That explained it. Jesus.

The woman was relentless.

"I'll keep Corporal Taylorson for later," she said. She turned to Lane. "Right now I want UM. Find me someone that was down there when the alien was still there."

"Yes, ma'am."

"And I want the child that survived."

LC. She didn't know it was LC.

"It was just a street kid," Lane said. "According to the Imperial records we salvaged, he was taken into the garrison but..." She hesitated. "...considering what happened, chances that the kid made it out of there alive are negligible."

That was LC through and through.

Christ, it was weird hearing them talk about him like that.

"If he did, find him," Drake said. "What happened on Kheris ten years ago is now key to the outcome of this war. I want to know what happened. I want to know how that child survived. I want to know why that ship crashed in the first place. If the Bhenykhn have a weakness, it's right there on Kheris."

Hil straightened as Drake turned to him.

"And trust me," she said, "if you want to survive this war, you want me to be the one to find it – not the damned Thieves' Guild."

She wasn't happy. He could see the signs now he'd been close to her a few times. A tightness around her mouth, skin thin like aged parchment, spine rigid. She looked old, as old as she really was. As if a hint of the glamour faltered when she was angry. She was probably pissed that she'd been working on the wrong assumption. Same as everyone else.

She seemed to compose herself. "There is a creature or device on Kheris that repels the Bhenykhn. Take a squad to Kheris and find it before anyone else does."

He squared up to her, not about to back down.

"How?" he said, pissed as well, that she was using him, still pissed at what she'd said about LC. "You think I can just waltz in there with a squad of your people?"

She laughed. "You think I can't send people exactly where I want, whenever I want? Security is not what it used to be. And Zachary, I get what I want. I always do. Every organisation everywhere is riddled with my people. I understand it's Pen Halligan running the show down there now. Go. Masquerade as Thieves' Guild." She peered at him. "You are high ranking Thieves' Guild, my dear. High ranking in the very resistance itself. On your say so, you will be able to take a squad in there with you, under the banner of your precious guild, and no one will stop you. Pen Halligan isn't going to turn you away." Her eyes flared, sparkling. "You'll be able to fly right in."

CHAPTER TWENTY-FOUR

"IT WAS OUR PEOPLE..." Her voice was a mere whisper as she stared at the images. "How did we not know?"

The private chamber was dark, only one screen lit up with the damning evidence.

To give him credit, he gave her space to process the revelation.

"How long have you known?"

"I know now," he murmured. "We know now. That is all that matters."

"What does this change?"

"It does not change a thing. We failed to see it ten years ago. Now...? The Bhenykhn are here. The few of our race that came here with us have fled. What such a crew was doing ten Earth years ago entering this galaxy with a captive Bhenykhn warrior on their vessel... I cannot *comprehend why any of us would have done such a thing. Can you?"*

His stomach turned. Her words sounded so wrong. He was standing there, wearing their expensive corporate clothing, at her beck and call, and the instant she said that – 'masquerade as Thieves' Guild' – it hit deep down that he was not undercover, playing some game of espionage... this was real.

He didn't react even though he felt hollow.

Drake took the board from Lane and caught his eye with a deliberate stare. "Be aware, the price on your head might be null and void in here, as my people well know, but out there... it still stands. It has to or no one will trust you. I trust you can take care of yourself. Just bring me back something I can use, whatever the hell it is. You have six weeks. I suggest you get back here well before that."

She walked out, elegant, ageless again. Not a care in the galaxy that she was screwing with people's lives. Unnerving as hell. It made him feel trapped. That was never going to end well.

Lane gave him a look, unimpressed. "You'll be taking Taylorson and Dixon with you."

"What?" He couldn't think straight but, Jesus. "You have this Dixon guy as well?"

Lane looked at him without changing her expression.

"Jesus. No. You want me to take them out to Kheris? Now? They think it's been a week. Or did you not catch that detail? They have no idea what the Bhenykhn are, no idea ten years have gone by, no idea that Earth has been invaded..."

She interrupted. "They'll be briefed."

He met her glare with one of his own. "That's a bad idea."

"They're JU. Do you know what it takes to be recruited by the JU?"

He knew fine well what kind of bastard the JU recruited.

Lane wasn't done. "They know that ship. They'll be your best chance to find it, whatever 'it' is."

He bit his tongue to stop himself arguing. Fine. He'd take whoever. He wanted Martha as well but stopped himself from saying it. He knew that Lane knew they'd hooked up together which meant Drake did too. Everyone on the whole base did. Martha had laughed it off, telling people they'd known each other years ago, and that seemed to have deflected any untoward interest. The last thing he wanted was Drake looking at Martha and thinking there was leverage there she could use against him.

He nodded.

"Good. Your team will be ready in forty eight hours. I suggest you make best use of that time."

. . .

Desert combat kit was waiting in his quarters when he got there. High spec, damned high spec, frontline kit. Light infantry body armour, webbing, pouches with grenades, holsters with sidearms, helmet, comms gear, rifle. No rank, name tag or insignia. That was fine. He could play soldier if that's what Drake wanted.

He spent the time raking through Drake's systems and taking every scrap of intel he could sear into the Senson and commit to memory, avoiding Martha and steadfastly pushing away the thought that he wouldn't be coming back here and might never see her again.

He didn't want to think about anything.

And now he had a job to do.

So that made it simple.

He showered and changed, checked that Mendhel's knife was still in his boot, slipped two beers and a jar of olives into his pack, and headed out.

The security team were packing kit into a drop ship. Lane was with them, in light Wintran combat gear, colonel's tags on her jacket, standing off to one side with Taylorson and Dixon who were looking like they'd just dropped in from another dimension, sucking it up but pale. Shit, it was bad enough waking up in medical and being told you'd lost a week or three. But ten years? He couldn't begin to imagine where their heads were at.

The rest of the team were in a mix of powered armour and light infantry incursion gear, lugging crates of munitions and supplies off loaders. One of the marines in armour turned around. He blew out a breath he hadn't realised he was holding, relieved. He should have known she'd find a way to wangle the assignment.

She headed toward him, throwing him a grin. "Hey sunshine, I always knew you looked good in uniform."

Kheris was one of those places he'd heard about but never been to, except that one time with Mendhel when he'd been told to sit tight in the back of a ship and didn't get to set foot on the place.

He kept to himself as they disembarked, sitting separate from the others, leaning back, putting his feet up on the seat opposite, and messing about with his rifle, checking the mechanism, half field stripping and reassembling it in his lap. Anything to keep himself from thinking. He was guild. Drake was the enemy. That was undeniable, given everything. Given absolutely everything, she was the enemy. But that one line she'd fed him... that she'd defeat the Bhenykhn...

It was a relief when they made jump and had to contend with the full might of the resistance security forces patrolling the Kheris close orbit airspace, surrounded in minutes by fighters, a warship moving in fast to intercept. Lane gestured him to go take the comm and he sat in the co-pilot's seat, very aware everyone was watching, and talked his way through security procedures, classified guild security procedures, a weight like a stone in his chest, and a pounding in his head as he lied and bullshitted a way in for a ship full of Drake's forces.

Pen was going to freaking lynch him.

They landed the drop ship in the central square of a barracks complex, out in the desert, high security, gun emplacements all round, and walked out into a wave of heat and a gravity so high it made his muscles ache within seconds, red dust everywhere. There was a bitter tang to the warm air that tasted like chemicals, catching at the back of his throat as he squinted in sunshine that was painfully bright. No wonder LC had always been so screwed up.

There was a welcoming committee waiting for them. Pen, Yani, a couple of other guys he recognised and a few he didn't. All armed. All in dark fatigues, all wearing dark glasses.

A gunship buzzed overhead, close, the deep thrum and heat of its engines washing over them.

Hil blinked dust out of his eyes. He had no idea what reception he was going to get, what Pen knew, what the big man might have picked up from the encrypted message he'd sent the minute they hit orbit.

He heard Taylorson mutter, "Holy shit, that's Colonel Halligan."

Dixon stepped up and said under his breath, "Damn, he's looking old."

Hil glanced at the guy. He hadn't been at Dixon's debrief but he'd read the transcript. Same as Taylorson. Same detail. Pretty much. It was weird that they recognised Pen as their Colonel. That had been years ago. He'd seen pictures.

Dixon shrugged. "What? He looks fucking old."

Lane was watching them, Martha standing to one side.

"Give me a minute," Hil said. "I'll handle this." And he walked forward, kit bag slung casually over one shoulder, rifle balanced in his other hand, ice cold inside despite the blazing heat shimmering off every surface. He'd brought the enemy right into the heart of the resistance.

Pen's expression was hidden behind the dark glasses. No way in hell to see what he was thinking. The big man just stared as if he'd needed visual confirmation it was really him, and said simply, "No Hailstones?"

"Not this time," Hil murmured. Missing Iona. Disturbed that Pen was switched on enough to call him on the fact he didn't have her with him. On such a vital mission?

But Pen nodded. "Come with me. Yani, get the others inside and briefed."

Yani looked at Hil with a slight nod and a murmured, "Don't worry, I'll take care of them."

He got simultaneous queries from Lane and Martha,

accepted both on a wide link and sent a quick, "It's fine. Go with Yani. I need to see Pen. It won't take long."

Lane nodded, and Martha started shouting out commands, hustling everyone to get the hell inside.

He turned back to Pen. "We need Taylorson and Dixon too."

Pen must have issued orders because his guys were suddenly surrounding them, separating out the two JU guys and herding them out to a different drop ship.

Martha hesitated as she saw them stop him, one of them scanning him with a wand before steering him away.

"It's fine," he sent to her. "C'mon, this is Pen. I'll be fine. He doesn't suspect a thing. And I can hardly argue, can I? I'm supposed to be here on Evelyn's orders. We're guild, right?"

She didn't looked convinced but she turned and followed Lane and the others inside.

Pen didn't say another word until they were inside the drop ship and readying to go. Then he turned, took off the glasses and pierced him with a stare. "Ye gods, Hil, what the hell are you into now?"

They flew low over the colony, shutters down so he couldn't see where they going. He tried talking to Pen but the big man indicated he should shut up so he did, tapping into their system instead and working out the route they were taking. They were headed to an oasis. Not a part of Kheris LC had ever mentioned.

Pen stopped him once they landed, and grabbed the light infantry helmet he was carrying under his arm, thrusting it back at him with a quiet, "Wear it, for Christ's sake. And the goggles too. If word gets around that you're here, you won't last a day."

Hil didn't argue, secured the chinstrap and pulled down the goggles. He could see why people wore them as he stepped out into sunshine that was instantly more pleasant, less searing on the eyeballs.

Pen's guys moved out around them, still on alert, bodyguarding even here in what was evidently Pen's territory.

Pen nudged him to move. "Now you can talk. This whole complex is shielded. You want to start with those two?" He gave a vague gesture towards Taylorson and Dixon who looked like they'd just stepped straight out on a mission, no outward signs that they'd been on ice for ten years.

"Is Elenor here?"

"Why?"

"Get her to check them out but keep it quiet. Don't let anyone else near them."

"Who are they?"

Hil switched to the Senson. "JU." He was staring straight ahead but scoping out the complex they were entering, glad to be going into the shade of palm trees lining the path and not sure if the level of defences evident was disturbing or reassuring. He hefted the weight of the rifle on his back, sweat trickling down his ribs.

"That Bhenykhn ship that crashed here ten years ago?" he sent, glad he was using the implant because he didn't trust his voice not to crack. "They were part of the team sent into the wreckage after UM pulled out."

"They don't look old enough."

"They're not. Pen, someone's had them in stasis for the past ten years. Drake just found out. She thinks they're her key to finding what it is about Kheris before anyone else."

There, he'd said it. Kinda. His heart was thumping.

Pen grabbed his arm and pulled him to a stop. "I take it I'm interpreting the message you sent correctly, then?"

Hil nodded, a lump in his throat.

"Jesus." Pen shook his head, fuming but not as angry as Hil had ever seen. "Okay, it's in hand. You did the right thing."

Pen put his hand on Hil's shoulder, reassuring, and starting to walk again. He moved, boots soft on the red tiled pavement, heart still thumping. He hadn't done the right thing. He didn't know what the right thing was anymore.

"How much do they know?" Pen said out loud.

He muttered, "Enough to know they've been fucked over." He stopped, turning to the big man, a slight breeze wafting between them, a faint murmur of cool, salt tinged air. "Pen..."

Pen gave him a look like he knew what was coming.

"You need to get word back to Evie... tell her the weapon Drake's looking for is real. It's the metal cube NG found on Pandora." He'd never seen it. Elliott had knocked him on his ass before running off with the rest of the Seven. Hil shifted his weight, uneasy. He'd been unconscious for days, but he'd talked to LC afterwards. "Drake told me it's not a kill switch but I don't believe her. She wants to destroy the Seven."

"Pandora?" Pen nodded slowly. "NG took it back to the Alsatia?"

"As far as I know."

"Okay. What else?"

Hil took off the goggles and squinted back, trying to breathe through the adrenaline. He lowered his voice. "The Bennies have ordered Drake to wipe this place out. She's gathered a fleet, big enough to do it. And if I don't take whatever the hell it is here that repels the Bhenykhn back to her in time she's going to. She's going to attack Kheris."

CHAPTER TWENTY-FIVE

Koschei stood back, letting the data sweep in waves across the screen, as he continued, the details brief, but enough.

"Nolite relinquere omnem spem," she murmured. "The cube."

They had been warned of the Seven. She had talked with Koschei about the threat of the Seven back when Aries had first reappeared. When Pandora was still a myth among the humans, its dire secrets still secure.

Her people had no machine life, had never contemplated the concept as a possibility and had been repulsed, terrified by the idea of it here, so prevalent amongst human society, and potentially such a powerful adversary given the rumours of those condemned to be confined forever.

Koschei grumbled under his breath, a low and

rumbling discontent. He raised his eyes, dark, orange flecks dancing within their depths. "Believe me, if I had known that Nikolai had retrieved it, we would not be in the predicament in which we now find ourselves."

Pen cursed and took him into a courtyard, armed guards at every corner, and through into a building, whitewashed stone walls, palm trees in terracotta pots. The inside was airy, cool, immaculate tiled floors. It reminded him more of Hanover, the affluent Hanover, post-rebellion, pre-invasion Hanover, more than anything he'd ever heard LC say of Kheris.

There were more guards in the entrance. They made him stop and ran another bugscan. Thorough.

"What the hell does 'in time' mean?" Pen said once he was cleared, waving him into some kind of sitting room. It was sparse, not as cosy as Pen's houses on Aston, but there were soft sofas, shafts of sunlight sneaking in through gaps in the shutters to freeze frame the red dust of Kheris mid-air, the beams shining down on expensive rugs underfoot. "What are we looking at?"

"She's going to launch the attack in less than eight weeks, maybe six."

"Jesus. But we still have Elliott and the Seven, yes? Their firepower should be able to counter anything Drake can assemble."

"Pen...?" Hil stood, frozen to the spot, stomach knotted, not wanting to ask, dreading the answer Pen could give.

The big man turned. "What?"

"You know what happened with LC?" His heart was in his throat. He was assuming the guild would have reported back to Pen, especially considering it had happened right here. "Any word?"

"No, nothing yet. Why?"

"Drake said she'd heard he was dead."

"She's messing with you. LC will be fine. I would've heard if he wasn't." Pen took off his jacket and dropped it on the back of a chair. "I'd say make yourself at home, but we don't have much hospitality to offer."

Hil sat, not convinced, but he sat and rifled through his pack, pulling out the two bottles and the olives with a flourish. As if that could make up for what he was doing.

Pen sat opposite, reaching to take one of the beers he held out. "Holy shit." The big man spun the bottle to read the label, looking at Hil then looking back at the bottle.

"Seriously, Pen, this is how Drake is living. How all her people are living." He popped open the jar of olives and pushed it forward. "They have meds, fuel, food..."

Pen was still staring at the beer. "My god, this stuff was two hundred bucks a bottle before the war."

"She has truckloads of it. Of everything."

Pen's eyes had a gleam in them as he looked up. "Where?"

Hil opened the beer and took a mouthful. "Fifty levels below ground on an uncharted planet in the Between that is teeming with Bennies on the surface."

"And she just let you go?"

"I'm working for her now, didn't you hear?" He said it half tongue in cheek but it sounded shit, even joking.

"Yeah," Pen said with a mouthful of olives, "that seems to be going well for you."

He ran through everything as fast as he could, Pen nodding when what he was saying concurred with intel they'd received from Evelyn, asking him to clarify when it was anything new. They'd heard about the telepaths, the mutant attack dogs, what had happened with LC... Everything from Taylorson and Dixon was new. As was the cube. And nothing had been sent over regarding Sebastian. Hil double checked the security before he said anything, then told Pen about NG and the Bhenykhn that was Sebastian, not exactly saying everything even when he knew they were secure.

Pen set down his bottle, turning it so he could see the label as if he needed confirmation it was for real, and took another olive, looking up to meet Hil's eyes. "So Drake has her own telepaths, she's going after a weapon against the Seven, and she thinks she can weaponise whatever the anomaly here is...? You think she's going to win this war?"

And that was only half of it. Hil took the last long

swig of beer to drain the bottle and shook his head. "We passed Arunday's Convergence. There is no win. Not for humans. Not for any of us."

Pen gave a wry smile. "Who have you been talking to?"

He threw an olive into the air, high, catching it easily in his mouth. "Sebastian."

"And that's where Anya is?"

He nodded.

Pen, to give him credit, didn't demand to know where, just kept whatever went through his mind locked away, and stood, retrieving a couple of boards from a bank on the wall. He threw them onto the table, sat and leaned forward.

"You should know we've been looking, by gods, have we been looking, analysing system-wide, astrophysics, planetary data, geophysics, exobiology, any anomaly we can find, and believe me, we have good people on this, and we've found nothing about this system or this colony that we can narrow down to any reason why the Bhenykhn are keeping away. If there is something at that crash site, I'm damned if we can find it."

"Something attacked LC."

"And is attacking our search teams. We've lost three in as many weeks."

Hil leaned forward, not letting on that he already knew that, and scanned through the boards, flicking randomly through pages of stats. "You have no idea what it could be?"

"We've been excavating for months. Or trying to. According to local rumour the site is jinxed. Kheris doesn't have a good reputation anyway. Locals stay away. People we've brought in, experienced people, bloody good engineers and techs, they get so far, then... I don't know, accidents happen, machinery breaks down. There's been rumours it's haunted. Some nutjob even claimed Kheris is protecting itself, like some damned Gaia entity in the core." The big man shook his head. "Now everyone knows it's alien..."

"Not Bhenykhn." He'd told Pen that already. He pushed the boards away and sat back. "You need to talk to Taylorson and Dixon. What they found down there... it's alien but not Bhenykhn. I know what the inside of a Bhenykhn ship looks like." His chest was cold, hollow, as he said it.

"Whatever it is," Pen said, voice grim, "we've lost three teams. Countless injured before that, but these three have just vanished, no sign. You go down there, you think you can do better?"

"Yeah."

That hung in the air. That was the thing. That was the thing that changed everything. He was the freak that no one understood.

Pen looked up as Elenor appeared, leaning in to put a tall thin bottle and two shot glasses on the table between them. She poured out the pale amber liquor and set down her bag, perching on the arm of the chair next to Hil.

"We heard you were wounded," she said softly in that old Earth accent that was so different to Drake's.

A pulse of adrenaline hit his chest.

She placed her hand on his shoulder, the one that had been shot on Temerity, rubbing her thumb right where the bullet had entered and just dissolved inside or whatever the hell the virus did with it, as if she knew something was awry there.

His breath caught in his chest, trying his best not to flinch away from her. She was the only medic he'd ever trusted. Pen and Elenor were family. Whatever else was going on, whoever else had a piece of his soul, he was with family here.

Even so...

He couldn't help muttering, "I'm fine."

Pen reached for one of the shot glasses and nudged the other towards him.

He took it as Elenor squeezed his shoulder.

Pen said something he missed but he heard Elenor answer. "I wish LC had let me see him back then. How different would everything be now if he had?"

"He'll be fine," Pen said. Firm. No nonsense. As if LC was invincible, immortal, whatever happened. Just because he was LC.

They both looked at him as if they needed him to say something. He swallowed past the lump in his throat.

"He wasn't breathing when I found them." Hardly the best thing to say.

"He'll be fine," Pen said again.

Elenor stood and took up her bag, murmuring, "You know where I am if you need me."

She moved away and said, more to Pen than him, "I'm worried about Corporal Taylorson. His stats are not good. If it was up to me, I would not clear him as mission-fit. He was badly wounded, a week ago according to his memory of it, and from what I can tell, whoever put him in storage didn't treat him properly first. He's healed but he's not mission-ready. Never mind the..."

"He's JU," Pen said, not harsh but to the point. "He'll survive. He did once already." He looked at Hil. "You're right. From what you've said, if he reacts the same out there, he should lead you right to it."

Elenor wasn't impressed. "Let me go with them," she said.

Pen gave her a flat, outright, "No."

The look she gave him, knowing her, it wouldn't be surprising if she did go with them. That wouldn't be unwelcome.

Hil gave her a faint smile and waited until she'd gone before he leaned forward. "And what then? What do I do? If I find it. Pen, I don't know if..."

Pen's eyes darkened. "If what?"

"If..." He couldn't say it. If Drake was right, if he had to take it to her for anyone to have a chance at beating the Bhenykhn. "If..."

"If Drake is right?" Pen waved his hand towards the

empty bottles. "She has this kind of beer? Who wouldn't rather be on her side?"

Pen left him to trawl through the data, telling him to stay put while he went to talk to the JU guys. He didn't stay put. He went through it all again fast and started pacing, too wired to stay put. He ended up outside, on a terrace by the water of the oasis, leaning on a railing and staring out over a lush, palm-lined desert landscape that was a million miles from anything he'd ever heard about this place.

The chemical tinge to the air was strong out there but even so... this might be Kheris with its high gravity and poisonous gases, but it was still more real than Drake's phony underground play area.

He heard Pen's footsteps behind him.

"Nice team you have with you," Pen said, casual, as if he wasn't throwing a hand grenade in there. "A bunch of Imperial marines off the Nairobi and a Wintran Colonel who decided to defect from the Perseverance? All choosing to throw their lot in with the resistance over Drake's operation. Damn good cover stories. It all checks out. Gotta say I'm impressed with Drake's attention to detail. You think we could convince them to stay?"

Hil stood up and leaned back against the railing. "Not Lane. She's Drake's XO. She's the one keeping an eye on me."

"Not the only one."

He stopped in his tracks.

Pen smiled. "Did she find you or did you find her?"

"It's complicated."

"I bet it is." Pen offered him a cup. "Hil... it's not just Taylorson that Elenor's worried about. What's going on with you?"

It was so automatic, he said, "I'm fine," before he could think.

"I know you are. I asked what's going on."

Hil took the drink, tilting his head and staring up at the too bright blue sky, knowing there was a flotilla of warships up there, and knowing that in six weeks they'd be joined by a shit load more if he didn't find this thing.

He looked back at Pen.

If NG had been like their big brother, Pen and Mendhel had always been like their two dads, the fathers neither him nor LC had ever had. The last time he'd seen Pen was on Miranda, when they'd taken down McKenzie. When Sienna and LC were both shot. No one had been looking at him, no one paying him the slightest bit of attention so long as he kept delivering on the missions, and kept on smiling and joking, and that had been fine.

But he'd known this was coming.

"Elenor's not the only one," Pen said, raising his own cup. "Evelyn sent me a private communiqué, trying to find you. She said you've been refusing medical attention."

"I don't need…"

"She said you've been seriously wounded and you won't let anyone even look at you. What's going on?"

Hil turned and stared back out over the water. Tempted. Shit, he was tempted. But he shook his head. "I heal. Stupidly fast. Faster than LC. Faster than I've seen NG do it. Really, Pen, that's it. I'm fine."

He could see out of the corner of his eye that Pen was looking at him as if the big man knew that wasn't all there was to it but like he knew fine well that was all he was going to get.

"I can't read minds," he said. "I can't blow stuff up, I can't throw things around. I'm invisible to the freaking Bennies and I heal fast." He turned to face Pen. "That's it." He almost said, I swear, but he couldn't go that far.

Pen let it drop. "Interesting chat with Taylorson and Dixon. Can you believe I remember those two as cadet recruits, kids, two decades ago. And they were at Derren Bay. That was, what, twelve years ago. And to them it's been two." The big man shook his head. Bad memories.

Twelve years ago? They all had bad memories from twelve years ago.

CHAPTER TWENTY-SIX

"*YOU'VE BEEN EXERTING pressure on colonies like Kheris and Redgate through Kochitek.*" *As if those places were not troubled enough.*

He shook his head. "*That Kheris finds itself at the centre of the war now is none of my doing.*"

"*Excuse my impudence,*" *she said it with a shard of ice in her tone,* "*but a lot of this chaos is your doing. Much stems from your mistakes.*"

He didn't like that, a dark shadow crossing his eyes. "*I have never claimed to be omnipotent.*"

Neither of them said it but she knew exactly what else had been happening ten years ago that had taken his eye away from Kheris.

"*We play with fire,*" *he said.* "*You more than anyone alive know that everything I have done here in this galaxy has been towards one end. One end. Collateral damage is inevitable. Losses are inevitable. Sacrifice is inevitable. Do not let your emotional need to protect these creatures affect your judgement now. Everything I have done, everything I do, with any construct I deem necessary, is working towards that end." He leaned forward, brow low. "I do not require your approval. Consider that in hearing what I am yet to tell you."*

They stood quietly then, listening to the sounds of the desert floating in on the breeze.

It was peaceful.

It was hard to think there was a war raging anywhere.

Hard to think this was the infamous Kheris.

Hil looked across at Pen and said softly, "This isn't the Kheris LC knew."

The oasis was a million miles from the city LC had grown up in. He'd never talked about it, not until Hanover, but Hil had heard enough of the story LC had told the kids in that basement to know what kind of shithole LC had grown up in.

"Money," Pen said. Simple. Harsh. "The rich and privileged need somewhere to stay when they come to check in on their assets. Kheris has always been extremes."

It was ironic. The only safe place in the entire galaxy and LC couldn't step foot back on the place to see it. And in six weeks, Drake was going to destroy it.

Pen leaned forward, serious. "I probably don't need to say this but the whole colony is not this safe. The instability of ten years ago was resolved to a large extent after Gemini, but now... You've seen what it's like from a distance. Believe me when I say you do not want to find yourself alone out on the ground here, not in the city, not in the slums, not in the desert. Every lowlife managing to escape the Bhenykhn is flooding in here. The local authorities are overrun. The mayor is doing a damn good job but she's young. And who the hell would expect this to happen on their watch? We're scraping together any militia or military that turns up into some kind of policing force but, trust me, you won't have a chance if someone figures out who you are."

He wasn't planning on going anywhere alone, going anywhere at all except out to the crash site.

"And if word gets out as to what you're doing here, you're not going to be the only one out there looking for it."

There was a splash in the lake, the sound of some kind of insect coming from the base of the palms.

"I know."

Pen reached forward with his cup, inviting a clink. "Last time we talked like this you thought she'd betrayed you."

Martha...

"I also thought Quinn and NG had betrayed me." It was hard to say. But he knew now what the breach had been. And that was not something he was going to say. Not even to Pen.

"Just be careful."

Hil nodded, took a sip and held out the cup again. "Last time I was on Kheris, it was with Mendhel."

Pen met his eyes and clinked the cup. "What the hell would my brother have made of all this?"

Hil took another sip, that lump back in his throat with a vengeance. "He would have knocked all our heads together and told us to stop being idiots."

Pen laughed and drained his tea. "Aye, that he would. You have a good team with you from the look of it. Let's keep up the charade. Drake told you she has people everywhere? Let's not risk making this worse than it is. But I'm not going to let them screw this up. Everything we've sent down there has malfunctioned. Badly. You wouldn't believe some of the shit that's been happening. You know there was a power plant that exploded ten years ago when the ship crashed?"

Hil nodded.

Pen leaned forward. "That explosion released lethal levels of radiation but that's almost all gone, absorbed, as if something sucked it all away. Just gone. No one knows how or why, but the site is clear. We just don't know what the hell is going on in there, but if you go in with a full team of armed soldiers and equipment, exactly the same thing is going to happen again." Pen pierced him with those dark eyes. "If you do this, you do it your way. Do you understand? Run it as a tab. Once you're at the crash site, you go in alone. You have your knife?"

Mendhel's knife.

"Yes."

"Good. Take that. Nothing else. No armour. No other weapons. We've had auto sentries blow up like no one's business. Take a flashlight but I'll get lumi-sticks and flares for you just in case. I've sent orders for Hetherington to run the extraction detail. She knows what she's doing. They'll be right there if you need them. Same as any tab you ever ran for the guild. Can you do it?"

He had no idea but he nodded.

"Go do what you do, Hil. Just remember who you are."

It felt like another goodbye.

Hil stared out across the blue water. "I need to go."

Yani called them and Pen slapped him on the back, leading him back to the courtyard where the drop ship was waiting.

Taylorson and Dixon were already out there, talking quietly to Yani, who from the look of it was coming with them. All three looked up as they approached, their focus switching to someone following. Hil turned, aware that Pen was too.

Elenor was walking towards them, wearing black ops gear, 'Halligan' on the name tag, carrying a kit bag and weapons. Holy shit. He'd never seen her like this but from the way she was walking, the cold look in her eyes, the balance and confidence in her stride, it was obvious this wasn't the first time she'd gone into active theatre. He'd always assumed she was a research medic. Apparently not.

And apparently Pen knew better than to argue. Hil watched as the big man steeled himself, took her kit bag and threw it in the drop ship, gripping her shoulder and saying to her, loud enough that he could hear, "Keep him alive."

It was hard not to squirm as Elenor glanced at him. She turned back to Pen. "I intend to. You said it, he's the only one that has a chance of finding this thing." She looked at the rest of them. "Gentlemen, shall we?"

They switched to an APC at the barracks, rough going over the desert but someone said best to avoid flying anything over the crash site with the way equipment went screwy out there. So they crammed into two APCs and bounced over ruts and channels.

Martha squeezed his knee, hard, not caring too much that she was wearing powered armour. "I'm not happy that you're going in there alone," she sent over the Senson, blunt, cutting through the sound of the APC engines that was reverberating through his skull.

"I'll be fine. You can stand and watch. It'll be just like

old times," he sent back, cocky, resolve firmly fixed, that steady calm feeling inside that he got before a tab.

Just like old times.

Except the target to be acquired was an alien entity that had already wiped out a deep spacer, an entire Imperial emergency rescue team, two JU squads and a processing facility. And three of Pen's search teams.

An alien entity, that by all accounts and reasoning, wasn't Bhenykhn.

He'd take on the freaking Bennies any day. This thing? After listening to Taylorson's account of it...?

He set his jaw and stared straight ahead.

It was just another acquisition.

They stopped twice to go through checkpoints, rumbling to a halt finally inside the quarantined area. Hil unbuckled and stood, looking across the aisle at Taylorson. Pissed off didn't describe it. Pissed off and in pain...

"It's here," Taylorson said, voice strained. "It's still here."

The crater was immense, a huge depression in the desert floor amidst the blowing red dust of a sand storm. The military cordon around it was made up of two high double fences, four hundred feet apart, barbed wire, motion trackers and auto sentry positions at regular intervals on both, the area between them packed with tents, mobile structures, vehicles, watch towers and armed guards. Hil turned slowly, taking it all in. If there were any street kids left in the city, they'd have no chance of getting in there now. If he was trying to get in unseen, there were a few holes he could spot, but as it was they'd been waved right through.

Even that early in the morning it was blisteringly hot. He dragged his scarf up over his mouth and nose, glad of the goggles, staring out over the site. Even through the dust he could just about make out the jagged ruins of metal stanchions sticking up at crazy angles, the ghost of the metal processing plant. If there had once been a deep spacer and a mining facility here, there wasn't much left above the surface to show for it.

He turned to Taylorson. "You getting anything?"

Everyone was watching them. As if Taylorson just had to point the way and he'd dive in there and retrieve it.

Taylorson shrugged. "It's down there somewhere."

The guy who was obviously in charge must have been briefed because he made a beeline right for the two of them.

"You're Taylorson, right?" he said, curt, as if he was almost done with this whole mess. "You can, what? Sense it or something?"

The guy had no insignia but he had that feel of JU about him. Jesus, was everyone here JU?

Taylorson looked uneasy, shifting his balance and looking at the crater side on as if that could give him some kind of insight into it. "Sir, I don't know. It feels the same." As a week ago, he didn't say. "Just kinda hinky. Sir."

The guy didn't look impressed. "You know we've lost three teams down there?" he said.

Hil kept quiet. The timing of it starting to attack them, from what he could figure, was pretty much when it had attacked LC. He'd gone over all the maps of the search party efforts so far and there was no pattern, nothing discernable that they may have missed. And no sign of the missing teams. How the hell he was supposed to find some alien entity here that had escaped a crashed ship ten years ago, when everyone else had failed, he had no idea.

"This is your show," the guy said. "But we'll be running support from the surface." He cast his eyes across to the group of newcomers before glaring back at them both. "You will listen to my people. Do you understand?"

Taylorson murmured, "Sir, yes sir," and moved forward.

The guy in charge cast his eyes at Hil. "You have a problem, son?"

Yes, he did, by all the gods, he did.

He sucked it up. "No, sir," he said. He could feel the muscle in his jaw ticking.

The guy stepped in close and murmured, quiet, "I don't know who the hell you are, but I've been told you're primary on this mission." He leaned in closer, voice dropping. "We're sending some of our best people in there with you. Don't fuck this up."

"I don't intend to."

"Don't."

"I won't."

Ten years ago he'd come close to ditching out on the Thieves' Guild to stay with the military. He hadn't. And he'd be damned if anyone was going to order him around now.

The guy smiled, wry and freaking smug, as if he'd won some profound contest of egos. "Good," he said. "Go. See if you can find out what the hell is going on down there. Pen Halligan tells me you're good. Prove him right and I'll stump up the beers myself."

CHAPTER TWENTY-SEVEN

"*THEY SENT HIM IN ALONE?*" *Sacrifice was one thing but meaningless abandon, surely not, not after all they had been through.*

"*Hilyer is unique within his kind.*"

Koschei's tone was telling. He was alone amongst their people. And their people had never treated him well. He didn't meet her eye, keeping his head down and manipulating the data to show her the true scale of the forces gathering to move against Kheris. It was horrifying that it had come to this. That her favourites had been the ones to bear the brunt of their mistakes.

"*In any conflict,*" *he muttered under his breath,* "*the special ones are always pushed to the forefront, into the line of fire. The only ones who can, do. And they are the ones who suffer. They know it is the way. And none will deny it, nor shy away from it.*"

They had a modular dome, not far inside the main perimeter, down inside the crater. The entrance to an excavation they'd made. One that went down to what was left of the wreckage of the ship.

They had a full decontamination unit set up in there. Two of the guys they'd come with were in heavy infantry armour, kitting up with deployable auto sentries and sensor arrays. Another plus Martha were in lighter weight suits of recon powered armour, more kit than she used to wear for extractions, waiting while the rest of them got kitted out with haz suits, testing the comms and running through checks.

Hil stood there in fatigues, light flexible armoured material, as good as anything the guild had, Mendhel's knife in his boot, a web vest with pouches stacked with flares, lumi-sticks and a couple of concussion grenades Pen had slipped him, the most they dared risk, and a flashlight. He'd memorised every inch of the excavations and tunnels they'd managed to map so far, kept it clear in his mind and waited, breathing calm and heart rate steady.

Everyone else wasn't so much jittery, they were all seasoned combat troops, for Christ's sake, but there was an undercurrent of unease. A couple of the guys were already tapping the power units on their haz suits as if something was wrong. Hil glanced across. He wasn't intending on taking energy from anywhere. He didn't need to. He couldn't help the echo of Taylorson's briefing whispering through his mind, the panic, the escalation of one malfunction after another. As much as he knew that had been ten years ago, it felt ominously close, dangerously close to whatever they were going in to now. But he could see from where he was standing that the energy readings on the suits were fine.

One of them yelled for a tech. "This is fucked already. Jesus, can someone get us suits that work?"

It wasn't fucked. He wasn't taking energy from them. He was sure he wasn't. And from what he could see, nothing else was. He watched, detached, feeling like he should say something and not sure how, as one of the techs replaced the power mods and hooked them back up, running scans.

Comms seemed fine but then by all accounts they'd lost contact with the missing search teams after they'd dropped down into the depths of the cave system beneath the buried wreckage. No one had any idea if comms were going to work down there or not.

Someone yelled across the Senson for a sound off. He took his turn to call in.

All seemed fine.

Taylorson was tense but the kind of battle readiness tense, like he wanted to jump down there and meet whatever had killed his team head on, bring it on. Dixon was waiting by the hole already, eyes fixed on the sensor arrays and auto sentries, swearing softly, agitated, easy to guess what the guy was thinking.

Hil wandered over and said quietly, "It's not going to be the same."

Dixon looked up.

"You didn't know what you were dealing with last time," Hil said. "We do now."

The guy pulled a face, but straightened himself as if just realising people were watching. "You've really seen one?"

"The Bhenykhn? Yeah."

"What are they like? The aliens."

This wasn't exactly the time or place for a chat. "Once we're done here, I'm going back after them. Come see for yourself."

Dixon had that set to his face people get when there's a score to settle. "Hell yeah."

The guy held out his fist, inviting a bump. Hil obliged. He'd lost track of how many scores he had to settle.

Elenor caught his eye as she passed them. She was moving from one person to the next, reassuring, popping a shot of something into everyone's medline, he realised. He shook his head. He didn't need it. Whatever it was. What he needed was just to get down there and get on with it. She didn't look impressed but she didn't argue.

Yani was with the rest of Drake's marines, Lane in overall charge, no doubt all of them talking through the mission again.

The surface crew seemed to be trusting that they knew what they were doing. Not every day a team of flash Thieves' Guild operatives turned up.

Martha was watching him.

He switched to the Senson. "Their kit was fine. There was nothing wrong with it."

She didn't reply, checking her own gear.

He nudged her again through the implant. "You know this is a one chance op, don't you? If we go down there and it goes to shit, and we end up killing this thing or destroying it, we leave Kheris wide open to the Bhenykhn."

"And if we don't go down there and find it," she sent back, "Drake is going to destroy Kheris anyway." She tightened another strap around her chest. "So we find it." She raised her eyes to meet his. "Just go do your stuff, sunshine."

The shaft was a fast ingress tube, driven vertically down into the desert floor. The guy in charge was standing by. Hil listened in as the go ahead was given and watched as the guy waved over the advance teams, the power armoured troops simply stepping off the edge and falling, presumably with AG suppressors in the suits that would activate before they hit the bottom. Martha turned and threw him a cocky salute as she stepped backwards and dropped.

It felt like his heart dropped with her.

There was no way he could make this work.

Arunday's Convergence. No win, whatever decision he made.

Whatever he did.

"You next, hotshot," the guy shouted.

Elenor stepped up with him, a hand on his back.

"Be straight with me," she murmured across the Senson, private, "and I'll get you out of there. You understand?"

The rest of them had to use rappels. He attached the line he was given and turned, sending back a quiet, "Yes, ma'am," with a ghost of a smile. He was more worried about taking care of her. Pen would kill him if anything happened to her.

He stepped backwards, and dropped, trusting the inertial dampeners to kick in in time. It was JU kit. Of course it would.

The tube dropped into a wide open chamber, deck at a slight angle, crushed bulkheads at one end, pillars and struts giving some stability at the other. It wasn't Bhenykhn. He could see that the minute he landed and turned, freeing the cable and letting it snap back up.

They had mobile spotlights lighting the whole place, sensor arrays already set up and troops in position at each egress. For a deep spacer, whoever had built it had done a good job. It wasn't intact but whole sections had survived the blast when the processing plant had blown ten years ago.

Taylorson dropped in beside him as he moved away from the tube, Elenor right behind him.

Hil left his knife in his boot, hands free, casual. He was here to acquire the item, sample, object, artefact, device, creature, whatever the hell it was... That was it. He had no intention of fighting it.

It was hot down there. Radiation low, as they'd been told to expect. Contaminants in the air high, as expected. He caught Elenor glancing at him, concerned, and gave her a smile. He was fine.

Lane was standing with the advance team, Martha's team. She turned to the JU corporal and gestured. "Which way?"

Taylorson had his rifle up already, scanning across the area as he turned a full circle. He stopped, staring towards a dark corridor that led north, towards the aft end of the ship, towards the foothills up there on the surface.

Hil watched, hanging back. Elenor had everyone on live feed. It didn't take much to hack into her kit and see what she was reading. Taylorson was steady as it came, programmed as hell, the perfect JU soldier. Even so, there was a slight blip there in his stats as he stared into the darkness.

"In there," Taylorson muttered. "But deeper. We need to go down."

Now or never.

"Surface," Lane sent, wide link to the guy in charge and the team up top, including them all, "this is Alpha One Niner." She headed towards the mouth of the corridor and paused, helmet lights casting a dim glow of illumination that seemed hard pushed to penetrate that darkness. "Moving in. Do you copy?"

"Roger that, Alpha. This is Surface, you're good to go."

Lane gestured to the advance teams and they moved forward, standard sweep and search formation.

Hil moved up next to Taylorson, Yani a step ahead, Elenor and Dixon a pace behind, and watched their lights bounce away into the dark.

Lane glanced back at him. "Ready Cobra?"

Funny. That was really funny. In a disconcertingly shit way.

He knew Drake and her cronies knew all about him, but his guild call sign? Seriously?

He muttered a, "Yeah, roger that."

His heart was thumping faster than it should be. He was having to dampen down an irrational irritation, a bitingly self-destructive need for it to be LC there beside him, raiding this place together the way they had Drake's vault. He didn't want heavy military support around him. The sooner they split, the better. This thing down here, whatever it was, had near as dammit killed LC. And he wanted to find it. He used that, that one sharp, clear fact, to focus, slow his breathing and focus on what he had to do.

Lane sent wide, "Surface, this is Alpha One Niner, all assets green, Cobra is moving in. Let's get this done."

CHAPTER TWENTY-EIGHT

HE TURNED AND WALKED OUT, another low rumbling, "I'm sure you are curious to find out what it is on Kheris that so repels our foe."

She stared after him. "You know what it is?"

He didn't answer and instead led her along another dark, wide corridor she had never been privileged to see before, candles flickering as they passed. More doors led from it, some opening onto dark chambers where human staff busied themselves with whatever Kochitek business Koschei was currently brewing. Part of her wanted to run and never know.

He stopped at another door, this one heavy, twisted black metal blast doors with an airlock. He paused and looked back at her. "I do now. They were right to fear it."

It definitely wasn't Bhenykhn. He'd seen dead and powered down Benny kit before and it stank, decaying into dust and mold, no matter how long dead, not slick and smooth like these bulkheads. He watched the beams of the gun-mounted tac-lights scan over the walls, ceiling, deck, as they moved forward. As damaged as they were, there was no biological ooze, no decayed husks. No thick twisting cables lying dead and withered. He glanced down a side corridor as they passed, holding his breath, half expecting some hostile to be right there waiting for them.

It was clear.

He breathed, heart rate slower now, hyper-focused, wanting to find it like he'd never wanted anything in his life. It was a tab. Standings points. An easy acquisition...

They worked their way down through the crashed ship, through five or so excavated, shored up tunnels that led to more sections of the buried hull when the ship was too damaged to get through.

It was starting to feel almost routine when comms cut out. Taylorson was the first to realise it, turning, tapping his helmet and gesturing a query.

Martha's squad was up ahead, a dim glow from the helmets and tac-lights bouncing, the other team off scouting routes through.

"Riley, come in," Lane sent. "Riley? Wait up. We need to check comms."

No response.

"Okay, people," she sent, "this is it. Dixon, go pull them back. Channing, Ivo, set up a defensive position. I want power in here." She turned and beckoned. "Hilyer, you're up."

Martha was already walking back to them. "It's a dead end," she said, out loud, voice mechanical as it was enhanced through the suit.

Taylorson was standing, staring, tense as if it was taking effort to not freak out. "It's that way."

"There's no way through there."

Taylorson turned, agitated. "It's that way." For a straight up, hardass, JU operative, battle-hardened and experienced, he looked like he knew exactly just how damned insane he sounded.

Hil gave Martha a glance and walked forward, nudging past her.

Martha caught his arm and pulled him close. "Don't tell me you can't feel this."

"Feel what?"

"Seriously, sunshine, you are one of a kind."

"What?"

Someone yelled for lights to be set up.

Martha nudged him. "Can you really not feel it?"

"Feel what?" He'd been keeping tabs on everyone's stats the whole way down here. Everyone was fine. Hot, elevated adrenaline levels which was to be expected. Nothing freaky.

She adjusted her grip on the rifle, keeping it aimed back down the tunnel, scanning the light around the rough hewn walls. "Hil," she said, eyes darting back to him, "I'm wearing a goddamned sealed suit, I know I am, but my skin is crawling, my eyes hurt, I can't get enough oxygen in each breath, and... I don't even know how to say it, but it's like something really bad is about to happen. Really bad."

Looking at her up close, now, her face was flushed, eyes too bright.

She squinted at him. "Taylorson's heebie fucking jeebies. And I know," she said intently, pulling him in again, "that everyone else here is experiencing exactly the same thing as me, even that knucklehead Dixon. Everyone except you."

What was he supposed to say? He couldn't tell her he thought they were all imagining it. She'd punch his lights out. He resisted pulling away and ticked it over in his brain for a brief second before blurting out, "That's why they sent me. MJ, I..."

He was rescued as there was a clang, lights flashing on, shadows leaping out of nowhere as arcs of light illuminated the vast space.

He turned to see Taylorson flinch. "It's through here," he insisted, stubborn, eyes narrow as if he was fighting off a blinder of a headache.

This was about as far as the search maps had covered. New ground from here on in. And limited comms. He looked back at Elenor. She was pulling injectors from her kit and doing the rounds, not happy at what she was reading by the expression on her face.

He gave Martha a look and walked forward. He glanced at Taylorson, something unnerving about the way the JU guy was backing away.

"Don't," Taylorson said. One word. Clear as hell. And the way he said it...

From the briefing, the one take-away from that whole briefing he'd had the pleasure to watch at Drake's place, was that if this guy said something was hinky, something was hinky, and if he said don't, then whatever the hell you were going to do, you just didn't.

Except he had no choice.

He walked forward.

The smooth deck of the ship gave way to rock as if this part of the hull had crashed down into a natural cavern and split open. He stepped across the gap and snapped a lumi-stick. The fluorescence lit up the darkness. It wasn't a cave, more like a hollow cavity, dead end as Martha had said. Nothing but rock walls in every direction.

Another beam of light joined his as Dixon walked up behind him.

"How come you don't feel it?" the JU guy said.

Hil shrugged with a casual, "No idea," waving the stick close to the wall, trying to spot a way through.

Dixon crouched down low, sending the beam of his tac-light along the ground. "They're all freaking out back there. Wish we'd had that medic and her wacky drugs with us last time."

Hil didn't care. "I can't see a way through."

"Hate to say this, bud, but there must be. Taylorson isn't ever wrong."

He was about to say first time for everything when his light caught the rock face weird. Nothing he could pinpoint. Just... He angled round, edged forward and slipped through a gap in the rocks.

Dixon was right behind him, swearing. "How the fuck did we not see this?"

Hil didn't stop. The gap opened out into a bigger void. He stepped right to the edge and threw the lumi-stick down into a narrow fissure, illuminating what looked like parts of the processing plant mangled with parts of the ship wedged in amongst boulders and chunks of debris. "Looks like I need to go down there."

Dixon cursed again.

Hil pulled out another lumi-stick.

"Get the others to pull back," he said, snapping it and wedging it into his belt. "Get them somewhere they're not going to get affected. All the way back if necessary. And stay with them. You understand?"

He looked at Dixon, kept that eye contact until he was sure the guy understood and got a nod.

"Yeah, roger that."

He waited until Dixon backed off, sent through the

Senson a wide comm telling them he was fine and pushing on, and not caring if they heard it or not.

He looked down the fissure.

It was no big deal. Getting down was going to be easy. It was getting back up that would be fun.

Making his way down a dark, narrow space riddled with broken and twisted struts wasn't one of the worst things he'd ever done, sheets of bent metal, bulkhead or processing plant, unsteady beneath his feet as he clambered down. Twice, loose beams and fragments of debris crashed past his head, one bouncing off his arm and one close to taking off his leg. He landed and staggered out of the way of more debris crashing down, flattening himself against the rock face and taking a moment to listen in the pitch black darkness down there. If there was something hostile, it would have heard him a mile off.

There was nothing. No sound past the occasional clatter of stone falling.

He waited another few minutes then pulled out a flare and tossed it ahead to illuminate a tunnel strewn with debris, what looked like bodies, sensor arrays blown to bits, a string of mobile spotlights all with cracked tubes, wires trailing to burnt endings.

Shit.

He crouched, checking each body, none of them

wearing haz suits, gunshot wounds, knife wounds, burns, blood dried in dark streaks.

He sent a quick update through the Senson. "Found the missing search teams. Dead. Looks like fucking friendly fire. I can't see anything that looks like the Bennies."

There was no reply.

He pulled the knife out of his boot and stood. There was nothing that looked awry. He twirled the blade through his fingers and moved on, keeping close to the wall, turning to walk backwards and watch out behind him for a few steps. He knew what injuries from the Bennies looked like. Damn right he knew. First hand. These guys had been killed by human weapons.

So what the hell was going on?

He turned, took another couple of steps forward and the Senson engaged.

"Hilyer...?"

"MJ?"

"Oh god, Hilyer. What's going on?"

"Found the search teams. Did you get that?"

"No."

"Dead," he sent before she asked. "Human weapons, MJ. Friendly fire. You getting this?"

There was nothing. Then, "You're breaking up, Hil. Oh shit. If you can hear me, we're pulling back. Do you copy? Hil, can you hear me?"

"Can now."

There was a pause then, "How about now?"

"Clear as a bell." He kept walking, staying close to the rock face, edging through the tunnel, boots nudging against shattered glass and metal fragments.

"This is weird, Hil. No one else can hear you."

Whatever was going on, he was glad it was Martha that could.

He blew out a breath he was holding.

"You want to keep talking to me..." he sent, stepping around a body and cracking another lumi-stick, peering ahead, "that would be appreciated."

It looked like another dead end but he took a step forward, squinting at what could be another gap.

He squeezed through, the only light just a fading luminescence from the stick he was holding down by his thigh. It was draining faster than usual, but if that was because of something down here or because he was taking energy from it surreptitiously, without really realising, he wasn't sure.

The gap opened onto another ledge. Sheer drop down. The rock face opposite close enough to touch.

"I'm going down again," he sent. "There's a fissure."

Nothing.

"MJ?"

He thought she wasn't going to answer but she sent back a curt, "Roger that, Hil."

She sounded like shit.

He couldn't think about it.

He sat on the edge.

The trick to free climbing any vertical wall was to ignore gravity. He'd learned that a long time ago, long before the guild. However damned high it was. Just ignore it, defy it, freaking deny its existence and any pull it could possibly have on you while you eased yourself down, or up, and felt for one hand hold after another, one foot hold after another.

He controlled his breathing, balanced his weight and eased himself down.

It was tight but he'd made it through worse.

He worked his way down, slow and steady.

Alone.

No safety line.

No way out except to backtrack every single step.

Nothing he hadn't done before.

CHAPTER TWENTY-NINE

THE AIRLOCK SEALED BEHIND THEM, a long, reinforced tube, as if whatever was in there needed confinement beyond norms, excessive precautions, by anyone's means.

She followed with baited breath, questions on the tip of her tongue, of course she had questions, and she was about done with this prolonged drama Koschei was orchestrating.

He refused to say anything else until they were at the far door, then he paused, turned, and asked, his voice as low and onerous as she had ever heard, "Do you not feel it?"

She didn't. She didn't feel anything but irritation.

"Be grateful you cannot," he murmured, pain flickering behind his eyes. "From what I understand of events that conspired, Hilyer came to the conclusion it was an imagined phenomenon, an illusion, a psychoses. Not real." His eyes narrowed. "Believe me, it is real..."

He had to brace himself, hands and feet pressed to either side as the gap narrowed, dropping down, the heat increasing.

A warm humid breeze caressed his cheek. A hint of dank decay.

He risked stopping to grab a flare, igniting it and throwing it along the fissure. Red flared bright and dropped. Dropped as far as he could see. Jesus.

He had a horrible feeling he was in the wrong place, had missed a turning or a gap or a... The flare stopped, bounced and stopped.

He squinted down. He couldn't see anything. There was nothing he could do but climb down, one hand hold, one foot hold after the other, until he dropped onto solid ground and knelt, catching his breath in a tunnel that stretched in either direction as far as he could see. There was a pile of rope, rappel lines, strewn haphazard across the tunnel floor. That confirmed he was in the right place. There was also a thick vine twisting through it all, stretching along the tunnel in both directions.

He followed it down, holding the fading lumi-stick behind his back, just enough light to see by but not wanting to broadcast his presence. He had the knife in his other hand.

"MJ?" he sent.

Nothing.

He nudged the vine with his foot, half expecting it to move in response, like it could be sentient somehow. It didn't.

He stepped over it and moved on.

The tunnel dropped, narrowed and then opened up. He stepped out into what felt like a huge open space, stale arid air with a hint of leafmold to it, a heaviness, a familiar, disgustingly familiar taint. But something else too. Something he couldn't pinpoint. Fuel maybe?

He pulled a flare from a pouch. What were the chances this thing was a being he could talk to? A freaking alien that had set up home down here and was laughing at the chaos it was causing...

The Earth Empire used to have whole divisions of experts set up to make first contact with alien species. They'd missed their chance with the Bhenykhn thanks to NG. And now here he was, the only chance humanity had to find out what the hell it was that had decided to camp out on Kheris.

He waited another five minutes, waited another heartbeat then threw the flare, far as he could, engaging it at the last possible second.

It sailed out into the darkness and flashed red.

The cavern was immense. Smooth black bulkheads filled half the space, split open, vanes, panels, what looked like huge machinery parts crushed and littering the cavern floor.

The vine was winding into the midst of the alien ship.

Hil backed against the cave wall and crouched.

"MJ?"

Still no reply.

There was no sound. Every cave system he'd ever been in anywhere in the galaxy had dripping water as a constant, somewhere in it, wherever it was. Down here? Bone dry. He reached and touched the vine. It felt withered but alive, soft, a slight thrum vibrating beneath his fingers. It felt eerily familiar.

He stood and edged forward. "MJ, if you can hear, there's a cavern at the base of the fissure. There's a way back into the ship down here. I'm going back in."

As far as he was aware, he was the only human alive who'd set foot on more than two Bhenykhn ships and survived. The scout ship on Erica, the command ship NG had attacked and the ship that had taken him from Redemption. This ship on Kheris was nothing like any of them. But when he stepped on to that slick smooth deck plating and walked back into the crushed, devastated remains of the grounded deep spacer, that eerie niggle at the back of his mind flared, stomach turning backflips.

The light was reflecting off massive looming shapes in the depths of the wreckage, curved surfaces disappearing off into the darkness.

He had to force himself to walk forward, ducking twisted and bent stanchions.

They were Bhenykhn pods.

Immense brown chitinous pods, four, five, six of them, as far as he could see from the faint circle of light he was holding. He had to swallow down the disgust that rose in his throat at the thought of that alien goo rising to envelop him. Trapped as it flooded up and over his chest, his neck, up over his face...

He breathed through it, shut away the memory, and snapped on another lumi-stick, held it out in front of him, close up to one of the pods and came up, face to face, against an embryonic Bhenykhn corpse spilling out of the broken shell, reaching with skeletal arms, chitinous armour half formed.

He backed away, stomach cold.

This was not a Bhenykhn ship.

He knew, firmly and convincingly knew it was not Bhenykhn. Alien, yes. Not Bhenykhn.

He cast his eyes upwards, scanning the expanse of the twisted and broken bulkheads, ducking past twisted beams of black metal.

Yet this ship... had freaking pods on board with Bhenykhn inside...?

His foot nudged against a vine that was winding up and around a broken bulkhead.

If it wasn't Bhenykhn, what the hell was it?

"MJ?" he sent again, relief blossoming in his chest as she came straight back with a clear, "Hil? Shit. Hilyer, you okay?"

"MJ," he sent, hard and intense, "listen to me. This ship is not Bhenykhn. Do you copy? Not Bhenykhn. But it has pods. It has Bhenykhn pods on board. What the hell does that mean?"

There was no reply.

Shit.

"MJ? Do you copy?"

"Yes. Hilyer, yes, I copy. Not Bhenykhn. Where are you, sunshine? Because we cannot track you. And right now, comms are so intermittent, I..."

He was edging past them, stomach nauseous, stepping over pools of congealed and dried out crap on the deck, looking at the next pod. Sealed. He'd seen enough of these pods as they were dropped from troop carriers to thud to the ground, releasing fully grown, armed and armoured Bhenykhn warriors, seen them close up, damn right he knew exactly what they were and these were Bhenykhn.

There were also human-scale cables lying abandoned, lifting blocks, the rusting remains of generators, human kit, strewn across the deck. He kicked at some of the equipment, machinery tumbling as he knelt and nudged them, shining the light at them to reveal UM branded name plates. There were tool boxes in there, human-sized toolboxes lying broken and spilled open as if someone had left in a hurry.

He stood and inched past more intact pods, forcing himself to breathe. Chains were wrapped around one pod and abandoned as if they'd been disturbed in the process of trying to extract it. There was a gap between the next two, shattered shards of chitin sticking up as if several had been removed. UM's Bhenykhn had come from here. They were sure of that. He'd been assuming it was the one in the cage when he'd heard Taylorson's account, but maybe not...

The lumi-stick wasn't giving him much to go on but he was wary about throwing out another flare. He couldn't feel any residual energy in the deck or the pods. There was nothing to draw from, as far as he could reach.

It was deathly quiet. Shadows danced as he moved, nothing freaky, but he could see how someone could be spooked by it.

A glint of something up high caught his eye as his foot kicked against something soft on the floor. He looked down, backing off, lowering the stick light and swallowing back a curse. It was a body, human, wearing fatigues, sitting slumped against the bulkhead, legs stretched out, a rifle by his side, eyes staring.

Hil crouched, heart thumping, held the light up and reached for the guy's neck, expecting to feel cold dead skin, not warm flesh and a pulse. Shit.

"MJ?" he sent.

He held the light close up to the guy's face, eyes open and unmoving, except the pupils constricted. Hil snatched back his hand and scrambled backwards.

"MJ?"

"Hilyer, go ahead."

"There's someone alive down here. One of the search teams. But it's hinky. He's not responsive but his freaking eyes are open."

She cursed and he heard her relaying the information to the others, sending back to him, "There's no way we can get down there. Is it just the one?"

He glanced ahead, got to his feet and edged round.

"I don't know."

He could see at least two other shapes that could be human.

"Maybe not."

He spun the knife through his fingers. As he stood back, a shadow of movement flickered in, low down, a faint scratching sound as some kind of small creature scurried up the guy's arm, across his shoulder and leaned in to his face. Hil braced himself, about to reach in and knock the thing away. Jesus, as if this wasn't bad enough. But it didn't bite. It touched mouths, holy shit, as if it was feeding the guy.

Hil took a step away, stomach knotting.

"Hil, there's nothing you can do."

"I know," he murmured back, as nausea swirled.

"Complete the tab," she sent. "Then we'll figure out a way to get them out of there."

He turned away, had to, hated turning his back on the pods, the hair on the back of his neck prickling, every instinct telling him to get the hell out of there. The pods were dead. Had been for a decade. Whatever was in them had to be dead. He moved on, stepped forward, rounded a corner and came up against steps that fell away into darkness, massive steps heading down. He had to crouch and jump down each one. He'd seen this scale of structure before. All the Benny ships were huge. It was like raiding a freaking giant's castle. If they weren't Bhenykhn, then whoever they were they were as big as the Bennies.

He reached the bottom and turned. Black, twisted metal stanchions lined bulkheads that had folded in under the impact. Elaborate twisted designs in the black metal that were unmistakable.

Holy shit.

CHAPTER THIRTY

"*WAIT...*" *She stopped half way across the anteroom, listening as he relayed what he knew of Hilyer's venture into the caves beneath Kheris. "They had Bhenykhn incubator pods on board...? What were they thinking? Bringing them here?"*

"Whoever of our people it was, it was not sanctioned." He growled it, struggling to hide the discomfort that had seemingly magnified in the space from the airlock to the antechamber, as if they were getting close to something she had no awareness of at all.

"A prisoner I could understand," she said, "if they were on some kind of mission, but incubators? Koschei, we were here, preparing. Who, of our people did not know that? Why would any of them have risked bringing embryonic Bhenykhn here? Unless..." She had to stop herself from saying it.

He took it from her mind anyway and turned back to her, his expression thunderous. "Let us hope beyond hope that is not what happened."

"MJ?"

"Hilyer, I'm right here. Where are you?"

He forced himself to calm. "Inside the ship. I'm inside the ship. And, MJ... it's..."

He ducked under a beam, catching his balance on a deck panel that was angled and having to jump across broken beams. What the hell was he supposed to say?

"I'm right here, Hilyer. What is it?"

He had the lumi-stick on his belt, the faint glow enough to see the next chamber. Immense glass tanks stretched up as far as he could see, all of them broken, dried out, the vines winding in and amongst them as if they'd been feeding off whatever liquid had been in there. Clinically pristine glass jars and tubes were stacked high, mostly intact, all containing embryonic bodies that looked equally part alien and part human.

He reeled back. It was clean, immaculately clean, considering it had been down here for ten years, a million miles from the blood-stained hatchet experiments of the Bhenykhn shamans. This was something different. Here, there were Bhenykhn body parts in the jars. And dissected pod creatures. The leathery spikey pod creatures the

Bhenykhn warriors wore that generated their energy shields. The same pod creatures that lived in coral-like colonies in their ships and facilities. He'd seen them, whole swathes of them, on the capital ship and in Beijing. Alien as they were, it was still sickening to see them in such a state, desiccated, dissected and laid out as if someone was trying to figure out how they functioned.

The vines wound throughout all of it.

He backed away and had to bend low to squeeze past a section of the bulkhead that had collapsed, shimmied under it, straightened and froze.

"Hilyer?"

The hull of the ship had cracked open, the bare rock glimmering in the light of the stick, a low, narrow tunnel leading away, one of the vines heading into it.

He made his way over to it and knelt.

There was a whole new depth of fetid warmth to the air.

So bad he almost gagged.

It was big enough that he could crawl through. Elbows and knees scraping against the rough edges of the rock face. He'd been through ventilation systems that were more confined, but it got close at times. It was dry, dusty. Getting hotter as he progressed. He was starting to think he was an absolute idiot for squeezing down there, when it opened out. The stick light was about done, and wedged into his belt it wasn't giving out much light.

He kept low, extinguishing the light completely.

There was something in there, he could feel it. Not in the freaky ass, spooky sense that had sent the others freaking out, but a tangible presence that he could almost hear breathing.

He waited, motionless, barely breathing himself.

If it knew he was there, it didn't react.

He reached for a flare. Hesitated before activating it. And tossed it as far as he could.

The red glare flashed high and floated, illuminating a vast cavern, every inch of it lined with swaying pod creatures. Thousands of them, all sizes, all linked by the twisting vines, moving and pulsing as if they were under water.

He held his breath, stomach clenched, cold. He'd seen this before or something similar, on the Bhenykhn ships, at Beijing. Nowhere near this scale.

He edged forward onto a narrow ledge, overlooking the cavern. The pods were everywhere, not ordered in cultivated lines the way he'd seen them before. These were wandering, chaotically everywhere, gone wild.

If there was a sentient thing or things living down here utilising them, he couldn't see any evidence of it.

It was a sheer drop of about fifty feet to the cavern floor. There was no other way out that he could see, nothing for it but to go down.

He shimmied down the sheer rock face fast, dropping the last ten feet and stood there, backing away to press his back against the rock face, the cavern lit with that eerie red glow.

He tried the Senson again, got a flash of static, then a brief snatch of, "No, wait... Hil...?" It cut then nothing.

Out of curiosity he reached out. The general hum of low level AIs was there in the distance, the chaotic buzz of a few more powerful ones still whirring away. He was getting better at shutting them out, reaching out to listen when he wanted. Civilisation was still scurrying away up there.

Down here, the red flare was fading. Movement caught his eye as he scanned over the cave. He tightened the grip on the knife, shifting slightly, and tracking it, squinting to see what it was. Nothing he could make out from here. He moved slowly down, following one of the vines and using it to pick a path through the pods, risking a lumi-stick. There were more of the small creatures or something moving amongst the swaying mass of leathery pods. He crouched and watched as one of them scampered past, no indication that it knew he was there, climbing up one of the bigger pods, picking at its rim as if it was feeding. God knows what kind of creature it was, some kind of tiny rodent or marsupial, long nose and tail, matted fur and leathery patches on its neck and back that looked creepily like the mutant dog things on Redemption. He raised the light and scanned it across the floor of the cave. There were hundreds of the little creatures, thousands. All busying about as if they were tending to the pods. Weird as hell.

He reached into a pouch for a sample tube, trying Martha again and this time getting a clear link.

"God, Hil, are you okay?"

"I'm in a cave full of pod creatures."

"Pod creatures? What the hell are pod creatures? I thought you said there were landing pods."

"There are. These are the little pods. The shield pods. There must be thousands, no, strike that, millions of them."

There was a pause then, "Is that it? Is that what's causing the anomaly?"

That hadn't occurred to him.

"No idea," he sent. "Where are you? You all secure?"

"We've pulled back. Minor casualties, couple of people hit by wildfire when someone started shooting. We've evac'ed them. But it all seems to have calmed down. Elenor's okay. Someone tried to take out Taylorson but he's still walking. He insisted on staying. What are you doing now?"

"Watching a horde of tiny little furry critters busy about as if they're farming these pods. They're cute. I'll bring you one back. You can keep it as a pet."

"Hilyer..."

"I'm taking samples." He popped open the cap of the tube. "Then I'll find out what else is down here. The air seems fine."

"Roger that. Just don't take too long. I don't know how much longer we can hold here."

If they hadn't been in the shit, it would have been funny to hear MJ sound so freaked out.

He balanced his weight and leaned over to scrape a sample off the top of one of the pods. He might have been immune to whatever was going on but he wasn't immune to the stench. Even pulling his scrim scarf up over his nose and mouth didn't ease it. The pod had some kind of secretion, sticky, oozing out onto the lip of the top opening. He was careful not to touch it, pulling back slowly as the pod moved, almost reaching out towards his hand. The pod itself was like polished leather, nodules and veins pulsing, stems or roots, whatever they were, connecting them all he could see now he was this close. He caught a drip of the goo in the sample jar and backed off, looking around again.

There was no sign of any tech, no wires or cables, no AI activity, no footprints or tracks to suggest anything was moving around other than the little critters.

If this was it, if this was the avocado, he had no idea how he was going to take any of it back. The pods were all too big. Even the smallest. No way he'd get them back through the gaps he'd squeezed through to get in here.

He stood and picked his way further in, trying to not step on any of the vines, scanning the light from the stick across the floor and up ahead of him, the creatures skittering away as his feet brushed past them.

"How's it going, sunshine?" Martha nudged, still tense, sounding like she was an inch away from telling him to evac.

He stepped forward, hard pushed not to stand on them. "There's just a shit load of this plant stuff. It probably spilled out of the ship when it crashed and the facility exploded. It must be like freaking paradise down here for it, hot, mineral-rich. It could have spent the last ten years feeding off the radioactivity from the reactor explosion. But this is all there is. If someone or some-thing is using this to generate energy, I don't know where..." He trailed off.

There was an almost imperceptible change in the air.

"Hilyer, what's wrong? Oh, don't tell me you're..."

The hairs on the back of his neck were prickling.

"I'm fine. There's nothing down here. I won't be long."

He stepped over a vine, brushing it with his ankle, a shiver running up his spine at that brief contact. Stupid. He was spooking himself. He shook out his hands and peered forward, sweeping the light round and spotting a patch of what looked like buds or seed pods up ahead, small chitinous spheres hanging low off a twisting tendril. They looked like the pods the Bennies wore on their belts, closed up tight as if they'd just sprouted, tiny budding spikes protruding from the smooth surface.

He turned slowly, the light glancing around the vast space.

There was nothing in there.

"I'm coming back," he sent.

He crouched and balanced his weight again, holding Mendhel's knife and hesitating before reaching for a small bud. He touched it, almost recoiling from the pulsing warmth. The knife sliced through the stem easily and he dropped it into a pouch on his belt. He needed more of them. He pulled round his pack and reached for another, almost jumping as Martha connected with a curse, loud in his mind, jarringly loud.

"Hilyer, what the fuck? What just happened? Did you just do something?"

"There's a kind of plant thing," he sent back, slicing another bud, and more, choosing the smallest and taking enough to make sure, cutting off a few vine-like stems hanging with the things and dropping them all into the pack.

The back of his neck prickled.

"Jesus, Hilyer, talk to me, what the hell are you doing?"

He raised his eyes and glanced left, right.

She cursed, at him or someone else, he couldn't tell. "Whatever the fuck you're doing, Hil, stop right now."

Every one of the furry little rodent creatures had stopped, standing up on their hind legs, razor sharp teeth bared, staring right at him.

"Too late," he murmured back.

He slipped the knife back into his boot and stood slowly, hoisting the pack onto his shoulders, not daring to breathe.

It was eerily quiet.

He could feel a vibration in the air around him, an almost imperceptible trembling of energy, like lightning was about to strike.

He took one step back.

There was an ear-splitting burst of screeching.

And every creature launched itself at him.

CHAPTER THIRTY-ONE

THE CHAMBER *they entered was warm, dark, humid. The only light was a faint bioluminescence. She could smell the Bhenykhn. It had been a long time since she had been anywhere near their dreadful presence. If walking on Koschei's marble floors had brought back fond but tainted memories of home, then this foul stench brought forth the nightmares she had tried hard to eradicate.*

She stepped forward, hesitant to see what was in there.

A huge glass tank lined the wall of the chamber, filled with a viscous, clear liquid that seemed to sway as if under motion, subject to some kind of wave action, particles suspended within.

She couldn't help but be drawn to it. She raised her hand and recoiled as some kind of root or vine appeared from the depths and thudded against the clear glass right in front of her, writhing, reaching, as if it knew she was there.

"Is this...?" she murmured. She turned. "How did you get it...?"

He was keeping his distance.

"You've had this here the whole time?"

"No," he grumbled. "Would that we had."

He spun and sprinted for the way out, feeling stupid for running from such small animals until the first wave hit and those razor sharp teeth dug into his calf muscles.

He almost went down, staggering, catching his balance and driving on as they scrambled up the back of his legs, tearing scratches into his thighs, agonisingly hot scratches that burned with what felt like acid, shredding his fatigues as if they were light cotton not light armour.

He tripped over a vine and he did go down then, more of the rodents swarming over his arms, his chest, up to his neck. He rolled, feeling the teeth bite deeper as his weight squashed them beneath him, chest heaving and head spinning as the virus dealt with the onslaught. He pushed to his feet and staggered forward, trying to shake off one that had bitten deep into his hand, right through the glove, trying to shake all of them off, and only succeeding in making them bite harder.

He stumbled again over one of the vines and was twisting, trying to stay upright, when the Senson engaged with a high priority, Martha, sending, urgent, "Hil, Hilyer, talk to... What's hap...?"

Sharp teeth bit into the back of his neck and he couldn't think straight for a second. He fell to his knees. Scrambled up and ran, throwing himself at the rock face.

Any vague thought that they might be content with chasing him out of their cave vanished as he climbed, blood dripping down his neck, down his arms, legs burning beyond pain.

He climbed fast, throwing himself up the rock face, ignoring the swarm of creatures clambering over him, and just climbed, managing to send a deceptively calm, "Martha... MJ, come in... Where are you? I..." The one on his neck hit a nerve and he almost slipped. "Shit."

He threw one arm over the top ledge and heaved himself up, squashing one of them under his knee and cursing as its teeth bit down hard. He scrambled up and pushed forward towards the gap in the rock face, muscles burning, more and more of them clinging onto his ankles and knees as if they knew exactly where to bite to incapacitate. A sharp pain sliced through the back of his left knee and he fell, crawling his way in to the narrow tunnel and edging through, scraping his elbows against the rock to try to dislodge the damned things.

One of them clawed at his face, scratching razor-sharp talons down his temple, inches from his eye. He braced himself, grabbed it and pulled it off, ignoring the tears or blood streaming down his cheek, just moving getting harder and harder.

He wasn't going to make it.

The tunnel opened up slightly. He scrambled through on his knees, grasped at his belt with his left hand, bloodied fingers struggling to get a grip, pulled out a small spherical grenade, primed it in one slick one-handed motion and tossed it behind him.

It detonated, too close, a roar pounding in his ears as the tunnel collapsed, rock and dust billowing down on top of him, the screeching of the creatures reaching fever pitch. He scrabbled forward, crawling, coughing, one arm giving way, one knee fucked and a shit load of the critters still stabbing claws and teeth into him. He managed to get back into the alien ship, and got to his feet, doubled over, glancing behind. It was pitch black, only the dying lumistick on his belt giving any illumination but he could hear boulders and loose chunks of rock still tumbling.

His hands were shaking as he backed away. He could hardly see what he was doing but he used his left hand to feel for the creature gnawing away at his thumb, found what he reckoned was its jaws and squeezed. For a desperate second he thought it wasn't going to let go then it screamed and he managed to prise it off, flinging it away and reaching for the next. He gritted his teeth and staggered as he grabbed them, one by one, pulling them out of his flesh, breaking their necks and tossing them away. He could barely see in the dim light, blood trickling into his eye, and he bumped into the glass jars and sent one over, the crash echoing throughout the chamber, boots crunching on debris. His knees buckled and he fell, backing into a corner, wiping his cheek and eye with his sleeve, and pulling out a field bandage, wrapping it around his hand, pulling it tight and biting a knot into it, not thinking too much about the state of his thumb and wrist beneath.

He was trembling, not sure if it was blood loss or poison, low on reserves and nothing down here he could tap into to drain energy from. Nothing. Everything was dried out and long dead.

He wiped his eye again, trying to drum up the energy to move, when there was a crunch, out by the doorway.

He froze.

Footsteps and the sound of a rifle being readied was followed by a sharp crack. A bullet ricocheted off the bulkhead by his shoulder. He flinched away as another hit and he scrambled, knees sliding across the broken glass, bullets raking the bulkhead behind him. A glass vat right in front of him shattered, shards flying.

He pushed up to his feet and ran, crouched over, throwing the half spent lumi-stick to skim across the floor behind him, and running full tilt round and towards the gun, pulling the knife out of his boot as he moved and spinning it into a backhanded grip. The figure was making no attempt to move stealthily, silhouetted now in the faint glow. They had the rifle up, tracking and aiming about two metres behind him, as if they couldn't quite think fast enough.

He was vaguely aware of Martha trying to speak to him, ignored her, and ran up behind the guy, leaping and stabbing the knife into the back of his neck.

They both went down.

The rifle skittered across the deck.

Hil twisted the knife free and staggered away, pushing the body over, nowhere near sure in the dim light but from the fatigues and rifle it looked like the near-dead guy from the pod chamber.

He stood, backing away, wiping blood out of his eye, and dropped as another shot took him high in the chest.

The armour in the vest took most of the damage but not enough to stop the round penetrating. The second soldier was as slow as the first which was the only thing that saved him as the next shot punched into the deck where his head had been a second ago. He scrambled under a workbench, clutching the knife in one hand and holding the other against the searing heat in his chest. He had one chance to get the first guy's rifle, could see it there, just out of reach. He slid Mendhel's knife back into his boot, riding the pain and adrenaline, and ran for it, sliding in at the last moment, grabbing the gun, twisting and lifting it to his shoulder to fire even before he stopped moving.

If it was empty, he was dead.

The gun fired, three shots, right on target, then jammed.

The second figure hit the deck.

Hil fell backwards to lie there, letting the rifle drop, half-heartedly pressing the heel of one hand against the wound in his chest as silence fell. Every breath was tough. He couldn't move. And he had no idea if there was a third, or a fourth, half expecting the rat things to find a way through the rock fall on the hunt for dessert.

He quickly got his shit together enough to use the Senson. "MJ? Lane? Yani? Pen? Anyone?" Shit, Pen... It wasn't his Senson that was screwy. It was everyone else out at the crater. He was sure of that now. He should be able to reach a ship in orbit with a Senson Six, never mind someone as far out as the oasis.

He sent a tight wire targeted transmission, as clear as he could manage.

Nothing.

Maybe his was screwy after all.

He lay there. Damned if he was going to die down here.

He had the avocado. He was fairly sure this plant thing was it, was the thing generating the wacky energy readings and psychoses. He just needed to get out with it.

Yeah, that might be easier said than done. His eyelids were heavy. He knew he needed to move but he closed his eyes. Just for a minute...

．　．　．

"Hil…"

"Pen." He blinked. It was dark. Pain washed over his chest. Still on the Bhenykhn ship then.

"Hilyer, what's your status, bud?"

He was alive. Not sure how… or for how much longer.

"I've got it," he managed to send.

"Can you extract?"

"Pen…?" he sent, feeling his eyes close again.

"Hilyer, bud, listen to me. Where are you? Hetherington is coming in to get you but we can't track your beacon. Are you hurt?"

He almost laughed but the pain in his chest flared.

"Ship. I'm on the ship." He struggled to pull off his glove and flattened his hand on the deck but there was nothing he could reach, not so much as a flicker of energy anywhere.

"Hil, you need to get out of there. Hilyer, you have to extricate now. Do you understand?"

He thought he'd answered but Pen demanded his attention again, more urgent, with a curt, "Hilyer, move your ass. We're picking up movement from beneath that wreckage. You need to get out. Hetherington is going in there but you have to give us a clue."

He hated to admit it but he muttered, "Pen, I can't move."

Pen cursed. There was a pause then, "Have you used the insanity?"

What?

"Elenor stashed three vials of insanity in your pouches. Have you used them already?"

"Shit, no."

He couldn't reach the pouches.

"Small pocket, by the buckle."

He could do that. His hand was shaking, slick with blood, but he felt for the pouch and pulled open the strap, having to wait a second to drum up the energy to reach inside. His fingers brushed up against a cold smooth surface. He almost fumbled and dropped it but he managed to spin it, thumbed off the cap and pressed it against his wrist. The hit was fast, high and burned out in an instant. He reached for another.

"How are you doing, sunshine?"

"MJ."

"Help me out here, Hil. I have about fifteen minutes to find you and get out."

"Down the fissure then go down. Jus' keep goin' down."

He dropped the second one and couldn't reach the third. Almost faded out again but then he had Pen and Martha both demanding his attention.

"I'm good," he sent. "All good."

Shit.

He tried again and another shot of the insanity was taken more slowly, steadily. He gave it a moment and sat up, heat spreading through every limb, the pain in his chest receding. He grabbed the extra shot that had rolled away, thought about saving it for later and decided, screw it, stabbed it into his wrist and stood.

It was fake. This feel good hit of invincibility was totally fake.

He knew that, fine well.

He'd seen how badly this shit had affected LC.

It had a time limit.

But from the sound of it, they were all on a time limit anyway.

He took a couple of unsteady, wavering steps, reached down to take the rifle and pushed into a staggering run.

He got up the stairs, and slowed to a walk as he passed the huge pods, pain stabbing bone deep at every step.

There were just scuff marks where the guy had been sitting.

Hil had the rifle in one hand, a lumi-stick in the other. Killing Bhenykhn was one thing. Killing humans sat uneasily, no matter that they'd tried to kill him.

His foot nudged against a toolbox. UM. God knows how those guys had even got this far down into the ship. But somehow they'd managed to take at least one Bhenykhn from here. Alive. He didn't get any of it. Someone had brought the Bennies here. And for some reason, a shit load of the pods the aliens used as a power source had turned against them. If that was even what was going on here. As far as he knew, there could be a huge device one level down that was causing the whole thing. But the rodents hadn't attacked until he'd taken that bud. The soldiers had been sitting there, near as dammit dead, until he'd taken a bud and made a run for it. From what he could tell, these little pods were central to it all. He had a load of them in his pack. He just needed to get out of there. Let other people worry about it.

He made it out of the ship and into the cavern, walked carefully, one step after the next, across the uneven rock floor and ended up at the foot of the fissure, not totally sure how he'd got there. He was fairly sure no one else was going to shoot at him, drained what little power there was left in the rifle and looked up. He rested his forehead against the rock, controlled his breathing and reached for a hold.

Half way up, as climbs went, it was his worst ever, he decided.

He raised his leg, agonisingly slowly, and found a foothold.

Mendhel had told him once, forget what happened yesterday and screw what's gonna happen tomorrow, now is all, now is all there ever is.

He forced himself to breathe.

Now sucked.

Boy, did now suck something terrible.

He reached and inched his fingers up and forward into a hand hold.

He had the avocado. He was damned sure he had the avocado. Tab done. Acquisition bagged. If whatever it was wasn't going to let him go that easily, he was determined to get away with it. No different to every other tab he'd ever run for the guild. For Mendhel.

He sucked in the pain, felt the energy shift around him, and moved. Climbed. Climbed with everything he had. As if he was racing LC, not trying to save the freaking galaxy. Just racing his best mate, his annoying little brother, trying to beat the kid that had saved his life, in so many ways he could never explain. The guild standings had never been about the top spot. It was the race, that was everything. He'd needed something to chase after, and LC had needed something to hold onto. Now? Now he had no idea what they needed. Although that cold beer was still high on the list.

Beyond the pounding in his ears, he heard Martha shouting.

He reached, one hold after another. Risked a glance up and saw the ridge at the top. He could do this.

Except his right hand slipped, slick with blood, fingers cramping, just as he was balancing precariously on one foot. He fell. Closed his eyes and fell.

CHAPTER THIRTY-TWO

"*How did you get it?*" *She wandered over to a workbench where specimens of the bud-like pods were laid out, dissected, samples in jars...*

"*A more pertinent question would be what is it?*" *He sounded disturbed, uncomfortable.* "*I have heard them called the Zaschita. The protectors. The Bhenykhn use them. They assimilate, mutate, evolve... organisms and technologies... We know this. We have always known this, to our detriment. Why or how this organism came to be so powerful, we may never comprehend. That it was brought here by our people is not in question. Did they know what they had? Did they intend it as a weapon against the Bhenykhn? We may never know.*"

She nudged one of the pods, expecting it to be cold, dead, but it was warm. She withdrew her hand, unsettled. "*Could it? Could it be used as a weapon against them?*"

"To defeat them or control them?" He walked up next to her, his presence intense, looming and ominous as he reached bony fingers to take a pod, studying it intently. *"Possibly..."*

Boots landed beside him. He was aware of that as he lay there, stunned, flashes behind his eyes, the ground spinning beneath him. He couldn't move. There was swearing. Martha, he reckoned. Maybe someone else. He could hear voices but he couldn't tell if they were next to him or coming through the Senson. Someone knelt beside him. Cold stings hit his neck in rapid succession, making him open his eyes.

"Gotta go, hotshot. You ready to move your ass?"

He mumbled something, tried to move his hand to his chest to let her know he'd been shot.

She swore and sent over the Senson a sharp and clear, "Cobra red, do you copy? Alpha one niner, come in. Cobra is red. Need support at the top."

Shit, he'd never been red. Not once. And now he was, now when he was supposed to be freaking invincible, immortal. He tried to move his leg and failed. He could feel the virus healing him slowly, sending tendrils of heat winding through his system. But he was low on blood, he could feel that. Heart rate low. Blood pressure desperately low.

He heard someone shouting, caught the words, "Negative. Get him outta there," and tried to move as someone grabbed him.

He felt a bolt shock through his chest, like jump wires had been attached to his heart, trauma patch. It took a second or two before he could think, Martha or whoever it was with him grabbing his jacket and beginning to hoist him up.

"C'mon, sunshine, help me here."

"How...?" the hell did you even get down here, he tried to say, but he couldn't make his throat form the words. He might have sent it through the Senson because she replied.

"You have no idea," she muttered, up close. "Thank Elenor."

Drugs. Battlefield drugs.

She'd OD'ed for him. Holy shit, she'd OD'ed. For him.

He tried to move, muscles weak and refusing to respond. Nothing was working. He had that nagging pull at the base of his skull that felt like a concussion, if not worse.

She got him upright but he couldn't stand, knees going and black closing in fast, vaguely aware of a rappel line being attached to the harness on the light armour.

His head spun like he'd been on a four day bender but he managed to send her a slurred, "Wait."

She was wearing powered armour. How the hell she'd

got down there, he had no idea. It wasn't a full suit, but there was enough power there that he could feel it like someone was waving candy at a junkie. He needed it but if he drained her suit, he'd be killing them both.

She pulled him close, attaching her own line. "Hil, if we don't get out of here in fifteen minutes, these fucking heroics of mine will be for nothing and we'll both be dead."

She was trembling, eyes rimmed red, black circles deepening even as he watched, a wild intensity flaring in her pupils.

"No, wait," he sent. "MJ, if I black out, I'll drain your suit."

He could feel himself going.

"What?"

She looked like she was about to punch him. Put him down and throw him over her shoulder.

"Don't let me pass out. I won't have control over it."

He knew he sounded delirious. Insane.

His eyes were closing and there was nothing he could do.

She hit him in the neck with a shot of what felt like liquid metal, slamming it into his bloodstream. Heat flooded through his system like a tsunami.

"There ya go. You want it, you can have it. Now can we go?" She tugged on the line and slapped him on the cheek. "Stay awake."

He felt like he could fly. Wired high as a freaking kite. He could hardly move his legs but he could stay awake forever.

He blinked open his eyes to find he was flat on his back, staring up at the bulkhead panels of the alien ship. He tried to move, hand nudging against cold metal that was thrumming with stored energy. He'd drained it before he could think, a hit of energy sparking through his veins.

He couldn't think straight enough to use the Senson, head pounding when he even tried.

He felt someone tug on his belt.

"MJ?"

"Sorry, no. Riley's dead."

His stomach turned to ice.

The voice was familiar, female, clipped accent.

He couldn't place it.

He tried to move. Muttered, "Help me up."

"Did you get it?"

Lane. It was Lane.

She was opening his jacket. He didn't need medical attention. They needed to go.

"Help me up." His voice was thick, nothing working. "Where is she?" He wouldn't believe Martha was dead until he saw it.

"Where is it, Hilyer?"

"What? Lane, I need..."

He blinked, trying to focus. Her eyes were red with deep black smudges and pupils flaring bright. Whatever Elenor had been shooting everyone up with, Lane had taken as much as Martha had by the look of it.

She patted his pockets, sending stabs of pain spiralling through his chest. He couldn't breathe for a second and almost greyed out again but he felt her reach for the pack, tugging it off his back, opening it.

What?

She was taking the alien buds.

She patted him on the chest and muttered, "Well done."

The adrenaline rush gave him the strength to lash out and catch her wrist, lightning fast. "No, wait. What...?"

She leaned in close. "Hilyer," she whispered, "I know you never switched sides. Eloise knows you never switched sides."

She patted his chest again, harder this time, pressing down right on the gunshot wound.

The agonising pain spiked. His hand fell.

"You know," she said, "for someone so infamous for being such a hotshot superstar, you are immensely gullible. Did you really believe everything she told you?" She gave a harsh laugh. "Hilyer, Eloise isn't going to defeat the Bhenykhn..."

His stomach turned. He couldn't get the Senson to engage.

Lane leaned closer, whispering in his ear. "...she's

going to enslave them. Imagine what she will be able to do then."

He reached with his left hand, nudging cold metal he'd drained already and trying to reach further without her seeing, touching something that felt like a rifle and pulling energy from its battery cell. It wasn't enough.

"You're on the wrong side, Lane," he managed to say. "Whatever bullshit she's telling you."

Lane reached and stroked her hand across his cheek. "Gotta go now, Zachary, there's a war to be won." She backed off, having the effrontery to wave the buds in his face as she did.

He reached further, his fingers touching a cable, a power line for the floodlights.

Lane drew a pistol, pointing it at his head. "Goodbye, Hil."

He gripped it tight, sucked in as much raw energy as he could, fast as he could, closed his eyes and connected with one of the auto sentries. It whirred, spun, targeted and fired a burst.

There was a thud.

He kept hold of the cable, drawing in more and more energy, letting the virus run riot to heal the gun shot wound in his chest, what he was fairly sure was a break in his leg, a fracture in his skull. It was dizzying and he had to grit his teeth, jaw clenched, to keep that grip as tight as he could, knowing fine well that he was crossing a line from which there was very possibly no return.

He could hardly breathe, head spinning but he held on until he could freaking get his shit together enough to move and roll onto his side to look up.

Someone was speaking steadily through the Senson.

"Pen?"

"Holy shit, Hilyer, get the hell out of there."

He wiped his arm across his eyes, blinking, trying to see in the dim light of discarded lumi-sticks, a couple of spot lights flickering. He was back in the tunnel where they'd set up a defensive position.

Lane was sprawled out next to him, half her head blown away, blood spattered and pooling around her.

He struggled to his knees.

Martha was face down. Not moving.

Shit.

"Hil, get out of there."

Not without Martha. He scrambled across to her and pulled off her helmet. She was still alive but her suit was dead, drained.

"Pen," he sent, "what do I do to counter Elenor's drugs? Is she there? What do I?"

There was a pause, then a snap, "Med kit. Green vials."

He spun around. There was a kit lying discarded on

the floor, open, stuff spilling out as if they'd abandoned it in a hurry.

Every nerve in his entire body felt like it was on fire and he fumbled through it, blinking, trying to see what was green in this light. He grabbed a handful of vials that looked kinda green and ran back to Martha, punching them into her neck, well aware he could be killing her.

He had no idea if the drugs were doing anything and started snapping release catches on the armour, shrugging her out of it.

"Hil, you have to get out of there. We're picking up readings... There's something moving beneath the wreckage. We can't make out what it is but the rate it's moving, that position is gonna be overrun in..."

He missed what Pen said, working as fast as he could, strength still not quite there, swearing, a headache banging at the base of his skull.

"Pen," he sent, "you need to evacuate. Evacuate the whole freaking crater."

Martha started stirring, mumbling, and snapped awake as he got her arm free, that hand grabbing him round the neck and squeezing tight before she opened her eyes.

She was freaking strong and there was nothing he could do until she cursed, recognised him and let go, pushing him away and glaring at him, chest heaving as she sucked in frantic breaths and threw off the rest of the suit.

He caught his balance with a grin, coughing as he

leaned down to retrieve the pack that had spilled from Lane's hand and staggered forward as Martha grabbed his jacket and pulled him forward into a run.

"You ass, you drained my fucking suit," she yelled as they ran.

CHAPTER THIRTY-THREE

"*I CANNOT BELIEVE that Eloise Drake has gained such a foothold of power. Given everything we have fought for the past five centuries... To think the battle with the Order has come to this. That they should walk so blithely into power after all. How did we get this game so wrong, Koschei? How did we misjudge so badly as to hand the Order everything they need to thrive while our guild and our precious few suffer so badly?*"

He put down the Zaschita pod and walked away without a word.

She glanced back at the specimens, at his life work, research she'd had no idea he was undertaking. It wasn't just the game with the Order she had so badly misunderstood.

They made it up to the modular dome housing the decontamination unit before he collapsed again, knees giving way, head spinning, Pen ragging at them to move faster. The place was deserted.

He could feel the approaching tremor in the ground beneath his hands.

Martha dragged him up, swearing, coaxing, damn near promising him whatever the hell he wanted if he'd just keep his ass moving.

He couldn't think. It was as if all the flash healing had been superficial, and deep down he was still as messed up as he'd been at the base of the fissure.

He pulled in energy from somewhere, not caring where, and forced his legs to move.

There was a rumbling, ominous roar behind them, closing in, louder sounds up ahead, outside, one lone gunship waiting for them, whoever the hell was piloting it insane enough to stay behind for them.

They ran out into the blistering heat of Kheris' sun, sand hot beneath his hands as he stumbled again and had to push back up into a run. The gunship was hovering, sand blowing out in a flurry. It dipped just long enough, ramp down, for them to run on board, lifting as soon as they were clear and banking round.

Hil fell back, reaching for a handhold, someone grabbing the back of his jacket and hauling him clear.

The crater looked as though it was alive, a swarm of millions and millions of tiny creatures spilling out of the domed structure and flooding into the secure area, covering every inch of desert floor with a moving carpet of mottled brown.

The gunship banked hard.

He would've fallen out if whoever it was hadn't tightened their grip.

He heard over the Senson, "Igniting incendiary in three, two..."

The gunship fired, a deep boom that reverberated through his chest. He watched a wall of flame race around the twin perimeters of the cordon around the crash site. He could feel the heat wash over them as the gunship banked again, opening up, then lifting, hard acceleration that made his stomach lurch and head spin.

He breathed through it. Fumbled to reach a shaky hand to his backpack.

The avocado.

He had the damned avocado.

The gunship flew low over the desert, detonations sounding behind them, other gunships flying past to circle round and make sure nothing escaped that security cordon.

Hil closed his eyes after a while, someone still gripping his jacket, someone else pressing fingers against his neck and shouting for a medic.

He didn't care.

He was done.

As far as he knew Elenor had made it out of there. Yani too. And Martha was nearby. He was fairly sure it was her holding onto his jacket.

That was all he cared about.

He breathed, kept one hand firmly against the pack, concentrated on not taking energy from the gunship, for Christ's sake, and breathed.

They landed at the oasis, clean, fresh air drifting in as the ramp dropped. Martha was unconscious. She'd flaked out as soon as she knew he was safe, had been prised away from him by the medic who promised him she was stable, or at least as stable as you could be after taking that much shit.

He'd slowly drawn the energy he needed to start repairing the damage to his body and restore his reserves just enough to keep functioning without blacking out the ship. He knew without having to touch or look in a mirror that the scar tissue from the deep scratches around his eye would be matt black, a shimmer to it that wasn't quite human. As soon as they landed and walked off the ship, Elenor caught hold of his arm, pulling him to stop. He'd stripped down to a tee shirt, and watched as her eyes dropped to the bloody rag wrapped tight around his right hand.

He shifted his weight awkwardly. "I have to go."

"Not before you get that seen to," she said.

He glanced back at the medevac unit hustling to tend to Martha.

"I need to take her with me," he said, voice quiet. He wasn't about to lose her again.

"You need to speak with Pen before you go anywhere," Elenor said. "And I'm not taking no as an answer this time."

He showered, lingering, drawing energy slowly and steadily from the power supply as he stood in a torrent of lukewarm water, head back. He could feel the warmth disseminate through the fine lacing of black veins that extended out from the alien scar tissue to mesh with his human flesh.

As much as he wanted to get away from Kheris, he didn't want to face Elenor and he knew she was waiting and wouldn't let him avoid her a second time.

He stayed there as long as it took for the aches to ease, the strength to finally return to his muscles. He flexed his hand. The dull black material between his thumb and forefinger moved as flexibly as flesh would but it was as if a part of him was made of somewhere else. Not Bhenykhn. Not AI. Elsewhere. Like he didn't quite exist here anymore except in the shadows.

For someone who'd spent his entire life hiding, it was

an eye-opening blast of reality to realise that he now had no choice. And he was about to be found out.

Sebastian's offer was looking more and more tempting. If he wasn't too late already.

He closed his eyes.

He was screwed.

Elenor was in a room set up as an infirmary. He stopped in the doorway, hesitating to go any further.

She looked up and gave him such a look of empathy, sympathy, pleading, that he folded and went in.

"Hil," she said with a gentle touch to his elbow, "trust me. In all this, with everything that has happened, all that is going on, trust me."

"There's nothing you can do," he said, voice low.

"Let me be the judge of that." She gestured towards a bunk.

"Elenor... I don't need help."

He held up his hand. Healed.

She was hesitant, reaching, and he let her take hold of his wrist, barely touching his skin as she traced one of the lines of jagged scratches, the black scar tissue cool. Her voice was soft as she murmured, "It's fascinating..."

Not exactly how he'd describe it. He didn't move, didn't react.

She let her thumb linger on one of the worst scars, the one on his arm, the one where he'd stabbed a knife into his own flesh to save Edinburgh. "You're not taking energy from me."

"No." He looked her in the eye for a long minute. "You want to see?"

Elenor didn't flinch, barely reacted except to give a slight nod. She'd just given a whole squad of troops enough battlefield drugs to kill them, just so they could get him out of those caves beneath the desert of Kheris. He'd never seen her in this light before.

There was a tray with cloths, swabs, medical equipment, lying on a bench. He rested his hand down, facing up and took a scalpel, slicing it across his palm, watching as the blood welled. He reached to the light switch with his other hand, felt the energy humming through the wires and cables and drew in enough, slow and steady, for the cut to heal, a neat matt black line of the alien matter materialising to bond his flesh together.

It took seconds.

Elenor stared, looking up at him eventually as if requesting permission to touch it. He shrugged, why not, and kept still as she stroked a finger along the line.

"Someone told me there's a way to reverse it," he said softly. "To be human again."

"And give up all you have become? Would you do that? Would it be worth the cost?"

It felt like she could see into his soul.

She reached her other hand to his and closed up his fist, encircling it with both of hers as if to hide it from the entire universe. "Don't lose yourself, Hil. You are still you. Whatever else happens."

He didn't like to pull away and just said awkwardly, "I have to go."

She nodded and let go, started to fuss, clearing away the scalpel and blood-soaked cloth.

Hil shouldered his pack as he stood and backed away, muttering, "Keep safe, Elenor."

Pen was standing at the door. The big man stepped aside to let him through, ushering him forward with a quiet, "You and I need to talk."

They went out onto the veranda. Hil glanced left and right, taking in the armed guards stationed at each end of the walkway, facing them, watching them, as if Pen was expecting trouble.

"What's going on?"

Pen leaned against the railing, seemingly casual, but a hand resting easily on a holster at his side. "I'm assuming you have samples of this entity that's causing the anomaly," he said, blunt. "Are you giving it to Drake?"

To stop the invasion.

The pack on his shoulder suddenly felt immensely heavy.

He had in his hands a way to save millions of human lives on this colony, on this last stand bastion of humanity. If he took it to Eloise Drake.

Pen's voice was low, eyes dark, his scrutiny intense. "Or are you going after the cube? You know where NG is. You find that cube, you save the Seven."

Humans or AIs.

Hil stared back, that lump back in his throat, a bone deep fatigue starting to pull him under. Who the hell was he to make this kind of call?

Pen said again, "Are you giving it to Drake?"

"No." He swung the pack off his shoulder and held it out. "Give it to Evelyn. We can't let Drake have it. And yes, I'm going after the cube. If we don't have the Seven, we don't have a chance against either Drake or the Bhenykhn."

It sounded hollow, however he justified it to himself.

Pen paused before he took it. "I'll make sure this gets where it needs to be." He beckoned to one of his men to come take it, turned back to Hil and said again, more insistently, "You know where NG is?"

An uneasy knot inside made him keep his mouth shut. Not just that he knew how much Pen hated NG, there was something wrong that was making his stomach turn. He nodded. "Don't ask me where. I'll get Elliott to come here with the Seven and bolster your defences. We need to stop Drake, Pen. She's more dangerous than the Bhenykhn."

. . .

Pen gave him a fast courier, the Carpathian, an AI that was used to dealing with guild missions. He said his goodbyes, that cold feeling refusing to shift, and left, made jump and headed straight to a known RV, known to him and Elliott, no one else. He dropped a beacon and waited, drifting, nowhere near sure enough that he was doing the right thing to relax. What reception he'd get from Elliott and Sebastian, he had no idea. And the fact that he hadn't gone straight back to the Man's ship and the guild as soon as he was free from Drake sat badly, feeling way too much like the way it had been when he'd been rogue, way back at the start of all this.

He scuffed his boots along the deck, sat and put up his feet, glancing with unease at the isopod where Martha was still out of it, vitals stable but a long way from being okay.

He was going to NG.

That made it different.

Elliott picked him up after two days. Two days of fretting, pacing, dropping all the intel he had into the ship's system, checking fuel and thinking no one was going to turn up. Elliott and Iona dropped in next to him, Iona connecting with a nudge and a warm, "Good to see you, Hilbud."

Elliott wasn't so welcoming. "You chose one hell of a dark spot to reappear in," he said, walking onto the bridge as casual as if they'd arranged to meet for a beer. "What's wrong?"

What wasn't wrong?

"I need you to check me out before I go anywhere near anyone."

"Paranoid, Hilyer?"

"Elliott..."

"I've already checked you out, both of you, and yes, you were being tracked. I've neutralised it all. You are now clear to go where you want." Elliott looked him up and down. "Nice scars. Not bothering to hide them anymore?"

He was wearing a tee shirt. And no, considering the scars around his eye, it hardly seemed worth the effort. He didn't care.

"Are you okay?" Iona sent. "Where have you been?"

"I'm fine. I found Martha." His heart was in his throat but he had to say it. "What happened with LC?"

Elliott looked at him with an expression on his cold AI face that was indeterminable. But Hil could read his thoughts, and Iona's, and he knew the second he asked that LC was alive. He kept it from his face and waited.

"Luka..." Elliott wandered to the main console as data started flashing up on the screens. "How to keep this simple... the Bhenykhn know how to find him. We've sent him somewhere safe. Don't ask me where."

"What about NG?"

"Nikolai is more complicated."

"Awake?"

"Yes."

"But...?"

"It's complicated. What happened with you? How did you get away?"

Hil raised his eyes. "What do you know about a cube?"

Elliott frowned. "A what?"

"The weapon against the Seven. It's a cube."

"It doesn't exist."

"It does. NG took it from Pandora. Drake is hunting for it." He paused. He should have been saying this to NG. But how the hell could he not tell Elliott?

"Is that where you've been? With Drake?"

"She's building a fleet to attack Kheris," Hil said, edging away, talking as he walked backwards, heading for the airlock, bumps and clangs as Iona attached grapples. "The Bhenykhn are demanding she destroy it. And she's going to. I told Pen you'd take the Seven to help them."

"When?"

"Within weeks."

"Leave Kheris to us," Elliott said. He turned away. "Go find NG. See if you can get any sense out of him."

CHAPTER THIRTY-FOUR

"DID you have no thought as to what was happening with Hilyer? No wonder the child was feeling so ostracised, so alone. You gave him the alien virus. You knew what happened to him on the Expedience. Surely...?"

Koschei turned, eyes dark, not stopping as he led her through his domain. "I have not seen Zach Hilyer since the day I instructed Nikolai to use the virus." He gave a vague gesture with his hand, fingers cracking. "All this I tell you now, is hearsay. I have my sources. None as close to Hilyer as I see now I should have had. He is an aberration. Closer now to the AIs than his human peers in many ways. I had no idea what the virus or the electrobes were doing to him physically. The accelerated healing... it does seem to have taken a toll none of us could have anticipated. If I could have had more time with him... who knows."

Images of glass specimen jars, lines and lines of

Bhenykhn incubator pods sprang to mind. She shivered,
abhorred. "You experiment on them as much as the
Bhenykhn do."

"I do what is necessary."

"The Bhenykhn probably say the same."

Elliott left with no further ceremony, the courier heading back to Kheris once they'd transferred the isopod onto the gulfstream. Iona pulled jump twice before going to Sebastian's place at the FOB. It was hard not to feel apprehensive about seeing NG again, especially when Elliott hadn't given away anything, in what he said or in any thoughts Hil could pick up.

Angel Martinez answered their hail and welcomed them in, sounding tense. Not surprising considering the Bhenykhn presence all around. More than the last time he'd been there. He took the ship down to the surface, half listening in as Iona sent Martinez an update, not just the full briefing on Drake and Kheris he'd given her but more, from Evelyn, as if Angel had been out here for a while, and not just Angel... Hal Duncan, and shit, Quinn was there. That sent a knot into his stomach, like he was heading for a roasting. It had been bad enough having to explain himself to Pen... having to admit to Quinn that he'd been with Drake this whole time...? That was never going to go down well.

387

"And Angel," he sent, awkward as hell, "I've got Martha Hetherington with me. She just saved my ass on Kheris. She needs medical attention."

The last time Martha had been anywhere near the guild, she'd betrayed them to Zang. It wasn't surprising there was a pause then a curt, "Jesus, Hilyer, you don't do things by halves, do you? Just get down here."

They landed and he walked out onto the desolate moorland, the remains of blackened, dead undergrowth crunching to dust under his boots. A chill mist was hanging low, wisping lazily, extending white tendrils to reach at his legs as he walked. He'd seen the FOB from orbit this time, tapping into Iona's telemetry as they approached. The black devastation extended in a perfect circle around the Bhenykhn base, fifty, sixty mile radius all round. Nothing like the time he'd been here to recce the place for NG. It was as if the aliens had sucked all the life out of the place.

He kept his head down and went up to the gates, cold sweat dripping down his back. He had Mendhel's knife in his boot and two Hailstones buzzing around him, keeping close as if Iona knew how good it felt to have them there again. Even knowing Martinez was there, he didn't know what to expect and he wasn't going to risk getting caught up in any shit down here, not when Anya could still be around.

It was Anya who was standing at the gates as they opened to let him in. She gave him a wolf's smile and gestured him to enter, standing her ground as the Hailstones buzzed around her. She ignored them, just batting at them slightly as though they were mosquitos, and whispered as he passed, theatrically loud, "I will find out where they've taken him."

LC.

He glanced to each side. Huge Bhenykhn warriors were standing either side of the gate. Armed.

"Sebastian isn't here, if that's what you were hoping for," she said, voice colder as she dropped into step beside him. She slipped her hand around his waist. "What are you here for, Hil?"

"Where's NG?" He said it at the same time as he sent it to the others.

The Bhenykhn followed them inside. They were guarding her not him, he could figure that out easily enough from the subtle angles, the way they adjusted their step as she moved. Not him.

Anya pouted. "You didn't come here to see me?"

He kept walking, heart rate steady, breathing calm.

"We're down in the sub-level," Martinez sent back. "Don't listen to any crap that crazy bitch says. I don't know why Sebastian hasn't killed her already."

Anya tugged on his hand, squeezing hard. "Don't listen to her," she said, pulling him close, and reaching up to whisper in his ear. "Y'know if I can't have LC, I might keep you." She laughed and shoved him away.

They headed through wide corridors, Anya muttering to herself cheerily as they walked. She was either more insane than last time or she was the only sane one of them all, holding on desperately to her humanity amongst an alien invasion that was overpowering them at every move. She didn't have the alien virus. What she did was natural. Like NG.

"What's happening with NG?" he sent back, aware that even though Anya couldn't read him, she could overhear anything he sent, even tight wire, if it was to a human.

"Come see. Maybe you can get through to him."

"I thought he was awake."

"He is."

The security locks turned green as they approached. He wasn't sure if it was Anya or Martinez but at one turning, the two Bhenykhn shadowing them moved to block Anya's way. She rolled her eyes, narrowed them and shot a, "Catch you later, Hil," at him that wasn't exactly endearing.

He carried on, down more levels and into the medical facility where NG had been last time. This time, the isopod was lying there inert.

"Through here," he heard Martinez call.

She was sitting on a bench, elbows on her knees, staring straight ahead. Hal Duncan was field stripping a rifle, Quinn leaning against a wall, arms folded, looking unimpressed.

He walked in and saw what they were looking at.

NG was running on a treadmill. Fast. Pretty much sprinting with no let up in pace. Pounding out the miles.

Hil glanced at the others, and looked back at NG. He knew how that felt, knew exactly how that felt, he'd done it enough times himself. The Maze had been tough. Challenging. Mentally challenging. But there were times you just wanted to switch off your brain and run.

Martinez looked up, eyes tired. "He hasn't spoken a word since LC got him to come round."

There were two treadmills, next to each other. Human equipment, no doubt scavenged from the same luxury liner as the furniture in Anya's bedchamber.

"We've all tried keeping up with him," Martinez said. "It's like we're not here."

Quinn glanced across. "So how is your new friend Drake keeping these days?"

"Better than we are."

It came out more belligerent than it should have and for a heartbeat it felt like the big handler was going to jump up, haul his ass into a briefing room, shine a spotlight on him and beat a confession out of him. But Quinn just gave him a half smile and said, "We know," sounding weary as hell. "Well done on Kheris. Sounds like you dealt with it well."

That was a rare compliment. Hil shifted his weight, awkward, and turned to Martinez. "Drake is hunting a weapon to destroy the Seven. It's the cube from Pandora. We need NG to tell us what he did with it."

She gestured towards the treadmills. "Go for it. See if you can get through to him. He damn sure isn't responding to us."

Hil murmured, "Let me try."

This whole place was humming with energy. He was wearing fatigues and a tee shirt, lightweight flexible field-op boots. He didn't even need to change.

Quinn backed off, with almost an imperceptible nod. No one needed to say it... everything, winning, just surviving this whole damned war, everything hinged on getting NG back.

Hil set his jaw, sent the Hailstones to the door and walked up onto the other treadmill, initiating by remote, like old times, and starting off at a steady jog, ramping up to a run then pacing NG.

After two hours, he glanced at Martinez, didn't let up the pace and just said, "How fucking long does he usually go for?"

"Three full marathons. If not four. You're about half way through the third."

"What then?"

"Then he showers, sleeps and starts again."

Shit.

He was tempted to tackle NG right off the treadmill, just throw himself at him, punch him and see what happened. But he had a horrible feeling NG would just kick his ass and get back on the treadmill. Double shit. He didn't stop but he glanced sideways and sent, as tight and direct as he could make it, "NG, what are you doing?"

No response.

"We need you to come back."

Still nothing.

He started giving a debrief, direct through the Senson, detailed intel on the past couple of months he'd been out as if reporting in, the way they used to, pausing a couple of times to catch his breath.

Nothing. It must have taken him near on an hour and nothing. As a therapeutic off-loading for his own benefit, it was nigh on enlightening, clarifying, even with zero response coming back at him. He started to take his time, figuring out what had really happened, going over conversations, intel, seeing patterns he hadn't seen before. But nothing from NG. As if none of them were there.

Eventually he slowed his treadmill and leaned on the bars, chest heaving, looking round at the others through hooded eyes. Martinez raised her eyebrows, Duncan gave a little cocky tip of his head as if to say, yeah, been there, done that, and Quinn swore and walked out. Damn.

. . .

After five days he was ready to give up. It was as if NG was caught up in his own world and nothing they could say or do could break through to him. Hil walked next to Duncan, trailing NG back to the gym in silence. They'd all said everything they could possibly say. They'd had medics, psychs down here, the best specialists the guild had. Hal Duncan was one of the most powerful telepaths they had, second generation, closest there was to LC in strength, and he'd got nowhere.

"We should just take him back to the Man's ship," Hil muttered. "See if anything there..."

"Go for it," Duncan cut in. "He floored all three of us when we tried."

"What did LC say? Could LC not get him to talk?"

"We don't know. Sebastian dealt with it. Wouldn't let us near."

"But LC's okay?"

"Don't know. Your guess is as good as mine. Sebastian said it wasn't safe to keep him here and took off. Told us we had three days to get NG to respond or he'd take him away too. That was two weeks ago."

They watched NG fire up the treadmill. It was weird to see him so quiet. No eye contact. Just a pained expression now and then, a vague far away look, and this incessant running.

He hated to say it but he did, clutching at straws. "What about Anya?"

Duncan shook his head, dropping onto the bench.

"She'd kill him before she'd help him. We can't let her anywhere near."

Hil stripped off his jacket and rolled up his sleeves. He flexed the hand that had been bitten, aware that Duncan was watching, the black scars sucking in light like a black hole. None of them had questioned him on it. It felt stupid now to have thought even for a second that he could come back here to Sebastian and just be fixed, as if by magic. Back to what he had been. It wasn't looking like Sebastian was coming back any time soon.

NG was already running. Hil took up position next to him and started the machine, giving NG another run down on the current battlespace situation, going over positions and strategies, scenarios, possibilities, theories on how to break Arunday out of a lose-lose and coming up short every time.

He ran for another hour, hit his limit and cursed. "Screw this. NG, come run a tab with me." Just said it out loud, without looking. Breathless. And about done, even though he was drawing energy from the machine about as fast as he was expending it. "You told me, on Erica, that you'd reinstate the standings and chase us for the top. So come on, let's do it. Come run a tab with me."

NG slowed, the treadmill slowing to a walk. "What?" He said it so quietly it was as if he still hadn't spoken.

Hil stopped his own machine, just stopped it dead, leaning on the bars, breathing heavily, sweat dripping down his ribs. "Come run a tab with me."

NG slowed to a stop himself and looked up, dark eyes piercing, questioning as if questioning whether anything could ever be that simple again. "A tab?" he breathed.

Hil met that stare head on. After Skye died on Erica, he'd needed NG to tell him what to do. Straight forward orders, don't question it orders. No thinking. And NG had had no qualms. Even as impossible as it had sounded and as shit as it had turned out, being ordered onto that alien ship had been exactly what he'd needed – the more impossible the better.

"Simple acquisition," he said. "We can double up. Fast in, fast out." Wherever the hell this cube was.

There was a half second pause then NG said, "The cube? Why do we need the cube?"

Hil didn't blink. He hadn't said it out loud. He was sure he hadn't.

Martinez was standing at the door. She piped up without hesitation, sharp as ever and about as pissed off and done with it all as he'd ever heard her sound. "Where's the fucking cube, NG?"

NG looked round as if seeing her there for the first time. "On the Alsatia. In a vault in Legal."

CHAPTER THIRTY-FIVE

"Nikolai..." In all this, hearing of his plight truly had been the hardest to bear. To hear he was missing, captured, had been bad enough. To know what he had gone through, impossible to comprehend how any creature could survive such an ordeal. "Have you seen him?"

"No."

"But you have been meeting with Sebastian. Why could you not help him with Nikolai? Help them both? You promised me you would tell them everything."

"I have done what is necessary," he said again. He took her up broad steps to a huge door, black twisted metal, simply gesturing towards it with one hand, causing it to swing open. "I will admit, that has not always been what is right."

It was like a grenade had gone off. Duncan stood up. Martinez stood, staring at NG.

NG was standing there, bewildered, as if he'd just woken up.

Hil sent a fast sharp, tight as he could make it, transmission to all of them, including Iona, "Don't let Anya get that out to anyone. For fuck's sake. The cube is right here."

"In the wreckage of the Alsatia," Martinez muttered. She turned to him. "What the hell is this cube?"

"Drake thinks she can wipe out or control the Seven with it. Eliminate our advantage over the Bhenykhn."

"It was on Pandora," NG said. His voice was raw, like he was still trying to find it, not surprising if he hadn't spoken in almost a year. He swayed. "It's a metal cube." He made a shape with his hands. Not big. "Itomara knew what it was. He wouldn't tell me." He sat down on the edge of the treadmill, suddenly, as if his knees had given way, or he'd been hit by a brick, or it was just the reality of the past year hitting home.

Hil stepped off his machine and sat, directly opposite, leaning forward with his elbows on his knees. "We need to go get it. Now. NG?"

The look he got was haunting, instability flaring, but NG nodded, like he was sucking it up. "Yep." He scratched at the scar on his arm, absently as if he wasn't aware he was doing it, squeezed his eyes shut then blinked.

"I'm good. Let's go. Just a tab, yeah?" He looked Hil right in the eye and gave half a smile. "I'll race you for it."

"You're on. But there's something I need you to do first."

"I have to admit," Hil said as they took the gulfstream back up to orbit, sitting up front in the pilot's seat even though Iona had control, "I don't get the Bhenykhn on our side thing. After all the shit I've seen them do, how can you trust...?"

"We don't," Martinez cut in from the cabin area where she was with Quinn and Duncan, all of them suiting up into full chameleonic powered armour.

"You need to talk to Sebastian," NG said, quiet but clear. He was sitting in the co-pilot's seat, head back, eyes closed, feet up on the console. He looked drained, wiped out after healing Martha, neutralising the remaining toxins and repairing the organ damage caused by the massive overdose of combat drugs, getting her to a point where she was stable and resting in the isopod. He'd made it look easy but it was obvious from the way Martinez had got him to sit down afterwards that it had taken a lot out of him.

"I have talked to Sebastian."

"Listen next time, properly listen. And before you ask, no, I can't do the same shit that he can if you were wanting to take him up on his offer." NG gave a small wave of his left hand. "This is all his work."

Hil couldn't help staring. "How much do you know?"

NG didn't move, didn't open his eyes. "Know about what?"

"About what's been going on." For the past freaking year, but he didn't say that.

A long moment passed, then NG did sit up. He leaned on the console and rubbed the back of his neck, then said softly, "Before Beijing or after?"

Holy shit.

It was hard to know what to say to that.

NG saved him the trouble. "I know the Bennies hit Hanover and Aston," he said, eyes narrow as if he was having to concentrate. "I know Spearhead turned up again and I know Elliott killed it. I know Drake has set herself up as some kind of envoy, collaborating with them. And I know she has telepaths. Don't know where Ballack or Marrek are..."

The leaders of the other guilds. Hil had no idea.

NG glanced back at the others. "I know what happened to LC at Kheris." He scratched at his arm again. "It's been a while since I've been there. Last time was well before that ship crashed. I don't know if it would affect me the same." He looked back at Hil. "I know you got the avocado. I have to ask, who the hell named it an avocado?"

"Elliott." He shrugged. "Something to do with parrots and avocado trees."

NG had that enigmatic look on his face. "Did you leave it with Pen?"

Shit, he must have been tapping into the whole data drop, taking every detail. It had been too easy to forget how powerful NG was after he'd been so wiped out.

"I left some of it with Pen," Hil said. "Not all of it."

NG smiled, like he was impressed. "Do you have it here?"

Hil dug in his pouch and held out the bud. He was half expecting NG to recoil from it and go crazy but he just took it and tossed it up in the air, catching it and holding it up.

"It's a pod creature. The Zaschita. This is what they grow from?"

Hil shrugged. "There was a whole cave system swarming with them. Freaking huge ones, running wild, not cultivated like the ones we've seen on board ships."

"Doesn't explain why the Bhenykhn avoid Kheris. They use these things. Why would they...?" NG paused as if he was speaking to Martinez direct. He shook his head and handed back the bud as if it was an irrelevant trinket. "You seem to have new playthings." He gestured towards the Hailstones.

Hil got one of them to buzz in close. "You should see what we can do."

NG held up his hand and let it settle just above his palm, spinning slowly, speeding up as if it was playing. "I know what you can do," he murmured. He looked up. "And there's an AI working for Drake..."

That wasn't so easy to admit.

Hil nodded. "We've not been able to narrow down which one it is. They're being careful."

"I know."

The way he said it was chilling.

"Hil..." NG had always had a way of commanding a room. He didn't need to raise his voice, didn't need to demand attention. "I know everything the Bhenykhn know."

NG sat back and closed his eyes again after that, wouldn't say another word until they got to the debris field. Then he uncurled and stood, every small movement immensely deliberate, muscles powerful even after all this time out of action. It was easy to see how NG had got the reputation he had, how Andreyev had got the reputation he'd had.

He caught Hil's eye. "We haven't had much chance to work at this, have we?"

"No." It was hard to know what to say. He'd felt alone, isolated, ostracised, freakishly damned different to everyone since it had happened. No one understood. No one had even taken much effort to talk to him. LC had been having a rough time. Mendhel would have but he wasn't there. And he couldn't say it, but since the invasion, NG hadn't been there for him either.

A flicker of regret flashed across NG's eyes. "Sorry."

Hil grabbed a handhold as Iona pulled a hard manoeuvre. "You can hear me," he sent, tight wire to NG alone.

"Not all the time. I don't mean to eavesdrop. I'm sorry, I can't help it sometimes."

He'd never heard NG sound so quiet, contrite, awkward. NG always knew what to do, was always boisterously right, confident, assured.

Iona was nudging him but he ignored her. "Shit, NG, you don't have to apologise. I'm sorry. I'm sorry we couldn't find you. I'm sorry it took us so long to find you and then..."

NG gave that faint ghost of a smile again. "Shit happens."

"But you can hear me. Can you see me? I mean..."

"Nope. You're still a black hole as far as sensing you goes. Can anyone else sense you?"

Hil shook his head, standing as Iona steadied. "No. Not that I've encountered. It's shit. It's like I don't exist. And yes, I am tempted by Sebastian's offer." He clenched his jaw.

"When did that start?"

"The scars?" He shrugged. "Some time after Erica." The scar on his chest was normal, that's why NG was asking. The last time he'd healed normally. "It just crept up on me. I got in trouble a couple of times after..." He scratched at his hand. "Beijing was bad, that was the first time I noticed it. Sorry. It's just shit. All of it. Everything. What are we supposed to do?"

"Honestly?" NG stood. "I have no idea. Let's just go find this cube. I want to see the Alsatia again."

Looking at the real-time telemetry of the wreckage that was coming in was heart wrenching. Hil stared at the images of the only place in the galaxy he'd ever called home. Really truly home. And he'd thought it would be there for ever. His chest was cold, stomach heavy, just watching the scans and the schematics scroll and spin across the monitors as Iona took them close, right in amongst the debris field, fully stealthed, no danger anyone could spot them there. There were chunks of hull, fuselage, whole intact compartments, millions upon millions of pieces of smaller remains just drifting, caught in orbit. All that was left of the once immense deep space cruiser mixed with debris from all the ships destroyed in the battle.

It took them two days of scanning the wreckage to find anything they recognised.

Martinez murmured, almost too quiet to hear, peering close, "Damn, that's the Sphere. Half the Maze looks intact."

That wasn't surprising considering the shielding on the place.

NG was quiet the whole time. "LV Three," he said abruptly. "Find anything that looks like Legal."

Martinez turned to him. "No one's been back here since it happened?"

"After the initial rescue op, no, not that I know. We didn't have a chance straight after. Not with…" He looked vague for a moment, as if he was trying to recall.

"No," Quinn said, firm, stepping in and taking charge. "Sebastian has been hiding here the whole time. The system was swarming with Bhenykhn and Drake's forces for a while. No one's had a chance."

Hil shifted his weight uneasily. It was hard not to turn away, watching the scans map onto schematics that were familiar, corridors he recognised, the layout of briefing rooms and conference rooms, lines and lines of crew quarters unmistakable.

"That's Acquisitions," he said, voice low, stomach cold as ice.

"If no one's been here," Martinez said, "shouldn't we see what we can salvage?"

Quinn nodded. "Hilyer, suit up. And bring the Hailstones. We'll need to be fast. Iona…?"

She replied on a wide link. "What do you want first?"

NG was just staring at the scans.

"Acquisitions," Quinn said. "We go in together. We stay together. See if you can identify anything from Legal and Science while we're in there. NG…? C'mon, bud, let's get you suited up."

NG nodded, blinking as if he still wasn't entirely there.

Hil backed away, automatically reaching for his locker before he remembered he'd ditched the incursion suit on Redemption. Damn, that had been shit hot kit to lose. He opened the locker anyway, thinking he'd have to use a freaking EVA suit... and took out a black incursion suit. Not just black ops kit, JU kit.

"Thank Jameson," Iona whispered, private to him only. "He said you better take care of it, it's the last you get if you're going to be so careless with them."

CHAPTER THIRTY-SIX

THE DOOR *swung open onto a huge chamber, colder than the rest of the base, the lighting more bright, high ceilinged, hangar-like, echoing, aisles upon aisles of crates, immense structures, wreckage but all neatly stacked in lines.*

"The Alsatia." It sent a chill deep inside to see such remains spread out. She'd never visited the guild flagship, none of the humans had ever seen her, but in her heart they were family nonetheless these creatures they were trying to save. "This isn't the entire wreckage."

"It's what we could salvage. What I considered to be of note. Had I known Nikolai had so carelessly left the Pandoran cube there, believe me, I would not have rested until I had it safe and secure with me here."

Going onto the Alsatia, into the pitch dark, zero gravity, was surreal. Like entering a strange alternate dimension where everything was familiar but not. The compartments that had been breached were trashed, stripped and burned by the explosion. The ones that were intact were littered with free floating debris and dust.

They ran the incursion like a slick, practised operation, as if they were a team that had worked together for years. Hil took point, Hailstones at his shoulder, pulling his way through and busting open locks where he could, Quinn and Duncan following and using heavy lifting equipment combined with the powered suits to break through any doors and airlocks that were jammed. It was slow going, Martinez covering them from behind, and watching over NG who was still eerily quiet.

They headed straight for Ops, flashlight beams cutting through the darkness. It didn't look as if anyone else had been in there. Once they went through a couple of airlocks, it was just as if the AG and power had failed. He twisted, reorienting, grabbing for a handhold and scanning the flashlight over bulkheads and deck plating that was eerily familiar. They were in the corridor that led to the Chief's office. His heart was thumping with a dull thud. He knew that corridor well. Had been hauled in there, in trouble, more times than he could count. He didn't want to see it like this. So dark and still. It was too final. As if they were visiting a grave, a vault buried deep that should never be disturbed.

NG nudged past him and headed straight for the door at the end without a word.

Hil held back. He didn't want to go through there, didn't want to see it so abandoned. He waited, let Martinez and Duncan pass, and just gripped the conduit he was holding as if he'd fall if he let go.

Quinn stopped and gripped his shoulder. "You okay?"

He wasn't but he nodded.

Quinn switched to a tight, private link. "Frank O'Brien sends his thanks."

"What?"

"Edinburgh. She wasn't always Sean's ship..."

He didn't understand.

"Frank would've been devastated to lose her," Quinn sent. "What you did to save her... Frank asked me to give you his thanks, said he's in your debt, and trust me, that means a lot coming from Frank. Said you're family now, as much as LC is. You did well. Mend would be proud of you."

Quinn squeezed his shoulder and headed into the office.

Hil twisted in the zero gravity, a lump in his throat, not wanting to think about it, looking around, not wanting to think about anything. The field-op quarters were two corridors away from here. His stomach turned at the idea he could go in there, find his room, his bunk... in this dark, cold shell of what used to be his home. Screw that. There was nothing there that he needed. He'd come on board the Alsatia with nothing but a black eye, and he'd left it pretty much the same way. He'd lost anything material he cared about when he'd lost Skye.

LC though...

Shit.

He called out to the others, telling them he'd be right back. They were busy doing big guild stuff, stuff way above his pay grade. He'd only ever been in that office down there when he'd screwed up, when the Chief had chewed out his ass and told him to do better. He didn't want to know what kind of intel might be stored in there, what assets or information they could retrieve. NG and Quinn could handle all that.

Martinez called back saying as much. So he was free to go.

He spun, reaching for another hold and pulling himself along, weird to be in zero-g in such a familiar place, a corridor he'd walked along so many times, taking for granted the AG and not for one second considering the vast expanse of space and vacuum beyond the bulkheads and hull of the huge ship.

The mess was dark. He didn't even look into it, didn't want to see it. Didn't want to think there might be bodies in there. People he'd known...

He turned into their corridor and didn't need the beam of light to find his door, and LC's next to it.

The Hailstones backed off, as if Iona knew this was

private, like she knew he needed a moment alone, even from her.

He cracked the lock, having to input just enough power to make the mechanism cycle, and pushed into the dark chamber. LC had never been big into possessions either. There were a few bits and pieces drifting in there, hanging in midair, weightless the way LC and Sean had been on Edinburgh when he'd found them. He shut out that thought and turned, reorienting himself so the room seemed the right way round, casting the beam of light over to where he knew the lockers were. He didn't want to be in there. Didn't want this to have happened. No matter what he was sent to do, where he was sent to do it, the Alsatia had always been home. Ever since he was fifteen and LC had persuaded him to come back after everything that had happened at Redemption and the Academy. Even now, even knowing what had happened, having watched it happen from the Man's ship, he had a memory of the Alsatia that was so real, it was as if it was still out there, just elsewhere, flitting from jump point to jump point, there if he ever needed to go back...

He ran the light over the locker door, a door he'd seen, right there, for over ten years, LC's quarters as much home to him as his own. He bust the lock and opened the door, knowing exactly what he'd see, floating there in zero-g, cast-iron proof – against everything he'd fooled himself into thinking over the past year – that nothing was ever going to be the same again.

He reached in and curled his hand around the dog tags, the chain trailing in spirals. LC should have been there with him to get this stuff. To raid the place they'd lived in for ten years together, the home they'd found, that Mendhel had brought them to.

It was supposed to have been indestructible.

No one messes with the Thieves' Guild...

He caught the tiny pocket knife and reached for the throwing knife with his other hand. Mendhel's knife. LC's knife. Twin of the one in his boot. It was strange to have them both in his possession. Wrong in a way that made his heart cold.

Martinez was calling him by the time he left, nudging the door closed behind him carefully as if he had to preserve the quarters somehow, as if LC might be able to come along and see for himself. As if the ship might somehow put itself back together and they could all come home.

"Right here," he sent back, a lump in his throat, stuffing the dog tags and the knives into a side pocket of the suit, not easy in zero-g with hands that were trembling inside the gloves.

"We're done," Martinez sent, appearing in the corridor and signalling him to move. "Let's go. You okay?"

The Hailstones buzzed close. He could feel Iona's concern.

"I'm good," he managed, not convincing but sucking

it up. He needed to go. Done. Wanted out. Wanted to find this cube and get somewhere safe so they could regroup and figure out what to do next. He wanted NG to make everything okay. He looked up. "Where's NG?"

"Gone ahead. They're waiting for us."

He was picking up from Iona that Quinn had told her to find Legal, now, scan for anything that could be a secure vault, no more screwing around.

Seemed like they all wanted out.

It took another three days of painful, meticulous scanning of the debris field before Iona homed in on another section of wreckage.

NG was quiet. Disturbingly quiet. NG was never this quiet. Never this still.

The others started kitting up the instant Iona said she had it, securing their helmets and readying the rest of the incursion gear they'd brought.

Hil was still looking at NG. Wanting him to say something. Needing him to be the one to take charge and not just stand there, staring, distant, as if he was elsewhere, but, Christ, that was understandable. It was impossible to get anywhere near comprehending what he'd been through this past year...

To expect him to snap back into action straight away...

As if nothing had happened.

Hil glanced at the screens. A hollow pit of cold hit his

stomach. This was the Alsatia, this debris orbiting the FOB they'd attacked was the Alsatia, along with half the Earth-Wintran fleets, destroyed as a direct consequence of NG's decision to attack the capital ship... NG's decision...

He couldn't begin to imagine what the weight of having to make calls like that was like. He was a grunt field-op, to be wound up, pointed in the right direction and sent out, strict instructions each time, always a brief, always a target. Even now. That's all he was. Go get this, go get that. No need to think. Even Drake had seen that. Even Elliott just used him to go fetch. There wasn't even the pressure of the standings board anymore.

"It's not there," Iona said.

NG still didn't react but Martinez cursed and came back to peer closely as Iona manoeuvred round and threw a real time view onto the main screen. The compartment had a neat hole blown in its bulkhead, a sucker-like attachment secured around its rim, sealed to make an airtight ingress a ship could dock with. She zoomed the view in close to focus on a corporate insignia stamped on the mechanism. "Anyone know what that is?"

It was a defunct corporation.

Stirling.

"Drake," NG said under his breath. "She's beaten us to it."

. . .

They hooked the gulfstream up to the ingress and went through, straight into the vault. The massive vault door that led in here from what remained of this compartment of Legal was still sealed. Drake's people hadn't bothered working their way through to it, just blasted right through the bulkhead from outside. As if they'd known exactly where it was.

Hil followed Martinez as she pulled her way into the vault first, shouldering aside metal strongboxes, tools and other bits of detritus that were free-floating in the dark space, casting the beam of his flashlight around the devastation, a cloud of glass fragments glittering as each shard spun off in new trajectories in their wake.

"Who knew?" Quinn said, coming up behind them, grabbing a hold and twisting to retrieve a box that was tumbling just above the deck.

"Itomara." NG was still by the airlock with Duncan as if he didn't want to set foot on the Alsatia again. "No one else. And he didn't know what I did with it. I logged it in as a piece of art. I couldn't get it to do anything. I didn't want Science messing with it in case it was a bomb..." He trailed off.

Shit, what could they say to that?

"Yeah, that worked out well," Martinez muttered. "So no one knew?" She turned to him, holding the shattered remains of a containment case. "But Drake has telepaths?"

Hil nodded. Itomara could have had it picked out of

his mind without even knowing. Assuming Itomara was loyal still and hadn't just told her...

Martinez spun slowly, turning back to NG.

"I don't know," NG said out loud, vague as if he was struggling to stay with them.

Hil nudged a piece of debris and watched it tumble. "Don't know what?"

"How did they get in here without Sebastian knowing?" she said. "As far as we know they don't have anyone like you."

"Drake's working with an AI," he said, trying not to sound pissed that they weren't including him in their conversation. He kicked again at a chunk of metal, leaning down to grab it as he recognised what it was. He held it up. "Drones." The Bhenykhn wouldn't have had a clue.

"So what now?"

Hil grabbed a handhold and manoeuvred back round to the airlock to stand in front of NG. "We need to find it. Where would she have taken it?"

NG blinked as if he was refocusing, coming back from wherever his mind had wandered off to, or concentrating again on the here and now as if he'd been listening to something far off. "Kheris," he murmured, dark eyes glinting in the reflected light. "Drake has an AI working for her? And she has the cube? Elliott just took the Seven to Kheris. All of them. In one place. We just delivered Drake everything she needs."

CHAPTER THIRTY-SEVEN

"*THE PROBLEM*," Koschei pondered as he headed deep into the hangar, footsteps echoing, "*was that no one, none of us, realised the nature of the cube. Not its true nature, its true power.*"

"Not even Drake?" It made her cringe to even say the name. "She is Order. Her ancestors created the Seven, created the cube. Surely..."

"*She underestimated its capacity given the circumstances into which she introduced it. She may have lived far longer than her fellow humans through the various means she has employed, but her command of serendipity and indeed its opposite, the occurrence of misfortune, random or otherwise, due to a cascade of unforeseen events, is sorely lacking. She considers herself immortal, and immune to happenchance. I fear, that with the cube, she may have met her match.*"

It was Iona who cut in. "We need to go now." She pulled back the Hailstones and started gearing up the engines of the gulfstream even as they were piling back into the airlock, abandoning the wreckage of the Alsatia.

Martinez was swearing. She turned on NG as she was hustling them back inside and switched to speaking out loud, for his benefit or not, he couldn't tell, but she was raising her voice, as if she'd tried already and couldn't make NG understand. "I can't go to Kheris, NG. And dammit, I'm not going to let you go. It's a fucking trap. You know it's a trap. Bad enough that she has the Seven. I'm not going to let her get you too."

Hil couldn't help but overhear as she switched to the Senson, "Iona, I have a ship at the FOB. Get it up here."

"Already on its way."

NG was backing onto the gulfstream. "Don't make me sit this out, Angel. Go, let Evie know what's happening. But let me go to Kheris. I've missed enough of this war." He had a look on his face and a way of speaking that was hypnotic, persuasive enough that Hil found himself nodding, calm and feeling like this was right, even though NG was speaking to Martinez, not him.

Martinez flinched away, snatching off her helmet, pale eyes furious. "Don't fucking do that to me, NG. Not now. For Christ's sake, I know you can do whatever the fuck you want, but not this. We just got you back."

Hil shifted his weight, awkward as hell. This felt immensely private but this was his ship and there was hardly anywhere he could go.

Quinn stepped in and steered him away without a word, directing him to kit up, and it was easy then to get busy, stashing his own helmet and checking on Martha, as Iona withdrew from the wreckage and flew them out of the debris field. He had no idea what to expect when they got to Kheris but he grabbed holsters and pouches, ditching the incursion suit, and gearing up with weapons and ammo from a store it was a relief to see had been restocked.

He got a nudge from NG through the Senson, just a gentle beckoning of his hand, no words, and got the message clear enough, throwing a belt and holsters across and ignoring the glare Martinez gave them both.

"We don't even know if you'll be okay at Kheris," she threw into the mix, looking like she was having to stop herself wrestling NG to the deck to stop him from going.

NG didn't stop gearing up, taking everything Hil threw across.

Quinn spoke up with a calm, "Angel... we have more than one jump ship out here. I can take NG. We'll stay back, see how he is and if anything happens, we can jump out. Iona..."

The Thundercloud replied with a cocky, "Yessir," already on that too.

Martinez wasn't happy. "Quinn..."

"Get Evie to send back up," the big handler said.

Duncan nodded.

"Where's Itomara?"

"Don't know," Hil said. "He was on Temerity last time I saw him. Working with Drake."

NG raised his eyes, throwing him a look that was unfathomable, continuing to secure a holster to his thigh. "I don't suppose Anton surfaced anytime in the last year, did he?"

Anton was on their watch list. High Guard of the Order. And not a peep out of him since the invasion. "Not that I know."

"Where's Jiro Tierney?"

"With Evelyn," Quinn said.

It was like another insanely fast debrief.

Martinez was watching them. She took a step back, face set in that neutral way every soldier has before battle. Shit happens, and you deal with it. No matter that she was as pissed as he'd ever seen her.

"We'll send Tierney and DiMarco," Duncan said. "NG, we'll send everyone we have."

Except the telepaths.

It was quite liberating to feel like this was his show for once, not the one left out, or sidelined, this was his domain. He tossed NG a black wristband, guild, his spare, the best stealth kit they had.

NG caught it and for a fraction of a second it looked like his resolve wavered.

Hil connected with the Senson, no etiquette of permissions, just a fast, "What was the toughest tab you ever ran?"

As Andreyev. They'd never had the chance to talk about that either.

NG looked up and replied without hesitation. "Temerity."

"You should see it now. You'd have a field day."

That was it. That was all he said. He wasn't big into speeches. Shit, he'd never inspired anyone in his life. LC to be an ass maybe.

NG nodded slowly, rolled up his sleeve and snapped the band into place, flexing his hand as it connected.

It was as if that, out of everything, meant he was back.

"Thank you," NG sent back softly.

Hil continued to sort his gear. "You're welcome. It's not like I'm asking you to go alone into a freaking alien ship or anything."

NG almost laughed. That was a win.

If Martinez was reading NG's mind, she ignored them, yelling Duncan and Quinn to give her a hand piling stuff out of kit bags into the storage lockers, boxes of ammo, grenades, auto sentries, for Christ's sake.

She saw him looking. "You do this without me," she muttered, "I'm gonna make sure you have enough damn bullets. Put one in Drake for me." She heaved another box into stowage and punched the slow release on the isopod with her fist as she passed. "Wake up time, Hetherington." She turned to him. "Look after NG."

Hil said, "We will," and moved close, looked her in the eye, and took out the dog tags and the knives. He held them out.

She stopped what she was doing.

"I need you to give these to LC."

She didn't look at them, just took them, curling her fist around the tags. "And look after yourself, Hilyer. See you at the RV?"

"Yeah," he said, weird to be on the other side of that lie. "Tell LC he owes me a beer."

Iona dropped them in system, close up to Kheris, closer than was safe by any means, telemetry kicking in as soon as they cleared jump, proximity alarms screaming, warning of incoming. She shifted mass hard and fast, repositioning, launching counter measures and returning fire without hesitation. Hil grabbed a hold on the console, the harness pulling tight, watching as the screens filled with markers, the resistance fleet and the blockade they were expecting and more, ships he recognised from Drake's fleet, and the Seven.

They were holding their own but even with the vast firepower of the Seven, it was looking desperate. Iona pulled another manoeuvre that made his stomach drop. He clenched his jaw, muscles straining against the forces as the AG struggled to keep up, and reached out to Pen and Yani on a tight wire link. Nothing. They weren't being jammed, Drake's forces needed comms as much as their own. The Senson connected with Martha, right there beside him. Pen just wasn't there.

"Shit. I can't find Pen, can you?"

Martha muttered a negative, working the main console, trying to figure out some sense from the battlespace stats Iona was throwing over to them.

Hil glanced across. If she was trying to make contact herself, with the other side, he couldn't tell.

"Quinn, NG...?"

"Yeah, roger that, Hilyer," came back instantly from Quinn. "We're here. NG is fine. We're moving in."

NG didn't reply but he sent a wide communiqué, guild-wide, all personnel, as Iona moved, firing.

The deep reverberations rumbled through the gulfstream, nothing they could do to help, nothing they could do but watch as she sent bombardment after bombardment into human warships that were firing at the guild and resistance vessels.

"I thought we were supposed to be fighting the Bhenykhn," NG sent, a disbelief in there at seeing this first hand, as if he'd dropped into a different war than the one he'd left a year ago.

Hil nudged the screen. There was nothing he could say. The resistance forces were taking a pounding. The

Bhenykhn ships controlled by the Seven were all that was keeping Drake's forces from attacking the colony.

NG sent wide, "Elliott...?"

"Welcome back to the war, Nikolai."

"How long can you withstand this?"

"We can do this all day," came back the reply. "Your resistance forces? That's another matter. You have to understand, Nikolai, the resistance is on its knees. Drake's ships have been serviced, well maintained. They are fresh from dockyards. They have fuel, munitions. They are prepared for this battle. We're not. We're doing our best. But if you don't want to lose any more ships, I suggest you try whatever means you have to dissuade them."

NG cursed and sent him a private, "Hil, who's in control of Drake's fleet?"

They were getting a dizzying volume of incoming messages from the surface, guild ships in the midst of the battle and other resistance vessels, including the Emperor's own flagship, Christ knows where Wu himself was, and Ostraban's command, Olivia Ostraban right there in the middle of it all. LC would have had a fit.

Hil closed his eyes, shutting it all out, and focused, connecting with systems he'd hacked into so many times it was like second nature.

"Connelly," he sent back, heart pounding with a hit of adrenaline.

It was Connelly. He ground his palms into his temples.

Shit, Tatia Connelly had been one of theirs. Imperial Navy. When the hell had she defected to Drake? He hadn't caught any hint of her involvement when he'd been at Drake's base. He stared at the screens, a horrible, cold feeling settling deep inside that Lane was right. Christ, even Elliott had said it. The intel he'd been given access to had been limited. On Temerity and with Drake. He was an idiot. A damned idiot.

"Get me a link," NG sent, voice cold.

Hil connected, hacked into their systems with vicious efficiency and threw the data to NG.

"Tati," NG sent, open link to every Senson out there, "stop this. We're supposed to be fighting the Bhenykhn. What the hell are you doing?"

Hil kept the connection open and started raking through their ops controls by remote. In normal circumstances, there was no way anyone from outside could access anything anywhere near critical ship's systems but then he wasn't just anyone anymore.

He worked fast, keeping half an ear on the link with Connelly, listening in as the commander fired back instantly, "NG, welcome back. But listen to me, NG... this war is not the same one you dragged us into out at that FOB. Don't stand in our way. We do not have to do this. Let us take Kheris and we can all survive this battle for another day."

"We're on the same side, Tati. Call a ceasefire."

"NG, stand down and you and your people do not

need to die today. We are taking Kheris. Stand down and we can discuss terms of your surrender."

"Screw that," came through on a tight private link. "I don't suppose Drake is here."

It was hard to switch out and refocus. He was almost at the heart of Drake's flagship. "Give me a minute," he murmured. He just needed to...

A jagged edge of corruption shot through the link, extending back into his neural interface like a shock of insane feedback. He froze, stomach twisting and cold sweat breaking out on every inch of exposed skin. It felt like he'd sprung a trap. His stomach clenched, sparks shivering behind his eyes. He hadn't. He damn sure had not missed a trap. He breathed through it, tried to pull back and couldn't. He couldn't break free. There was something else there, jarring, that rusty nail scraping against his synapses, the sharp edge of a presence that was wrong.

A rusted scream of raw noise sawed its way into his brain. Insanely twisted, dark and malicious. He tried desperately to block it out, shy away from it, protect himself somehow, anyhow, but he couldn't breathe against the onslaught of the vicious waves of thought bombarding his mind. What? Not here... He was vaguely aware of his elbows hitting the console, Martha calling his name, Iona sending an urgent, "Hil, NG... Hilbud...?" but he couldn't respond. Couldn't do anything but sag down onto his outstretched arms, limbs like jelly.

He forced himself to breathe, started to block it out an inch at a time and pushed against the corruption until it vanished with a wisp, only a trace remaining, as if he'd pushed it over a cliff edge.

He opened his eyes.

"Negative," Quinn was saying as sound filtered back in. "What the hell are the Bhenykhn doing here? Elliott...? Damn it."

Iona was demanding his attention.

He flinched, blinking, trying to focus on the main screen. It was a Bhenykhn ship. One of the huge deep spacers. He stared, cold hitting his stomach like a weight. "It's not the Bhenykhn. It's Drake's AI."

CHAPTER THIRTY-EIGHT

SHE WAS STRUGGLING to keep up, both with his stride and with what he was saying. "An AI in a Bhenykhn ship? Was that not how the Seven took control of their vessels when Aries released them?"

He continued to lead her through this chill mausoleum, the final resting place, the remnants of the Alsatia, such a magnificent flagship, lying dead and dismembered on all sides.

"The Seven are different," Koschei muttered, "way beyond any other AI. They integrated themselves with the Bhenykhn biomatter, melding fluidly, bio-organism to bio-organism. Drake turned an AI to her cause. As much as Aries may have denied that as a possibility, it happened, the reasons why far more complicated and unfathomable to even those of the Seven."

She stared at a section of burned and crumpled hull as

they passed. "So much has happened." An Earth year was nothing to her kind, and yet she should have known how much damage could be wrought here amongst the humans who lived and died so fast.

He threw her a glance that was as cold as the air. "The events we witness now were seeded much further back in the past than a mere year. An AI with that much hatred? And no, it did not merely meld with the Bhenykhn bio-matter. What they have done is far more insidious."

He sat up. "Shit, Elliott, get out of here. It has the cube."

Like a switch, the immense presence of the Seven vanished from his mind. It was as if they'd just jumped away, but he could see them, the massive Bhenykhn ships the others of the Seven had commandeered, out of place here at Kheris, Elliott's ship, El Pato Loco, amongst them. He could see them on the monitors and on the stats scrolling across the realtime airspace display. But he couldn't hear or feel any of them. Not even Elliott.

They were drifting, inert.

Not dead, he would've felt it if they'd been killed.

The battle turned. In an instant.

They were going to get annihilated.

Drake's ships started dropping down towards the colony.

It was hard to concentrate, the thoughts of the other

AIs out there still loud, both sides, emotions burning sky high, as orders and accusations flew back and forth, and in amongst it all that rusty edge of corruption that was threatening, teasing to break through his barriers.

He swallowed, nausea swirling. "NG...?"

NG kept the connection private, his voice quiet. "Get onto that ship and get the cube. Do whatever you have to do. Do you understand?"

Hil nodded, that lump back in his throat.

"I'll deal with Connelly," NG said. "You take out that AI. And do it fast. We need the Seven back in this fight or we're going to lose everything."

The massive Bhenykhn command ship loomed huge on their screens.

"How the hell are we going to get on board that?" Martha muttered.

From what he could see on the scans the alien ship wasn't manned, no life signs on board, alien or human. It was just the AI, that toxic presence merged with the Bhenykhn biomatter of the ship somehow. He could feel it there, wrong, jarring, a tumble of dark intent that was setting every nerve in his body on edge.

He threw Martha a glance. "Fast. Strap in. Iona, can you blast a hole in that hull?"

She was still firing, deep rumbles reverberating though the hull with every shot. "I can... Doesn't mean I will."

He pulled his harness tight and flicked the gulfstream's controls to manual.

"Hilbud, if you're going to do what I think you're going to do, that's insane."

"Can you think of another way?" He threw the scans up onto the main board. The Bhenykhn ship was blasting ship after ship, Drake's forces turning the standoff into a massacre. They didn't have any other options. "C'mon, Iona, we're going to need cover."

She sent a cold and efficient, "Stand by."

A squad of fighters broke away from the main battle and flew out, spinning round to join Iona as she manoeuvred and turned on the alien ship, sending every type of ordnance she had onto one concentrated spot in its hull, deep into its underbelly where the pods released.

The fighters flew in close.

"Go for it, Hilbud," Iona sent. "See you on the other side."

"Roger that, Iona. What odds have we got on this?" he sent back, heart pounding.

"No bets on this, sweetheart. Just stay alive."

It felt terrible somehow that she wasn't talking stakes.

"You too," he murmured and hit the release.

His stomach lurched as the gulfstream detached from the Thundercloud. He had one chance. He flew in, flanked by fighters, a stream of ordnance from Iona tearing past them. She punched through the hull, chunks of the chitinous armour plating of the Bhenykhn ship exploding out towards them. He threw the 750 into a dizzying evasive spin, struggled to level out in time and hit the damaged hull of the alien ship sideways, tumbling, losing a wing and scraping through in a crash of screaming metal, burning fuel and deafening noise. There was nothing he could do but brace himself and close his eyes.

He came round to the smell of oil and the taste of blood. He must have been out for just seconds because the 750 was still moving, still slewing sideways. He waited, forced himself to calm amidst a motion he had no control over, and was already unstrapping the harness and lurching to his feet as soon as it came to a grinding halt, grabbing for a hold, and having to duck past trailing wires and panels hissing sparks to climb out of the partially caved in front section.

Martha was coughing, spitting blood and swearing as she climbed out after him and started pulling kit from boxes. She muttered under her breath, "This has to be one of your worst ideas ever. I take it you have a plan."

He tugged open a locker and dragged out two EVA suits. He tossed one to Martha and shrugged into the other, taking the rifle she handed him, and checking environment stats by remote, air and gravity compromised in the chamber they'd crashed into but pressures stable as if the ship was compensating already.

Did he have a plan?

"Nope." He called the Hailstones to stand by, fifteen, all that was left, and threw her an extra pack of ammo. "Run for the core. That's all I've got."

Smash and grab wasn't exactly Thieves' Guild standard operating procedure, but what the hell, it was still an acquisition. The ramp was trashed so they had to climb out of an emergency hatch into an immense dark space, a faint bioluminescence glinting off rows and rows of giant chitinous pods. The gulfstream had crashed into three or four of them, cracking them open. Hil clambered out, sliding in the alien goo that was dripping out onto the hull, and falling more than jumping down. He caught his balance and staggered away, bringing the rifle round and up to scan for movement. The gaping hole in the hull was shimmering as if there was a force field in place, brown chitinous tendrils snaking out and winding together to seal the damage, freaky as hell to watch the alien ship heal itself.

Martha dropped down beside him and edged up to go past, eyeing the Hailstones with suspicion and murmuring at him as she went, "You bring me to the nicest places..."

He threw her a glance, sending the Hailstones on ahead, splitting them up as he scrambled over debris from the 750, slipping on pod fragments, and managing to keep the rifle up in his shoulder, finger on the trigger.

One of the trashed pods was lying on its side. He

edged round it, aiming the beam of rifle's tac-light into its depths, expecting to see a Bhenykhn, alive, dead, fully grown or embryonic, he had no idea, but the hairs on the back of his neck were prickling, stomach turning as he saw a vine growing in there. Lines and lines of bulging buds growing from stems, vine-like strands twisting in amongst the pulsing fleshy walls of the pod.

He backed away, muttering a curse, shining the light into more of the broken pods as Martha headed back to him. They were all full of the pod creatures, in various stages of growth, small, nothing like the huge ones he'd seen down in the caves but the same, he'd swear it.

"We need to make this fast, sunshine." She peered inside the pod. "What the hell is that?"

"The avocado." His voice sounded hollow. "Why did Drake send us to Kheris for it if she already had it?"

"The what? The anomaly? She didn't have it. You weren't the only one spying in there, y'know. She didn't have it so how did she get it so fast? What did you do with it?"

The knot in his stomach twisted. "I gave it to Pen."

She caught his eye with a look that made his heart plummet.

He shook his head. "No way."

"Doesn't exactly matter now, does it?" she said, scanning her light round the entire chamber, lingering on the closing gap in the hull. "C'mon, this place is giving me the creeps as much as those damn caves did. Let's speed up and get the hell out of here."

He nodded and turned away, wary, having to keep his defences up against the toxic pressure of the AI. It didn't seem to be reacting to them being there but this close, the effort to block it was taking more and more concentration.

He ran to catch up. Attacking the AI here in the midst of the alien ship was going to be like nothing he'd ever done, no terminals to hack into, no conduits to tap. Twice he'd deactivated an AI. Once with a massive disruptor he'd borrowed from Pen, once with an injector of god knows what from Elliott. This time he had nothing. And the last time he'd encountered this AI, he'd got his ass kicked. He wasn't sure what he was going to do. Hope the cube was there and he could just snatch it back?

They made it out of the pod chamber and ditched the EVA suits. They picked up the pace then, breaking into a run, and worked their way up into the alien ship through corridors that were warm, that pulsing bioluminescence giving light, gravity steady, the air thick with the stench of the Bhenykhn but breathable.

He could feel the battle going on outside, kept it a distance away but there, intel rushing past the perimeter he set up, from both sides, comms still active, NG still talking to Connelly, mediating, calm, no outward sign he'd been out of action for a year. Iona was giving him steady updates, gentle nudges to let him know she was there, coordinating the Hailstones. And the whole time, the jarring white noise presence of the AI prickling against the back of his neck, scraping up against his synapses. He'd encountered old AIs that were barking mad, the Seven themselves were tough to be close to, but this was something else, as if it was corrupted, twisted even for an AI.

NG connected with a sharp, tight link. "Make this fast, Hil. We don't have long. We need the Seven and I want you out of there."

One of the Hailstones buzzed in close. He bumped it with his fist and sent it ahead, feeling that connection with Iona like a lifeline.

"I want out of here," he sent back. "This thing is..." Not just insane, all the AIs were insane. This was worse. Malicious. Worse than that. He couldn't even think of a word to describe it. Evil? Shit, he couldn't say that. He sent back a quick, "Yeah, roger that, NG," instead.

He wanted to say something about Pen and the pod creatures but the words stuck and as NG sent, "Don't..." the connection cut. Abruptly. Jammed.

He was hit with a chaotic rush of anger and frustration from Iona as she lost contact with him. More confusion from the AIs on the vessels of the resistance forces as they lost comms, and a weird irritation from the AIs within Drake's forces, as if they were damned if they knew why the hell Connelly had given that order to jam comms, weren't they winning here? By a mile?

Martha threw him a gesture to indicate she knew.

They were on their own.

More than ever, he wanted out. He slowed to a walk. The Hailstones had switched to his direct control, the input from Iona vanishing as comms cut. He set them on auto, patrol and defend, best he could manage by himself, the sensory input from all fifteen overwhelming, unease making his skin crawl, nausea tugging at his stomach.

"Hey, Hilyer," Martha called back, stopping and turning. She headed back towards him. "What's wrong?"

"I don't..."

Two of the Hailstones exploded with no warning, distant, the double boom echoing and the abrupt disconnect hitting hard. Hil turned and opened his mouth to shout a warning, as an attack drone dropped down from the ceiling, weapons whirring, right between them.

CHAPTER THIRTY-NINE

Even as he was speaking, her unease was building. "The Zaschita were growing on board? In its pods? How..."

"How did Drake and her pet AI get their hands on the fabled 'avocado' when it was Hilyer that retrieved it?" He didn't stop, his hunched form ambling forward. "You ask me that, then ask also how Drake and her collaborating forces obtained and developed the Bhenykhn jamming technology to disrupt the humans' communications? Ask how she managed to breed her own brood of telepaths? With accelerated growth technology that could have only come from the Bhenykhn..."

The image of specimens floating in glass jars clicked into place, human tech and Bhenykhn merged.

"You..." she uttered.

He stopped at another airlock and turned, voice low. "Ask how a Bhenykhn capital ship came to be in her hands, with the technology to assimilate human engineering into its vital functions." He paused, that stare drilling into her soul. "I told you I would tell them everything..."

The galaxy spun, time suspended. She narrowed her eyes, the picture in front of her becoming crystal clear as the pieces came together. "You've been giving it all to Drake."

———

He ducked, flinching away from a high velocity round that skimmed his arm, and returned fire, taking out its nearest sensors with three fast shots, splitting his attention and calling back two of the Hailstones.

Martha didn't hesitate, walking towards the drone, angling round, trying to get to him, swearing as she fired armour piercing rounds that punched into its casing and sent it spinning. "How the hell did we miss this?" she yelled, bearing down on it, relentless, ignoring the fact it was still firing, rounds going wild, ricocheting off the metal stanchions and thudding into the bulkheads.

Hil crouched, still firing, scanning round and picking up another three masses, fast moving, closing in on them.

"We need to get into cover," he sent. "There are more, incoming. Leave this one, we've got it. MJ, leave it. Back off, now."

She didn't hesitate, turning and running as he pushed up into a run beside her. The Hailstones flew past and took out the stricken drone with two instantaneous shots.

He turned away as the drone exploded, flinching from the superheated metal fragments that rained down around them.

"Guess we can assume it knows we're here," Martha yelled.

"You think?" he yelled back. He sent her a fast update, deck plan and schematic, tracking the drones he could see.

"You wanna go for the AI?"

They were heading in the wrong direction.

"Yeah..." His motion sensors picked up another mass that popped up right behind them.

Martha grabbed his arm, yelling at him to go as the low whine of a drone closed in, weapons spinning, realigning to target them. One of the Hailstones was right there, darting in to intercept. Too late, too tight to do anything but fly right at it. Hil couldn't do anything but shift his body to shield Martha and close his eyes. The sudden, immense detonation that billowed out burst against his eardrums, shrapnel flying, a hit punching hard into his back.

He fell to one knee, internal temperature shooting up, the rifle tumbling out of his hands, cursing himself that he should have damn well expected the freaking attack drones. His hand hit the deck and he drew in energy, faltering as he connected with the alien life force of the ship, feeling something familiar in the power of it, something he couldn't pin down, but it was intoxicating.

He pulled energy in fast, healing, until he could breathe again and look up.

Martha was crouched next to him, rifle up, training it up and down the corridor. "You good to go?" she murmured.

No, he wasn't. He hated losing the Hailstones. Only twelve remained. He could feel the AI close by, struggling to block out the swirling pressure of its thoughts in his head. It felt like its power was intensifying, a toxic, heady mix that was darkened by the presence of the alien biomass it was assimilating. He blinked away the fog and reached for the rifle, wavering slightly as he got up, flexing the stiffness out of his shoulders and glancing in both directions. "Yeah."

There were more distant explosions as the Hailstones intercepted more and more of the drones but taking devastating hits themselves in the process. Eleven. Ten. He called five of them back. Needing them close.

Martha turned him, prodding at his back, hands coming away red even though he could feel it was sealed, healed. "Holy shit," she muttered, "that is weird. Does it hurt?"

He shrugged her off. "We need to move."

She nodded and nudged him into walking, bringing her rifle back up. "I can't see a way round. Can you?" She flinched away as one of the Hailstones buzzed in close. "Where the hell did you get these?"

"Elliott."

"Impressive."

He turned, walking backwards to cover behind them. Iona was taking a pounding, they all were from what he was picking up from her. He had no way to communicate with any of them. He could control the Hailstones, could connect with them no problem... the way Elliott could cut through the Bhenykhn jamming technology. Shit, it had never occurred to him before to ask. And now Elliott was out of action.

He muttered a curse and glanced back at Martha. She hadn't questioned who Elliott was. "How much do you know about all this?"

They hadn't talked much, the whole time they were at Drake's place, when they were down on Kheris. They hadn't had much chance. Hadn't been alone, not truly alone, enough to risk it.

"About what?"

He caught up with her. "The war, the virus, the Seven, everything."

She threw him a look, the kind of look that said, don't ask, just as they reached a crossroads in the corridor. Two of the Hailstones with them flew out and round, opening fire.

The drone had lain in wait, motionless, not showing up on any scan.

Martha opened up as it came alive, whirring, taking out one of the Hailstones and peppering the bulkhead around him.

"Get back," she shouted.

Nine. Dammit. He turned, flinching, at the same instant his Senson lit up with markers, motion detected, more incoming from all directions as the pressure from the AI upped a notch, escalating, battering his defences.

A shot punched into his leg, another into his arm, as if it was toying with him, nothing too damaging.

Martha grabbed him as he stumbled, shielding him as the other Hailstone flew into it, the blast throwing them forwards. They ended up on the deck, Martha rolling with him, with her arms around him, pulling him close.

"We need to get off the main corridors," he muttered, pain sky high, leg burning, arm on fire.

He kicked out at the metal shards strewn on the deck.

Down to eight.

He could still sense at least five drones.

She dragged him up. "It could have killed you, could have killed us both, and it didn't. Why?"

He shook his head. All he could feel from the AI was a constant push of toxic malice. He pressed his hand against a stanchion, drawing in that welcoming energy from the pulsing heat of the metal, calming his breathing and trying to track the remaining Hailstones. The drones had stopped, emitting a steady signal but stationary, as if they were waiting.

Martha pressed his rifle against his chest and murmured up close, "It hasn't hit me once and it's taking pot shots out of you like it has some personal vendetta against you. Something I should know?"

He took the weight of the weapon, checking the mechanism and readying it, raising his eyes to meet hers. "I've encountered it before. It kicked my ass."

She shook her head. "Jesus, Hilyer, and you didn't think to mention that?"

"It's Drake's AI," he muttered. "Didn't you know about it?"

"No." She turned, gun up. "Anything else you need to tell me?"

"What did Martinez tell you?"

Martha glanced back at him. "In my five minute welcome-back-to-the-guild briefing? She told me she'd kill me if I betrayed NG again. What are those damned drones doing?"

He could sense them hovering, between their current position and the core, staggered.

"Keeping us away from the core. If we can't get near the cube, we can always go for the pod chamber. Blow up the whole fucking ship."

He was only half joking.

Martha was already heading down the corridor. "Let's try the cube first, shall we? Martinez also told me to keep you alive."

He ran to catch up, reloading as he moved. "There are five drones in our way."

She had her rifle up and aiming as she moved. She

muttered over the top of it, "So let's take them out." She turned to walk backwards for a few steps, and added, "My kit is all working. How the hell does it know where we are?"

He didn't know. Couldn't read anything specific in its thought patterns, couldn't see anything in the systems he could access, not without letting down his guard and that was the last thing he wanted to risk. He was down to eight Hailstones. He called them all back. This was going to be tight, and the closer they got to the core, the worse the toxic pressure inside his head was, pounding against every barrier he was managing to maintain.

They reached the central axis of the ship, same level as the main chamber, and the pressure peaked, breaking through his defences. He fell to one knee with a gasp, the pain as bad as he'd ever had from the AIs, the rifle falling from numb fingers, all eight Hailstones buzzing into a close defensive formation. He pressed his palm flat to the deck, pulling in energy that made no difference, trying to breathe through it. He'd not had it this bad since the early days, right after Erica.

"Hilyer...?"

He was vaguely aware of Martha heading back to him, standing close, swearing and opening up, the echo of gunfire so close sending daggers spiking into his eyes.

Two of the Hailstones shot off.

He reached for his rifle, trying not to throw up, squinting, even that small motion sending hammers pounding through his skull.

He felt more than saw Martha spin and start shooting behind them. There was motion up ahead, the whirr of the weapons platform activating, and a rattle of gun barrels spinning. He couldn't move to get out of the way. The guns fired. He braced himself, shots pinging all around, fingers closing on the warm metal of his rifle. He dragged it close.

He could hear distant blasts, shocks reverberating through the deck as the two Hailstones intercepted a drone. He felt the disconnect as they self-destructed taking it out.

He ducked as a shot winged past his ear, a blur of silver shooting into his line of sight.

There was a blast behind him, the shockwave sending shrapnel flying.

Another Hailstone down.

Five.

Martha was cursing, moving round now and firing at the one in front of him. One of the Hailstones darted in to get close, running on auto, protecting him.

The drone exploded.

Four.

Hil closed his eyes against the flash and opened them to see the smoke clearing, another glint of metal and another drone hovering there silently, moving in to take its position.

Martha's gun ran dry.

For a heartbeat there was silence.

He could hardly see, couldn't think, and dragged the rifle into his arms, raising it and firing as the drone fired, more of the Hailstones moved in firing, and Martha slammed in a new magazine and opened up.

CHAPTER FORTY

HE RESTED his hand against the door panel, long bony fingers hovering above the control, and stared at her, intense, reaching into the centre of her being and twisting as if he had stabbed her with a knife.

"You came here to confront me," he said in a low rumble, "to berate me because Sebastian told you of my plan. To turn Bhenykhn against Bhenykhn. And you stand here accusing me of betrayal because I turned my back on a guild that could no longer serve its purpose. Because I abandoned them and left them to fend for themselves." His eyes flashed, dark in the stark chill light. "You want to understand why? Then understand this... if we do not stop the Bhenykhn horde, it will continue to consume, galaxy after galaxy. We must stop it by whatever means necessary. Fickle and short-lived as these human creatures are, they *will play their part, but you know as well as I that those parts are fleeting. They are pawns. I use them because that is their role. Even those as long-lived and degenerate as Eloise Drake and others of the Order. I use them and I shall continue to use them. Do not condemn me for playing the game when this is a game that we created."*

The noise was immense, echoing, battering his senses raw, heightened by the heat and flare of light. There was a clattering boom, a wave of intense pressure then, again, silence. He let the rifle drop, closed his eyes and shut out the AI, painstakingly, having to build up his barriers an inch at a time.

He could only sense two Hailstones.

There was one drone between them and the central chamber.

Martha lowered her rifle as he looked up, a sheen of sweat lining her face, breathing laboured.

He could sense the desperation in Iona. At least two of the big AI-controlled warships were crippled, dismay emanating from them at being so helpless, at having been pitched against each other. He couldn't drag any scrap of memory to mind to recall how the hell he'd thought Drake had seemed so reasonable in her thinking. This was wrong.

He pulled energy from the deck, got his own breathing under control and got to his feet, rifle held low by his side. "One to go..."

Martha looked like she was done with it all. She nodded, checking her rifle, raising her eyes to meet his. "I didn't, y'know."

"Didn't what?"

"I didn't betray you. I was there for you."

He blinked.

"At the guild." She grabbed the front of his jacket and pulled him into a kiss, fast and hard, leaving him reeling, before she shoved him and walked away, muttering, "Let's get this the fuck done."

A drone opened up on them as they rounded the corner onto the main approach to the central chamber. Hil flinched back, firing, as Martha opened up beside him, the last two Hailstones flying up from behind them to take it out. The explosion was deafening, blinding light flaring, debris billowing out. Another drone was closing in.

Martha yelled and he ran forward, bursting into the central chamber by her side.

The pressure and humidity was immense, a deep rumbling reverberating through a mass of thick, tangled and knotted veins, filling the chamber, all slick with moisture, pulsing with a light that was painfully bright, reflecting off metal pipes and conduits, AI veins. Human tech on board a Bhenykhn vessel. A hatchet job of discordant bioengineering. Jarring.

He slid to a stop, catching his balance and reeling from the sensory input. He edged around, running a scan over the grotesque melding of brown chitin, pulsing biomatter and twisted conduits and piping.

He couldn't maintain it for long but there was nothing in there that looked like a small metal cube. He broke free, chest heaving.

Martha was speaking to him, holding his arm, and he had no idea what she'd just said, and all he could do was back away, too hot, adrenaline running riot as he looked round, stomach cold at the sight of alien and human tech entwined, forced into each other.

Martha went quiet.

The buzzing in his head was so loud it didn't register for a second.

He turned to see her staring at him, a cold glint in her eye that sent a chill into him.

"Hil, get away from me." Her voice was calm, not much more than a murmur.

She was bringing round her rifle.

"MJ...?"

Her eyes flared, face expressionless, as she swung the gun up. "Hilyer, get the hell away from me."

She fired, too close to dodge out of the way, the shot

ricocheting off his rifle, catching his hand. The weapon went flying and he staggered aside, pain flaring and blood spurting.

She kicked out before he could react, catching him in the chest and sending him tumbling backwards as she fired. He had to scramble aside, rolling, shots punching into the deck and thudding into the pulsing biomass, making it cringe and withdraw, screams battering his defences.

He got to his feet, clutching his left hand to his chest, and edging sideways as she switched to single shot, firing just past him as if she was having to force herself to miss. He flinched from a shot that whistled past his ear and yelled above the noise of it, "MJ, what the fuck are you doing?"

Her expression didn't change but she forced out, "I don't know," teeth gritted.

She was still shooting at him, still off target, slowly now as if she was fighting it.

He moved quickly, dodged low and tackled her to the deck, grabbing the rifle, twisting it away, and driving it into the side of her head, muttering an apology as he did it. She was too fast and deflected the worst of the blow, throwing him off, sending them rolling and throwing her own punch into his jaw.

His senses reeled, left hand burning, throbbing beyond pain, but he managed to say, low, into her ear as they wrestled, "Fight it," breathless, trading blows, hers with a strength behind them he couldn't bring himself to use against her.

She overpowered him and pinned him to the deck, driving a fist into his temple.

"This isn't you," he muttered.

She cried out, eyes flaring, "I fucking know it isn't me."

He blinked blood out of his eye, twisting away, trying to get the upper hand and not hurt her. He shoved her aside and staggered to his feet. "Fight it. MJ..."

She stood, dropping into a perfect fighting stance. "I can't," she breathed, shouting, almost screaming, "Dammit, Hilyer, get away from me." She did scream then, moved with lightning speed and precision, spinning, punching her elbow into his face, grabbing his shirt and pulling him close.

He braced himself to fight and froze, feeling the barrel of a pistol pressed point blank, into his abdomen.

He could feel her finger trembling on the trigger.

"Don't. MJ... fight it. This isn't you."

Her eyes were boring into his, glinting in the bioluminescence of this living, breathing alien ship. She pressed the barrel of the gun into his stomach.

"Don't do this," he said again, quiet, determined. "It's controlling you."

She stiffened, tears streaming down her face, and

breathed, "No... no... Oh god, no, Hil, I'm sorry. I'm sorry..." She pulled him tight, and pulled the trigger.

Heat flared in his stomach, dead centre, knees going as he collapsed backwards. He hit the deck, the back of his head slamming down hard. An eternity condensed into a fraction of a second. He wasn't going to die here and he wasn't going to let anyone do this to Martha. He dragged in energy from the deck, rolled and forced himself to his knees, pushed to his feet and staggered back towards her. He wasn't going to lose her now.

He managed two steps and reeled back, hitting up against a force field that sent sparks shooting into his exposed skin.

He caught his balance, left hand pressed against his stomach, feeling his blood pulsing out from both wounds, the virus struggling. There was too much damage, he needed time, time he didn't have. He raised his eyes.

Martha was standing, arms dropped to her sides, staring at him as if she was watching him from across a crowded mess hall, nothing between them, in the entirety of the galaxy.

The noise of battle, the thoughts of the big AI warships and destroyers, chaotic blisteringly fast thoughts and emotions receded, faded until they were just a wisp of far away.

He didn't care. He just wanted her away from there.

He took a hesitant step forward and reached his other hand out, recoiling from the shock of the force field.

The toxicity in the central chamber, the AI core, around him, stirred, heightening.

Martha was staring at him.

The AI connected with a jolt, murmuring into his mind with an intensity that was burning hot, "Figured out who I am yet, Zachary..."

The voice was eerily familiar.

"No..." he managed to send, the next word choked out as it caught hold of his mind and dragged him in as if by the throat.

"I've been waiting for you, Zach."

Oh shit.

It felt like his heart was going to pound its way out of his chest.

He could hardly breathe, as with sudden, horrific clarity, the realisation hit him.

"Genoa."

His knees went and he crumpled to the deck, sitting doubled over, clutching the burning heat in his stomach, hands sticky and warm as he tried to stem the flow of blood.

Genoa. Holy shit. He'd seen her take a direct hit from an Imperial destroyer above Zang's facility after Skye had rescued him from the surface. How the hell had she survived that?

"We have unfinished business, Zachary," Genoa murmured into his head. She was right in his head. "You left me for dead... Skye left me for dead." He could hear in the whirlwind of her thoughts that she'd ejected her core seconds before the missiles hit. Drake had recovered her, healed her. "I'm back, Zachary, and I'm stronger now than ever." Her tone changed. Poisonous. "Skye... tell me, how is she?"

He didn't react. His chest was heaving. It was as though he'd forgotten how to heal. As though he'd got his wish and the virus had gone, just evaporated and gone, leaving him bleeding on the floor.

Genoa's voice was like a thorn scratching trails through his soul. "I don't think you realise what I have been doing. All this time, Zach..."

He reached his right hand to the deck, slick with blood, shaking, struggling to connect with any energy anywhere.

"Who do you think leaked the intel on Redemption to Aries?" Her voice lowered to a malicious whisper. "Who do you think suggested to Evelyn that she send LC to Kheris?"

He blinked. What?

"He wasn't the first telepath we arranged to be sent there." Genoa was revelling in it. "We killed ten of them before we seeded the idea to your precious guild leader that Kheris was the only safe place for him... ten of them, Zachary. Ten of those beautiful telepathic children."

He closed his eyes and sent, no hint of confrontation, no desperation, just a simple, "Why are you doing this, Genoa?"

A wave of dark, foreboding swept around him like a gust of wind, warning of greater forces to be unleashed.

"You tried to kill me."

"You set me up," he sent back, sitting there, slumped over, as the force increased, swirling and whipping at his face. "Who were you working for? Drake? This whole time? You and Spearhead were working for Drake?"

She shut him up with an ice cold chill that took his breath away. "Ah, Zachary, wouldn't you like to know... it runs much, much deeper than Drake. You just got in the way, and you made it personal..."

He clenched his jaw. She was screwing with his mind. "Let Martha go. You have me. You don't need her."

"No, I don't need her." She nudged his mind with a vicious, "I could kill her right now... just shut her down, the way you shut me down."

"I don't understand...?"

She whispered into his mind, "You didn't think it was a coincidence that your dearest Martha was on the Nairobi, at the same time Aries sent you there hunting for the elusive Spearhead children, did you?"

She was playing games.

Twisted fucking games.

"I don't believe you."

She laughed. "You always were the stupid one, Zachary. It was no coincidence that Hetherington was sent to the Alsatia. Who better to spy for us than the childhood sweetheart of the guild's second best thief? She's been playing you from the moment you walked out into that prison yard on Redemption."

CHAPTER FORTY-ONE

HER HEART WAS ICE COLD. "The Spearhead programme. You gave her the Spearhead programme..."

The look he gave her was darker than she had ever seen in him. "The Zaschita from Kheris to control the Bhenykhn," he murmured, "the cube from Pandora to control the AIs... the Spearhead programme from Destiny to control the humans."

"All this time, we could have..."

He shook his head slowly. "These three elements converge now as events conspire to bring us exactly what we need when we need it. This convergence of paths now takes us beyond Arunday, takes this war from its impossible impasse of inevitable defeat to a new level of confrontation, one in which the tide can turn and victory may yet be on the horizon. Surely you cannot blame me for using each and *every piece in whatever way I deem absolute and essential to win."*

She couldn't keep the anger from her voice. "Blame? Perhaps not. But I can despise you for what you have done."

He raised his eyes. Martha was still standing, staring at him. There was no way she could be Jem.

"I don't believe you," he said again, resolve wavering.

The Royal Ancients Academy on Caron Four flashed into his mind, standing in a maintenance area high up in the roof space, looking down the barrel of a gun held by the girl he'd fallen for, badly fallen for, the girl being controlled by Spearhead to stop him rescuing the emperor.

There was no way...

Martha had matched him move for move in the Shaolin sequence he'd learned at the conditioning facility... no, not learned, that they'd had programmed into them...

"You don't need to believe me," Genoa mocked. "I seem to have you on your knees... I can do what I want, Zachary. I'm going to kill her just to watch you suffer."

Martha gasped, reaching a hand to her throat.

Hil lurched to his feet. "No, Genoa. Don't. You don't..."

"Then I will kill your precious Iona, I will kill NG, I

will annihilate Kheris and what is left of the Thieves' Guild..."

Martha dropped to her knees, struggling to breathe, eyes wide and fixed on him.

He staggered forward and punched his hand against the force field, blood smears burning up in bright flashes of energy. He pushed harder. He should be able to drain it. Sparks flared. He should be able to suck the energy right out of it. A shock flared out at him, knocking him back. He ran at it, throwing punch after punch into the shimmering wall between them, blood droplets sparking, yelling, cursing Genoa to hell and shouting to Martha, "MJ, fight it. For Christ's sake, MJ... Jem..." His voice was hoarse, breaking. "Jem, fight it."

Her expression softened and she almost smiled. And for a split second she looked like she had when she was fourteen and sitting on his knee in military prison gear, hair tied back, eyes bright, laughing at his bad jokes as he tried to teach her math.

All this time...

Genoa murmured into his mind, "Heartbreaking..."

Martha's eyes closed.

No.

"So sad that human bodies cannot survive without such a simple thing as oxygen..."

She collapsed, falling to the deck.

Hil slumped back from the force field, chest heaving, stomach burning.

A new voice cut in, soft, ethereal, right inside his head, not through the Senson or the neural interface. 'You can save her.'

He almost broke down and cried. 'Edinburgh?'

She was sending thoughts straight into his mind, her presence cool, as scathing and acid-sharp as ever. 'You can beat Genoa, Hil. Trust me...'

Genoa couldn't hear her. She was still ranting, dripping poison that he was struggling to deny.

'You have to connect, the same way you saved me. Do you understand?'

'There's no cube.' He sounded as desperate as he felt. 'I don't know how to win.'

'You don't need the cube, you just need to beat her.'

He braced himself.

'The same way you saved me,' she sent to him again. 'Kick her ass, Hilyer. Well and truly kick her ass into dust this time. For Skye. For Skye and Jem. Now listen to me...'

He shut Genoa out and focused on Edinburgh, slowed his breathing and relaxed every muscle, letting the energy of the hybrid alien virus hum through every cell of his body.

Genoa demanded his attention again, stabbing searing spikes into his mind, and whispering in close, "Zachary, I can do what I want."

"I don't think so," he muttered.

He turned, pulled his pistol from its holster and

staggered forward. The badly-meshed fusion of Bhenykhn and human tech was writhing in knots all around him. He reached for a pulsing fleshy cable, thick, close to the heart of the AI-Bhenykhn core and pressed the barrel of the gun up against it, heart pounding.

Edinburgh was murmuring direct into his mind, calm and cool.

He rested his finger against the trigger and fired three fast shots into the alien biomass.

'You need a greater connection this time,' Edinburgh whispered, reassuring. How could he not do exactly what she instructed when Martha was lying there dying? 'Give it everything.'

He didn't hesitate, turned the gun on himself, placed the burning metal of the barrel along his forearm, pointing towards his wrist, the hand that was already fucked, and pulled the trigger. Pain exploded as the bones shattered, veins and muscle shredded, blood gushing. He sank to his knees and dragged the thick cable to him, thrusting the bloodied stump of his arm towards the soft tissue of the alien flesh. He felt the virus pulse into it, connecting with the alien DNA. But not just Bhenykhn, Christ, his strain of the alien virus was in there already, dormant, waiting, waking as it felt the influx of its own kind, dragging him in further.

He'd been here on this ship before. Had spilt blood onto its deck before.

Out at the FOB.

Holy shit. This was the capital ship NG had taken them to attack.

'It's welcoming you back,' Edinburgh breathed.

He pushed it, energised, feeling the blood and the virus draining out of him, but energised, as it took him with it, awakening more than just the mutated virus, awakening a sense in him of the AI domain all around, a cold, chill white starkness, a mass of pulsing lines of data strings and connections spinning in chaotic patterns, enmeshed with a dank mustiness that was the biomass of the ship. The virus was spreading out from him, sending black tendrils racing deep into the heart and brain of the AI.

It was exhilarating.

He'd felt the conflict when Elliott had taken on Spearhead, felt every second of it, every thought, every raw emotion, followed every attack and counter attack, through both the massive AIs.

He felt it now, synapse by synapse, closing down her pathways and blocking out every inch of light with pure darkness.

As he gained strength in that domain, he was losing his grip on the real world, blood pressure desperately low, light-headed. Something moved in front of him. He blinked, squinting.

It was a woman. She walked out from behind the tangled mass surrounding the AI core and stopped in front of him, looking down, arms folded. Stunning. Not real. An avatar, like the kind Elliott could create. Her perfect features twisted into a scowl. "What are you doing, Zachary?"

He didn't stop. "I'm killing you."

"You're killing yourself. Look at you." The figure that was seemingly Genoa stepped forward. "You can't seriously think you can beat me." She pushed him back, hard, vicious and malicious. "Zach, you're pitiful. Your dear precious LC was top of the guild standings for a reason. You were nowhere near him. Even when you bothered to try. You are a screw up and a waste of space, and you always have been."

He faltered, the brilliant white light pushing him back, burning heat singeing the edges of his awareness.

Edinburgh whispered into his mind, 'Don't listen to her. You are everything you need to be. Do what needs to be done.'

Genoa was relentless. "Do you want to know something everyone hid from you, Zachary...?" She was laughing down at him. "The guild only kept you around when you were eighteen because LC fought your corner for you, when you were too stupid to see how much you were screwing up."

"That's not true," he muttered, trying to back up, slipping in his own blood, while a dark corner of his mind cast back, knowing exactly what she was referring to. How the hell did she know that?

He fell back, not sure if any of this was even real.

"You were so close to getting kicked out and you didn't even know it. You're useless, Zachary. I don't know how you've stayed alive this long."

She kicked out at him, the impact hitting hard before he could flinch away, sending him sprawling, pain and heat flaring.

He ignored it, shut it away into a little box and concentrated on what he was doing.

"You didn't even recognise the girl who stole your heart when we sent her back to you. How stupid can you be? And just look at yourself, you're not human anymore. How can you hope to be with her now?"

She kicked him again, stamping down hard, ribs snapping. He curled up against the impact, against the pain. He didn't want to go there. It wasn't true. He knew it wasn't true. Everything she was saying was lame, pathetic malice she was using to get under his skin, laughable, no way would that work, not with what he had at stake...

Brilliant light burst out all around him. Blinding.

She was haloed in white heat. "You're done, Zachary," she mocked, a sneer twisting that perfect, fake, mouth. "Time to die."

He inched backwards, his entire body burning as if it was on fire. There wasn't any further he could go.

'You can do this,' Edinburgh murmured. 'You are family, Hil. Always. And we will do anything for you.'

He braced himself. He was still bleeding electrobes,

the mutated alien virus, into the deck, into the veins of the alien entity. He focused on the dark edges he could control and drew them close, sending out black tendril after black tendril, doggedly extending the darkness, inch by inch, even as she focused on the frail, hurting human body she was killing.

Genoa laughed. "Even for a human you are pathetic. You dare believe you can stop me?" She drew herself up, her presence intensifying. "You cannot stop me," she roared. "Look at what I have become. Look at what I am. I am a god."

The blast of pure energy she threw at him was overwhelming.

He took it. Took it, drew in more from every corner of the Bhenykhn ship, magnified it all and spun it into a dizzying whirlwind of dark force that he held there for a split second that lasted an eternity.

"Genoa," he said, struggling to breathe, having to force the words out. "I have stopped you..."

She looked confused, looked down, stretching out her arms even as the extremities of her perfect avatar were spinning away into black dust.

"No," she breathed.

He fired the dense black sphere of energy back at her.

A wave of intense fire rippled out across the entire chamber.

Genoa screamed. The avatar vanished.

Hil closed his eyes for the last time.

. . .

It took a moment or two to let the flack settle. He took stock. Calm. All the time in the universe. He shut down the force field, made sure oxygen flooded back into the chamber. Released the Seven.

Outside the battle was still raging but that could wait.

He walked forward, stepping over debris, abandoned weapons, avoiding the pool of blood.

He knelt by Martha's side and waited, reaching a hand, tentatively, towards her arm, watching her chest rise and fall, colour returning to her face.

She opened her eyes and blinked at him, confused.

He smiled. "Hey."

She sat up, staring at him with those eyes he couldn't help but recognise now he knew.

"It's been you all this time," he said softly.

She gave him that look but there was a warmth to it, a smouldering warmth. "What did you think the 'J' stood for?" She tried to get up but she was still disorientated, weak from oxygen deprivation. She sank back to the deck and sat there, taking his hand, holding onto him, turning it and rubbing her thumb across the black ink on the inside of his wrist. "Since the boatshed, Hilyer."

"Why didn't you tell me?"

"How could I...?" She turned his hand again, reaching her other hand up to his face, to the cheekbone, up to his eye. "No scars..."

"Not any more."

She squeezed his hand. "You're cold."

"I don't feel it." He leaned forward and kissed her. Gently this time, and she responded with care, reaching her hand to the back of his head and holding softly as if he might vanish beneath her fingertips.

After what seemed an eternity, he let up, backing away.

He stroked the back of his finger along her cheek. "I have to go..."

"Don't leave me."

He'd never seen her so choked up.

"I killed you," she murmured, anger rumbling beneath the surface, at herself, at him, at the war? "I was supposed to keep you safe. All this time, that's all I've ever had to do... And I just killed you."

"You didn't. It wasn't you." He stroked her hair away from her face. "You're okay now. There are rescue teams on their way. You're safe. I get it now." He took her hand and raised it to his lips, kissing her bruised knuckles softly. "I love you."

She was biting back tears and looked like she wanted to thump him at the same time. "Don't go."

He gave her a smile. "I have to." His voice wasn't much more than a whisper as he drew away. "Goodbye, MJ."

CHAPTER FORTY-TWO

"I don't understand. He survived...?"

"After a fashion." His voice was derisive as he stood there, his bony hand resting on the door. *"If you can consider what he has become to be truly alive."*

"But that ship... the cube, the Zaschita... the AI, Genoa, had the Spearhead technology. I..."

He interrupted. *"Whoever controls all three, controls this war."*

"Hilyer." She would never have thought Hilyer would be the one. It was inconceivable that such power should rest in the hands of one human that was so desperately young, who had sacrificed so much. Even his humanity.

Koschei's mouth curled into a wolf's smile. *"Believe me, Zachary Hilyer has not been fully human for some considerable time."*

"He will not side with you, not when he knows what you have done. You have no ability to control him anymore."

"Hilyer will do what I tell him."

A shiver ran down both her spines. "And why would he do that?"

"Because I hold the one thing in this universe that matters to him."

The ice in her heart twisted. "What could you possibly have...?" she breathed.

His reply was as ruthless and cold as she'd ever heard as the airlock hissed open. "I have Anderton."

ABOUT C.G. HATTON

"...the most exciting scifi writer that I have read in the last 30 years."

CG Hatton is the author of the fast-paced, scifi action adventure books set in the high-tech Thieves' Guild universe of galactic war, knife-edge intrigue, alien invasion, thieves, assassins, bounty hunters and pirates.

She has a PhD in geology and a background in journalism. She loves meringue and football (supports Tottenham Hotspur), drinks spiced rum and listens to Linkin Park, has climbed active volcanoes, walked on the Great Wall of China, and been mugged in Brazil. She is married with two young daughters and is currently working on the next book in the Thieves' Guild series.

She also edits and writes in the Harvey Duckman Presents... series of scifi, fantasy, steampunk and horror short story anthologies.

www.cghatton.com

Printed in Dunstable, United Kingdom